THE
OTHER
SIDE
OF
PARADISE

Vanessa Beaumont

MAGPIE
BOOKS

A MAGPIE BOOK

First published in the United Kingdom, Republic of Ireland and
Australia by Magpie, an imprint of Oneworld Publications, 2024

ISBN 978-0-86154-777-7 (hardback)
ISBN 978-0-86154-869-9 (trade paperback)
eISBN 978-0-86154-779-1

Typeset by Tetragon, London
Printed and bound in Great Britain by Clays Ltd, Elcograf S.p.A.

Oneworld Publications
10 Bloomsbury Street
London WC1B 3SR
England

Stay up to date with the latest books,
special offers, and exclusive content from
Oneworld with our newsletter

Sign up on our website
oneworld-publications.com

To Wenty,
for being a very different kind of Englishman

PART I

CHAPTER ONE

London, 1921

When Jean looked back on those first few months in London, the prevailing emotion was one of embarrassment. Embarrassment at the attention she received each time she entered a room. Embarrassment at the number of eyes always upon her – the piercing eyes of mothers and grandmothers, making a quick calculation of her possible impact on their children's lives, appraising her height, waist, weight of silk and turn of ankle. Embarrassment at the curious eyes of her female contemporaries: would she be friend or foe? Would she bring a breath of fresh air to a room that had long seemed stifling to them? And the men, young and old alike, taking in her dark hair, her slim build, strong nose and angular face, her fine-boned hands. All those eyes knowing exactly who she was, who her parents were, who her grandfather was, what her extraordinary, near-perfect prospects were. It had all felt so embarrassing.

Her parents had arrived a full six months before her, her father taking up his post as American ambassador to the Court of St James, her redoubtable mother Elizabeth by his side. Jean had merely to arrive and be introduced.

The introductions had started as she stepped off the damp, carpeted gangplank on Southampton docks to find herself greeted by the awkward young man from the embassy. He put out his hand, barely making eye contact as he directed her trunks and bags to the car, opening doors and giving instructions to the various attendant staff as he went. 'Not too choppy on the way over, I hope?' he asked, but he didn't wait for an answer, continuing to mutter comments about the weather addressed to no one in particular. When they had settled into the back of the car, however, he seemed to relax, his relief palpable in its steamy fug. His task had been accomplished, and Miss Jean Buckman of 455 Madison Avenue, New York would be safely conveyed to her parents' ambassadorial residence without incident.

The Buckmans had chosen not to make their home in the usual official residence of the American ambassador, for that was not quite large enough for the scale of her mother's ambitions. Rather, they had decided upon a grand private palace on Park Lane; the president had, of course, given this decision his blessing, and her mother's offer had been impossible for the owner of the house to refuse. And that was Elizabeth Buckman's way: always to achieve one's ends, with an unbending charm and the surety of limitless finances to smooth away any tiresome impediments. And so Jean found herself living in a vast, Vulliamy palazzo facing Hyde Park, with four large drawing rooms, countless smaller ones, not one but two libraries of note, a ballroom of considerable scale, and enough bedrooms to allow her parents to host each and every visiting dignitary and quite possibly the president himself. Jean had heard it said that by the time the clock in the entrance hall chimed nine in the morning, her mother already knew which Americans of import were in London and had arranged for their appearance at her elegant, chinoiserie salon within the hour.

Jean knew that she was even more of a commodity here than she had been in New York. She could feel the weight of it at the first Saturday-to-Monday she spent in a picturesque Queen Anne house that sat proud and perfect amid the manicured slopes of a Hampshire estate, its gardens a Repton delight, each room giving onto a peerless aspect of English Arcadia beyond. She could sense the anticipation of the house as her parents' car had snaked down the drive to be presented by the tableau of servants awaiting their arrival. She had heard the fussing of the hostess as she was ushered inside by the butler, had blushed at the fanfare with which she was introduced to their only son, who stood awkwardly at the bottom of the grand staircase, waiting for the gallows.

That night at dinner she looked down a table groaning with silver polished by a silent army of gloved hands, a chorus of censorious family portraits standing sentinel above.

The portly gentleman to her right, cheeks mottled with drink, leaned in. 'My dear, you are quite the guest. I have dined at Appington more than twenty times, but never have I seen Lady Danby use the Sèvres.' He looked across the table to his hostess and smiled at her benignly, before dabbing at the corners of his mouth with his napkin and dropping his voice. 'They've sold at least half of the estate already. And there's an attic sale planned for next week, which they've tried to keep out of the papers but of course we all know about it. Clearing things out for young Alexander, as Lady Danby put it to me earlier, with a valiant attempt at nonchalance. Maintaining the facade of the charmed English life can be an exhausting occupation. Her hair has gone quite grey from the effort.'

The gentleman on her other side leaned across to congratulate his friend on this incontrovertible truth. He tapped Jean's
arm knowingly. 'The Dollar Princesses may be the stuff of fable
now, but we can all see where your mother's' – he searched for
the word, alighting on one with a greasy smile – 'munificence,
shall we call it, might be put to good use.'

His friend leaned in closer. 'We have heard rumours, quite
splendid ones, about the scale of her entertaining. Much needed,
after the gloom of the last few years.' He gave a snort. 'I do
hope an improvement on dear "Walled Off" Astor, living at
Cliveden with a staff of a thousand all in perfect livery, but not
a drop to be drunk!'

'But what plans she must have for you, my dear. I can recall
the Double Duchess, the tour de force of my mother's day.
Consuelo Yznaga as was, who bagged the Dukes of Manchester
and Devonshire.' His face fell. 'Both my sons are already married. Fearfully sensibly, I might add.'

The man on her other side went on, undeterred. 'Oh, but
your dear mama would have known the buccaneers, Minnie
Paget and Jennie Jerome, women famed for the persuasive
powers of their American charms over the powerless British
peer. Little Alexander Danby' – and here he gave a smirk for
her benefit – 'should be so lucky.'

On they went, back and forth, forth and back, these men who
debated the impact of her arrival in England as if she were some
filly at a thoroughbred sale. It was a game to them, the novelty
of her appearance between them livening up the interlude
between overcooked beef and the next glass of average claret.

After the ladies' part in dinner had drawn to a close and they
had arranged themselves artfully around the drawing room in
a practice as familiar to them as breathing – a foursome taking

their places at the card table, a trio warming themselves by the fire, another cluster standing around Jean's mother, captivated as much by the scale of the diamonds at her neck as by her conversation – Jean could sense that though the voices were discreet, the smiles were watchful and acid was waiting none too patiently on the tip of every tongue. At moments like this, she felt the intensity of society's gaze upon her as if it burned her skin.

'Elizabeth Buckman's family *are* California—' one woman uttered to her neighbour through pursed lips.

'With more money than God—'

'Oh, and half of San Francisco as their back garden, I'll have you know.'

'And don't forget the family newspaper, which she was kind enough to buy for her husband. Thanks to his wife he has Washington's ear, and the rest of America it seems.'

'My dear, my husband tells me that in New York they have hospitals, libraries – even working men's hostels, where men get turfed out of bed at nine in the morning to encourage hard work and straight living – all built and run in her grandfather's illustrious name.'

They were looking at Jean now, fixing her with eyes as inscrutable as stones.

'In London, though, it mightn't be quite the same.'

'Quite. What does all that money *mean*? Her father the ambassador, intimate of politicians and the King. What will she do next? Twenty, unmarried and living in London for the foreseeable…'

The wife of one of Jean's companions from dinner, catching her eye, beckoned her over to where she was sitting, tapping the seat beside her insistently.

'How do you intend to occupy yourself here in England?' the woman asked. Her voice dropped. 'Please God, don't let it be Alexander Danby: he's quite peculiar. But with a father like his, a cousin of my husband's in fact, one can't really be surprised. Odd blood there. You ought to meet some girls of your own age. My niece, Mary, have you come across her yet?' She didn't wait for an answer. 'She's a frightful bluestocking. Biding her time at a worthy little bookshop in Mayfair, which fills me and her mother with despair.'

A smaller woman, with watery blue eyes frozen in a look of perpetual concern, abandoned Lady Danby and another woman by the fire and turned instead to join in the conversation, ignoring the peevish looks she left behind.

'My daughter Polly works at a boutique on Walton Street. She trails from thing to thing and from party to party. I'm a horror for saying it, but she's dumpy and dull and I dread her getting caught out in this frightful game of musical chairs – not enough men to go round after the war and the music bound to stop at any time.'

Another lady was now drawn in from the card table and Jean could feel the rest of the room growing quieter, some valiant voices persevering with stories they wished they could abandon in favour of the real interest at hand. This last lady, looking over to Jean, eyed her beadily.

'You should have seen the first presentation at court after the Armistice. What a mix. Some straight from the schoolroom, tongue-tied and chewing at their nails, others brazen and confident, skin brown and weather-beaten from driving ambulances in France. Hearts a little hardened: brothers lost – promises broken… A life lived but then taken away.'

The lady next to Jean on the sofa leaned in, her voice quiet, insistent. 'End the whole circus of expectation. Just marry, and then you can make your own life within it.'

'Oh really, Sarah. Who will it be, though? These boys must all seem so awkward to Jean. None of that delicious American spark we've heard about. But don't worry, with an Englishman it's rarely their true nature. There's life buried beneath the reticence—'

'Although too much life is usually the result of the port after dinner—'

The conversation was broken up by the reappearance of the men. The alchemy of the room changed in an instant by the opening of the drawing room doors, and a curtain of port and stiff collars descended on the female conversations that had preceded it, as if they'd never taken place at all.

As the weeks in England turned into months, Jean did go on to meet the daughters of these women. She was introduced to them at parties or balls or little fashion shows, introduced by their mothers, keen to let some of her American 'charm', as they euphemistically called her money, rub off on them. Jean found many of these girls to be amusing and astute, aware of the possibility of change despite what their mothers said, yet unable to do anything with this, as if they had been given an old draft of a play. They read the words out loud, confidently too, but somehow the lines felt wrong. The effect was a clumsy self-awareness and a desperation for someone, anyone, to take the lead, to do something different so they could follow suit. But in reality this question of who to marry was all the sport they had. The promise of freedom and autonomy was no more than the scent of blossom on a breeze, gone as soon as it arrived. Although the world had shifted imperceptibly on its axis since the war, the rules were still the same.

*

Jean stood in the picture gallery of her parents' house at another party given to celebrate her coming out. She had made her pilgrimage to the palace several weeks before, but still there followed a never-ending round of gatherings to mark the occasion. The evening was warm and the windows were open, drawing little gasps of delight as guests looked down on the gardens that her mother had lit with a thousand paper lanterns, dancing like moths in the gentle breeze. Every doorway and inch of wall inside was draped with garlands of gardenias and arrangements of roses of white and deep pink, each bud chosen so that it was at its most splendid as the procession of guests made their way up the vast double staircase and into the gallery. A harpist, dressed as Aphrodite in a gown and wreath of gold, was playing the guests into the ballroom as they were announced to their hosts. Jean heard her mother's voice tinkling over the noise of the room: 'Just a little affair, nothing to write home about.'

But in the midst of all this – the swirl of entertaining, the talking and charming, a world she had been brought up to inhabit supposedly as easily as a second skin, in the midst of this evening whose real purpose was essentially the revelation of herself, dressed in a pale pink chosen to offset the roses perfectly – Jean felt weightless. Glass in hand, cheeks flushed, she listened only absently to conversations, sipped champagne that tasted of nothing.

She found herself talking to a pair of grandes dames, pearls drooping like wilted flowers on their pale, sunken chests. The shorter of the two was gesturing to a pair of boys standing in the corner, faces red with drink, laughing uncontrollably at some joke between them. 'The men you girls will marry, see how flippant they are. So careless. It's an insult to the sacrifice

of those who went before. And they should know better. A year
more and the war would have claimed them too. They ought
to behave with more reverence...'

As they talked on, Jean allowed herself to close her eyes.
She could have been anywhere. Her real self, the part that lay
beneath, felt untethered. It didn't bother her, but it gave her this
curious feeling that at any second one part of her, the thinking
part, might float away, and that the shell she left behind could
go on doing the work of being Miss Jean Buckman utterly
adequately, with no one knowing the difference. Perhaps it had
been the same in America, perhaps she simply hadn't noticed.
Hers had always been the role of acquiescent daughter, the foil
to her more difficult older brother. Less than beautiful, far more
than plain, kind and self-contained, Jean's life had been one of
graceful ease, steered with precision by her omniscient mother.
It had passed in lunches at the Colony, dinners with the Goelets
or the Phippses, summers at Newport or at her grandfather's
estate in California. But listening to these women talk, in this
room that marked the apex of her mother's ambitions for her,
it was as if a breeze had blown right through her and she was
weightless and so very removed.

Then her mother Elizabeth's eyes had been upon her, catching this absence, and she had seen the tight smile she knew well,
and the room contracted again and the airless feeling evaporated as the women's faces before her – still talking, mouths
moving – returned to focus. Her mother eased herself into
the conversation with a perfect bon mot, a flash of laughter, a
gentle but firm reminder of someone that Jean really ought to
meet, and she ushered her away from the ladies still berating
the youth in the room with enthusiasm. And when Jean and
her parents were sitting together at dinner the following night,

at a little table laid out for the three of them in Elizabeth's small salon, discussing the great success that the evening had proved to be, her mother fixed her eyes on Jean, not unkindly but with an intensity that gave no room for her meaning to be misunderstood.

'Though it may seem different now that we are in London, my darling, the business at hand is the same, just dressed in that peculiar English way. It is the season, like all the others that have preceded it. Boys will meet girls, marriages will be made. It is that time. It is that time.'

Jean nodded, hearing the words, felt that her father was nodding too, felt that everyone she had met in this country would have nodded if they could hear, but as she lay in her bed later, thinking about all the people she had spoken to, all the interactions she had had, thinking about this season at hand, as her mother had described it, as if it were a sort of clerical matter that needed attending to, it seemed to her that all of this doing and dancing, all of this being, was not creating anything of permanence. Like cracks under the glaze of an old porcelain vase, her life when viewed from far away looked like it had a pattern, intricate and fine, but up close there were fault lines that Jean felt might not take the pressure of a human's touch.

CHAPTER TWO

Jean stood at the entrance to the Savoy, new shoes pinching at her heels, swathes of mink at collar and cuffs too showy, where one of her mother's dressmakers had suggested a more exaggerated silhouette, all the rage apparently in Paris. She found that small suggestions were constantly being made by her mother here in London – tweaks and additions that were never so great that they gave Jean cause to doubt herself entirely but were enough to make her sit a little straighter, to feel her mother's eyes always at her back. Her parents' car had dropped her off, and the stubborn rain meant that there was no time to hesitate. A doorman was waiting with umbrella unfurled, so she stepped forward under its protection and into the building. She loathed entering a room alone, having to establish herself, to find someone to introduce oneself to, the conversations cast out like ropes from a boat in the hope that one of them would be taken up.

The dining room was full already, tables packed, but she was shown instead to the bar, where people were resolutely not sitting down, gathered instead in clusters, drinking and talking and sizing up the company. She was presented with a sea of backs until a smile was bestowed and a space made for her, and she let out a silent exhalation of relief. She was squashed up next to a pair of men, boys really, deep in conversation, oblivious to her presence beside them. One was leaning on the bar, his hair smooth and dark, and he had a silver cigarette case in his hand that he habitually flipped open and closed. Seeing Jean was alone, he offered her a cigarette, which she declined with a shake of her head.

'Edward Warre. How do you do?' He smiled briefly when she introduced herself, and took a sip of his drink. 'You'll be here all day unless you know the man. He has a knack of ignoring newcomers. Could be something to do with the crowd that comes here now. He does a good sidecar, it's what my sister always has.'

'A sidecar would be perfect then, thank you.'

He had the barman's attention almost immediately, who lowered his head to take Edward's order, giving him a quick smile of recognition before busying himself with glasses and bottles as the pair stood side by side, the space between them strangely intimate.

'Who did you come here with?' Edward asked.

'Alone, actually. My parents know our host's parents, so it was suggested that I come and meet him and some of his friends. Some people my own age. I've just moved here from New York.'

'Well, in summary: Johnnie's fine but quite dull, and his father staggeringly so. The ones to know if you want to have a bit of fun are those two.' He gestured to two young men smoking at the other end of the bar. 'But certainly not him.' His head flicked to the right, and she glanced at a bespectacled blonde boy standing alone, fiddling with the glass in front of him, feigning concentration.

The question of what to say next hovered, but he sidestepped it neatly.

'I think you'll find you and I are next to each other at dinner. But nothing worse than saying everything now and leaving us stuck when we sit down. I'll leave you with your drink. But remember what I said about our friend on your right. Once engaged, you'll never escape.' He gave a quick half-smile and, picking up his drink, moved away.

But when they were shown to their seats, her host had swapped the placement to put Jean next to him instead, and Edward was somewhere in the middle of the table, in a group of young men that seemed to know each other well and grew more raucous as the evening progressed. They would beckon over the waiters more and more frequently, calling for more drinks, and at some point a glass was smashed and a cheer went up. Jean, seated at the well-behaved end of the table, was bored, her host as dull as predicted, talking her through his maternal American grandmother's family tree in painstaking detail, but Jean caught Edward looking across at her, and there was his brief smile again, snapped away before anyone else might see it.

Edward Warre was a name, once heard, that came up often. Followed often too by a place, the family house, Harehope, its name spoken in an offhand way that assumed knowledge. She'd mispronounced it at first, found herself corrected with an amused smile: 'It's Hare-up, as in up and down. Don't say the "hope", darling, or you'll never get invited.' And in the way girls did – the flutter of excitement, the spinning of a thread of connection or flicker of engagement into something more – Jean took that brief exchange at the Savoy and amplified it. This was a world where a glimpse of a shoulder, a smile at a lunch or the offer of a dance might be all there was, a flash of something to be eked out in the weeks and months to come. So Jean began to look out for him at parties and dances, and the following week she saw him again, this boy who'd made her smile, who had confidence and shyness in equal measure, somehow captured in the simple open and close of a silver cigarette case.

She was at a dance given at a house on Belgrave Square, their hostess an American lady with an insatiable zest for staging costumed parties of elaborate theme for the young. They found themselves next to each other as ices were passed around, crammed into the corner of a room where chairs lined the wall while Jean sat, an uncomfortable Cleopatra with a crown of gold laurel that pinched at her temples, the clatter of costumes and music and talking making her head ache.

He was sitting with friends, his back turned, but the group had broken off to talk to some others and Jean and he were left as a pair, perched on a pair of small, ugly chairs that must have been hired in for the occasion. Edward wasn't in fancy dress, but he had a tinselly crown set far back on his head. He looked bored, tapping his foot impatiently.

'Who have you come as?' Jean asked tentatively.

Edward turned, a flash of recognition when he saw her face, then a look of confusion.

She gestured to the crown.

'Oh, this? A friend said I wasn't allowed in unless I'd made some attempt at a costume, so I gave a girl who was leaving a winning smile and got this in return. Does it suit me?' He looked directly at her, his face serious.

'As if you were born in it.'

He laughed, taking it off and turning it in his hands. There was a long pause, but just as Jean felt she ought to fill it, he looked at her again. 'How do you find all of this?'

She wasn't sure if he was referring to the party in particular or life in London in general, and his expression gave nothing away, so she took him to mean the latter.

'If I'm being honest, strange.' She paused. 'Sometimes fun, sometimes overwhelming. I'm never sure if I'm doing what I ought to be, or whether in fact there is anything one ought to be doing at all. Which I suppose is a much more worrying thought.'

He smiled, looking down at the crown again. His lashes were long and the skin under his eyes was dark. He gestured to the room. 'Some people seem to make a life out of doing not very much, and to be having a perfectly good time. I'd say our delightful hostess could make a business out of it.'

She laughed. 'True. And you? Are you having a perfectly good time doing not very much?'

'I suppose so. Though I prefer being at home.'

'Not London?'

'God, no. I can't stomach too much of London. Home is Harehope, our place in the north, wilder, less noise, fewer dress-up parties.' That flash of a smile, gone as soon as it appeared. 'Perhaps you should come and see it. Give you more of an idea of what England is really about—' One of his friends was standing over them now, moving from one foot to the other, seemingly agitated by the empty glass in his hand. Edward excused himself from Jean, but as he pushed his way through the throng, he turned. 'You ought to come and see it for yourself.' And then he was gone.

For the duration of Jean's conversation with him, that feeling of lightness that had characterised her time in London seemed to telescope into something else. There was something tangible in the process of wanting to get a reaction from that serious face with its downturned brown eyes, the small patch of red at his cheeks. She wondered if perhaps she could now gain satisfaction from the routine of her life – a lunch somewhere, a tea somewhere else, a dinner or a dance, a rhythm that she had found strangely oppressive – if it might give her an opportunity to learn more about this boy.

Stories about Edward were easy to come by from any number of women she gossiped with at lunches or parties. He was known in that way that everyone was in London, gossamer-thin threads that connected each person she met; a sometimes impenetrable mass of cousins and second cousins and connections by marriage, all trotted out as glibly as if they were directions on a map. She was at a charity bazaar in aid of the wounded soldiers in a down-at-heel concert hall in Kensington a week or so later. Tables were draped in white, with arrangements of carnations hastily being placed by harassed-looking women as Jean and her mother arrived. Elizabeth was welcomed as she always was – the noticeable deference, the slight parting of a crowd to make way for her indomitable presence; the curious looks that followed when her back was turned: who would she talk to, where would she sit? 'One must never leave one's placement to chance, my dear. The wrong sort of people will descend like wolves,' Elizabeth had said to her in the car, patting her hand firmly, and so a place for Jean to sit was found beside a grey-haired, powdery-skinned dowager who smelt strongly of lily of the valley, a type Jean had become familiar with in London.

The dowager nodded briefly at Jean as she took her seat, taking in the entirety of her in one practised glance. 'So you're

soul perhaps, deprived, like many of his contemporaries, of any opportunity to prove themselves against the overshadowing presences of their brothers and cousins and fathers, that older generation immortalised for eternity, whose bodies were left to rot in sodden fields, in landscapes pocked and scarred, but whose sacrifice was so enormous, their deaths so vile and ugly, so senseless, that they threatened to eclipse utterly the living left behind. And in her conscientious way Jean began to work on this portrait, to shape it and perfect it, to fill in small details here and there, and if, when she held it up to the true subject, it didn't quite match, she would push away any doubts and turn back to her portrait.

Meetings between the pair continued after this, carefully choreographed by Jean's mother, who had turned the not-inconsiderable force of her attention onto this new friendship. There were several days at Ascot in June, where she and Edward stood together in the royal box, sharing a race card, Jean fascinated by the pageantry on display in contrast to the muscular horses, skin slick with sweat, oblivious to the starched perfection of the enclosure and the wild approval of the crowds. Edward's knowledge of horses was encyclopaedic, and he seemed to take pleasure in advising her on the winners, or the endless gossip and tips from owners and trainers and punters that were pounced on and sifted through like panners looking for gold. This confidence, when he was on firm ground, seemed to alternate with an uncertainty, an impatience to get away from any light that might be shone on him.

There was a chorus too, watching these scenes unfold with gimlet eyes:

'Oh, he's not terribly good with girls. Doesn't have the faintest idea how to talk to them.'

'But he's in that set – they do everything together, a little circle that lets no one in.'

'I can't bear his sister. A vicious little thing when she wants to be.'

'But that house, that house. The faded grandeur of it. It's so deliciously romantic. And those eyes. One wants to know so desperately what they're thinking. Perhaps he needs saving.'

Jean listened, she observed and she wanted. Attraction and sympathy were worked on in equal measure, and that hint of a connection, however tenuous, felt like a hand stretched out across a great divide. If she could only grasp it, it might pull her across to the promised land of real life that must surely lie beyond.

The next week there was a dinner given by Elizabeth Buckman for mutual friends of the Warres, the guests chosen to reflect the Buckmans' flawless connections – the Roxburghes, the Sutherlands, Grace Vanderbilt – who were artfully dispersed among the other twelve guests to give just the right impression of position and *politesse*; and finally there came the anticipated invitation to Harehope.

A letter was carried to Elizabeth's desk by one of the footmen, brought to her as she sat, the morning's correspondence spread out before her. It was a square of cream paper, small and neat and edged in gilt, with only a line or two of elegant script looping across its breadth; it was a thing of little consequence, but from the look of quiet triumph on her mother's face, something to be distinctly pleased about.

CHAPTER THREE

It was the edge of the perimeter wall that ran along the roadside that she saw first, its stone grey and worn, gently heralding the place. Their car turned a bend and they were through vast stone pillars and past a gatehouse, a small castle in itself, and then they were being pulled into the house's orbit. A drive wound them in, curving through a park studded with elm and ash, proud witnesses to the family's travails over the centuries. Another bend and Harehope was revealed to them with a flick of drama as its architect surely intended. Jean felt a flash of dislike for the sullen pile now before her. But as they drew nearer, something changed, an alchemy of the house in its landscape, and though it was not beautiful, it was of substance, its stone a mighty expanse of grey under an overcast sky, and there was a defiance to its solidity and permanence that demanded respect. Beyond, she knew, stretched only moorland – no houses, no roads, just mile upon mile of wild, untended nothing that ran behind the formal gardens, on and on, as if the house were teetering on the edge of the earth. As their car pulled into the porte cochère, there stood the butler, back straight as a rod, face like a stone, impervious to the great sploshes of summer rain on his shoulders.

Edward's mother greeted them at the head of her assembled staff, and Jean felt the whole performance begin once more. She could sense the familiar anticipation in the hallway, the tension of a household primed to receive, and she knew how this would proceed, as it had done countless times before. Edward stood at his mother's side, hands in the pockets of his tweed suit, affecting nonchalance, though she saw a knot of tension at his jaw, and he rocked back on his heels as he waited for his mother to take the lead in receiving the guests. This particular dance had begun, but there was no doubt as to who was the choreographer.

'Tea is in the drawing room,' Lady Warre announced before turning abruptly, Jean and her mother expected to follow.

The room they entered was vast, a faded beauty, with walls of a pale yellow silk and great swags of thick red damask at each window. Its floors were polished oak, with an enormous Aubusson laid over, worn thin in patches from years of use. The low grey light that came from the dank day outside added to an air of tiredness, as if the room had given a large sigh, shoulders sagging from the simple effort of being. At the far end of the room triple-height windows gave on to the formal lawns below where Jean could make out a flash of stone, a fountain, its water a trickle. A round table groaning beneath an elaborate display of cakes and sandwiches, as yet untouched, sat in the window.

Edward followed them in, casually taking a log from the basket beside the fire to throw on. 'Jean, you'll be staying in the Chinese Room. Stokes, will you take her bags there?'

His mother, taking a seat on one of the two faded brocade sofas, gestured to Elizabeth to sit on the other. 'No, she won't. That room's got two outside walls, and we don't want our American guests complaining of chattering teeth. Stokes, I've moved Miss Buckman to the Green Room.'

Edward looked down, cheeks red, momentary authority snatched away. The insouciance he had possessed at the Savoy dissipated in an instant.

Without turning to her son, Lady Warre gave a small, almost imperceptible flick of her hand and said over her shoulder, 'Edward, go and let your sister know the Buckmans are here.' She beckoned to one of the housemaids to bring over tea, and then turned her attention to Jean and her mother.

As Lady Warre and Elizabeth talked, Jean had the chance to observe this woman properly for the first time. She was dressed in the old-fashioned style, in a blouse of pale cream voile with delicately buttoned sleeves, tucked into a full navy skirt; she was whippet-thin, upright, her wrists as delicate as china, the pearls around her neck heavy on her translucent chest, her eyes a piercing blue. She sat, utterly still, her face a mask as Elizabeth regaled her with details about their journey it was abundantly clear she had no wish to hear.

That afternoon, Jean and Elizabeth were shown around the house's interior by Edward as his mother looked on: objects of interest, paintings of note – their pride a vast, murky Dutch old master that hung in the entrance hall; and then the inevitable gallery of disapproving family portraits, the proud, pop-eyed stares of those eighteenth-century figures whose felicitous inheritance of land seamed with coal had brought the family its rush of wealth; next came the furniture and tapestries, grand and tired, inhabiting the same place for eternity, the walls and floors sagging and buckled beneath them. The house had been the Warre family home for several hundred years, each generation adding or subtracting to the building with varying degrees of success, but the main body of the current hall was Palladian, mid eighteenth century. It was vast, a great block of northern stone, with wings that fanned out and dimly lit corridors that ran on for an eternity, where they ended unclear; rooms giving onto rooms onto rooms, footsteps echoing across stone flags warped and uneven with age. Some had the stale air of disuse, of windows hastily opened and dust sheets thrown off for their arrival. Jean noted that the King's annual stay at Harehope on his way to Balmoral was mentioned more than once by her hostess, and the superb hunting ground the estate possessed was pointed out, not quite in passing.

Edward's older sister was part of their assembled group. Charlotte, widowed just before the Armistice, spent her time between Harehope and her home in Hampshire. She looked very like her mother, that same pronounced thinness, with translucent skin that veins threaded through like blue silk, and dark, almost black hair. She was still dressed in mourning for her husband, a flattering black crêpe de Chine, and she inhabited the house with a territorial presence. She and her mother were often to be found together, muttering about the servants or where lunch might be taken, conspiratorial in their plans.

Jean found herself alone with her that night before dinner, Charlotte seated at a card table in the drawing room with a half-worked puzzle before her, Jean standing awkwardly behind, looking on. As Charlotte talked, her voice a bored monotone, her two young boys appeared briefly to say goodnight, hair combed and smelling of lilacs and talc, and a perfunctory kiss was bestowed on each before they were ushered out again. Jean felt Charlotte looking her over, appraising her and her mother, waiting for a trip-up, a delightful little revelation of poor American manners.

'When my brother Charles died, we were all utterly bereft, but then when Father went too, it flattened us. The one following the other, then my husband. Funeral after funeral, mourning for one only to mourn for another.'

Her hand hovered over the pieces, a large ruby hanging heavy on her long, pale fingers. She didn't seem to want a response.

'I don't think any of this can carry on.' She waved her hand impatiently, indicating the room filling now with guests, a butler and several footmen standing silently at its edge, poised to assist. 'How can it? All the best men gone, and everyone bankrupt by war. And look at the servants, busy living a wartime existence, doing their bit and making their way, and then they're supposed to go back to how it was before. Did you hear about the Duke of Portland at Morven's coming of age? Made a speech about how all of this must come to an end. No more houses, no more estates. And look at him – ten thousand acres of Nottinghamshire and Welbeck's collection. If he's in a bind, where on earth does that leave us?'

She looked up now at Jean, with a cold curiosity.

'Perhaps it isn't the same for you, though. Everything is a bit more transient, I imagine, coming to it all so recently. Perhaps the thought of losing it all mightn't mean as much.'

Charlotte let out an exclamation of delight. Seizing a piece, she slotted it neatly into its place, and smiled as if the last sentence had been said by someone else entirely. Looking down at the little black Pekingese in her lap, she ruffled its ears.

'Well done, my little angel. Well done! Frightfully clever, aren't we.'

The conversation, it appeared, was over.

At dinner, Edward's mother sat at one end of the polished mahogany table, Edward opposite her, in the place only recently vacated by his father. Elizabeth was on Edward's right, and Jean watched as her mother performed her traditional dinner set piece. The faux humility about life in America, her exaggerated admiration for these great English houses of such age and eminence – though Jean knew she loathed their archaic plumbing and ancient, threadbare linen – then the laments about the problems with her house in London, though of course there were none, this last part connecting Elizabeth, in her eyes at least, with the more prosaic problems she imagined lesser beings had to endure. Jean could see Edward's eyes flick down to his own mother as he feigned interest, only adequately well.

Jean was placed between two of Edward's friends. The group of three had stood around before dinner, smoking by the fireplace, their familiarity a wall between them and the rest of the room.

'We've known each other for years,' the young man on her right announced cheerily. He was reed-thin – all elbows and angles, and endearingly absent-minded with the use of them – and she had seen him earlier greeting Stokes the butler like an old friend, slapping his back when he had walked into the drawing room, blithely unaware of the discomfort he left behind. He was now attacking his food with enthusiasm.

'Freddie Byam-Hughes,' he offered, wiping his mouth on his napkin after swallowing a large spoonful of soup. 'Been coming to Harehope since I was old enough to shoot. We were in the same house at school. I always preferred a few weeks up here with the chance of some grouse to hanging about in Hampshire with my father breathing down my neck. I haven't seen Edward quite as much, though, since he left Oxford. His father wasn't best pleased about that. Not that he would show it. His old man couldn't say boo to a goose.' He lowered his voice. 'Not like the delightful Lady Warre. Warmth personified, wouldn't you say?'

'Yes. I'm not entirely sure what she makes of my mother. Or me, for that matter.'

'I think that's rather her thing. A glacial superiority. Dripping into every room so the temperature of the house drops below freezing.' He smiled. 'Not hard in these parts. So what do you make of Harehope? Quite far north if you're not used to it.'

'Well, I was shown the stables this afternoon by Edward, which he seemed to enjoy considerably more than this afternoon's picnic—'

'I never know why they insist on looking at that dreary ruin. I've done that picnic countless times over the years in pouring rain or blazing heat and it's never improved. But the stables. Edward would sooner live there than the house, I should think. Probably holds a bit more sway.'

The young man on Jean's left turned briefly to interrupt, clearly having had an ear on their conversation. He had that peculiarly English trait, opinions blunt to the point of rudeness but delivered with an elegance of manner that made it look like art.

'Sway? Edward's got quite enough of that, thank you very much. Lord of all he surveys at twenty-one, without having to pull his finger out. I'm sure he didn't even have to arrange this little gathering – no offence, of course.' He briefly dipped his head in Jean's direction. 'But for the war and Charles being killed, he'd have ended up in that godawful house on the edge of the moors. The bleakest place I've ever seen. But now he's here at Harehope instead, bum in the butter, and aren't we, his dearest friends, revelling in his change of fortune.' He took a slug of his claret before presenting his back firmly to Jean once more.

Freddie shrugged. 'He's right. But Edward's got to make a go of things. It was an embarrassment that he didn't finish Oxford. Charles was so brilliant at it all, effortlessly so. Not the easiest thing to follow. Harehope is Edward's now, in name and all that. Though he'll have to prise it from his mother.'

Jean looked at Edward now, still listening to Elizabeth, with that inscrutable face of his. She did find him attractive. He was handsome in a sharp, off-centre way: his eyes were dark, watchful, with hollows beneath his cheekbones. He was lean, and there was that dissatisfied energy to him. Watching him mount a horse earlier, she could see he had a natural ability and a connection with the animal he rode, the unspoken bond between muscle and mind immediately apparent in the horse's quick and easy response to even the smallest flick of a rein. And Jean had been told by her mother that Edward's interest in her was clear; that the invitation to Harehope would not have been made were it not.

Another course came, glasses were filled, the turn was made, and then abruptly Lady Warre stood, ringing a delicate silver bell that sat at her right hand. Edward stood too, mouth opening to say something, but his mother clapped her hands briskly and asked the women to retire before he could speak.

Freddie leaned in. 'I told you. He'll have to prise it from her dead hands,' he muttered.

And here was Lady Warre, ushering the women firmly out of the dining room, directing a footman to a napkin dropped on the floor, reminding the butler which port the men were to have, either unaware or unwilling to accept the new world her family inhabited, as she stepped over her son's futile attempts at establishing himself in this house she still presided over.

As they sat around in the drawing room later, his friends mobbed him up with enthusiasm – for Jean's benefit, she felt – but everything they said, every conversation begun or story shared, every memory or joke or quip, came back to Harehope. As she sat in the faded elegance of its drawing room, which had held countless variations of this evening, with countless outsiders rejected or accepted, indifferent as Harehope seemed to the changes in the world beyond its ancient walls, she understood that this house was the heart of it all. Harehope was the thing that lent Edward his confidence. It was the symbol of who he was, and uneasy though his hold, so recent and so fragile, it made him. He couldn't captivate a room with his wit nor master his mother, but he had a conceit, a confidence, an ingrained superiority over the world directly drawn from the hundreds of years his family had spent on the land he now possessed.

Walking back to her bedroom, relieved to excuse herself after a long day, Jean took a wrong turn down a dimly lit corridor and found herself on the threshold of a large, square room. Its walls were lined with books, and an armchair of the softest red, worn from use, was turned towards an empty fireplace. She was drawn instinctively towards the shelves; they were crammed to bursting, filled with copies of Aeschylus, Sophocles, Euripides, books wedged on top of books, spines worn, pages thickened and uneven with use; Herodotus, Thucydides, Xenophon, the *Iliad* and the *Odyssey*; names she knew and many she didn't; bound files placed on a low chest, the top one neatly labelled A FEW ANTIQUITIES FROM MACEDONIA. This was once a library alive with use, no shrine to vanity, and at the centre of the room's simple mantelpiece sat the most delicate pot Jean had ever seen, black figures dancing across its deep red clay, hands linked, heads flung back in ecstasy, as if bringing their spirited, faraway world into this well of cool, English reserve. She knew at once that it was Edward's brother's room, and Jean felt a sudden wave of sadness for this young, vital man whom she had never met, all his passions and quirks tidied away and left to petrify in this museum that had long closed its doors to visitors.

She felt someone's presence in the room behind her and turned to see Edward standing in the doorway.

'We never properly got the chance to talk, Charles and I. He was always that much further on – off at school while I was still running around in short trousers, and then off to war. You know he was mentioned twice in dispatches. He was very outgoing, popular, but he had this mind. I think he was quite special. He converted the room into his own library after he came down from Oxford. Working with one of the estate joiners, choosing the wood, laying it all out, intricate plans that he spent forever over. And once it was done, he'd spend hours in here on summer evenings. Excavations into another world, I suppose. Mother didn't know what to do with it all after he died. So we've kept it as it is. It's swept every day, I think.'

He gestured to her to leave the room and then followed, closing the door behind him.

'Would you ever sit in there?' Jean asked. 'Perhaps it would be like sitting with him for a while.'

'It wouldn't seem right. It was very much his. It feels private somehow.' He looked ahead, giving away no emotion as they walked down the dim corridor. It was hung with enormous oils of stags sprawled on the fell, the light so poor that in the gloom the animals looked to Jean like beasts from a child's nightmare.

'It must be so hard for you – for you all.'

There was a flicker of tension at Edward's jaw. He ran his fingers quickly through his hair. 'It's hard when one is reminded always of Charles. Not simply that he's gone, but somehow that it's me that's left.' And he gave her a brief sideways look then – the tiniest revelation of self, snatched away as quickly as it was given – before he walked her up the stairs to her room.

She knew then that this family was paralysed, suspended between the ages of dead son and living, between a world before the war, when everything could drift on in the perfect light of a summer's afternoon, and the grim reality of today: Edward now in charge, a bleaker world, his position unstable. The realisation was something that appealed to her. Here was the thing she could tend to and make good, a young man who needed her – not just for her money, which threatened to eclipse her at times, but for her love. This was the cause of his distance. This would be something for her to mend.

And when he left her politely at her bedroom door, that sideways look and the glimpse of the empty fireplace in his brother's ossifying library stayed with her long afterwards.

CHAPTER FOUR

The visit to Harehope had been deemed a success. This was quite clear from the relish with which her mother relayed details of the trip to her confidantes – 'My dear, there was not a ceiling without damp, great circles of brown, but oh! the gardens. Divine, quite divine.' Yet the reality of what Jean had felt with Edward was so fragile that she kept turning over snatches of connection, trying to work them into something more before a recollection of another quite different conversation, marked by cool restraint, unpicked them all again.

In a draughty drawing room on Charles Street, at another dinner before another dance, in a room full of boys and girls not quite saying what they meant, Jean and Edward found themselves together again. She approached him, shyly; a quick smile, a sip of a drink, a moment before they were called to sit down.

He spoke first. 'My mother didn't put you off? Girls can find her fearsome. Some of Charlotte's friends won't come back to Harehope at all. It's not what she says, but what she doesn't.'

'The opposite might be true of mine.' Jean paused. 'She can be rather overbearing.'

'She puts on quite a show.'

'I've grown so used to it that I don't notice it any more. I suppose English restraint puts it in high relief.'

At one remove from the conversation, she listened to them swap stories of their parents as if they didn't exist themselves. Gone were the ages of chaperones, but one seemed to stand between them nonetheless. And there was an awkwardness to him, an almost palpable uncertainty beneath the confidence. For all the utter rightness of his manners, his knowledge of precisely what one ought to do in any given circumstance, his perfect breeding that allowed him entry to every room, he still cleared his throat before he spoke, looked always to his friends for their reactions.

Freddie came to join them then – a kiss for Jean, a brief shake of the hand for Edward – and she could sense Edward's relief as his friend took over the talking. And when dinner came and she was placed next to Freddie, he seemed to know what she was thinking.

'He's a funny one. My oldest friend, but I'm not sure I ever know what he's going to do or say. I suppose he operated as something of a free agent as a child. His mother ignored them all, and he was surplus to requirements anyway, with Charles there, always out in front. Edward was left to do as he pleased, and no one bothered much.' He smiled. 'I wouldn't wonder if you and he aren't a good thing. For him, I mean. Beyond the obvious, of course. He'd hate me saying it, but it might bolster him a little.'

And her mother had settled on the idea. Despite Elizabeth's protestations about Harehope's rooms, whose temperature seemed to hover around freezing, she was drawn to the Warre name, to the standing of this family whose money was in decline but whose position was certainly not.

'He's a dear, isn't he? That fine face, trying to be in command when his mother's like the admiral of the ship, blasting out orders from that tiny little body. Think what you could do for him, Jean. The life you could have with him, my darling daughter.'

And they danced again at the Savoy, the band playing a song that sent the young rushing to fill the floor, and she felt a tension within Edward amid the noise and the laughing, felt there were things he would like to do or say but didn't yet know how. That was what marriage would do: it would liberate, it would unburden them of the sense of others always watching; it would set them free, wouldn't it?

'Oh, you'd be a fool not to,' girls in powder rooms with laughs of glass would say, not quite to her.

'A lot of the good ones are gone.'

'If you don't marry in your first season out, you'll be dragging around your parents' heels for eternity.'

And then they'd dance off and all that would be left was a strange silence within the noise and the acid taste of too much champagne, and Jean would feel suddenly, clearly, that to pursue this, to persevere with whatever this thing was, was the only means available to her of entering real life. Without it, she would always be at the edge of things, the gauze of propriety keeping everything at bay. She had always felt hampered by the air of who she was that hung about her. Her mother, her name, her great, great wealth, was like a mantle around her shoulders, and until that was removed, she feared she would be caught in aspic, observing only.

And so she and Edward had walked along the Embankment that night, in a group of bright young boys and girls, cheeks red and eyes shining from the dancing and the sweet taste of spirits, happy simply because the evening was warm and there was another party to go to. Then they were standing alone, leaning against the stone balustrade, catching their breaths with the Thames flowing strong and silent beneath them.

The voices of the others were further away; snatches of laughter, someone being mobbed up, and Edward leaned forward and kissed her. His lips on hers, rough somehow, his breath on her face, warm and sweet.

He pulled back then, looked at her. Not a smile, but his face was a question. And so she had smiled for him, had put her hand in his, and they had walked the last part of the journey together in silence. And this subtle shift in status had been noted, had been marked down in society's ledger – an invisible work of untold weight – in thick, black ink for all to see.

CHAPTER FIVE

Jean was lying on her bed, a book open and unread beside her. The blinds were lowered against an afternoon sun defiantly laying great strips of bleached white across her room. The house on Park Lane was a place of two parts during the hours of daylight. Downstairs, in the state rooms, as her mother grandly called them, guests were being received, history made in the figures of substance hourly called up its great stone steps. Young men from the embassy, the hopes of her country's future, with fine minds and intelligent faces, walked briskly along corridors they knew were steeped in influence and power. On Jean's floor, however, several flights of stairs up, all was quiet. Legs stretched out, head resting on her hand, she would allow herself to day-dream. This time away from the curious gaze was sustenance to her, carrying her through the endless engagements – her mother's evening sport – that would inevitably follow. Elizabeth Buckman rarely came upstairs during these hours of industry, so when she appeared at Jean's door, chest rising from the exertion of bringing her not inconsiderable girth up the four flights of stairs, and urged her daughter to hurry down to her salon, Jean knew that she was being called downstairs in a real sense, that the in-between she had inhabited – a child in all but name, her freedom only existing as an expression of her mother's wishes – was drawing to an end; she could feel it in the tiny droplets of perspiration at her mother's forehead, in the grip of the handkerchief in her hot little hand.

Jean followed her mother down corridors where young men now stood aside, door upon door opening until the final set was pinned back, revealing the inner sanctum of her mother's salon and her father standing in front of the fireplace, a look of vague worry on his face. He would be desperate to escape this room, filled as it was with emotion and untrammelled female excitement.

Elizabeth seemed to fizz with pent-up joy, her face straining to contain itself. She spoke, as usual, for the pair.

'Jean, dearest. Father has been at Edward's club for lunch, and he has asked for his permission to marry you. It's simply wonderful. We shall have a wedding! Robert, do tell her.' The hint of impatience was barely concealed.

Her father nodded. 'Edward seems like a sound young man, and your mother is, as you can see, very taken with the idea. I'm assuming this is in accordance with your own wishes too?' His eyes were hopeful, willing on an answer that would tie up this matter and release him.

The tension in Jean's stomach dissipated, for it had happened, this thing that had been on her mind for several months. But what replaced it was unexpected. A seminal point in her life was upon her – windows flung open, life to come in. Events had been working towards this, gradually gaining momentum, and yet now it had arrived in this room that smelt overwhelmingly of freesias and her mother's cloying scent, it had somehow fallen flat.

Her parents' eyes were upon her. She could see how ready they were to accept this shift in her status from daughter to wife, as natural as the flow of a river to them, out and into the mouth of a waiting sea. She caught the almost imperceptible shrinking of her mother's eyes – the fear that the plan she desired for Jean might not be brought to fruition. *It must, it must, there is no other course*, those eyes said.

'Yes, of course, Father, that's wonderful. Thank you, thank you so much. That's wonderful. It really is.'

The relief at her reply was clear, her father giving her a kiss on her cheek before excusing himself, and Elizabeth was like a dog unleashed, free and away, running through lists of people and clothes and dates and notes to be written, all punctuated with the briefest of exclamations addressed in Jean's vague direction – 'Oh, how marvellous, oh, what fun we'll have.'

'I think we ought to invite the Goelets to dinner this evening, don't you, darling? As they were here that night we all met? And perhaps Lady Warre and her daughter would come again when they are next in London? Perhaps a little party – well, a proper party – to celebrate the engagement. Oh, and the peonies will be just perfect for that. A peony party! How delicious.'

Jean sat to the left of her mother's desk, in the small armchair with its tight lemon-yellow upholstery and the firm but not too firm stuffing that her mother insisted upon, and let her mind empty to try and unpick what she could out of all of this. How strange to make a decision of such magnitude at one remove. Not to see Edward. As if she were extraneous to the whole thing. She wanted to talk to him, to ask him what he felt, to put her hand in his, to kiss him again, but instead it was for her to sit in this chair, listening to her mother, agreeing when required, making suggestions when needed, as a succession of people began to file through the salon and the afternoon progressed, a never-ending procession of women kissing Jean, congratulating Elizabeth, patting Jean's hand, touching her cheek, their words and good wishes like playing cards mounting up till the pack was all there and the event was a reality.

As tea was being cleared, the fire re-laid for the evening and the room making its ritual change from day to evening, Jean found herself talking to a cousin of Edward's who had heard the news and had to stop by; the conversation felt rather transactional, Jean handing over pieces of information that the girl pocketed immediately like coins. Jean's mother and one of her oldest friends, an American married to that most prized of all possessions, an English duke, were chatting in the corner of the room, Jean only vaguely apparent to them now, so enraptured were they both by the far more real presence of a Wedding to Arrange. Elizabeth's voice had dropped, but Jean could hear her still.

'Oh, it was her destiny, Mary. She doesn't know it, but the procession of the Buckman name across the water and into a fine English family…the foundations were laid years ago.'

'Of course! In everything you've done—'

'That I have arranged – not her father, I might add, but me – from birth to now.'

'But like the finest of dresses, you can't see a stitch.'

'Well, it's the hand of God at work, my dear. And what if Edward's a little awkward? Isn't that the English way? Some charm to be found in the eccentricity, and frankly, the arrogance—'

'Oh, Elizabeth, mother of a daughter to be wed, a prize in itself these days, and into quite a family. Well, thankfully there's no ageing father and unseemly handover to worry about. That's quite the wedding gift.'

And so the announcement of their engagement was placed the next day in *The Times*. A lunch for fifty followed at her parents' house. A trip to Paris was arranged to shop for her trousseau and to have the first of three fittings for a dress of the finest duchesse satin that France could provide. Yet Edward and Jean were rarely alone. They did kiss again – brief, spare, chaste – and they went to dinner several times among a group of his friends, to the Savoy again or the Berkeley, to a party held by Freddie Byam-Hughes at his parents' house on the corner of Brook Street, and at each a never-ending succession of unfamiliar faces approached them, beaming, hands outstretched, congratulating the pair on their news, thumping Edward on the back.

She kept looking to Edward to see if he felt the same, to remake that second of connection that would carry her through a hundred absences, but he never seemed to look up at the right point, never caught her eye when she needed him to. And so she left it, and turned to the matters at hand: the invitations, the dress, the planning, the guests. The construction of an edifice so grand and assured that no one noticed she couldn't find the door to enter it at all.

CHAPTER SIX

It was July, and after a damp June there had been a run of almost unprecedented heat and sun since the beginning of the month, the barometer in the hall at Harehope stuck at VERY DRY for weeks. A celebration of Jean and Edward's engagement for the tenants of the estate had been arranged, and a house party pulled together to make it more palatable for the family. The lawn was beginning to yellow with patches of scorched and lumpy grass that the under-gardeners would toil over fruitlessly. Borders were beginning to wilt, and even the guests were tiring of cheerful commentary on the weather. The river was as low as anyone could remember and fishing was out, leaving the men snappy and bored at the lack of sport to fill the hours of daylight. Those staying gathered in knots, waiting politely for instruction from their hosts, who were nowhere to be seen.

Jean sat with her mother in the drawing room, waiting for Edward to finish a meeting taking place in his study.

'You look so nervous, darling. Smile a little.' Elizabeth wore the voice Jean knew well from childhood, warm and smooth as butter with the unmistakable hint of steel beneath. 'I can see that the formality of those two gentlemen is unsettling. But they are simply doing their job. Your father had to go through the same thing before we married, although if I recall, there were three of them and Robert looked, for the first time in his life, utterly terrified.' She lowered her voice. 'Come. It is a gift, this thing we can bestow. Our home in New York, Newport, the newspaper. That was my gift to your father, and look at the joy it has brought us.' Then the slightest of shadows falling, the shift in the room as Jean knew that the image of her brother Oliver had come to their mother, the darkness that appeared always at the edge of their perfect family portrait. 'You are giving Edward a gift that will change his life immeasurably. Your challenge is to be delicate in how you bestow it. Never let him feel you are in charge, or at least let him take the lead in situations he feels he needs to. I can see that Edward may struggle with this a little more than your father. He doesn't have quite the same talents to build on, if we are being direct, but he has this place, this house, this estate that you can' – the hint of a smile danced at the edge of her mouth – 'enhance.'

Jean nodded. She knew her mother's family wealth was, in essence, limitless, in what it could buy and in what it could achieve. It had guaranteed them a place at the table that was New York society of the 1860s: a hard-won seat that, once attained, was gripped with determination; today, the interest on their capital alone, doubling and trebling as each month passed, would allow that position to continue in perpetuity. But in this house, in the figure of those two men from her grandfather's bank sitting with Edward now and informing him of quite how blessed this union was, Jean wasn't sure if it was a gift entering or something more insidious, something alien finding its way into this place that had survived unassisted for so long.

The door opened, and Edward came into the drawing room in his shirtsleeves, the cotton crumpled and damp from the heat of the airless study. He wouldn't look at Jean but rather addressed her mother: 'They say they have all they need, and so I think the suggestion was we'd have lunch before they went back to London?'

Elizabeth rose, delighted that the meeting was over. She gave Edward a pat on the arm as she passed. 'It wasn't so bad, was it, my dear?'

The group made up an awkward little six as they took lunch in the morning room, where smaller numbers would dine. The lunch passed like stagnant water, with Lady Warre unable, or unwilling, to find the correct register to address these men who were undeniably trade but had mysteriously found a place at her table. Elizabeth, however, used to her work as an ambassador's wife and able to create atmosphere out of a paper bag when it suited her, kept her end up, asking questions, laughing delightedly at even the whiff of a joke, clapping her hands together in delight when Edward so much as opened his mouth.

One of the men from the bank, a Mr Bennett, an owlish figure for whom lunchtime chit-chat was an impossibility, was addressing Jean with great seriousness, having been studiously ignored by Lady Warre.

'The question of a house in London did arise in our discussions. Of where you and Lord Warre might like to live in town after you are married. I believe a possible house has been posited by Mrs Buckman.'

Lady Warre looked sharply at her son. 'Is that so? How kind of Mrs Buckman.' She turned to Elizabeth. 'And where have you been thinking my son might live?'

Elizabeth, oblivious to the acid in her host's voice, smiled. 'Robert and I have been told by several people of your family's house on Park Lane coming back up for sale, and wondered whether that might be of interest. A possibility too good to resist?'

Even Alice Warre was taken aback. She took a sip from the glass of water before her. 'Our house? It would, as you say, be quite something to have it back. It was in the family for over a century before my husband sold it.'

Unperturbed, Elizabeth continued as if she had suggested buying a bag of apples. 'Jean, darling, I think that would be lovely. Don't you?'

Jean looked to Edward, who was concentrating on his food.

Alice – such a gentle, girlish name for someone who was the opposite – gave a brittle smile. 'And what other little wedding gifts did you discuss in your meeting, Edward? Do tell.'

He cleared his throat. 'Come, Mother.'

Mr Bennett, who seemed only able to react in the literal, nodded gravely. 'We discussed one settlement from Mrs Buckman that Lord Warre would like to put towards the house here, and we discussed, only briefly, the possible purchase of further moorland in Scotland. And then there was mention of paintings and furniture that might be required for the London residence, once agreed upon.'

On he went, his voice as efficient as it was dull, running through suggestions Edward had made, in private, as to how this marriage might be put to use, of how he intended to spend the largesse Elizabeth Buckman was generously dispensing, painfully unaware of the discomfort it was now causing. Jean saw Edward shifting in his seat; knew his mother would be unable to contain her distaste at the direction of the conversation.

Edward stood up. Cheeks red, unable to look at his mother or Jean, he addressed Mr Bennett. 'Thank you, I think we have heard enough from the meeting. If you are to catch the afternoon train to London, it would be a good idea to get your things ready. Someone will be waiting in the front hall to take you.' He left the room quickly.

His mother stood to follow Edward out. 'Thank you both so much. I must say, I am not accustomed to lunches such as this. Most enlightening.'

Jean sat that evening in her room before dinner. The heat from the sun was gone but the air was heavy and damp, the quiet broken by the occasional roll of thunder, so distant one wasn't sure what it was but carrying with it the expectancy of release to come.

The house itself was quiet, as people had retired to their rooms to prepare for the evening. She could hear the gentle closing and opening of doors down the corridor, the sound of voices as tables were laid, glasses put out, windows opened, cushions taken in from chairs outside as the weather threatened to break.

She sat at the mirror at her dressing table, face scrubbed clean and hair held back by a silk band of pure white. Stripped of everything, the girl that looked back at her was so young; so unfinished. And yet all this tension, this change at Harehope that seemed to pull at Edward, to grate on his mother, had been brought about by her and her alone: by this girl of twenty, with a face scrubbed clean and eyes carrying uncertainty.

Jean had never contemplated until now how much her decision to marry could recast the dice for someone else; how her acceptance had diverted the Buckman river to a new course. It was so strange to feel herself a vessel through which funds poured and lives were altered. She was a classical goddess, changing her form and those around her. For the awkward little signing session that afternoon had transformed everything into Edward's: in an instant it had become Warre wealth; an alchemy of Californian gold to northern coal and back to gold, in a seamless flow that began in the foothills of the Sierra Nevada and would culminate in her walking into the drawing room tonight in a perfect silk dress that hung ready for her now, draped in jewels that lay in open boxes before her, to stand before a young man who exhaled his cigarette smoke into the air like a knife, taking her in as she stood before him: a golden vessel to be turned and inspected and emptied out.

CHAPTER SEVEN

Jean's Aunt Elaine, a fly in the ointment for Elizabeth Buckman at this time of unparalleled celebration, had arrived at Harehope the following morning. Elaine Radcliffe was her father's sister – a tall, handsome woman, with the same high forehead and strong nose as her brother, forty-four and, more importantly to her sister-in-law Elizabeth, a divorcee. The whiff of scandal that still accompanied Elaine in certain circles meant she was intolerable to Elizabeth. The New York society Mrs Buckman presided over was not known for its spirit of forgiveness. As long as Jean could remember, Elaine had always lived alone.

Elaine asked Jean if they might escape the other guests and go for a walk along the stretch of river that ran closest to the house. There was a mown path cut between banks of wild-flowers that was pleasant, even though the water was now so low it barely covered the rough stones of the riverbed. Elaine had clearly been enjoying her tour of the English countryside prior to her arrival at Harehope, amused by the formality that accompanied every occasion of the day, however small, from breakfast alone in her bedroom to the elaborate tea in the dining room for which the guests would assemble in another change of clothes. Everything was faintly ridiculous to Elaine, and Jean had seen her watching Lady Warre and Charlotte talking that morning with a barely concealed fascination, as if it were all a diverting play rather than a scene from what was soon to be Jean's life.

They walked in easy silence for a while before Elaine looked across at her niece. 'I'm sorry I put your mother's hackles up so terribly. I don't have to do anything at all to get that imperious look of hers.'

'I think it's that you don't mind what she says to you. It's quite a rare thing.'

'Well, I'm sure she's told you that by God's good grace I can't attend your wedding. Hence the invitation here, I suppose. I'm on to Italy after this little jaunt. And I'll see Robert down in London. Elizabeth let me know that no one of interest was here at Harehope and was very clear that I only stay a few days. So, now we are alone, tell me something. What does Edward do on days like this? I haven't laid eyes on him once since breakfast. Are there hidden tunnels underneath the house, transporting him to secret assignations with the other men, where there's more food and more drink served on more white linen?'

Jean laughed. 'I honestly don't know. I suppose he goes down to the river, although there's no fishing with the water so low. Or he has meetings with the agent. There's always some kind of business to attend to. You must have seen that officious-looking Mr Wisden lurking outside the dining room. The master of the long explanation when ten words would surely do.'

'Does he ever come and find you? Edward, I mean. Or perhaps that's not quite the done thing here?'

'Not really, no. I suppose it isn't. Everyone tends to do their own thing.'

'Perhaps he's unsure of what Miss Buckman might wish to do in her hours of leisure?'

'He's still very reserved when we're alone. Sometimes he talks, but he's much more himself when he's with his friends. Which I can understand – and I don't think the meeting with Mother's people from the bank helped much.' Jean was embarrassed by how weak it all sounded. She didn't want to have something that still felt untested scrutinised by someone as worldly – and blunt – as her aunt. She bent down to pick some of the heads off the wild garlic that had run riot along the path; crushing the leaves in her hand, she breathed in the bitter, peppery scent.

'But shouldn't you two be desperate to spend every second together? Waiting for your mothers' backs to turn before clasping hands and whispering into each other's ears?' Elaine was smiling, but it was clear she would not abandon her line of questioning.

'I suppose so. But it doesn't seem that's the point of the engagement. Rather it's endless drink parties and tea parties and incessant talk of the church and the dress. Once we're married we can do all of that. We can just get on with the rest.'

'My dear, I know you are twenty, and being the daughter of your mother, one might need to take two years off that. But you're about to marry this young man – and no doubt in some style. Can you tell me why you have decided to do this? It's not for his family, if my conversation this morning with Lady Warre has taught me anything.' Her bark of a laugh shot out.

'I want to do it,' Jean replied, tentatively. 'He's handsome, if that's what you mean. He seems to like me.' The last words came out as a question without her intending it.

'How English you sound! With your self-deprecation and apologies. I don't think you realise quite how good you are. You've been no trouble at all, always going along with what your mother has suggested, or what you think your father would want. Now you're going to marry some repressed Englishman because it's convenient for them too! My dear, at eighteen I married the right man, who lived at the right address, who summered in the right place, who had the right sort of friends. And then one morning I sat at the breakfast table and realised that this was my only life and it was being spent with a man who if I'd asked him to name one thing about me that he'd learned since we were married, it would have been that I didn't care for marmalade. Life is so brief, it's glimpsed and then it's gone. Decisions at your age are taken so lightly it's almost comical. Is it for your mother?' The bite in her aunt's voice was impossible to ignore.

'Perhaps. Perhaps it is, you know.' Her own voice sounded too quiet. 'I do like the idea of getting out from under her feet. Of it all happening and then moving on with things, without too much fuss.' Jean hesitated, unsure whether to continue. 'And have you heard about Oliver? He left Yale halfway through his sophomore year, demanding they find him a senior job at the paper. And he's only been in it two months and he's causing trouble – late and unreliable, missing for hours at a time. They're worrying so much about it. I can see it on Father's face all the time. What will become of him, all that potential wasted, the public nature of his failure. I can get away from all of that. And, you know, I feel sorry for Edward. He's the brother of this boy everyone worshipped, this boy who's gone, and I can see he doesn't feel up to the job yet. He's unsure of himself and he has that great burden of expectation, and I understand that. I really do. Look at Oliver.' She was sounding more sure of herself now.

'You're so good, so conscientious.' Elaine was smiling again, but her eyes weren't. 'What a waste, my darling. You could have been wild and wilful and driven every man mad here with your indecision. What fun I would have had in your shoes. But I see that you've done what you've always done – taken the right path, easiest for everyone – and no doubt it will make your parents supremely happy. But these moments of choice are fleeting. Use them wisely.' Seeing Jean's discomfort, her face softened. 'I understand how keen one can be to move on to the next thing, to avert the world's gaze, really I do. But in truth, you girls barely know yourselves at all. It's as if you exist only in summary, and beneath there lies a great well of the unexplored, the unmined. You all forge on, like the well brought up, dutiful things that you are, unaware of the dangers of making decisions like these without breaking through that crust. You'll remember these words one day, when you're an ancient old crow like me.' And she laughed, that quick, sharp laugh that only reaffirmed to Jean the truth being revealed to her, if only she would take it.

The path took them to some wooden steps set into the bank that led down to the river's edge. The bank was dry and uninviting, the earth crumbling from the lack of rain. A heron stood opposite, head erect, the great curve of its neck and beak in silhouette against the dry grass behind. Something disturbed it from its watch and in a second it was out and over the water, beating its wings in great muscular movements that revealed its scale – skimming low at first and then higher, wheeling left, away from the house. Jean couldn't take her eyes off it; the singularity of its movement, deft and decisive, and her eyes followed it, mesmerised, until the river took a bend and it was out of sight.

*

The depleted party dined that night at a table set up in the smaller of the drawing rooms. It gave on to the lawn, with large double doors that were kept open as they ate, the candles on the table drawing in moths that danced above the light and caused the portraits that hung about the room to close in on them, like that familiar chorus commenting on the drama beneath. The storm had not yet fully broken and the air was close, the men longing to take off their jackets, to loosen their collars. Guests talked in low voices, the dinner seeming to lack an obvious host. Edward and his mother expected their guests to take the conversational lead; that they had opened their doors to outsiders was, in their opinion, generosity enough.

Jean and Edward were next to each other, as custom demanded. When he turned to talk to her, following the change in partner his mother had signalled at the head of the table, his features remained impassive.

She spoke quietly so no one else could hear. 'I'm sorry about yesterday, Edward. I hated lunch too. It's a strange thing, all of this, but once it's all arranged, we can put it behind us.'

He nodded, a brief, polite smile. He had the flush to his cheeks he'd get in the evenings, a red mark just below the cheekbone, and he drank quickly, impatient to get the imposition of dinner out of the way, keen to return to the fug of cigar smoke and the easy companionship of male conversation. 'If you don't mind, I'd rather we didn't talk about it at all. As you say, it's done now.' His expression was painfully serious, and he looked so young. He was twenty-one – no sense of self developed yet and the Buckman stamp now firmly imprinted on him for all the world to see.

Jean looked up and saw her aunt's face between the glow of the candles, eyes on her and Edward. Her expression was unreadable, though Jean knew her thoughts. Her stomach contracted for a fraction of a second; she felt the possibility of another life, another choice, like a ghost's breath on her face. Then it was gone.

CHAPTER EIGHT

Seven months later

Jean stood, the collar of her coat buttoned high, the wool rubbing at her chin. Her skin felt raw and her eyes watered from the shock of the cold. The park was a flat grey, hard with frost, and the sky, heavy with the threat of snow, mirrored it, as if earth and sky were one and the same and this thin sliver of life – the house, the stables, the smudge of smoke from the chimneys – was just a scratch of ink on paper. The air was still and the sounds of the yard came clearly across to her where she stood, leaning against the stone pillar, head kept low for warmth. She could hear the dogs whining and yapping and one of the stable lads was shouting, his voice hoarse. She was too cold, out here on her own with no conversation to distract her from the bite in the air, and so she turned slowly back to the house. As she approached, the doors flung open and Edward, in shirt and breeches, was there, shouting for someone to find his boots. 'And have you seen my wretched jacket? I can never find anything, and everyone knows I leave at the same time every bloody morning.'

She had no idea where his jacket was, nor his boots, nor did she fully understand the pattern of life so normal to everyone else at Harehope but her. The wave of activity that swept through this house that was now hers each morning: her husband striding out in immaculately polished boots, crop in hand, jacket over one arm, to find the hounds, yapping and circling at the kennels in the yard. His mother too would join each day, the Dowager Lady Warre – famous for her fearlessness, her tiny figure upright, side-saddle, the liveried grooms fussing around her horse, each, to a number, terrified of her. The hunt met in front of Harehope most mornings and Edward was master of hounds, fearless, strident, position unquestioned when in the saddle.

Jean went back outside again, following her husband, jacket now found of course, and stood on the gravel as the throng gathered, the men talking in low voices, their breath freezing in the damp air as the horses pawed the ground and shifted, pulling to get away. As they came together at the sound of the horn and made off, the majesty of it all struck her, the order in the chaos as horses circled and turned till they found their position and streamed off, Edward in front, but then a wash of loneliness swept over her, the like of which she'd never felt before.

It was now late February, coming to the end of the hunting season, when Edward would ride out like mad every hour he could, from morning till dusk. Time did something strange here at Harehope: hours passed inside in a sort of dim silence, whole days going by, rolling into the next, each just as the one before it. Jean remained at the house, struggling to make headway with the servants who, to a number, refused to acknowledge her new position as Edward's wife, the lady of the house. Only yesterday she had asked why the tea in the drawing room was left out to get cold for an hour before anyone was there to drink it. Her question had been met with the same blank-faced response – 'It is how her ladyship did it' – and a bob of a curtsey. Her mother-in-law, though no longer living in the house, was a spectral presence that hung over every room, her name on the tip of every servant's tongue.

Jean had attempted to exert some control a month or so into her new life as Lady Warre. She had come downstairs, weaving her way through the kitchens, heads lifting and hands wiped hurriedly on aprons as she passed, looks of confusion followed by hurried curtseys as on she went, down corridors entirely unknown to her, where she had been told, reluctantly she felt, Mrs Hawkins' little study resided. A knock at the door and another face of polite surprise appeared. 'Lady Warre?'

'I'm sorry to disturb you.'

'Please come in.' The housekeeper ushered her into the small, neat room and waited awkwardly, unable to sit while her mistress stood.

'I felt we ought to have a conversation about how things are done in the house. Now that I'm living here.' How to do this, Jean had no idea.

'Of course. I had assumed that you were happy to continue with things as they were. But I do understand.' Mrs Hawkins waited patiently, head tilted to one side.

The list Jean had assembled in her head now felt too pathetic to articulate. For was this the extent of her role? To suggest the lighting of fires an hour earlier; to shift the changing of the flowers from a Monday to a Tuesday. And what was there to change – it all ran perfectly well without her involvement, this house that had done things in the same way for eternity, without the interference of a silly little girl from New York and Rhode Island who had never so much as hung up her own dress?

A smile hovered politely on the housekeeper's face. 'I wouldn't want your ladyship to trouble yourself unnecessarily with details. We do find the house runs well, and I'm sure you have more important things to concern yourself with.'

'No, no. I see that things are done very well. That's not what I meant.' Jean forced a bright smile. 'Perhaps if we could just light the fire in the drawing room a little earlier on cold mornings? And if I could go through what bedrooms we are to put guests in, that sort of thing. It's not much really.'

'Of course, m'lady. And I shall let Stokes and the rest know about the drawing room fire straight away.'

But as Mrs Hawkins, as her mother-in-law, her mother, indeed the entire sentient world would no doubt feel, the thing with which Jean was meant to be concerned, given that she had been married now for nearly a year, was producing an heir. Though money abounded, though the leaking roof was being attended to, though paintings of note were being acquired and cottages once quietly sold now publicly bought back, what the world required of her was to bring forth a child, and preferably a boy.

They had made a start, of course; a start so inept, so riddled with feelings of inability and inadequacy, of polite attempts and silence, that it hung over them both like a cloud. The first time she knew must be put down to experience, or lack of it, but it had continued like that, a thing of tension and of propriety, of failures that couldn't be expressed. It was of marks missed, God by how far, and yet they were in a contract to persevere. Jean knew nothing of herself – nothing of her own body, nor what it was meant to do or bring about in Edward. She had occasionally come close with a girlfriend to talk of what 'it' might involve, but the pathetic collection of half-heard and barely understood scraps that Jean held was entirely useless when it came to needing it, arming her only with a rigid anxiety. Edward was silent, his embarrassment at their failed unions worn as a sort of sullen distaste. When they dressed afterwards, he putting on his pyjamas quietly, buttoning the shirt methodically, she pulling the nightdress over her head and climbing back into bed, she wanted to cry for their growing inability to express. These were acts that seemed now to her cloaked in shame, Edward's body filled not with desire but with some urgent need for the whole thing to be over. In that, at least, they shared something.

As the weeks turned into months and these occurrences – for that was how they felt to her: occurrences that captured no part of her beyond her body in its most anatomical sense – failed to result in a pregnancy, a frustration had come to the edge of things. Edward wouldn't want to look at her afterwards, would often make an excuse and go and sleep in his dressing room. Eventually he had suggested a specialist in these matters be called, to see, as he elegantly put it, 'what was wrong with her'. A Mr Jenkins, a large, breathless man, his neck spilling over his collar, had been summoned from London at the recommendation of Edward's mother, and Jean was submitted to a variety of excruciating questions and perfunctory examinations.

'Physically, your ladyship is in excellent condition. A little undernourished perhaps, though one never knows what the fashion for eating is these days.' He gave an exaggerated sigh as he mopped his brow with a crumpled handkerchief. 'In my day, it was a glass of ale before breakfast.' He shook his head mournfully. 'I'm not sure it is the same today. I should think rest and time spent here at Harehope should do it.'

Jean had allowed Stokes to show him out and had sat in the drawing room a while longer, listening to the ticking of the ormolu clock, the creak and shift of the house, and the voice in her head growing louder and louder, hammering against the genteel silence. What Mr Jenkins had diagnosed was unhappiness – nothing more than her body, worn down by this pallid distance that sat between her and Edward, by her constant questioning of herself, failing to bring forth flesh.

She was the opposite of those fecund nudes in the Italian paintings that hung before her now; they were all fleshy curves and burgeoning desire. She was a rail of bones, taut and anxious, ready to snap. The more she thought about the idea of children resulting from their weekly unions, the more laughable the whole thing became to her.

And now here she was, a fur around her shoulders to keep the damp chill in the room at bay, another day of nothing yawning before her.

Stokes entered the room with his customary throat-clearing, followed by the parson, who was clutching a battered leather holdall and limping slightly.

'Lady Warre, so kind of you to invite me this morning.' Before Jean could remember if she had, he sank into the corner of a sofa, an expression of bliss spreading across his face. 'My joints trouble me greatly in this cold weather. Such a relief to sit in such comfort. Are you cold, Lady Warre? You look frozen through.'

'I'm fine, thank you. I'm not sure I've acclimatised to the house yet.' In fact, she dreamed of copper pipes dripping with steam; of living up to the caricature of her fellow country-women and bringing Harehope's plumbing into the twentieth century. Her mother-in-law might hate it, but she wasn't sure if she could spend another winter under sheets so cold they felt damp, waiting for a maid to make the sixth trip up the back stairs to make a single bath warm enough to wash in.

Stokes re-entered, carrying a whisky and water on a silver salver, though it couldn't have been later than eleven – 'Weak, I trust, dear man?' the parson enquired, eyes transfixed by the tumbler of liquid gold presented to him – and Jean stood while Stokes took charge of the fire that lay unlit and damp despite her attempt at change.

The parson cleared his throat. 'Now that you are firmly ensconced at Harehope, I wondered whether I might enlist your help in the choice of hymns and flowers at the Sunday service. The late Lord Warre made the decisions when he was alive, but I don't think your husband has quite the same...interest in the spiritual life...' His voice petered out.

'This was something Lord Warre used to do?'

'Well, yes. The religious life of the tenants and the surrounding villages does rather fall on the shoulders of the incumbent. Your husband has a duty to appoint the livings in five of the surrounding churches. It is a special bond between the land and those who are blessed enough to live on it; one of the many, almost imperceptible ties between the Warre family and those who live here.' He looked hopefully up at Jean. 'I think the late Lord Warre enjoyed that part of things. He was such a gentle man. The tenants here were very fond of him, he made such an effort, knew their names, would write to a widow or visit a cottage when the war took a son or grandson. He became terribly stooped at the end, but of course he had suffered the loss of his own son.' A cloud fell across his baggy face. 'Did you ever meet Charles?'

'No, I didn't. I've heard so much about him, I wish I had.'

'A quite brilliant young man. The hope of the place, if one is being candid. I think Lord Warre never considered a future without Charles. When Charles was killed, it was the end for him too. They were like islands, this family – Lady Warre, her husband, the children – but Charles was able, in his own way, to pull together the disparate threads. Perhaps it was their shared belief that all would be well with him at the helm that kept the family together. He had a warmth to his nature, an easiness with people.' He hesitated again. 'Not a characteristic perhaps shared with the rest of the family.'

Jean sat forward, the closest thing to a conversation she'd had in weeks opening up before her. 'I *have* found myself struggling with that particular family trait. I thought perhaps if I involved myself more, it might make things a bit easier, to feel at home, to have a greater sense of purpose.'

The parson nodded enthusiastically. 'The hunting can provide that, I am sure. The great outdoors.'

'Well, that's the thing. I'm not much of a horsewoman, I've barely ridden since I was a little girl. And within the house it's very much the case that everything is done as it always has been.' She looked up. 'I had wondered if I mightn't involve myself in the life of the tenants a little more, the local villages. My mother is a great one for that. I thought, perhaps, I could get involved with some of the charitable works that are done at Harehope.'

'Ah, I do understand. A noble suggestion. But her ladyship, by which I mean the Dowager Lady Warre, has rather a firm grip on that side of things. I wouldn't want to unsteady the ship there.'

'The local school perhaps? I saw on a walk last week that the building is not in the best condition. Some of the window frames looked rotten. I mentioned it to Edward, but he didn't seem to take much notice.'

He nodded, regretfully. 'Lady Warre has a group, the local ladies of note, as you might call them, that she very much has the whip hand over. All charitable works in the county tend to be done through her. The local schools, the hospital. I'm surprised she hasn't mentioned this to you.' He put his glass down on the little side table next to him and leaned forward, straining to get the momentum to reach the satchel at his feet. He gave her an encouraging smile as he pulled out a hymnal, holding it out towards her beseechingly. 'The early-nineteenth-century arrangements are most satisfactory, in my humble opinion. And even if your ladyship doesn't wish to choose, perhaps you might like to read the music and familiarise yourself with the words?'

That night she and Edward were to dine alone. He was late down, his bathing and dressing keeping him upstairs, and Jean sat waiting for him at a table laid for two in a small anteroom that led off the drawing room. Oval miniatures of the Warre family lined its pale damask walls, some silhouettes, some colour on ivory, and Jean sat, mesmerised by the sheer number of lives that had been lived here – of men, wives, children and grand-children, lives laid out like flies trapped in glass. How they had lived was long forgotten, perhaps never a thing of consequence at all, but what remained was the fact itself. That this family stretched back and back, seemingly forever. The surety of the place, its permanence giving it an inviolability, regardless of what ran beneath. It made her heart shrink a little, made her feel a tiny hand at her throat when the conversation of earlier came back to her: where did her place in all of this lie?

Edward entered, hair still damp from the bath, and Jean stood to receive a brief kiss on the cheek before he took his seat opposite her.

'How was your day?' Polite engagement was still their default.

'Do you really want to know?'

'Of course.'

'It was actually very good, despite the ground. We went all the way across to Stannington and up beyond there. Saw the usuals. Quite a decent gathering.' He looked to her.

'Well, the parson came to see me. Gave me a little talk on the code of *noblesse oblige*...'

He rolled his eyes. 'He would.'

'He came to ask me about choosing hymns and the flowers for the Sunday service, as apparently you won't. Then let me know, politely of course, that anything beyond that is still very much your mother's domain. Put a dampener on my suggestions of any kind of involvement. That it's not the done thing, or something like that.'

Edward was only half-listening, looking around for Stokes to fix him a drink.

'So I thought, if you didn't mind, I might go to London at the end of the week. There's not much here for me while you hunt and—'

'Is that what all of this is? Are you waiting for me to tell you what to do?' His voice had risen in irritation.

'All of what? I don't understand.'

'I've been watching you each morning these last weeks, and I can't decide whether you are unhappy or simply waiting for instruction.' He paused. 'There is no instruction. This is how life at Harehope is, always has been.'

Jean looked at the plate before her. She needed to try to explain to him how wrong this all felt. But how? 'You must see that we've never really discussed anything about what I'm to do here. We've just taken up this new life without talking about anything at all. When it comes to the house, anything I try to do seems to be met with the same response. That things run perfectly well as they always have done, without a need for me.'

'But is it such a hardship to live here at Harehope as things are? And your role, unless I am missing something, is to be my wife and hopefully the bearer of my children, to live perfectly happily here, and in London. And if London is your preference in the hunting season, then so be it. I'll come down in a couple of weeks, when it's over.' He wore a tight smile, but behind the effrontery it was pulling at him too.

Edward looked down at the table.

'It was made quite clear to me by those fellows from your bank that your life can proceed as it always has. Thanks to you we have houses, we have funds. We don't have children, but hopefully we can break the stalemate there soon. So don't for God's sake sit around pretending you need me or the pretence of domesticity to occupy yourself. Do what women do. Do what women of extraordinary means do. Just don't wait for me to tell you what that is. None of this should come as a surprise, surely?' His face was tense as he said these last words, his eyes filled with uncertainty even as his voice feigned confidence. She felt her stomach contract at the lack of understanding between them.

The restraint, the failed attempts at communication, the sex; he saw it not as something to be moved through but rather a thing they ought to accommodate, to learn to live with. To do more was beyond him. They were a stunted pair, so close to a life of connection but locked instead into this room of polite exchanges, of delicate evasion, that lay next door. A voice of protest rose but then could not find the words, so it fell away again, and that silence took hold. It held more power each time it lay between them, cementing their positions.

Stokes entered, a crystal water jug in hand. He filled each of their glasses, pausing briefly before leaving the room, the customary hint of enquiry.

'A whisky, Stokes, please. I'm tired tonight. And her ladyship will be leaving in the morning, so if someone could run her to the station. I'll have breakfast in my room tomorrow morning, if I may.'

CHAPTER NINE

Jean walked down the vast marble staircase alone, taking in the splendour of their London house, the paintings that she and her mother had chosen with the scholarly gentleman from Leggatt's when they had bought the house – a pair of vague, watery Venetian scenes, a dark view of Jacobean London which made her feel uneasy, and a de László of Jean on her engagement, filled with a promise and romance that seemed to her deceitful now. With each step closer to the drawing room she could feel the growing tautness in her stomach. Edward would be waiting for her in the smaller of the three drawing rooms in his perfectly pressed black tailcoat and waistcoat of brilliant white, his hair with its metallic glint of pomade. She steeled herself for another evening that they would embark on together, like a pair of beautiful carvings, brilliant in their shining detail, hollow and cold as a tomb.

They drove to dinner in silence, Edward smoking with the window down, the chill in the evening air causing the skin on her arms to pucker. His presence was so guarded, the air between them so uneasy, that the right words could never be found. All was stilted, over-thought and under-felt.

'Charlotte said she'd be at dinner tonight.' His voice was bored and he stayed looking out of the window as they passed the trees lining the edge of the park, bare outlines where spring was yet to burnish them. 'I'm thinking of going to Scotland for a week or two. I might take some friends to stay at the new lodge, Francis Stevens and possibly Freddie, to fish on the Tay. Stay in London or go back to Harehope, whichever you prefer.'

After two weeks spent apart, she thought something might have changed, but each evening had been the same since he had come down to join her from Harehope. She had tried with him, hoping that a party or a dinner to attend would bring them together, that small talk about the hosts or speculation about the guests might provide a different tempo to their life at Harehope; might break the habit of silence forming between them. She allowed the act of bathing and dressing, sitting at the mirror and making up her face, to soothe her anxious mind. This is what a marriage is, she told herself as a dress was held out before her to approve. This is how one learns the ways of one's husband. Incremental steps that would gradually bring them both to a place of contentment and knowledge. Tonight she had placed a gold bracelet on her wrist, the metal cool against her skin – a wedding gift from one of the hundreds of guests who had paid witness to their celebrated union, who had turned their faces to her, like so many hopeful sunflowers, as she processed down the aisle at the Chapel Royal.

Unaware of the stagnant pool Jean found herself in, her mother had been dropping an idea liberally into their conversations – 'just a little suggestion I had in mind, my darling'. But what was little to Elizabeth Buckman was not necessarily the same for the rest of the world, and what her mother desired most, what she had set her heart on, was for Jean to lay another piece on the family chessboard, to buy a house in France, 'near Nice perhaps, such a dear part of the coast'. She had been mentioning it more and more frequently, as was her way when the inevitable was before her, requiring only that it be taken up, as it ought, by her husband or her daughter. 'It would be the perfect project. It would get you out of England in this gloomy part of the year. Lots of charming people that you'll adore are doing the same.'

Selfless as her suggestion seemed, the house would mark the completion of Elizabeth's European conquest for her daughter. But it might do Jean good too, might break this strange habit of silence and tension forming between her and Edward.

Elizabeth had gone on, voice like cream: 'I've spoken to a number of people who take houses out there, who spend some of the winter and early spring in the South of France. The Elchos – do you remember divine Edith? Such a striking little thing, and her husband, I can't remember his name. Well, they are often there and Edith simply adored the idea of helping you and Edward find a house. Suggest it to him, won't you? A little present from your father and I. Such a delightful part of the world to spend one's time.'

Jean had not yet spoken of it to Edward. And what was there to fault? Another house bought for him, another Buckman gift bestowed upon him, though in reality the weight of this endless bounty was threatening to suffocate the life out of their marriage.

She kept her voice measured as she looked across at Edward, head turned away to the window as they passed Wellington Arch. 'I had an idea – to travel to France. Mother has mentioned that she and Father would love for us to buy a house down in the south. It would be a gift from them. A wedding present, Mama said.'

She waited.

'Edward?'

He looked across at her, the light from the street lamps catching the edge of his face, the perfect set to his jaw.

'Charlotte asked me the other night if you were getting bored of all this dreadful English parsimony. Go, go. I won't come. But perhaps that's the point. Paris will be unspeakably grim – a mass of hobbling soldiers and pale widows, tin cups upturned, and I don't know anything about the rest. But go.' Then he looked away, and she could hear the bitterness in his voice. 'And if your mother says we must have a house there, then who am I to stop her? How long will you go for? So I can tell people.'

'I'm not abandoning you, am I?'

'No, I see that. But we are just married, so I ought to have a line, don't you think?'

'I'm not sure yet. Mama suggested staying with Tommy and Edith Elcho, who I know are in Paris for the next month or so, and then going with them to Nice. To try and meet with a local agent to see what might be for sale. A couple of weeks, at the least.'

He nodded, his lips a tight line.

Their car had turned into Belgrave Square and was drawing up outside a house whose double doors were pinned open, the yellow light spilling out onto the street, a liveried footman waiting to bring them inside.

Edward opened the car door for her. He took her hand, a reflex of form not desire, and they walked in together: this perfect couple who had wealth, beauty, youth draped around their perfect shoulders, a pair for whom doors were always open, faces always delighted to receive. But like the silhouettes that hung at Harehope, though the outline was indisputably them, the interior felt to her impenetrable, their inner life still so obscured.

'Go. Go then,' he said to her with impatient eyes as they stepped inside, and then turned, with a different face entirely, to the group of young men idling in the hallway, waiting for his conversation, waiting to amuse him and to approve of him and to make him feel whole again. 'Go.'

CHAPTER TEN

A late-afternoon sun cast the colonnaded buildings that ran alongside the Jardin des Tuileries in that peculiarly golden glow that could only be Paris, as if the whole city was lit from within. Jean watched from the car's window as memories of her childhood passed her by, set against the piercing blue of a faultless sky. Past the Meurice they went, where she'd taken tea on winter afternoons so bitter her cheeks would be raw from the cold; on down the Rue de Rivoli, and then she was out in the vast opening of the Place Vendôme – and she saw herself, seven years old, coat buttoned and muffler on, one gloved hand tightly in her father's as she walked up the narrow stairs of a handsome building in the square's north-east corner, to his tailor, where a wall of cottons and silk bales seemed to reach to the sky.

Jean had spent four years in Paris as a little girl, her father the ambassador, Elizabeth Buckman at his side, electrified by all that this extraordinary, sophisticated belle-époque society could offer her. It was a reciprocal arrangement, for the city's finest paid lavish homage to this hostess whom they had first met when she was in her teens but who was now *une vraie dame, l'Americaine insurpassable.* At eight or nine, Jean would walk between the horse chestnuts of the Tuileries, the city's slate-grey skies her companion, its rooftops calling out for her to leap across them. She took ballet classes in a draughty drawing room somewhere in the 8th, Madame barking at her young students in her gravelly voice: *plié, plié, entrechat, plié*, all to the imperfect tune of an ancient piano. She watched her mother at Worth on Rue de la Paix as silent women, pinafored and pins in mouths, turned silk and chiffon into jewel-embellished works of art. These were disjointed memories, like splashes of ink on paper, of parties watched between banisters from the top of a giant staircase, of guests gliding into the courtyard of their *hotel particulier* like boats in sail, the glimpse of a vast wooden door, with a leering bull's head and twisted horns, disappearing from sight as the carriage rocked its way down the narrow cobbled streets on the day they left to return to New York.

The Elchos were, she was told, taking tea in the Ritz's garden, and she was shown at once to a manicured terrace – an oasis of cloche hats and pearls – where ladies and languid gentlemen were sitting at round tables, enjoying the afternoon pursuit of seeing and being seen. She saw Edith first, alert, upright in her round-backed wicker chair, ready to pounce; Tommy was slung deep in his, tea ignored, a glass of bourbon at his elbow and a paper, unread, in his lap. They took her in, her luggage, footman, hat, furs, with undisguised joy. Their next entertainment had arrived.

'Darling, settle in with us and let's get your things sent to your room. How are you? Travel palatable? Mother dispatched?'

Edith Elcho was a New York firecracker, the irresistible embodiment of old money glamour combined with an ability to make those in her brilliant, brittle company feel never quite enough. Jean's mother approved of her wholeheartedly. She was thin, striking more than beautiful, and had a lightning bolt of energy running through her veins; she was all gestures and wrists, leaning in conspiratorially one second then head flung back the next, a flash of teeth and a stretch of red lips, laughing at something horribly indiscreet. She had married an Englishman, Tommy: handsome, rich, well-connected and with his own particular attribute, a spectacular and self-celebrated indolence. The Elchos were always at the best party, always at the best table, Edith seated without fail at the host's right hand. They had the relaxed attitude of a pair who had nowhere to be other than where the mood took them.

'All fine, thank you so much. Mother was more than happy to see me go, but very keen to know about your mother and her recent trip to Rome. Frightfully jealous, she said; something about a lunch given for her with not one, but two cardinals in attendance?'

'Oh God, yes, she's right. Mama's written to most of New York about her European conquest – didn't manage to make her way to London to see us though, did she, darling?'

Tommy didn't look too worried by this turn of events, and smiled indulgently at Jean. 'How's Edward? Couldn't bear to leave the field?'

'Tommy, darling, it's such a relief you're so useless at all that,' Edith broke in before Jean could answer. 'All those ridiculous costume changes, and those enormous breakfasts, sideboards groaning with kippers when one has barely opened one's eyes...' She turned again to Jean and patted the seat beside her as Tommy gestured to a waiter for another drink. 'So – a house in France. That's our little *projet*. My favourite kind of trip, and we're always hoping more people will come and liven up our backwater. Now the Russians have gone it's just some stuffy Brits and a few of us Yanks left, though I did hear of a fabulous count, Ruspinov or Roskinoff, I can never remember, who washed up there last month, terribly dissolute and fabulously handsome. Apparently the countess had all her jewels sewn into her underclothes. But don't worry, darling. We'll find you somewhere near us, it will be such fun. Edward can go to Monte Carlo and have a little flutter, or there's always sailing if he's into that. What's that club they all adore in Nice, Tommy, dear?'

'Le Cercle Nautique. He won't like that though – wrong sort. But there are still a few people scratching around that might entertain you both.' Tommy sat forward now, and the sheen to his skin gave away the considerable amount he must have drunk already. 'Before long it'll be dead again. Too hot to see anyone after the end of April.'

The conversation gained momentum and Jean allowed herself to relax into their company and into the flow of drinks that would inevitably run into dinner somewhere fashionable, too late for anyone to be hungry but terribly of the moment. Nothing would be demanded of her, or of her real self, which was lying somewhere beneath the surface, bruised by her months with Edward but gradually feeling some light from the sun refracted into the water.

The champagne was cool and crisp, and when it hit her empty stomach it gave her a surge of energy she hadn't felt for months. Tommy went upstairs to change, and Edith ordered another drink for the pair of them.

'Now Tommy's gone, can we talk? I've been dying to hear how you are. I don't know Edward, but Tommy had that ridiculous face on him when his name was mentioned, which means he's absolutely the right sort. So how's it all proceeding, darling? No children yet? Ghastly question, but I'm only saying it before someone else does.'

'No. Well, it's been nearly a year and nothing yet. But I'm told to be patient, that it's quite normal.'

'And how do you find being married to an Englishman? The truth now. Don't forget, you and I are the same.' Edith took a sip of her drink. 'If I'm honest, Tommy came back from the war even more pompous than when it started. Don't worry though, it wasn't the fighting that did it – balls and bravery. No, no. He had a comfortable desk job behind the lines, with plenty of cognac and more *jeunes filles locales* than he knew what to do with. I should think it was the time away from me. Got away from my bossing him about.'

'It's all fine. It is. It's just not quite as I expected. Or perhaps it's that I'm not what he expected. At times I feel as if I'm missing some mark he's set for me.'

'Oh, don't we all, darling. We're American! And though we supposedly speak the same language, there's the inescapable difference in how we use it. Always feeling out of place?'

'Yes, or as if I should know what to do. Or say. I want to say things, sometimes so much, but I can never find a way to start.'

'Darling, it's because they'd rather say nothing at all. They're all scarred by their mothers and ignored by their fathers, and… oh God, you look so sad suddenly. Don't listen to me. I'm just older and jaded, and Edward is still a boy really and working the whole thing out for himself too. We'll find him a house in France, that'll cheer him up. Come on.'

But as the evening wore on, and they were crammed around a table somewhere that was too small for their swollen number, Jean's knees practically touching those of the man opposite, the table a chaos of half-drunk glasses and carafes, tumblers of gin and bottles of champagne, the men either side of her so close she could feel their breath on her face, she realised Edith wouldn't want to know about her petty melancholy. Why would she? Much easier for everyone if she was simply house shopping and nothing more. No one wanted a long face at dinner – now was the time to forget the gloom of the last years and sally out in a new dress and dance.

The evening became raucous, and Jean slipped away before the gang trooped off en masse to the night spot *du jour* in the 8th. She was taken back to the hotel by Tommy, ever the gentleman, though he was drunk and glassy-eyed by now, his hand flung out from the open window of the car, trailing the air, a beatific smile on his face.

'He's a lucky man, Edward Warre. A bloody lucky man.' He smiled blearily at her.

'Is he? It doesn't always feel that way.'

'Come, you're a little beauty. I'd make a pass at you if I didn't think Edith would scratch my eyes out for it. But why the sad face? What can you of all people be sad about?' His voice trailed off and he seemed to have forgotten the words he'd just spoken.

They were coming down the Rue Cambon to the back entrance of the hotel, where there was only the young night porter – skinny as a rake, eyes red-rimmed with tiredness – to let them in.

Tommy kissed her on the cheek as they stood at the bottom of the hotel's curved staircase, his face serious. 'I think he'd be a damn fool not to be out here with you.' Then a smile broke out and he turned and walked up ahead of her. 'But I must go to my bed before I make an idiot of myself. Something about this city always does it to me.'

Jean watched him climb the stairs, a little stumble then a pause to steady himself, humming tunelessly as he went. The way men like Tommy saw her, an asset that her husband had acquired, a vessel Edward now held in his hands – for she was his to hold, as she understood it now, to admire as Tommy thought he ought, or to place on a shelf – all of it rendered her powerless. Hers was to be observed; her part to play was conduit, not player. And she saw then, in the cosseted night silence of the Ritz, that this life she had was a passive thing. It was cast in gold and encased in jewels that shone and entranced as it was turned in the light, but the hands around it, which held it tight, were not her own.

CHAPTER ELEVEN

Dawn was breaking as the train snaked its way into Marseille. They had left Paris at dusk the evening before, Tommy silent and irritable from too much drink, their conversation outside the hotel snuffed out by his hangover. They had managed to find compartments on the *train bleu*, and porters and attendants had swarmed the platform, loading and checking their luggage, ushering them aboard. But in a conjurer's act the night had passed and the Mediterranean coast was now before them, bathed in the rose glow of an April dawn. Fingers of light spread out across a pale sea smooth as marble as they made their way through towns Jean knew only from conversations overheard – Saint-Raphael, Juan-les-Pins, Antibes – but then dawn gave itself up to the day and the sea changed again, transforming to a blue so true and bright and brilliant she felt she would never tire of watching it.

She joined Edith and Tommy for breakfast, the latter's mood now lifted by a glass of champagne, the dining carriage empty other than a portly French gentleman, nose in his book, and a young English couple, hands entwined over the table as they pored over their Baedeker. Newly married, she suspected with a lurch.

'It's rarely French you hear at this time of year. It's mainly the English, unless you go to Monte Carlo. Ciro's is full of Americans killing time before they make their way to Paris and London for the season. Nice and around there are the English toffs, the Aberconways, that sort, though we'll be lucky to catch them now. Most people will be gone by the end of the month.'

Tommy was warming to his subject, enjoying his role as imparter of wisdom to a gauche young girl.

'Edith and I love it here because it doesn't demand anything of one. Just enough people to have dinner with, a game of *punto* if you feel the itch, and otherwise long mornings, longer lunches. There's not much history here. Just promenades and sea and towns built for pleasure. And the locals are desperate for us to come – I think they've realised that we're the only real things here. For God's sake, the palm trees that everyone thinks are native were imported by an Englishman in the eighties.'

'There'll be plenty of houses for you to look at, darling,' Edith continued. 'We take ours for three months – rent it from an ancient *visconte* who never seems to use it at all. Lost his two sons at Verdun apparently and now can't bring himself to come back. The *guardian* is always trying to persuade us to buy it, but I'm not sure I'd know what to do with it for more than a few months. There's only so much of heaven one can take.'

They were approaching Nice now, the view from the window taking in the sweep of the Baie des Anges, the beach empty in the morning sun, the line of palm trees clearly outlined against the brilliance of the buildings behind them. It seemed to Jean as if the place was opening up for her. Every day could be a new day here; perfect, unblemished. The town stretched itself out before her, wanting to be appreciated, longing, she felt, to cast the spell it surely had cast on so many before her.

*

The Elchos' house was as she had imagined. The *visconte*, though bereft of sons, clearly had considerable money and style. Its plaster was the palest peach, its arches and porticos edged in white, and a Corinthian colonnade led out onto a wide terrace and to elegant gardens beyond. A sequence of lawns, each edged in elaborate borders, stepped down to a stone balustrade, beyond which lay a perfect vista of the sea and the red tiled roofs of Nice far below. The Elchos had perfected how to spend their time here, making their way through a day of elegant ease punctuated by meals on the terrace or down at somewhere popular with the right sort on the Promenade des Anglais.

Jean and Edith had spent the day being driven round various houses, a polished gentleman from Nice in charge of their itinerary: Monsieur Beauclaire, as he was charmingly called, a salesman of untold, and exhausting, enthusiasm.

'Ah, but this house is *spectacle*, the envy of every other owner on the coast,' he would say, conveniently forgetting the last string of hyperbole he had hung on a house they had only just left. 'It is a treasure, a prize, a gem.' And his voice would rise and his hand gestures grow more energetic as his description of the property reached a crescendo. He listed the provenance of each house with relish. Several Russian counts had inhabited a particularly grand address in Beaulieu that was looking for a new owner, and an American gentleman – and with this he gave Jean a jerky bow – had only recently put on the market another, perched in the hills behind St-Paul de Vence.

Jean had looked at four houses by the end of the day, each one of grand enough proportion and provenance to earn her mother's blessing but none with anything significant to distinguish it from the others; perhaps a longer drive, or a larger terrace, more elaborate topiary or a more decadent past, but the sum of them all had left her flat.

They sat around the table on the terrace that evening, drinking champagne in twisted flutes that Edith had started them on well before the hour that was generally considered acceptable. Tommy was making his way slowly up and down the terrace now, glass in hand, enjoying the sound of his own voice as he proclaimed the failings of some couple Jean didn't know.

'I find them, frankly, unacceptable. Not the right sort at all—'

Edith interrupted him with relish. 'Darling, she left him for one of Diaghilev's dancers – divine, and just twenty-two.'

'What do they see in all of that nonsense? Ridiculous costumes, music I don't understand. It's preposterous.'

'Preposterous to you, my dear. To others it's *art*. Art in its most unadulterated, liberated form.' Edith allowed the words to elongate in her mouth, watching the effect it had on Tommy.

'But did you really follow it all? And that party we went to after? I couldn't stomach the costumes on some of the men, and—'

'Oh, Jean, it was divine. If you could have seen it. A party I thought only existed in my dreams. Women dressed in reams of gold and silver, the men with roses and sprigs of jasmine in their hair, and these dancers…from the Ballets Russes—'

'I thought we'd never get off. A party on a boat is unspeakable, no mode of escape. And they ran out of anything acceptable to drink.'

'It didn't seem to stop you, dearest.' Seeing her arrow land, Edith rose triumphantly and clapped her hands together. '*À table, à table.*'

Dinner progressed, a seemingly infinite round of small plates – eggs in aspic, sole meunière, *côtes de veau* – on a procession of exquisite porcelain and elaborate silverware, Edith not remotely interested in the food on her plate but rather in goading Tommy, hoping gleefully for a rise. She was always impatient for a change in tempo, and the more Tommy drank the more it incited her to provoke a reaction.

'Darling, let's go up the coast tomorrow. We could go and see Sybil and Frank.'

'I don't think your mother would know them,' Tommy snorted, looking across at Jean, his eyes a little hooded from the drink taken.

'Oh, come on, it'll be fun. I haven't seen them in an age.' She turned to Jean. 'They left New York and moved to Paris a couple of years ago with their daughter in tow, renting a place in the outskirts near Fontainebleau. They would escape the city whenever they could to come down here. They bought a place up beyond Saint-Raphael, a little too off the beaten track for Tommy. Although they are' – and here she smirked, an eye on her husband – 'terribly stylish.' She said the word with great solemnity and then burst out laughing, reaching for her cigarettes.

The trio wandered out on the terrace and at Edith's suggestion walked down to the stone balustrade to take in the sea and the lights below. She liked the Elchos. They made her laugh, and there was something to say for the way they saw the world, plucking the fun from life like fruit from a tree, sharing it with those they liked if the mood took them, luxuriating in the pleasures available to them. But she knew for certain, after a day or two in their company, that her difficulties with Edward were beyond the realms of what could be discussed. Edith was a very different person to her, the type of American woman that a certain Englishman couldn't resist: sophisticated, arch, amusing, opinionated, always game for a party but with a carapace of confidence that rendered her unreachable. The anxieties that Jean could barely articulate to herself were too fragile to share with someone who saw the world in aphorisms and aperitifs. Tommy would pull rank; Edward was a White's man and they had been at the same house at school, shared friends, shared cousins – there was always that incomprehensible amount of impossible-to-follow family connections that linked someone like Edward to the rest of his world. Jean's lack of confidence in how the early months of her marriage had passed would have seemed ridiculous to him, trifling and whining and simply not 'done'.

Like a match struck in the dark, the flare of a realisation came to her and sent a glow around the terrace she stood on, lit up the faces of the elegant, sarcastic, clever couple standing beside her in the chill of a Riviera evening. She would not be able to outrun what she had come here to escape. It had followed her. Edith and Tommy were part of it, breathed the very air Edward breathed, drank the very water her mother did. This marriage of hers, this life of hers, regardless of the racing of her heart or the darting of her mind, stood around her like a fortress. Dressing it in the warm glow of the Mediterranean, or the life of Paris opening up like spring buds after the frost has gone, changed nothing.

CHAPTER TWELVE

'How utterly ghastly to be so efficient. What drama would there be in life if everyone did everything exactly when they promised?'

Edith was standing in the doorway of Jean's bedroom, leaning against the door frame, cigarette in hand, a robe of the finest cream satin dripping from her brittle frame.

'For all of Tommy's eye rolling, once a plan is made, he acts on it. We're leaving this afternoon, darling. You'd better pack your things.'

Within a matter of a day, Tommy had managed to secure them all an invitation to dinner and a room for the night with the couple, Frank and Sybil, up the coast, plus their promise of an introduction to an agent who knew all the houses available to rent or buy in the area.

As Jean packed, she struggled to shake off an unsettled feeling that had bled from her dream the night before into her waking self. She had been walking along the riverbank at Harehope in darkness, barefoot, feet damp from the grass. A light, coming from the fishing hut down the path ahead of her, drew her on, and as she grew closer the sound of voices travelled to her:

people talking, laughing. When she pushed open the door she was hit by a wall of heat. The tiny hut was crammed with people, talking and talking, glasses in hand, and Stokes moving between them, pouring drinks from a shaker. Her mother was there, sitting down on one of the hut's wooden benches; she saw Edith and Tommy, Edward's sister Charlotte, Edward's mother, more familiar faces and more unknown jostling for space, elbows nudging against her, but not Edward. Each time she tried to talk to someone, the same question would be asked: 'But where is Edward?' Not rudely but gently, politely, kindly. 'Where is Edward?' With a rising panic, not knowing the answer, struggling to recall where he might be, she would turn to someone else, only to be asked again, until everyone in the room was looking at her expectantly. A door opened and shut behind her, and she turned, hoping desperately to see Edward.

But the sound was her mind making the journey to wakefulness; the door opening and closing had been a maid down the corridor, and Jean had found herself awake and alone in her bed, her back damp with sweat and her head dense with half-remembered scenes. The pull of the dream had stayed with her all day, niggling while she had lunch, and she had gone back to it while she sat with Edith on the terrace, worrying away at it like a scab.

At five o'clock sharp – when Tommy was sober, he was fiercely punctual – she climbed into the back of their cream Delage, Edith with a scarlet silk scarf knotted around her head, long legs tucked elegantly beneath her. As they wound their way down the hill and joined the road that ran along the coast, Edith began and then abandoned attempts at conversation. The road's surface was bumpy and the combination of the engine and the air coming in the open windows made it hard for Jean to hear. So she was relieved to sit back and let her eyes drift over the view, pushing the worry back further and further, letting the buffeting of the wind in her ears and the infinite, untroubled line between sea and sky drown out the anxious voice in her head.

The journey took them an hour or so. They had taken a road that clung close to the coast. It stayed low to the water, passing by a little fishing village that edged the sea – CROS-DE-CAGNES, the sign had said – with boats hauled up on its pebbled beach and widowed old women in black sitting in a huddle on the steps of a municipal stone building. She could almost feel the sun's warmth on their lined faces as they sat, hands folded in their laps, chattering like sparrows. There were little rocky outcrops that ran right down to the water, and there was a pleasant scrappiness to the coast, torn and ripped and a little gnarled, before bursts of paler, pebbled bays would appear to soften its edges. She must have dozed off briefly, because they were suddenly climbing a much narrower road that wound back to the higher ground behind the sea's edge. Umbrella pines lined the route and the car threw up a fine dust as it made its way along the drive to the house.

Edith was talking now over her shoulder. 'Sybil is frightfully graceful, calm and self-possessed as a rule. Probably finds me a terrible gossip. Her husband is much more the host, if I remember from New York days. They had a perfect house in Southampton, right up on Meadow Lane, and always threw these perfect little parties, always the right people, never too many, no one brash.' Tommy was too busy manoeuvring the car round the tight bends to contradict her.

They drove between a pair of simple stone pillars, a pile of loose bricks wedging open the black wrought-iron gate, and a girl ran right up to the car. She must have been six or seven, legs like twigs, her brown hair cut short in a fringed bob just below her ears. She was dressed in a simple cream shift, clutching a handful of peonies.

'Mummy, Mummy, there's someone here in a big white car!' And she ran back down the gravel drive that snaked round to the front of the house. The view when the car turned the corner made Jean gasp. There was the sea, sparkling in the late-afternoon sun, a perfect tableau before them, close enough to touch. A large terrace ran around the front of the house, from which Jean could make out a narrow path that must have descended steeply down to the rocks and the water below. And there on the terrace stood Sybil Fairbank in a loose cotton dress, one hand up to shield her eyes from the sun, in her other a basket laden with more peonies. Her daughter was now by her side, trying to pull her mother forward towards the excitement of the strangers.

'Welcome, welcome, everyone to our little backwater. Edith, how kind of you and Tommy to come and find us here. And you must be Jean Warre?' Sybil stepped forward and kissed Edith before extending her hand to Jean. 'Frank will be out any moment, and he can help show you to your rooms. Have a drink – take it up to your room to change. He makes a refreshing little something with mint leaves and lemon.'

Her hair was thick and dark, her face broad and unlined, and her whole demeanour exuded a calm and ease that fed into Jean almost immediately, like salve on a burn. Tommy was pointedly carrying all the bags from the car, looking round in agitation for staff to pass them on to. When no one appeared to relieve him, he dropped them heavily on the gravel, wiped his palms on his trousers and put out his hand to Sybil.

Frank appeared from the dark interior of the house. Like his wife, he looked unruffled, in pale cream trousers and a fine wool jumper over his voile shirt. Tommy, in his double-breasted jacket and tie, was stuffy and uncomfortable next to him. He gave Tommy a gentle pat on the back and scooped up some of the luggage, beckoning them all to follow him inside.

'I hope Sybil has told you I insist you take a drink up to your room. We're rather low on staff here, so I shall be your valet, Tommy. Do let me know if there's anything you need.' He kissed Edith, and then looked across to Jean. 'A pleasure to have you here. I met your father once. He came and talked at Yale and I had a word with him afterwards. What an extraordinary man, what a father to have.' Grabbing her case last, he led his clutch of guests across the terrace and into the house, leaving the little girl to bring up the rear, hopping to keep up.

Jean's bedroom was clean and cool, with a red tiled floor and pale linen curtains that framed a balconied window. The view from her bed was a square of perfect blue. When she stood out on the balcony, though, it took in the lawn and terrace below, with its outdoor table and chairs and beds of rosemary and lavender that ran along its edge. The house was like nothing she had encountered before; it seemed to hum gently with life, and she felt as if she had just undone a dress that was too tight, her chest expanding, her lungs filling with air. She sipped the drink Sybil had brought and sat back on the bed, kicking off her shoes, listening to the sound of the little girl's voice below as she chatted away happily to her mother as the table was laid for dinner.

There were guests assembled on the terrace by the time Jean came down: a row of unfamiliar backs; women standing in the fading light, furs and stoles hung around bare arms. Sybil was sitting on a pale wrought-iron bench piled with faded cushions, her legs curled beneath her, drink in hand, a young man sitting to her left, head tilted as he listened. Frank was moving among his guests, shaker in hand, a little word for someone here, causing a ripple of laughter when he bent in fleetingly to a conversation. He introduced her to a pair of older men who switched from French to English for her benefit, and she smiled, keeping half an ear on what they were saying but letting her senses take in the place – the scent of eucalyptus and pine in the air, lavender from the bed that ran along the edge of the lawn – and the music drifting out from the open door of the drawing room, the gentle melancholy sound of a woman's voice and a lone trumpet accompanying her.

When they sat down to dinner inside, at a long table covered in a pale linen cloth, where the flickering candlelight danced off the glasses and the little girl's peonies now nodded from vases of brilliant crystal, she was placed opposite the man who had been talking to Sybil. 'David Carver,' he said simply, extending his hand across the table to her.

They were at the table's end, with no one at the head between them. It felt as if they were eating alone, and she had to lean in to hear what he was saying over the noise.

'Sybil tells me you're a fellow American.'

'You could say that, though I live in England now. I've married an Englishman, so I'm not sure what that makes me.'

'Well, I'm a confusion too, I suppose. Or a cliché, whichever you prefer. An American living in Paris for the foreseeable. And a writer. I'm with the *Paris Herald*, for my sins.'

She hesitated. 'I imagine you'd know my father then. Robert Buckman, of the *Tribune*? Our family paper, if that doesn't sound faintly ridiculous.'

'Who doesn't? He mightn't like you trading talk with a rival…'

She smiled and took a sip of her wine, cold and crisp.

'So what brings you here?'

'I'm staying with friends down the coast. My mother is keen on the idea of a house down here, so I've been looking at a few possibilities.' Another flash of embarrassment for how spoiled it made her sound in the easy simplicity of the dinner. He seemed unperturbed, leaning forward to make himself heard over the noise of the other guests.

'This place, the coast, it's captivating. Once you've been a few times, you can't stay away. And it's surely an improvement on Paris in the heat. The apartment I rent is tiny, cramped in the eaves of a building in a narrow little street in the Marais. Sounds wonderful on paper, if you're feeling poetic, but in reality the plumbing could do with being brought into this century and when it gets hot, the smells from the street rise up and it's all I can do to sleep at night. Are you familiar with Paris – in all its glory and imperfection?'

'I lived there as a child for a few years. We lived in the 7th. I only have snatches of memories.'

'And will you be down here long?'

'No, I've got to get back to England, to my husband.'

'He's not here?'

'No, no. He's in the country.' She paused. 'I think. Or with friends in Scotland.' She hurried on. 'But he didn't want to come here. Wrong time of year for him to travel.'

David said something that she didn't catch and so she sat forward in her seat to hear more clearly, and she was drawn then to the line of him, found herself observing him as she might a painting: the slight furrow at his brow, the thick blonde-brown hair; was he a little older than her? The act of observing made her aware of herself in turn, her face as she looked down at her glass, the smear at its rim where her lips had left it. His face when she looked up again was open, inquisitive, with eyes of an extraordinary mid-blue. There was something about him that she could not have articulated if asked, but that seemed to her, in that moment, golden. When the man on her right asked her something, she could still feel David's eyes on her. When she turned back, there was a smile playing at the edges of his mouth.

Dinner drifted to an end – David was pulled away to talk to the woman on his left – and the guests wandered out onto the terrace again, where the men smoked and drank tiny glasses of a dark local spirit, scattered around the large table dotted with lanterns that Sybil had lit from a taper. Jean had drunk more than she usually would, and the warmth from the fire in the small drawing room where she was now sitting was making her drowsy. Tommy, utterly lost in the fluid familiarity of the evening, was looking around for Edith. He was at sea in this gathering that had no coherency to it other than a casual confidence that Jean found magnetic.

David came in, looking for Sybil, to thank her. Sybil stood to say goodbye, kissing him warmly, and Jean found herself sitting, unsure of whether to stand too. But then his hand was on her shoulder. 'A pleasure to meet you. I hope you have some luck in finding your house. Sybil, you must know of the right place. You know everything down here.' He smiled, that easy smile again, and then he was out of the room, and gone.

CHAPTER THIRTEEN

A steep path, cut between jagged, limestone rocks, would lead her down to the sea. It was shaded on either side by a dense greenery that grew up above it, shielding it almost entirely from the house and lending it a damp, earthy darkness. Jean made her way carefully, wishing she had worn something more practical than the heels she had come in. She almost slipped, putting her hand out to the wall to steady herself and then feeling its cool stone, rough and reassuring. The path dropped down once more and she found herself out in bright, bleached sunlight, on a stretch of rough shingle, its stones grey and pale in the midday sun. It couldn't have been more than eighty yards across; it was more like a cove, with a steep escarpment of rocks jutting down into the water on either side, the sea bleeding from aquamarine and grey in the shallows into a perfect azure blue.

'The fishermen pull up their boats here in the late morning, and occasionally children from the town come and swim, *mais il y'a des autres plages, plus grandes, plus accessibles, qui sont pres d'ici*. You might get a sailing boat mooring a little way off in the evenings, but they'll usually be gone by dawn. It really is very private, Madam.'

The young man had driven out from Antibes to meet her at the Fairbanks' house. He had been less polished than Monsieur Beauclaire, a little more hesitant, embarrassed by Jean's youth; he was not much older than her, she guessed. He had only one house to show her – it needed a little work to the inside; built at the turn of the century, it had belonged to a Frenchman whose wife had died and who had let the place go. As she had walked around the house with the young agent, taking in the roses climbing above the front door, the jasmine running wild, she could see that someone had loved it once but that their mind had been taken elsewhere.

Something of the pace of the evening before had stayed on in her too. She felt as if she had slept better than she had in months, felt more connected to her body, to her senses, as she walked around the inside of the house. It was smaller than the others she had seen. Prettier, gentler somehow. Its stone was a soft yellow, and its windows had wooden shutters of a pale eggshell blue. The drawing room and dining room were elegant, though the curtains were faded, but the overall impression it gave was of generous spirits having inhabited it, of warmth and happiness.

'I'll need to confirm some things with my family, but I would like to make an offer.' The confidence in her voice surprised her. This was to be her house. She would love it, make it her own. The thought made her heart skip.

The young man, clearly delighted with his sale, began to make enthusiastic notes in his ledger while Jean wandered back onto the terrace. Beneath it ran a lawn, with a low hedge of lavender skirting its edge, and in the corner lay that secret hollow down to the cove below. The house, she was told, had a small amount of land to the back, and a full cellar if Jean wished to buy it.

'If I may, I'd like to take another walk down to the beach before you take me back.'

'Of course.'

She let her hands trail the wall as she made her way back down the path, confident now, relishing the prospect that this could be a daily journey. When she reached the beach there was a figure at its other end, where the agent had pointed out the public access from the narrow road. It was a man, hat and shoes in hand, trousers rolled up, and he was standing at the water's edge, rocking back and forth on his heels. Something about his posture was familiar, and she walked in his direction, putting up her hand to shield her eyes from the sun as she tried to make him out.

He turned to continue walking along the beach, and that was when she recognised him. It was David. The writer from last night. They drew closer but she had to stop, her stockings and shoes preventing her from coming nearer. He looked down, embarrassed by his bare ankles and feet, and smiled back at her, shyly this time.

'Good morning. How are you? Were you looking at the house up there?' He gestured in the direction she had come from.

'I was, and you know, I think I want to take it.' She looked down at her feet. 'Of course, I have to talk to my husband and my parents, but I love the position, and this beach.'

'I come here any chance I can, because there's never a soul here. You can sit and read, and it gets the sun from about nine o'clock until the late afternoon. There's a sweet boy whose father keeps an eye on the house, and he sometimes comes and plays here when he's not at school. And that's about it.'

'And you come down here when you're not in Paris?'

'As often as possible – I'm planning on spending more of the summer months here. Like I said, Paris isn't at its most enticing in the heat, and trust me, you can tire of the scene at the Boeuf sur le Toit. I'd rather be down here, by the sea. A few of us are planning on doing it. I'll rent this little place I've seen in town, it's dirt cheap, about twenty minutes' walk from this beach. It's not much, but it's got charm. I could walk here every day.' He hurried on, embarrassed. 'Or to the other little beaches nearby. And there's Juan-les-Pins, which is close, and has nothing much going on, but I like it for that. There's a little picture house where the baker's wife plays the piano, and there's barely anyone there from now. It's blissful.'

'I like the sound of that. I'm not sure I'd be here in the summer – there's an awful lot of nothing going on in June in London and then we spend August at home...but I should like to come here when I can.'

'It sounds like you have a plan then.' He put his hat back on, and tipped it. 'Look me up when you next come back.'

They said their goodbyes, and she left him standing in the shallows as she walked back along the beach and up to the house, where the agent was waiting with his car to drive her back to the Elchos.

There would be Edward to talk to, her mother to discuss matters with, papers to sign, deeds to be handed over, but all of these things seemed nothing to her. If she could only walk on that beach, and feel what she had last night, the detail of it all – the taste of the red wine, rich and smoky, the glow of the candlelight, the scent of jasmine in the air. There was a vividness and a clarity to it that she could barely express, but it was more real to her than anything she had experienced in months, maybe years.

CHAPTER FOURTEEN

The house was hers. Edward had approved, of course he had, for the gift was not in his giving and its acquisition had been hurried through, a reflection of her mother's delight at so splendid a choice. So hers it was, and Jean felt a novel pleasure at the possession of something that felt entirely her own.

Jean had been given a month to pull the house together, a blissful month when the subtleties of spring gave way to the riot of early summer, when yellow broom grew wild along the roadsides and the bougainvillea scrambled its way over stone and sun-kissed walls. She would start each morning in a simple silk shirt, a light cotton skirt – the days were already so warm by the time it was mid-morning – and she would walk through her new home, taking in each small detail, its novelty delicious to her, before wandering onto the terrace and down to the end of the garden for her first view of the sea. Her lungs would fill with the salt tang of the air and she would make her way down the narrow path and onto her beach, walking its length slowly, shoes in hand, each step bringing another small pleasure that would sometimes overwhelm her with its simplicity; just the silence of an empty bay, the gentleness of the early-morning sun on her face, the uneven shingle shifting beneath her feet.

She would take her breakfast alone on the terrace, at a large, pale *fer forgé* table she had bought from the previous owner. The *visconte* had offered her most of the contents for a meagre sum, keen as he must have been to rid himself of painful memories. Some of the furniture was too tired; other pieces were swooped on with delight by Constance, her decorator – 'utterly divine, darling; worthless but divine' – so charming in their age-old positions that the idea of moving them seemed almost sacrilegious. In the kitchen there was a huge wooden dresser that sagged in the middle from use, and gleaming copper pots hung over an ancient range. Jean found this room comforting, with its worn red tiles and the simple wooden table and chairs and she wanted to leave it just as it was. She had inherited, too, the previous owner's housekeeper. Marie had grey hair kept in a low bun, heavy pockets beneath her eyes, and a rasping voice from the cigarettes Jean saw her smoke every evening at the back of the house. Jean's French wasn't bad, and she was able to give Marie what seemed, from the housekeeper's shy smile, a passable speech about her happiness in buying the house and keeping her on.

They had commandeered the driver that Edith had used near Nice for the next month, and he and the car her mother had insisted on buying for her were at their disposal whenever they needed it. Monsieur Lechabret was often to be found parked in the shade at the bottom of the drive, napping at the wheel of the silver open-topped Rolls, his rotund body taking up most of the front's leather seats, a copy of yesterday's *Figaro* crumpled across his chest. He would leap up in his seat when Constance tapped him on the shoulder, rubbing his eyes furiously as he jumped out of the car to open the doors for them.

Constance, or the Honourable Mrs William Holmes, to give her proper name, was proving to be the ideal companion for Jean. She must have been in her mid forties, slim and handsome, married to an older man universally acknowledged as a bore of immense proportions and dwindling finances. Constance had used her natural eye for colour and design, as well as her substantial address book, to turn her talents into something of an industry. She had already decorated countless homes in London – always of 'dear, dear friends' whose names would then be dropped liberally into conversation to secure her next commission – as well as some houses in Palm Beach and several apartments in New York. Jean admired her taste and her decisive nature, but also her ability to speak her mind in absolute terms.

They had had dinner alone on their first night in the dimly lit dining room, the dark red faded silk of the chairs only adding to the gloom, and she had decreed what Jean needed to do.

'Darling, this house should be yours, and it shall be decorated as you like. Let's leave behind London and Harehope and all that and choose something in sympathy with the climate and the times. And don't go traipsing poor Olive and the like across the pond each time you come here – the girl looked like she'd faint when she stepped off the train in Paris. Your French is perfectly good, and the house feels looked-after so make good use of Marie and anyone she has. Edward seems like someone who won't want to be bothered by "shall I's" and "shan't I's". Let's crack on and do this together, so that it can cease to be a worry and be a delight instead. I know of a few people who are planning on summering down here, so we shall have some company for the next few weeks, and Lechabret can get us where we need to be. I think we shall enjoy ourselves immensely.'

Jean found the air of productivity and Constance's brisk presence in the house uplifting – the clack, clack of her heels across the parquet floor as she took notes and made measurements. There was the calm of Marie and her small coterie of maids too, dusting, unpacking Jean's things, showing Olive how to work the archaic laundry at the back of the house. By midday Constance would have done four hours' work and would be looking for a plan for lunch or dinner, keen to make her presence in the area known to whoever was deemed worthy of their interest.

Constance knew of Sybil and Frank through friends in New York and was keen to remake their acquaintance. A lunch was arranged at the large hotel nearby, persuaded to stay open out of season by the small number of visitors staying on as the temperature rose. Monsieur Lechabret shook his head in amazement when he was told where they were going.

'*Le monde, il change trop vite,*' he muttered to himself as he held open the door for Jean to climb in. A look of almost comic sadness passed over his heavy, jowled face.

The hotel – a flash of brilliant white against the deep greenery of its manicured lawns – was run by an Italian of easy charm, a seasoned host who chatted amiably to them as they made their way along the terrace and down to the loggia restaurant where they were expected. Apparently it was a novelty to him too to be open now, with guests lunching and dining beyond the season's traditional end. The dining room was open, with vast windows on all sides looking out onto the rocks and the sea glinting below, sharp as metal in the bright midday sun.

Simple tables, adorned with vases of flowers, were laid, and there was a small gathering of about eight waiting for Jean and Constance.

It was easy for Jean to arrive at something like this, as Constance immediately held the table's attention, dropping four names before she'd sat down, allowing Jean to take in the assembled group without their eyes being upon her. There were familiar faces from the dinner the month before – she recognised an older French couple, a distinguished man with an elaborately curled moustache, his younger wife, skin dark from the sun, silent and statuesque beside him. Sybil was standing now and gesturing for Jean to come and take her place opposite Frank, who was leaning back on his chair, his face bronzed, his hair wet from a swim he must have taken from the rocks that led down to the sparkling sea below.

Frank leaned across the table, gesturing at the empty place next to her. 'Apologies. We're waiting on David, always late. He's coming in overnight from Paris. We wired him yesterday and told him to come straight here. I believe you met him at the dinner at our house – charm personified, and as captivated by this place as any I've seen.'

He took a bottle of wine, droplets of water sliding down the label, from a bucket on the floor beside him, and poured Jean a glass. Its chill was delicious in the heat. 'So who is planning on staying here for the summer?' he announced to the table. 'It'll be heaven. You all know it. Anyone too stiff will have gone.'

Sybil looked up from her conversation with Constance further down the table. 'Just how I like it, darling.'

'The weather will be scorching, which will drive out any lingerers.' Frank was smiling as he filled glasses around him.

'Darling, I'm longing to take a drive further down beyond Cannes, I'm told there are some beautiful old fishing villages. Ravishing—'

'But of course!' The man with the moustache was snapping his fingers impatiently. 'You foreigners only scratch the surface here. I am amazed. Amazed by the laziness of the American or the English or the Russian visitor to our parts. They come south, from Paris, and they get out of their little carriage or their car or their train, and they are dazzled by the buildings of Nice, so mesmerised by the promenades and the palm trees and the glitter of it all, that they simply stop. And that's it. That is the Riviera that they write home about and spend their money in – at Monaco or Nice or Cannes. But go further down, travel on, go further, further, and you see what riches there are here, Le Dramont, Saint-Raphael, the sheer joy of St Tropez and the simplicity, the unadulterated beauty of Ramatuelle. If only they would bother to trundle just a little further.' He smiled indulgently as Frank filled up his glass, then shrugged. 'Their loss, our gain.'

Suddenly Sybil was on her feet, arms outstretched to receive a kiss, and there was David, with that smile of almost unbearable openness. A warm handshake for Frank, a nod to the other end of the table, and with a confident ease he was sitting beside her, taking a sip of his wine, face turned towards her.

'So, we meet again. I am delighted if it means you bought that house. What a place. I envy your choice.'

'I've come down for a month to pull everything together. It was all rather tired inside and needs some affection. We've been here a week, Constance and I, and it feels like a month already. She's quite a force.'

'Ah well, you've fallen in with the right crowd here. Frank, our conductor, bringing us together, making us our best selves, drawing out the perfect tune somehow. I always feel more of a man when I'm in Frank's company.'

It was true, the atmosphere did seem to respond to Frank's subtle direction, conversations coming together, reaching a climax of amusement, moving on before a subject grew tired. Even the food arrived as Jean's hunger peaked – plates of scarlet tomatoes, gleaming in oil, skins taut and scattered with salt; dishes piled with salted anchovies swimming in oil like gold; crevettes oozing with garlic – all arranged in artful chaos on a central table so one could help oneself, refreshing in its informality and so right for the mood of this place with its windows open to the breeze.

They were sitting now, plates cleared, little cups of a dark, bitter coffee before them, glasses replenished, relaxed by the wine and the heat and the company. David turned to Jean again, his attention focused entirely on her as the others chatted on.

'How's the beach? I've been thinking of it as I sit in the office in Paris. Those fishermen, chatting as they fix their nets and scrub the wood. The heat that everyone curses. I can never tire of it when I'm by the water. The English colonised this place fifty years ago and yet they'd never stay later than April.'

'Unfashionable, I suppose.'

'Unfashionable only because someone, long dead, once said so. So baffling to cling on to these accepted modes of being when everything is shouting, screaming the obvious – that things have changed, that there's pleasure to be had in breaking the mould.'

'But it's not always as easy as that. Things can be prescribed for one, I suppose.'

His face was thoughtful. 'I heard your brother has joined the family paper. Prescribed rather than chosen?'

She laughed. 'If I'm honest, the question I'm normally asked about him is whether he'll be lunching at the Brook or Pierre's.'

'Well, no doubt he's a Brook man, but the paper interests me a little more. I just wondered if it was always the plan for him.' He was serious, though she was finding the intensity of his focus on her distracting.

'I suppose it was, although he joined sooner than my father would have liked. Things haven't always been smooth where Oliver...' She paused, well trained in withholding what it was not done to reveal.

'You mean yours is not the life of gilded charm the world would have us believe?'

'Something like that. Father is, as you can imagine, quite a man. He's so revered, and—'

'That can be overbearing?'

'I'd always see Oliver standing awkwardly beside Father at a party, pulling at his cuff, or looking uncertain in a conversation which Father was leading, no place left for him. He'd have one eye on the great man, the other on the next drink.'

'So the rumours are not just rumours.'

'No, I suppose not. Although my mother would die if she heard it discussed among her friends, or anyone she held in high regard.'

'New York does seem to quake at her name, if the society pages are to be believed. Can't be easy being her only daughter. Is that why you're hiding away in the backwater here?'

Jean looked up, blushing.

His face fell. 'Oh, I'm sorry, I'm too frank for my own good. It's rude. Ever the writer. Tell me to be quiet, I'm used to it.'

'No, don't apologise, please. If I'm honest, it's refreshing. People either know so much about my family that it's poor manners to ask anything at all, or they know nothing and I flounder about how to explain myself without it sounding ridiculous.' She shrugged. 'I've struggled in England because of it. I felt there was already such a strong sense of who I was – and so many opinions on what that might mean – that it was hard to get beyond that.'

'Your husband managed it though. Or did he do it the English way, by saying nothing at all?'

She laughed. This feeling was new: of opening one's self, one's world, up for examination – not to present it as fact, a page in the social register as her mother would, but rather as something worthy of discussion, of thought, God, even of amusement.

The lunch was drawing to a close, and Constance came to stand behind her chair, signalling that it was time to go home. As Jean stood, saying her goodbyes, she couldn't decide if she had been there for hours or just a second, a brilliant snap of light that seemed to split everything into before and after.

CHAPTER FIFTEEN

Each day began with a cobalt-blue sky. A peach halved then quartered, its skin furred but its flesh cold and sweet; some correspondence to deal with, or a conversation with Constance on swatches of fabric; a drive into town with Lechabret to buy the newspapers or the flesh flowers that would come in from Nice by train. Time stretched each morning till Jean thought it would snap under the fierce heat of the midday sun, and then would give way to the loll of the afternoon rest, spent in the cool of her room under starched white sheets or reading outside on the terrace in the shade of the sprawling pine. Her mind became unfamiliar to her in these periods of rest, drowsy with the heat and the effects of the cold wine she would drink at lunch, and sometimes her dreams frightened her with their intensity. She felt aware of her body, how it responded to her tangled mind in these hours when her eyes were closed, but somehow she inhabited an in-between where anything was possible.

She had seen David now every day since she had been here. It had started with that lunch at the hotel nearly three weeks ago – the ease of their conversation, the way she could open up about her family, talk freely, laugh easily. The feeling had spread into her bones, giving her a confidence in herself that she had not known before and an awareness of each moment that felt infused with colour and scent and sound. The buzzing of the fat bees that hovered, suspended, over the lavender, the thrum of the cicadas at the edge of every thought, the gentle wash of the water over the pebbles on the beach, back and forth in a gentle, cleansing sweep as she sat with her feet in the water. And David: the sound of his voice, the way he sat, leaning forward when an idea seized him, hands clasped in front in enthusiasm, or behind his head, looking up at the sky, smiling with lazy delight at the blistering sun that played sentry to their every move.

The lunch had led to another dinner with Frank and Sybil, this time a more intimate affair, for many had been called back to Paris by life and its demands, despite the conversations otherwise. But not this small group, for whom reality and society and its circular demands seemed a far-off place; here all was possibility, ideas, with none of the conservatism of New York, none of its codes of behaviour, none of the strictures of prohibition. These Americans had seen less, endured less, of the horrors of the Great War – this part of France to them was freedom, opportunity. And it felt the same to Jean, too: there was a novelty to life here that was so invigorating, like a virgin beach walked upon, or the sea at dawn dived into. Everything with Edward, with Harehope, had felt inhabited a hundred times before, life lived over and over. Here all was new, untouched, untried.

So tonight was just Constance and Jean, the Fairbanks and David, sitting out under the stars, the candles on the table lending the evening a celestial glow, talking, laughing, Jean watching this man who seemed to confound everything she had thought she knew.

Jean sat beside him, looking at his face in the flickering light, the small bump at the bridge of his nose, the smooth skin, brown from the sun, the casual way he dressed, cuffs rolled up, shirt neck open, bare ankles, battered loafers. Here was an American, born on the same continent, born on the same coast, but different to all the boys – and men – she'd known.

David was leaning forward, lighting himself a cigarette, the eyes of the table on him. He had been talking about his family – he was from Boston, the son of an attorney; he'd been to Yale, though he was nothing like the blustering, ruddy-cheeked friends of her brother she had met at dances in her last summer in Newport.

'I'd moved to New York to write, but on my first day at the *Herald* my editor calls me into his office, congratulating me on being the youngest writer on the desk, and he has a look somewhere between guilt and amusement, and he tells me I'm to head to Coney Island, where there's a talking cat that needs reporting on. He has a straight face now, knowing that I got the job because of a series of pieces on the dying days of the Kaiser's Germany, but I've got no choice but to go and write three hundred of my finest on a talking ginger tom. Who, I might add, could not talk but could miaow to the tune of "Danny Boy", if one was being generous.'

'Where were you living then?' Constance asked. He had the group's attention. There was something appealing in his slight otherness; this writer, so handsome, so unencumbered, not quite of the same background as the rest of them.

'I was renting a small apartment in Greenwich Village with a college friend, in a brownstone with an ancient Irish woman who lived beneath us and who called us her boys. She'd lost her son in the Easter Rising.' He took a drag of his cigarette, exhaling slowly. 'She was wonderful, you know. We were her boys, and she would leave a pot of some stew or other outside our apartment door every Sunday night without fail, with a little note reminding us of the importance of a home-cooked meal.'

'Oh, but David, you're selling yourself short.' Sybil was leaning back in her chair, her legs on Frank's lap and tumbler in hand, letting the spirit within coat the edge of the glass as she turned it slowly. 'You got bigger pieces and travel pieces when you were in New York. I remember Helmut Everley telling me you were the writer he had his money on.'

'You know Helmut?' Jean was surprised. He was a figure she'd known only from soireés given by her father at their apartment. She would be brought in to greet the guests, 'to smile and scintillate', as her mother used to remind her as she nudged her into the room, before ushering her out when dinner was announced.

'As much as one can know him. But he was kind to me. He read some of my early pieces. He was the one that suggested Paris could give me some possibilities. To explore, to write.'

'What do you write about?' Jean's question felt naive, but David looked across at her and she could feel that he would have happily talked to her alone. That the others were just spectators, mere enablers of the intimacy growing between them that they could both touch the edges of but never articulate, because there was nothing tangible beyond the change in the air that moved between them.

'Well, for now I write what my dear editor suggests, or I should say directs. Expat life in Paris, fairly straight, steered forcefully away from any of the Left Bank artistic scene. But I'm working on some short stories, building on an idea I had. About Paris, the city, its hold on people, the freedom that's come after all the slaughter. Following a pair of brothers. It's just the germ of an idea for now. I feel there's a new way to tell these tales – straighter, more direct. Truer.'

'But you must carry on, make yourself the time. We owe it to these days, these nights to shrug off the old, inhabit the new.' Frank was standing up, going to retrieve another bottle from inside. 'I'd love to read some of your work.'

Jean could see Constance checking her watch, swallowing a yawn.

'Oh, they're not for public consumption yet. One day maybe. But for now it's the bread-and-butter writing. And the bliss of being down here. You know, I feel less and less like a foreigner each day I spend here.' David's eyes caught Jean's across the table and she wanted to agree, but said nothing. She just held his look, and that thing passed between them again, unseen by the rest, maybe even imagined by her, though she felt sure it was not.

They had found themselves meeting at her beach mid-morning. At first it had been by chance, and then it became an unspoken arrangement between them. Shy at first, they would greet each other like adolescents, hesitant before they fell into their rhythm, walking its shingle length, empty apart from the fishermen, then standing, barefoot, feet in the shallows as they talked.

She had asked him on one of those walks about France: why here, why now. Away from the group, those dinners where sometimes it could feel as if it was an artful performance – not the same as New York, so different to that, but still self-aware, arch, intellectual, contrarian. Here, they could both be more direct.

'I suppose I've always been one to get away. From home, from Boston, then from New York. Growing up the way I did – my mother had these bouts. Great passages of time where she would retreat to her room, door closed to the world. We called them bad streaks, but they were really her becoming so sad and sunken within herself that she couldn't do anything – she would barely leave the house, let alone have dinner with me or my father. But we never discussed it. My father and I just continued on politely while this silence stalked the corridors of our house. And it made me angry. That he wouldn't say a word about what was going on, nor think about why my mother might be behaving in this way. It just felt as if someone had laid a giant blanket over our house, muffling all the life within. So when I was old enough, I had to leave. It was sucking the breath out of me. And when I chose to go to Yale, not Harvard, where my father had gone, it was like I'd drawn a line between us. And, I'm ashamed to say, it felt good.'

They were standing now at the farthest edge of the beach, looking back down to where the path to her house began.

'I deferred my place at Yale to sign up to fight here in 1917. Father was horrified – I was so young, I was interrupting my studies. But he was wrong. All the blood and the fear and the horror I saw was worth it, for that feeling in Paris at the end. It was so alive, so free. I swore then that I'd come back. This was the place for me. It was all so different to the quiet control of home, to my father and his views of what one could and couldn't do or say. So when I finished Yale I moved to New York, and as soon I could, I put an ocean between me and all of that, came back to Paris, came here.'

David looked out to sea. She saw the freckles scattered across his cheekbones, the way he'd turned his collar up against the sun. London was battling against grey skies, heavy with guilt and grief, a generation trying to lift their heads above it all. Here there were no clouds, just the bright peacock blue of a May morning and the creaseless, perfect sea stretching out before them, aching with optimism.

He turned to her then. 'We're all escaping something here, aren't we? And this place, it gives us the freedom to do that, to—'

David stopped himself, looked down at the sand, but she knew their minds had met on where this freedom could take them. She knew she had passed a point too, that she didn't care what happened next so long as she could stay here, looking out to sea, standing next to a man who could unburden himself with so little effort, could shrug off the weight of something and return to the present as if he'd just dived beneath the water and come back up to the surface.

She had invited him back to lunch after one of their morning walks – it was on the edge of both of their minds, she could tell, but she knew he would never ask.

'Constance is away in Paris for a few days and Marie has gone to church, taking Olive with her as it's her day off. But I know she's left a simple lunch, tomatoes from the vine, some bread.' She looked down at her hands. 'You could stay?'

He had said yes. An awkward smile was traded between them. They had sat then on the terrace, had shared a bottle of the local rosé, and the intimacy of eating alone had made her feel reckless: the heat and the taste of the wine, the sound of the cicadas, grinding and loud, the cool of the shade after the blistering sun on the beach; all of it now seemed deafening to her. He had sensed it too, had become quiet when lunch had drawn to a close and the question of the impossible – the desired – hung, unspoken, in the air between them.

'I ought to get back. I promised Frank I'd go into Cannes with him this evening.' He ran his fingers through his hair, avoiding her eyes. 'I don't want to keep you. I'm sure you have things you need to do.' He stood, but he didn't move off as he said it, and his jacket lay untouched on the back of the chair.

She stood too, close enough that she could touch him.

'I ought to go,' he said again, but when he put out his hand to say goodbye, she took it in hers. They were close enough to kiss now. She felt desire, and something more than that – a decisiveness within that desire that she had never known – run through her, and it was as everything before had been a dreamless sleep, a half-life spent under layers of matter, obstructions to truth.

His eyes were there, open and blue, unflinching before her, and she felt a new confidence, a surge of something chemical. She knew then, as she kissed him on this terrace, hundreds of miles away from anyone she really knew, that what was happening had to happen; that it would continue and that she could not, would not, stop it. It would take her somewhere new, unclear, fraught with danger, somewhere she wanted to be no matter the risk. The glimpse of a world in colour lay before her, one from which she would not turn away.

CHAPTER SIXTEEN

A silk scarf tied knotted under her chin, a cardigan over her shoulders, Jean sat in the back of the car, relieved to be away from Constance and her opinions. The journey would take her through Juan-les-Pins and on the coast road to Cannes. The wind whipped her face. There was a mistral blowing, a cold, dry wind coming down from the mountains, clearing the closeness that had hung in the air for the past few days. The sea was ragged and choppy, and the pull and tug of the wind in the trees added to her feeling of unease.

Each time her mind was distracted by something – a bend in the road, a glimpse into a house with a curtain drawn back, a cloud of dust in the air – another image would snap across it, the intensity causing her to shift in her seat. The back of David's neck, her hands in his hair, his hands on her body. She could not associate herself now with the person who had done these things so willingly, so absolutely. Like watching flickering images of someone else entirely. A woman who took a man to her bed, who had given herself freely to him; who had lain with him afterwards, his arm across her naked chest, watching the thin beam of light that broke through the shutters, listening to the silence of her empty house.

After David had gone that first time, she had sat entirely still at the table on the terrace. Her hands shook and she took one of Constance's cigarettes, finding the act of lighting it and exhaling something to fix her fractured self to. Time passed, the sun's intensity waned; Marie and Olive returned, coming to say their shy hellos before returning to their rooms. Still she sat, upright and silent, bolted to the ground by the enormity of what she had done. She felt she needed to scrub herself, to shed the person who had done this thing so alien to everything she thought she knew of herself. But as much as she wanted to peel off this layer of dirt, she knew she couldn't. That what she had done – and would continue to do, she knew it even then – was the most fully conscious act of her adult life. She could not control it any more than she could the heat of the sun or the pull of the sea. It was in her and through her, and every second thought brought her back to it. And it was pure. An act more natural and instinctive than any upstairs in the house at Park Lane or at Harehope. She was wide awake with David, as if a dart had entered her body, piercing her core and allowing life, real life, to flow into her veins.

They had spent the afternoon together only yesterday, using another snatched few hours when the house was empty, before Edward arrived. They lay side by side, Jean's head resting against that dip in his shoulder that had come to feel like home. The clock in the hall chimed two, letting them know politely that they had a quarter of an hour before David would need to make his exit, erase himself from the marital bed that had never held her husband. Hands entwined, minds emptied by desire satiated, now filling once again with the anxiety of Edward's arrival, David kissed her knuckles.

'It sounds like I'm bitter about him coming, but I'm not, I swear. I just want to have you to myself. But I'll do it. I'll disappear like water into the sand, leave no trace…' He turned onto his side to look at her. The physical ease between them still had the power to confound her. 'You know, I've never needed to own things, never been possessive. I liked the way my life was a light little case that could be packed and unpacked easily. But now it's different.' He carried on, his hand trailing a path from her shoulder to hip. 'It's just so strange to me that he's coming out to see you, to see this house you're supposedly creating for him. But it feels as if it's ours, doesn't it?' He sat up then, pulling up the pillow behind him. 'Who is he? This man who stretches you out like a string that will snap?'

She had been careful not to talk about Edward, as if the mention of his name might conjure his presence into being. But then a wire had arrived announcing his arrival, and though he was not yet there his spirit somehow was, in the feeling that pulled at her chest and the tiny fingers of anxiety that began to tap away at her insides.

David stood up to dress then, pulling on his clothes, buttoning his shirt deftly, an eye always on the time. He kissed her quickly on the head. 'I know you don't know how to play this, but nor do I. I feel that somehow it's for me to know. Two years older, still unmarried. But I don't. I'm sorry. It's the truth. I feel like a child, confounded by a game whose rules I don't know and whose aim is unclear. So we're adrift, you and I.' He stood over her now, smiling a wan, tired smile. 'At least we're together in that.'

He turned and left the room, closing the door behind him, and she could hear the light jog of his feet on the steps. He needed to be away before Constance returned from a trip that Jean had engineered. The skill of the adulterer. Desire had armed her with lies and an inventiveness she'd never known she had. She had sat at the edge of her bed, the shutters open, the white heat of the afternoon stripping the room of all that had preceded it.

And now she was in the car on the way to meet Edward, and another image burned across her mind – David's face above her, pushing her hair out of her eyes so she could look at him, their urgency, how out of control they were – and now a jolt on the road and she was back in the present, the car pulling into the shade of the plane trees that ran alongside the entrance to the train station.

'Would Madame like to come to the platform?'

'Yes, thank you, I will.'

She glanced in her pocket mirror; it was still the same woman who looked back at her. She had taken some colour in the month she'd been here, and freckles were scattered over her nose and on her cheekbones. She removed the scarf and patted down her hair as she stepped out of the car, Monsieur Lechabret holding the door open for her patiently. The pair walked through the arch of the station building, through the busy concourse and onto the platform as the train was pulling out of the station, the screech of its brakes scraping against the inside of her brain. And there stood her husband. They walked towards each other like acquaintances; she offered him her cheek and his hand was briefly at her waist. Her heart tripped – he would see into her, sniff out her deception – but he just stood, waiting for her to direct them out of the station.

When they were in the back of the car, their knees touching as they jerked their way through the busy back streets clogged with market day shoppers, and they wound their way slowly back out of the town, she chatted nervously.

'Constance will be there when we get back. Do you remember her? I'm sure she said she'd met you in London.'

Edward nodded, eyes only on the traffic, taking in their slow progress with irritation. 'Is this normal?'

'I'm afraid it's market day, so it gets terribly crowded. But once we're through these narrow streets and out on the open road we'll pick up the pace.'

He said nothing further, so she persevered.

'You should have seen Olive yesterday. She had her day off and she must have spent it sitting outside a cafe in the sun. You know how pale her skin is. Well, she's now positively pink, a lobster. Constance suggested putting calamine lotion on it, but she refused. Didn't trust it. She's a silly thing. But the house is cool, lovely thick walls, and there's a terrace that's very pretty and one can have drinks there in the evening.'

She felt her voice rising with forced jollity. He was looking at her closely, and she had the sudden urge to be sick, a bitter taste rising in her throat. But she swallowed it down, folded her hands into her lap, listened to his account of his journey, his dislike of the food in the dining car, the failings of the other passengers and his valet's packing, his mouth pinched as he spoke.

When they entered the house and she walked up the stairs to show him their room and his dressing room next door, she felt his eyes on her back. She took in the crisp white of their bed, the shutters still open as the midday sun had yet to take the house hostage – and here was another image scorched onto her brain: her back arched, David's mouth on hers, his hands between her legs. She had to reach for the rail of the bed to steady herself.

Back downstairs, Edward was brusque, giving each room a cursory glance, moving on to the next with the briefest of comment. Marie came forward, bobbing a curtsey, and he nodded before making his way out onto the terrace, his hands behind his back, a landlord surveying a property he had no use for.

Constance appeared at the top of the stairs, and her rush of enthusiasms and greetings was a relief to Jean.

'So what do you think, Edward? Is it to your taste? We went with *l'esprit local*. I hope you don't mind.'

'It's charming. Not perhaps my thing, but that wasn't the point, was it?' He kissed her on each cheek before turning to Jean, the faintest of smiles on his lips.

'Can I fix you a drink before lunch?' Jean was desperate to keep moving, feeling that staying still would snare her in some hidden trap.

'A gin, thank you.'

He had sat down at the table now, pulling out his cigarette case from his inside pocket, and was casting around for an ashtray.

'How does one while away one's hours here? Apart from making house? Are the local gentry up to the Buckman standards?' He looked over her to Constance as he shook out the match. 'I'm afraid Jean wasn't much taken with the hunting set at Harehope.'

A wasp was circling the tumbler Marie had placed in front of him, and he batted it away irritably.

'Mother couldn't fathom who would still be in France at this time of year. I had to remind her that it was frightfully modern to come here now. I saw Tommy at White's last week and he howled with laughter. Said I might find the assembled crowd a little unusual. Not many of our sort left.' Pulling a handkerchief from his pocket, he wiped his forehead, glancing round for a valet that wasn't there. 'One needs a hat in this damned heat.'

Constance and Jean now sat at the table with him, Constance asking the right questions, about Ascot, his mother, Harehope; making him laugh, coaxing him into good temper. She was a professional at this, a master at listening to men with the perfect mix of deference and amusement. Jean could see the effect it had on Edward's abrasive mood. She hadn't seen him like this – speaking in a voice fractionally too loud for the small group, finishing his drink and beckoning for another almost immediately. She wondered whether he was uneasy at being on turf that was more Jean's than his; it was his turn to be the fish out of water.

She took one of his cigarettes, which he lit for her, raising his eyebrow at her new habit. 'I find it soothing in the heat,' she said.

Constance chattered on. 'We've been invited to a few dinners, Edward. Charming Americans who I knew from New York, and there's a hotel that's stayed open for the gang that are still here. One can lunch there adequately well. There'll be enough to keep you occupied, I promise. And besides, you'll want me out of your way so you two can be alone after all this time apart.'

Edward smiled briefly, looking to Jean, who felt her cheeks flame.

Constance leaned forward and patted her hand. 'Oh, you really are too sweet, my dear. It's all right, I'm only teasing. I shan't make any more comments like that, God's truth.'

As the other two talked, Jean sat quietly, trying not to look too closely at Edward. His face seemed to shift and blur the more she took him in. This man before her was not her husband, a person she was sharing her life with, but a foreigner whom she barely knew. And she was foreign to her old self too. The woman that had left London a month before was not the woman who sat here on the terrace, smoking a cigarette, the taste of another man still in her mouth.

*

That night the three of them had dinner, the candlelight casting shadows that made strangers of their faces. Jean drank two cocktails before dinner, relishing the burn of the liquid on her empty stomach, willing on its anaesthesia for the rest of the evening, dreading the moment they would have to retire to their room. Constance once again played her role to perfection, picking up the slack from the young couple who sat like polite acquaintances at the table, but even she seemed to tire of her role, and the trio broke up eventually, Edward and Jean bidding her goodnight.

They walked up the stairs, Edward's polished shoes marking his progress on the stone floor in time with the thudding of her heart. She felt that if he were to see her undressed, her body would reveal its secrets; that David's hands would have left some mark she could not hide.

He stopped at the door. 'I'll sleep in the dressing room tonight. You looked so tired at the end of dinner. Positively drained. I'll see you in the morning.'

She closed the door behind her and sat alone on the bed. As she listened to the sounds of her husband undressing next door, she opened the shutters and sat looking at the moon that hung, huge and low, over the water, as if it was being pulled down to earth against its will.

CHAPTER SEVENTEEN

The strange, disjointed *ménage à trois* – Jean, Constance and Edward – left the car and made their way down the small promenade that marked the main thoroughfare of Juan-les-Pins. The town was shabby and Jean felt that in the winter, with rain on its streets and a dark grey sea, it would be dreary. But in that magic hour of a summer's evening between dusk and dark, when the world possesses a perfect, muted luminescence, it was beautiful in its poverty and simplicity, and she wished she could sit on one of the benches that lined the walkway and listen to the sounds of the evening coming to life.

The promenade divided the beach from a chaos of low buildings that ran along its other side, and children were still playing on the sand although it was past eight o'clock. A little boy was batting a ball to his sister, her hair a tangled mess of salted curls, and a group of old men in shirtsleeves were playing pétanque, the game Jean was now familiar with from evening excursions, the delight when metal struck metal, a patting of backs and a nodding of heads, the simple pleasure of a simple game.

It was Edward's last night before he would return to England, and the trio had been invited to dinner in the small casino that had taken note of *les Americains*, who were still here as the heat grew more intense, and were serving dinner and drinks to any guests that would come. Constance had suggested a night out, for Edward to play *punto* and avoid too much conversation with the 'stragglers', as he liked to call the various people Jean and Constance had introduced him to over the week.

His mood had been sour; he was not one for sitting still, and without his usual pursuits to engage him, he withdrew. The heat irritated him and, with no male companion to talk to in the evenings, he was restless. He seemed irritated too by Jean's familiarity with life out here. He would snort when she spoke French to the maids, and made a point of disliking the Provençal food that Marie would cook for them and that Jean adored for its seasonal simplicity. He liked to form an alliance with Constance in conversations, isolating Jean wherever possible, and though Constance did her best to rebalance the scales, she was also required to play her role as deferential lady to her male host, as flatterer of moods and keeper of tempers. The atmosphere in the house was one of forced civility and taut nerves.

They made their way into the marble entrance to the casino, through the provincial-looking gaming tables, empty apart from a pair of bored young men, idly playing cards, their eyes flicking up briefly to the group that entered. They walked out on the terrace that ran along the back of the building, overlooking the beach, where tables were arranged at random and an ancient waiter was carrying a tray of drinks to the group settled at the terrace's furthest edge. A man was playing an upright piano in the corner, wiping his brow every so often as he turned the page of his music. The whole place had the charming air of an absent-minded aunt, and the waiters seemed entirely unfazed by the smartly dressed diners gathering to eat there.

The table was already strewn with glasses, and little *assiettes* of cured meats were sweating in the still air. Constance led the way, announcing Edward and Jean to the assembled guests – there was the usual flicker of interest at this young Englishman and his title – and the men got to their feet. As she took in the group before her, Jean's stomach clenched. David was among them, standing towards the end of the table next to a seated Sybil, drink in hand. His face was flushed red and he was looking down.

'We've been here a while – you must excuse us for starting without you.' A tall, elegant man with a handsome face and a smooth charm whom Jean didn't recognise was kissing Constance on each cheek, smiling broadly at the new arrivals. 'Drinks? It's still so hot one needs something to cool down. They're slow at bringing them, so we've been ordering two at once.' He was French, with an impeccable accent, wearing an eggshell-blue linen suit cut in the latest style, and he gestured to Edward and Jean to sit. The casual air of the dinner, something Jean was used to from her month out here, was not something Edward would enjoy. He loathed not knowing who people were before meeting them, finding something undignified about having to delve into people's backgrounds to establish who they were, and was entirely unpractised at putting himself in any kind of context. He took his seat next to Sybil and gestured to the waiter. Jean had no option but to take her place opposite David and next to a man she knew had been David's host for the past few weeks.

Her neighbour immediately struck up a conversation with her, lighting for her the cigarette she had taken from her purse, hands trembling. 'So David tells me you've bought Antoine d'Erlanger's place? It's utterly charming. I went to see it when

I heard it was for sale. I love that terrace, and your little beach.'

She nodded politely as he talked, her attention held instead by the conversation taking place opposite her. Sybil was asking Edward a succession of questions to which he was giving cursory answers.

'And the house here?'

'It was all Jean's idea. Her little project.'

'But I take it you are pleased with her choice? We came and saw it last week, and I think it's in an enviable position.'

'Well, it's certainly a change from England.' Edward seemed in no rush to elaborate, so Sybil persevered.

'And how long do you plan to stay out here?'

'I leave tomorrow. I believe the idea was for me to visit the house my wife has bought for me. It's the way it works apparently. She and her mother shop, and I am invited to survey the spoils.' He was smiling but his tone was cold, and Sybil took to studying the menu before her. 'Have you met my mother-in-law? Elizabeth Buckman?'

'I haven't. I believe my husband has met your father-in-law.'

'I see. Well, she seems to speak for the pair when it comes to family matters – or the releasing of the purse strings, at any rate. Funny you don't know her, though. As I understood it, there are only four hundred people worth knowing in the whole of New York and you could fit them all in Mrs Astor's ballroom. Isn't that the thing?'

Jean was watching David now, stiff and quiet opposite her. He was drinking quickly, and the easy languor that she knew so well was gone.

The evening wore on. Bowls of bouillabaisse were served, then *carré d'agneau*, the meat making her stomach turn. Jean chewed, she sipped, she smoked, she talked – but every ounce of her was drawn to the two men across the table. A glass smashed to the floor and she started, looking across, seeing that David had knocked it as he talked to Constance on his other side. His forehead was damp with sweat, and she could see droplets appearing through the linen of his shirt.

Edward was now holding court, his voice low and steady, and there was a polite, almost deferential silence along the table for the young English lord, so immaculate, so refined, and now for his pretty young American wife.

'How did you two meet?' their host was asking Edward, and the table was quiet, smiles of anticipation at the no doubt charming story they were about to hear. Edward looked to Jean.

'Go on, Jean.' Edward smiled. 'It seems your friends haven't heard. Do tell.'

'Oh, really?' She floundered. 'A dinner given by mutual friends in London, at the Savoy actually, and then we bumped into each other again, the way one does, at a party the week or so after. Our parents knew of each other, so things just happened after that.'

Edward nodded. 'Yes, I suppose things *just happened*, as Jean so elegantly put it.'

David was looking at Edward directly across the table. His voice was too loud when he spoke, his mouth a loose line. 'Her money for your title, you mean? I thought that cliché had been killed off by the war.'

'Perhaps not, if you still feel the need to articulate it.' Edward gave a tight smile, swallowing his anger at the slight, but the ripple it caused ran down through the guests, changing the temperature. It was unbearable to Jean. David's humiliation leached across the table to her.

Constance, an eye always on her clients' mood, alert to the currents that could swirl and change so quickly, clapped her hands together, rising to bring over the maître d' to oblige. 'Some music! We must have some music. We can't have the piano sitting there like something from the *Mary Celeste!*'

The pianist, none too pleased to have his dinner interrupted, was duly brought out from the bar, a cigarette dangling from his lips as he took his seat and started on a half-hearted tune.

Edward took out a cigar, biting off the end and watching Jean as he sucked the thing to light, the tobacco finally taking and its acrid smoke lazily filling the air around him. There was a sense of anticipation among the guests; the tension before a storm breaks. Conversations were started but went nowhere. Drinks were drunk without being tasted.

Now Edward rose, smiling as he stood, eyes still on Jean, his chair scraping against the stone floor. 'Darling, we must go. Please excuse us. I've got to leave early tomorrow, and Constance and my wife no doubt have work to do.' He walked round to Jean's chair, pulling it out from under as she rose automatically, eyes on no one, her pulse in her ears, as she turned her back on David and the table and followed Edward and Constance back through the building.

In the car, he sat in the front with Monsieur Lechabret, silent, smoking his cigar. Even Constance couldn't bring herself to talk, looking straight ahead to the pool of yellow that the headlights threw onto the road ahead. But as the car wound round the final bend that led into their drive, Edward looked over his shoulder.

'Do tell about our young American friend. We haven't seen him all week, but he seemed to have some strong, and not terribly original, opinions about us.'

Constance leaned forward, patting Edward's shoulder. 'He's nobody, darling. We've met him once before at some dinner or other. A writer, probably out of sorts because nobody reads him. Writers can be such bores.' She turned to Jean. 'Don't you agree, darling? Now I think we should have one last drink on the terrace before bed. Celebrate all our hard work.'

She carried on chatting as the car made its way up the drive, and Jean sat back in her seat, worried that the screaming in her head would spill out into the silence of the night. But the earthy whine of the cicadas in the still, hot air was the only sound.

As Edward held the door open for Jean and she stepped out of the car, his eyes were black as ink, but the look they held made her flinch.

CHAPTER EIGHTEEN

Jean was alone, sitting at the kitchen table, the heat of the day now gone. Marie was off for the evening, had left at six, hanging her apron on the back of the kitchen door and smoking her nightly cigarette by the gate before pushing her bike off down the drive, and Jean had wandered into the kitchen looking for a glass of water. She had sat down, unsure of what to do with herself, on her own in the house, waiting for Constance to return. It was just the two of them again, Edward having returned to England the day before.

She shifted in her seat as she heard the car turning down the drive, heard the open and shut of the door, Constance's bright goodbye to Monsieur Lechabret, and her efficient clip on the gravel as she made her way around the back of the house. Jean took a deep breath and ground the cigarette into the dish in front of her. 'Constance?' Her voice was too quiet to be heard, and she cleared her throat and called out again. 'Constance? I'm in here.'

The kitchen door opened tentatively and Constance put her head round, confused. 'Darling, what are you doing back here? Haven't you seen the sunset? It's ravishing.' She walked into the room properly, slipping off her jacket, standing now in front of the table, handbag on her wrist. 'Are you all right? You look frightful.'

Jean felt her face crumple, and she began to cry.

'Oh, dear one. What is it?' She pulled out a chair and sat down opposite Jean. 'Can I have one of these?' She gestured at the cigarettes that lay on the table in front of them. Jean nodded, wiping her tears quickly. Lighting it, Constance took a drag and then looked across at Jean. 'Let's have a drink, shall we? Never a good idea to countenance times of strife without something strong in hand.'

Constance reappeared with two tumblers and a bottle of gin. Pouring them a large splash each, she put one down in front of Jean. 'So...'

'Oh God, it's a mess. I don't know how to begin. And I'm so embarrassed...'

'If it's embarrassing or shameful, I imagine I've done it before. I was once young, I promise.'

Jean took a sip of the drink, the gin burning her throat as she swallowed. 'That evening, the dinner at the casino. I know you heard what David said. About my money and Edward's title.'

'The whole table did, darling. It seemed so out of character, although now I look at your face, I see I've been missing something. Have I? Been missing something terribly obvious?' Constance's face was so kind it overwhelmed her, and Jean couldn't hold back the tears.

'I've been such a coward. Edward has sniffed David out, I know it, this American who made those bitter, drunken comments. I know he saw the way David looked at me that night.'

'Did Edward say anything? Before he left?'

'No, he didn't. But he's no fool.' Jean looked up wearily. 'But that's the problem with us. What we don't say. What we've never said. A marriage of a year and we've never talked about what any of it means, talked about anything at all. It's been so lonely. And then I came out here and there was this place and David, and it seemed to change me. Showed me another possibility, another way to be, where one could be oneself, or a self I didn't even know existed. The release. And then the desire – no, more than desire, it's something more than that.' She rubbed her face roughly. 'What have I done?'

Constance listened and nodded, allowing Jean to talk on, letting her fill the silence with words that for so long had been suppressed. But when she had spoken her piece, exhausted, Constance took her turn to speak. She was measured, firm. 'These things happen, have always happened. They happened to me.' She laughed bitterly. 'I can't be in the same room as my husband half of the time. And that leaves a space for someone else. But' – and she fixed her eyes beadily on Jean – 'episodes like this must never be allowed to become rumour, gossip, dinner party whispers. That is the end of it all.'

She took another sip of her drink and then looked at Jean, her face soft, her voice quiet.

'Edward may not be the kindred soul you had hoped to find in marriage – my God, he's damaged. He'll never be his brother, I can see how that has snared him. But in your position you cannot let him endure the shame of others knowing what has gone on. You must end it. Now. David was something for out here, but he won't travel, darling. You must leave him behind. Go back to London, to Harehope, to the life you're meant to have. By all means keep this place as your escape from all of that, but not David, that's too dangerous.'

Taking in Jean's face, she clasped her hand across the table and gave a forced smile.

'One can't be fodder for his first novel, darling – too ghastly! Come on, my love, cheer up. You'll soon be busy back in London, and you won't even remember him.'

And so they had packed up the house the following day, Constance's job now done and the final pieces left with Marie to sort. Jean had not had the courage to see David again. She had been too cowardly. Couldn't countenance the goodbye that she knew had to come; the question of her return impossible to answer. This thing she had brought into being, it could not continue; she had been mad to think it could.

She had walked down to the beach on her last afternoon, had stood at their spot, taken in the lapping of the water, the shift of the shingle beneath her bare feet, the gentle sigh of it all. She had let her eyes drift out to the horizon beyond, to that perfect line where blue met blue and drifted off to infinity, had whispered a goodbye that no one heard but which was carried off in the soft breeze of a perfect Riviera day.

CHAPTER NINETEEN

The heather was rough, scratching through the woollen tights she wore under her thick tweed skirt. They were on an uneven track now, following the barrel-tummied pony that was loaded up with rugs and picnic hampers filled to bursting with sandwiches and cheeses, hams, fruit cake. Her stomach turned again at the thought of food, and she wiped her brow, damp with sweat. The sun was strong now, it was nearly midday, and she had been walking for over an hour, following the pony and one of the underkeepers, who was leading her to the spot for lunch.

She turned to look back down across the valley. The scale of the place always lifted her. Acre upon acre of rugged moorland, gentler and less dramatic than the Scottish moors, but she loved it for the way the majesty of the hill, its endless roll and swell of purple, tapered down into the lush greens and yellows of the valley below, where pockets of stone houses lined the brook and nubby stone walls marked out the fields. None of the other women had wanted to join the guns for lunch today, but Jean couldn't stay in the house; the silence of it pressed down on her like lead. The weather could change so quickly up here and she had heard one of the keepers saying it would be fine on the hill, so she had decided to make her way up there.

Another flip of the stomach, and she had to start moving again to distract herself from the nausea that had been building since her return to England. At first she had thought it was travel sickness from the long train journey up through France, the change at Paris, the queasy progress their boat had made across an unseasonably choppy Channel. But it had persisted in London, becoming more intense and harder to ignore. She had not been physically sick, but the feeling in the pit of her stomach was there from the moment she woke till she lay down at night. Nausea began to mingle with nerves as her mind made calculations. She was unused to the rhythm of her body, her monthly bleeds having all but stopped before she went to France, but this feeling could not be explained away – it was instinctive, the knowledge that something other was inside her, upsetting the balance. She had spoken to a girlfriend, recently married and the mother of a baby girl, and she had squawked with delight, congratulating Jean on news she and Edward must surely have been longing for. Jean had, indeed, been longing for a baby, something to make her marriage a concrete thing, for there to be something to show for the year they had spent together as man and wife, but that had been before France. Before David.

The thought of him made her wince. She would only let her mind go to him when she was in bed at night, the darkness allowing her mind to go down paths that the daylight would not. Thinking of their month together, those afternoons alone that had seemed shocking at first but then like a second skin. The desire, the intensity of it, a new world revealed to her, a new self opened up. And then the bluntness of the departure, no goodbye at all. Just a journey in misery, alone, back to a place which was supposedly home but felt more alien than it had when she first left.

She was back in England. She was back at Harehope for the foreseeable future and was – she was all but certain – carrying David's child. The reality was so shocking she had to snuff out her thinking mind like a candle sometimes to stop it racing down these grooves of panic. Edward would know it couldn't possibly be his. But how would he react to that? It was horrific what she had done: the ultimate betrayal, the failure in her duty as wife, but worse than that. An insidious lie growing in her womb. But would he turn her out if he knew the truth? How could he, when everywhere he looked her name was there, stamped into the paintings, the furniture, the servants' pay? She was at the centre of it all, the fulcrum on which the whole thing rested.

The underkeeper turned back to make sure she was still following. Jean wiped her brow one more time, and carried on up the track.

CHAPTER TWENTY

Jean stood by the window in Edward's study while he sat at his desk, still in tweeds from his day on the hill, distracted by a letter from London. The clouds carried the threat of rain, but the sun behind still burnished their edges in flashes of silver. She turned to look at him.

'I have something to tell you, Edward.' Her voice cracked like glass. 'I'm pregnant. I think it must be quite early – I feel quite wretched, this sickness…'

He didn't look up, but folded the letter and placed it carefully back in its envelope. 'So we are finally to have a child.'

'I have asked Mrs Hawkins to call out the doctor this week, to see if everything is all right…' Her voice trailed off.

He was leaning forward now in his chair, eyes fixed on her, but his voice was low. 'How are you going to play this? The innocent, until I force it out of you? Or the brave and defiant woman, knowing you have your own little trump card to play? What's it to be?' His eyes were bulging slightly, and she could see the letter in his hand shaking. 'I want to hear you say it.' His voice was low, deliberate.

She kept her eyes down. 'It's not your child.'

'I can't hear you, Jean.'

'It's not your child. I had an affair in France.'

Then came the first flare of real anger. 'Of course you did, with that weaselly man at that dinner. Staring at you across the table with his pathetic spaniel eyes. I knew it almost the moment I saw you at the station too, something different about you. The way you carried yourself. And now the thing falls to me, doesn't it? How am *I* to react? How am *I* to treat you, standing here, with that paltry little bump I can see you've been trying to conceal. Freddie's wife said something to me yesterday: that you were blooming, so beautiful, was there any news...' He stopped, and his face was twisted with rage, but also with the hurt he thought he was concealing. 'What kind of a woman does this? Who are you, Jean?'

'You never tried to find out.' Her voice was quiet and she didn't know if he'd heard her at all, because he was stoking himself now, goading his own anger.

'The way you tiptoed round this house, looking, always, for something from me. Well, now I know what you wanted. Was I not man enough for you? Was that what it was?' His voice rose as he struggled to contain himself. The worst she could have done to him, she'd done: stripped him of his pride, his sense of self that was so fragile, so dependent on the approval of others. 'Well, I won't let you humiliate me. Another example of what I can't do. I won't have it. So you can live with this vile mess you have created. And I will crush you and whatever reputation your hallowed family has if you speak of this to anyone. To all intents and purposes, this child will be mine.' His voice was low again, vibrating with hate, and he would not look at her. 'Perhaps you don't rate me as a husband. Perhaps you never have. A proxy heir who you've propped up with your cash and your paintings and your American "generosity".' This last word was spoken as if it was poison to be spat out. The chair scraped against the floor and he walked over to where she stood, close enough that she could see his chest rising and falling.

Everything until now had been suppressed, pushed down. Misunderstandings, rejections, loneliness, his sense of inadequacy, all of it left untouched, unexamined, stagnant water left to putrefy within him; the Englishman taught always that to be master of oneself was the victory to sound, not knowing that the battle was pointless, leaving himself maimed and weak when the true fight came.

'I will be what you already take me to be, Jean. I will take your money, and I will use it, and we will have this child, and it will be ours. And if it is a girl, we will try again – and again – and again – until we have a son.' Angry wells of spittle were gathering at the edges of his mouth. 'And you will never speak of what you've done. Silence will be your penance. And your bloody money.' The last words were muttered through his clenched jaw.

Momentarily stunned that her deed would go undiscovered by the rest of the world, she felt a warped elation at his acceptance, but then came a flood of guilt so great it threatened to drown her. Edward would absorb her deceit; what other path was available to them? He would enable her to hold up her head in society. But they were both now caught in a trap more ghastly than she had first envisaged. He would never love her, how could he, but this child who was not his and this money that was hers would bind them together forever.

Edward walked out, closing the door behind him and leaving her in a room she had never been alone in. Unsteady on her feet, she went and sat at his desk, lighting one of his cigarettes and staring blankly at the sea of papers before her. She exhaled, her nausea returning; and she held her head in her hands. The weather was closing in, the way it could here, a blanket of dense grey eclipsing the blue-sky promise of only a few hours before.

She had told him; he knew the truth; the game was on. But what world would this child be born into? Where its father was not its father, and its mother a cheat and a liar.

PART II

CHAPTER ONE

Harehope, 1924

Eyes a flash of a jay's feathers in flight; a swirl of dark hair at his crown; skin soft as kid; a cry that could crack her open. Until now, babies had appeared to Jean as vague and indeterminate bundles, each just as the one before, offered up for the requisite congratulation to be given, then handed back with relief. Her own, now here, was the opposite: a tenacious, determined presence, a mass of fierce individual needs and intense and unfathomable wants, all distilled into a body no bigger than an evening slipper. Jean held Alfie in her arms, in awe of the miracle of his body, of limbs and toes and tiny hands. He was eight weeks old now, holding his head up a little by himself. When he'd been undressed for his bath the night before, she had been mesmerised by the little legs, by his arms that made those small involuntary movements which caused him eternal pleasure and surprise. And those eyes that seemed to know the world already for what it was.

He was wearing the Warres' ancient christening gown, its length swamping him like a wedding dress, its lace yellowed in patches from age, the intricacy of its weave so fragile it felt like it might turn to dust in her hands. She handed him back to his nanny and watched as the older lady deftly wrapped him in the fringed silk shawl and then looked expectantly up at Jean. 'Shall we go, Lady Warre? They'll be waiting for us now, I should think.'

Jean nodded and the little trio processed out of the front door, Nanny Hodgson fussing with Alfie's shawl as she went. They walked along the front of the house, dwarfed by its vast facade of grey stone, and Jean glanced up at the row upon row of windows that stretched above her, the house's scale still able to catch her off guard; the great pediments which framed each window, the Corinthian columns of the building's middle that seemed to taper up to the sky. That was her favourite part of the house, where the true Palladian symmetry lay, before Edward's Victorian forebears had added and subtracted to the pile they had inherited, in wings of different lengths that sprawled out on either side.

On they went, feet crunching across the gravel in the quiet chill of the morning air, until they came to the edge of the east wing of the house, where a stone path, flanked by hedges of tall box – the pride of the gardeners – led them to the Warre family chapel. Edward, his mother, his sister, a scattering of friends, the parson, the bishop: they would all be waiting for them inside. Tenants of the estate too, for this baptism was an event essentially public in nature. The arrival of a son, the firstborn, heralded as if from heaven; the truth hidden from them all, a cruel joke from on high.

The reception of Alfie's birth had stunned Jean. The pomp and adulation for a boy who shared no blood with the soil on which he was feted. She had overlooked how important the firstborn son was in her adopted country. Back home, Jean and her brother were placed on more or less an equal financial footing, as her mother and uncle had been before them. Here, everything was funnelled directly to this mewling, infant boy, regardless of who or what came after, a much-vaunted child who – should she choose to – she might barely see until he went to school, as far as she could understand the nature of the nursery at Harehope.

She pushed open the heavy oak door to the chapel, felt the hush descend on the guests already sitting in its damp chill, saw the faces of the women she passed brighten as she made her lonely procession down the aisle, involuntary smiles spreading at a glimpse of this long-anticipated baby. Edward was standing by the stone font, in conversation with the bishop. The sun coming in through the stained-glass windows bathed it in a golden light that caught the dust, and the air was mossy, a little stale from lack of use, but there was the scent of roses too from a garland that had been placed around it. She had seen one of the gardeners carrying the flowers in from the glasshouse that morning, as if they might shatter into a million pieces at a touch, so fierce was his concentration. The tenants and old retainers, dressed in their Sunday best, were sitting deferentially at the back of the chapel, delighted at the chance to glimpse this boy who seemed to signify so much: hope, the circularity of life, freedom from death, like the *long live the King* uttered at a monarch's departure, without a breath to separate extinction from rebirth. Yet each word of congratulation given to Jean caused the knot in her stomach to tighten and pull, a tug of shame at the truth only she and Edward knew.

Jean stood now by the font, the cool of the chapel stone making her wish she'd worn a thicker coat as she held her son in her arms. She watched Alfie's eyes, determinedly blue – 'like his grandmother's', people would note as they took in his parents' distinctly brown eyes, though of course they knew nothing of who he was – and there were little creases beneath them that Nanny told her were tiredness. His eyelids flickered as they struggled to resist the descent of sleep, then closed as he finally gave in, soothed no doubt by the low rumblings of the bishop's voice as he read the words from the book held open before him, the hands of the young altar boy trembling at the task.

'Oh merciful God, grant that the old Adam in this Child may be so buried, that the new man may be raised up in him. Grant that all carnal affections may die in him, and that all things belonging to the Spirit may live and grow in him. Grant that he may have power and strength, to have victory, and to triumph against the Devil, the world and the flesh.'

The words washed over her like water, the meaning distant but the effect powerful: incantations of damnation and salvation, of the Devil and his hold, the fragility of infant life, the duty of those gathered. The bishop was looking at her; she realised the time had come for the anointing, and she held Alfie out to him, the old man's hands shaking a little as he received him. He held him up for the gathered to see, then dipped his head in the water of the font, cupping water and splashing it once, twice, three times over his head before briefly holding him up again and dabbing his forehead with a folded cloth. Alfie had woken at the shock of the water, and then emitted that cry that confounded Jean whenever she heard it, a sound that clawed at her insides as he begged in the only way he knew for it all to stop. He was handed back to her and she rocked him in her arms, shushing him gently as she'd seen Nanny Hodgson do so effortlessly, embarrassed by the eyes of all those people on her, this mother who knew nothing of herself, let alone of this child she rocked in her arms. The cry reached a peak and then gradually ebbed away, and Alfie's eyes locked onto hers, finding comfort in the connection.

She thought then of the letter that had come that morning from her mother, apologising again that she couldn't be there, congratulating Jean on what would be one of the happiest days of her life: *The gift of children, the next generation set on its path because of that love you and Edward share. It is a miracle, a blessed miracle. You will have made them all so happy, my dearest darling, by giving them a boy. A boy!* The letter had begged that Edward change his mind and include the Buckman name in Alfie's, but he had stood firm. And what power did Jean have over him there?

The congregation stood as one as the service drew to an end, the bishop processing down the aisle first, mitre on, crosier aloft, with the parson shuffling behind him, giving a bright smile to remind the gathered that this was really his domain, that the bishop was an unnecessary flourish. Those assembled were relieved that the formality was over; she could hear it in the chatter that picked up and spread like a ripple through the chapel. Now tea could be had – or better, a drink – and Edward could be patted on the back, with the hint of a smile that always seemed to accompany the congratulation: that it was Edward's virility, his strength of purpose, that had resulted in the arrival of the necessary boy.

Freddie was standing outside, hands in his pockets against the cold as he waited on the grass, letting the other guests pass with a friendly nod to those he knew. Edward and Jean stopped when they got to him, and Jean gave Alfie a little kiss on the forehead before Nanny took him off for his rest.

Smiling brightly, Freddie patted Edward on the arm, before offering him a cigarette. 'Well done, well done, old thing.'

Lighting it, Edward exhaled, keeping his eyes on Jean. 'Must be a relief, mustn't it?' Freddie, oblivious to the undercurrents, nudged Jean chummily, with a schoolboy smile. 'This'll get Edward off your back for a while at least, if you forgive the expression.' He took a drag of his cigarette, the smoke blooming in the air between them, and turned to Edward cheerily. 'You've beaten me and Rose to it. I'll never hear the end of it now. Time for a drink though. I'll head back to the house. One needs something stiff to kick off these stodgy affairs.'

He left the two of them standing, Jean smiling politely as the remaining guests filed by. Edward kept his eyes on the group now passing, and with a tight smile he muttered to Jean, a fraction too loud, 'How do you do it?'

She looked up at him, surprised at the tone when others were so near.

'When you know what this is. How can you do it?'

'Edward, we can't do this now.'

'Do you enjoy this?' He turned his whole body to face her. They were so close she could smell the tobacco on his breath.

'Of course not. You know I don't.' She felt tears prick at the edge of her eyes, swallowed to keep them at bay. 'I am sorry for all of this. You know I am. But I can't change it. We can't change it. You said as much. So we have to do this. We have to carry on. Try and make something of it.'

They turned and walked in silence back to the house. The path they took was flanked with rose hips, bright as blood, and when the house appeared before them, its stone warm in the sunlight, it seemed to welcome them, grateful to this pair for so diligently securing the next generation. Stokes was standing inside the front door, in his hand a silver salver with coupes of champagne offered for the small toast that would be made later by Edward. The last of the guests were already inside, so, without a word, they took a glass each, and its sharp acid taste was a relief to Jean.

She saw Freddie forcing Edward's mother to engage, extracting a brittle smile from her eventually; saw him compliment Mrs Hawkins on the flowers as she passed him in the hall, leaving the flush of pleasure behind; saw him remember the name of Mrs Hammersley, who no one ever remembered and who was standing looking lost, an empty glass in her hand. Freddie was so good at these things, far better than Edward, always talking to the people that needed to be talked to, sensing the ones that needed rescuing. He'd known them all for years.

He stood with Jean now, their backs to the fire as they watched the room: the gathering of local gentry, relieved to be included but now enduring the hour of standing around, the thirsty among them hoping to catch Stokes' eye, the bored waiting for the earliest acceptable opportunity to make their excuses.

'This will be good for Edward, you know. All of this.' Freddie dipped his head in the direction of the room.

She looked across at him.

'He can get on with it all now. His mother hasn't quite the bite she once had. Look at her now, behaving herself in the corner when before she would have been making sure everyone knew exactly who was in charge.' Alice was indeed sitting, upright, on a sofa, enduring the parson's presence beside her with barely concealed contempt as he leaned forward, cheeks flushed from absent-mindedly accepting Stokes' efficient offers of more champagne. 'Edward can take his rightful place now, you see. And you, of course – but you know what I mean.'

He gave an apologetic smile. 'The next generation secured. Edward's done that. And let's be blunt, that's part of the deal, isn't it? He can breathe a bit easier now, and you two can get on with enjoying being married. Must put a bit of a strain on things, until it's out of the way.'

She smiled weakly. 'I suppose it must for everyone, mustn't it?'

Freddie was looking closely at her now, and she could see the fine lines of light and dark that made up his hazel eyes. He took a small intake of breath before continuing, his voice a fraction lower. 'I know I said it to you before. About Edward not being the easiest. But now you've got Alfie, and his mother has been put in her place a bit, I really hope you'll settle into things here. You do look so worried sometimes. The weight of the world—'

She looked down, giving a short laugh. 'Do I?'

'Rose said she'd love to see you more in London.'

'I'd like that very much.'

'Well, I'll make sure she arranges that. It can be quite cliquey here, people who've known each other from birth, and love to remind one of that—'

They were interrupted by Charlotte breaking in, kissing Freddie quickly on the cheek, acknowledging Jean with the briefest of smiles. 'Freddie, darling. So good to see you. Have you seen the Hamiltons are here? Rose will die if she hears what happened to Louise at Elton. It's too killing.'

Charlotte embarked on a story that she knew excluded Jean, emitting great peals of laughter as she tapped Freddie's arm for emphasis, dropping her voice and leaning in so all Jean could see was the back of her head. So Jean drifted on, said hello to a few more guests, swapped nonsense with another new mother about dimples and bootees, went to look in on Alfie in the nursery, but all the while she carried Freddie's words with her, turning them over in her mind, feeling the truth of them. What all of this should have meant for her and Edward; the liberation they should have felt in the fulfilment of their duty to this place, to this house.

Later, she and Edward stood for photographs in the entrance hall, at the foot of the oak-panelled staircase where Warres looked down on them from every aspect, row upon row of them reaching to the ceiling, in frames of elaborate carved gilt, with high foreheads and unforgiving stares, in flamboyant cuffs and ruffs of silk, painfully reproduced by artists now long forgotten. Edward stood at her shoulder, directed by the photographer who kept up a constant flow of jolly banter as he edged them this way and that, minute shuffles and tweaks till he was satisfied, giving a delighted little clap of his hands. She held Alfie in her arms, asleep once more, and as they turned and smiled, in that split second as the flash went and the bulb popped, she felt the lie crystallise and Freddie's hopes vanish. Her husband's arm stiff at her waist, channelling only resentment and hate, his sense of self diminished further; she knew he felt it too. But the outer shell was now perfected, for all the world to celebrate.

Dressing for dinner that night had felt too much, so Jean had excused herself, taking her food instead on a tray in her room and then stealing up to the nursery floor as soon as she could. It lay at the top of the house, running the length of one whole side of the building, with windows that only started above an adult's head height, giving the run of rooms that made it up a dark, underground feel. Nanny Hodgson slept up there, as did another nursemaid, whose sole job was to launder Alfie's collection of miniature clothes and to bring Nanny's food up and down the five flights of servants' stairs, three times a day, notwithstanding her mid-morning biscuits and substantial afternoon tea.

Nanny Hodgson sat, head nodding, in the worn armchair, a tartan rug thrown over its back to cover the patches where the upholstery had rubbed thin from use. The door to Alfie's room was ajar, and Jean slipped past her and went in, pushing it open quietly, wary of disturbing him. He lay tucked into his bassinet, head turned to one side, arms raised up either side of him, which she now knew meant he was held in a deep sleep. He was tucked in tight, but the narrow dome of his chest rose and fell with each small breath. The ripple of dreams under his thin blue-grey lids held her there, and she felt the overwhelming urge then to protect him from anything, everything, each nightmare that would wake him, each cruel word spoken to break him. The fragility of it all overwhelmed her and she lay her hand gently on his chest. The touch allowed something instinctive to feed into her, the force of the bond between them that the shameful truth could not break through.

She remembered when she had first set eyes on him, as the fog of ether cleared and the doctor presented her with the small bundle, her son, a boy. As he watched her take in the enormity of it all he patted her shoulder. 'We've told your husband. Delighted with the news.'

Edward had come in half an hour later, when she was sitting propped up on a nest of pillows, her hair still damp with sweat. The nurse was fussing about the room; her presence holding Edward back. He had looked at Jean with a face strangely contorted, his jaw so tight it seemed mechanical. He had briefly kissed her on the cheek, his skin feeling cool as glass against hers, and he had smiled, a stiff smile, and muttered, 'Well done, darling' before leaving her. But what could he do? Another man's son, celebrated like a gift from the gods, the continuation of his family and all the promise of generations to come loaded onto this tiny stranger's shoulders. And so Jean had lain there against those pillows of softest down, in her bedroom that was suddenly wholly unfamiliar, as if the act of birth had carried her on a journey to an entirely new world, deposited her on a shore at low tide that stretched on and on to the horizon, where she felt loneliness bleed out before her to eternity.

Jean walked back out on to the landing where Nanny was sitting, head still nodding under a splay of chins. She sat in the chair opposite, not wanting to wake her but not wanting to go downstairs yet. The old woman was like a soldier getting rest where he could, though, and she slept lightly and stirred easily, sitting up now, rubbing her eyes, instinctively patting her hair.

'I'm so sorry, Lady Warre, I must have drifted off.' Little pockets of soft skin sat like crescent moons beneath her eyes.

'Don't apologise. I just had a look in at Alfie and then I couldn't pull myself away.'

'Oh, he's such a dear, isn't he? And what a good little sleeper, like his father was.' She smoothed her skirt, shifting in her seat to settle into the telling of one of her well-worn tales. Jean had learned that these stories were frequent, extensive and often had no need for an audience at all, let alone an attentive one.

'Oh?' Jean knew what was required of her.

'Oh yes, he was terribly good. A content little baby.' She paused. 'A little trickier when he was a boy, but that was to be expected. Needed to get himself heard, I should think, with an older brother off doing everything first and a sister who wanted everyone's attention.'

'Yes, I suppose. It was just me and my brother growing up. It was quite easy for me, I think.'

'Well, Lady Warre left me to get on with things up here, so I was sure always to try and keep everything as fair as I could on my floor. Not favouring Charles too much, which they all naturally did. Oh, but it was hard not to – he was such a delightful little boy. So full of joy, and terribly funny.' She looked up at Jean, small creases fanning out at the edges of her eyes. 'But that's another time, isn't it?'

She was settling into Jean's company now, and her face took on the glow that a conversation about her old charges always ignited.

'Now, I can remember when Charlotte was a girl, and Edward was learning to walk, so he must have been one and a half or thereabouts, and Lord and Lady Warre were away. Up with friends in Scotland, and I was here with all three of them. And, oh, there was a tremendous storm. So great that we lost several trees in the park, and one fell right across the gates to the drive. I sat up the whole night long, terrified that the children would wake and be frightened.'

As she half-listened, Jean felt herself being pulled into this house, woven into the fabric of Harehope, the history of it, with this marriage she had made, and now this child she had borne. She felt the reality of it suffocating her, the house on top of her, creaking and groaning with the weight of its judgement. And then the words of the service – the promises they had given before God to protect this child, to guide him to good and to right – holding her to it, but it was all a lie. He was hers, not theirs, yet he would carry their crest, their title, be seen as a measure of their success or failure. But she was his mother, oh, the pain and the bliss of it tearing through her till she thought she would break open.

She looked at Nanny and then to the window above her, the stars like flecks of dust behind the panes of glass that were thick and warped with age. The old woman's voice carried on, rising and falling, but Jean was drawn instead to the night that lay beyond the nursery. It was so black out there that she felt the darkness might pull her out and swallow her up entirely.

CHAPTER TWO

Spring gave way to early summer, dreary days where the rain fell in an endless fine mist that seemed to lie over everything like a veil, the sun only briefly appearing in bright fierce strokes that disappeared as quickly as they came. 'Dreich' was the word one of the gillies had used as he trudged out with Edward one morning, and it was so apt. The grounds were lush though, a panoply of rich greens, groaning with life, the leaves of the old oaks on the avenue seeming to reach out and touch each other, as if they were drinking not water but an elixir through their knotted roots. But Jean felt dried up, aged, alone. She would walk with Nanny as she pushed Alfie's vast pram up and down the drive like a boat, or sit in the window of the drawing room and watch as it was left under the protection of the beech tree, a muslin covering its hood, so that he could sleep in the fresh air. He was changing each day, each day astounding her with his infinitesimal progress, tiny steps forward in this journey that seemed to have slowed life down to a crawl. His father's interest in him was nil. Unsurprising for a father of any baby, but crowed upon by Edward's mother as if his disinterest were a thing to celebrate. But Jean knew the core of it, the revulsion at this celebrated boy.

Jean felt so tired, weighed down by the guilt, the relentless rejection by Edward. Her body too seemed like someone else's, a stranger's coat put on; the crepey skin at her stomach confused the familiar, distorting what she thought she knew. And she loathed that her underclothes felt tighter, felt self-conscious at the changes where her ribcage had widened to accommodate Alfie as he had grown inside her. Edward had taken to watching her at dinner, though, when guests were there, his eyes on her across the table as the candles flickered and low voices carried on all around them.

Tonight he had done the same, eyes fixed on her with an intensity that made her cheeks burn, caused her to worry that the others would notice as he barely listened to them talk on at either side, watching her as he drank, calling several times for more claret but never breaking his stare. She had slipped away as soon as she could after dinner, but now as she lay in her room and heard uneven steps making their way down the corridor, she found herself on edge. He had opened the door slowly and stood now in the open doorway, drunk, she could tell, from the intervening hour or two he must have spent in his study with the men, under the blanket of cigars and port. She had been reading, her knees drawn up before her, the lamp by her bed the only light in the room, but she was still confused when she saw him; they hadn't shared a room in months, Edward barely able to countenance proximity to her.

He was swaying, a cigarette in his hand, burned out, though he didn't seem to notice. He leaned against the door frame briefly for support before stepping in with an almost-trip.

'I've been talking to the boys, and they were saying how beautiful you looked tonight. Tired by motherhood, but still such a beauty.' His face was slack, his mouth a loose line. 'Do you think you're beautiful, Jean?'

He took off his jacket, letting it drop to the floor, but he was unaware of his actions, falling into the next with no memory of the one before. Then came his bow tie; he pulled at it impatiently before unbuttoning his shirt, rocking still, his forehead damp with sweat.

'I know you are, but do you know?' Edward walked round to her side of the bed. He was looking at her, his eyes someone else's, and he dropped the stub of his cigarette to the floor. 'I don't know what goes on behind those eyes.'

The last words came in a rush and he leaned down over her, his breath hot on her face.

'Not who you want. Not what you want.'

For a second she thought he was going to be sick, but then he fell on her, pulling down the blankets, grabbing at her night-dress, fumbling as he went to pull it up, his hands desperate to touch her flesh but the alcohol confusing intention and action. She was rigid, horrified by his urgency, by the self-loathing and desire battling each other. He pulled at his trousers and found his way into her, and then she turned her face away, each move and shift of his body driving her further from herself. Away from him, from this house. She thought then of France, of her beach, of its shingle and its sky that drifted to eternity, and she held herself apart from what he was doing to her, a tiny bit of her that would not submit.

When he had finished, he lay by her side, chest heaving. His skin was damp and his eyes swimming out of focus, and she realised how drunk he must have been to do this. He passed out then and she pulled herself up to sitting, drawing the sheet up around herself, and turned to look at him. His profile, that almost saturnine face, unquestionably handsome yet always set to hate when she was in the room. She was mesmerised, somehow above herself as she watched him, his chest rising and falling, rising and falling.

She was lying in her bed, in her house, beside her husband, but what had just occurred – the sadness of it, the desperation, his brutality, his weakness – felt as if it had happened to someone else entirely. The house was silent as a tomb, and all she had was the sound of his breath and the smell of him, of whisky and tobacco, sour and sweet, hanging in the air.

CHAPTER THREE

It was a Wednesday morning and the house was full to bursting. It was August, and there were shooting parties that would often last for five days at a time, with dinners each evening, breakfasts each morning, lunch on the hill, tea back at the house: a seemingly constant round of food and drink, gossip and laughter, and endless swapping of observations about the weather. Each new lot expected the best of their hosts, full of anticipation at the sport to be had, not realising that the house itself was like a circus in town – all glitter and stardust on stage, while behind the scenes moods were fractious and tiredness was setting in.

Jean had woken with the same feeling of inertia that had seemed to hang over her like a cloak of lead these last few weeks. Each movement was heavy, and when she knelt on the nursery floor to let Alfie sit on her lap as was her morning ritual, to let him pull at the loop of pearls at her neck, make the burbling sounds she adored, she had had the urge to lie down, to give into the tiredness that enveloped her.

A whisper entered her thoughts. Could this be? Surely it was too soon. But then it was breakfast, and as she helped herself to a plate of eggs and the steam rose off them, she felt her stomach roll. Another whisper, this time a fraction louder. She stood to say goodbye to the men as they left their places at the table, stood quietly in the bluster and noise as they gathered their things, eager to get out of the house and onto the hill. She was hot, felt pinpricks on her skin, a wave of ice came running down her spine and her vision grew dim, flecked with strange sparks of colour; she swayed, putting her hand out for the back of the chair behind her, didn't made contact; then darkness.

She was sitting on a chair by one of the dining room's open windows, and Edward and Mrs Hawkins were standing over her as she struggled to understand what had happened. A glass of water was in her hand.

Mrs Hawkins' face was pinched with worry. 'Are you all right, m'lady? You're still terribly pale. I'll call for the doctor.'

Jean's eyes met Edward's as she took a sip. Mrs Hawkins held out a cloth and Jean put it to her forehead. Her skin felt clammy, and the room too bright and close. 'Yes, that would be so kind. Edward, don't delay things on my account. Everyone will be keen to get out. I'll be fine.'

He nodded, his eyes on her, trying to read something. Then he left the room.

'Let's get you upstairs, shall we? I can call one of the girls to help us.'

'No, no, I'll be all right.' Jean stood up, the light-headedness returning, but she steadied herself and took Mrs Hawkins' outstretched arm.

The curious eyes of the housemaids followed them as they made their way upstairs, and her mind made calculations once more. She had had no curse since Alfie's birth, though perhaps that was not unusual. And this tiredness, the tenderness of her breasts, the swell at her stomach that hadn't shifted. She felt so unfamiliar with herself, with all the changes birth and motherhood had brought, that these signs had been lost on her. But she had heard that it was common to fall pregnant easily again – but so soon? They had only slept together three times, each time Edward so drunk he could barely stand, each time infused with a bitterness so strong she could taste it.

Mrs Hawkins was looking at her enquiringly. 'M'lady?'

'I'm sorry, my mind was elsewhere.'

'Would you like to wait in your room until the doctor arrives? He might be an hour or two at least. I can bring you some tea?'

'Yes, yes, that would be lovely. Thank you, Mrs Hawkins.'

The housekeeper left Jean at the door to her bedroom, and she went and lay on her bed, no energy even to remove her shoes. She simply closed her eyes, willing the growing nausea, impossible to ignore now, to leave her.

The doctor had confirmed it. After an uncomfortable examination that had made Jean want to scream as he had poked around inside her like a vet examining one of his more obstinate cows, he had stood over her as she lay in bed afterwards, an avuncular smile spread across his broad face. For this was a personal pleasure for the doctor, a sign of the absolute rightness of things in this house he had attended to for more than a quarter of a century. 'Congratulations, Lady Warre. And so soon after your first child. A fruitful marriage, a joy to see. But remember to rest now. No going up on the hill. Rest – and quiet – is my advice.'

That night, she told Edward, who was already dressed for dinner as she sat in her dressing gown. There was the glow of triumph at his cheeks, his virility no longer in question. She watched him tell the other men, as they stood around later having drinks, watched the news spread through the room, the murmurs of congratulation, the nods of *I told you so*. Darting little kisses, jealousy's bite just perceptible, were bestowed by the wives: 'Gosh, what a lot you've got to show for your marriage, darling, Alfie still only a baby. Well done you.'

She noticed too the nudging and jostling from Edward's friends as they mobbed him up; the knowing, chummy smiles, their comments not entirely out of earshot.

'Keeping yourself busy, old boy.'

'So kind of you to break away from the bedroom to have us to stay.'

And he had looked at her then across the room and there was a sense of power regained in the flinty stare. Oh, she saw it clearly then. He was just a boy, needing desperately the medal for the race, the nod from the teacher. This overlooked child who'd never been congratulated for anything. But she knew in her heart that this success of his, as he saw it, would change nothing between them. Strangers they would remain, for what could he ever know of tenderness, of intimacy? And listening to the murmur of after-dinner conversation in this great house of hers – guests still charmed to be invited in, to stand around in little knots and gossip and absorb the feeling of being very much on the inside – she felt like property. She was simply the bearer of another child for this family, her husband's name stamped firmly upon her; another body to be carried by her and then taken from her: a public symbol of the life of this marriage, though the smell of its decay was so real to her at moments like this that it made her gag.

The months progressed, her stomach swelling and the veins that streaked across that stretched, tight skin growing darker and more intense. The changes in her body were a source of conflicting emotions, of revulsion at times when she caught herself in the mirror, the extended belly, the swelling of her breasts, but then of awe that she alone was summoning this baby to being. Everything felt harder somehow this time, with her body depleted so recently by Alfie's birth. Where before her hair had been thick and lustrous, now it lay flat and limp, and she would find strands and strands of it in her hairbrush, or lying like a retribution on her pillow in the morning. Her skin too was sallow and she had lost weight – 'and condition', her mother-in-law had noted witheringly, looking at her as she would one of her less-pleasing hunters.

Christmas was to be spent at Harehope, her parents set to join for a few days from London. But then Jean had received a telegram. The bronchitis that had blighted her father throughout her childhood, requiring him to spend spells in Switzerland when they lived in Paris, or reluctantly to cancel public engagements to allow his lungs to recover, had returned. It had been a damp winter in London, December cold and wet – 'The climate doesn't suit him,' Elizabeth had fretted when they spoke on the telephone. And then came the news that they were no longer able to come for Christmas. They would spend it alone in London, more rest required by his doctor. *I'm so sorry to abandon you like this*, she had written. *And your first Christmas with Alfie, our darling grandson. We are devastated, I assure you.*

The household had stood around the tree in the hall on the last Sunday of Advent, an enormous pine felled from the woods, draped in velvet bows with a halo of candles glowing in the dying light of the late December afternoon. They had listened to the blessing of the parson, the well-worn words uttered to the tenants from the village, invited into the house for half an hour to sing carols. Edward loathed the tradition for its sticky sentimentality, hated having the house invaded by people he felt no obligation towards – 'Is it not enough that we house them, without having to have them tramp in here?' A boy from the village was chosen to sing the first verse of 'Once in Royal David's City', and he carried a candle, a halo of yellow in the dim light.

Jean held Alfie in her arms as she listened, letting him stretch out his hand to touch the tree's hard, green-black needles. She kissed his head, breathing in instinctively that smell of caramel and straw; watched him, captivated as he was by the flickering candlelight before him. Her son's first Christmas, and the contrast between what should have been and what was felt to Jean as bright and hard as the gleaming red of the holly's berries on the wreath at their door, like pricks of blood against the waxy leaves beneath.

Sheets of tissue paper and balls of twine and ribbon littered the study floor as Jean sat back on her knees, surveying her work. Unable to be with her daughter and grandson at Christmas, Elizabeth Buckman had made up for it in a procession of elaborate parcels that had been arriving for the last fortnight. Improbably delicate glass baubles for the tree that could have been from a maharaja's treasure chest, so brightly did they sparkle; a hamper from Fortnum's, crammed with jar upon jar of jams and gold tins of biscuits and silver boxes of teas and iridescent candied fruits; a parcel of the latest books from Hatchards of Piccadilly and a case of Warre's from Berry Bros., whose vintage had caused a rare release of emotion from Stokes as he had prised the lid from the wooden crate. The last parcel had arrived only the day before, straight from Harrods, containing a little coat of sky-blue wool for Alfie that she had wrapped in tissue, a collar and trim of navy and buttons of dark horn whose polish would have made a naval commander proud. The present's meaning would be lost on Alfie entirely, but it gave Jean a foolish pleasure to add more to the little pile she would have for him to open on Christmas Day.

She looked up as Stokes stood in the doorway of the room, clearing his throat. 'The telephone for you, Lady Warre.'

It was eleven o'clock on Christmas Eve morning and she wondered who could be wanting to talk to her now.

He seemed unwilling to leave the room. 'It is Mrs Buckman. I wondered whether you might like me to find Lord Warre?'

'No, thank you, Stokes. That won't be necessary.' But as she walked the short distance to the telephone mounted on the wall in a dark corner of the hall, Jean felt her pulse as if it were outside of her body and her hands were clammy as she took up the earpiece in her hand.

'Darling, is that you?' The voice at the other end was her mother's, but it was one she had never heard before. It was far away, lost and unsure, and Jean knew then that the worst had happened. 'Oh, Jean. He went early this morning. It had been a long night. His breathing was so laboured and his temperature so high that nothing would take it down. Then he was just too weak. The doctors held no hope for him. He drifted off and never came back.'

Though youth had abandoned her father long ago, leaving him with scant hair and a beard of grey, though his health was not perfect and she would hear his chest catch when his lungs were weak in a damp winter, Jean had not been prepared for this. What child ever is? The years of adult life collapsed in an instant, leaving only a son or daughter, a child looking up at a vast and unending sky above. The fact of his death, blunt and hard, was somehow impossible for her to absorb. She felt her chest cave a little, as if a blow had been taken right in its centre, and then a tiredness seemed to take hold of her at the thought of how it must all now be unpacked: the shock, the overwhelming sadness and then the memories; the book of her childhood to be taken from the shelf, to be examined, stirring up everything that had been felt but never said – why never said – for this man who, though remote in his way, had been the pillar of her world.

'Oh, Mother.'

Jean heard her mother struggle to contain herself, taking tiny little inhalations of breath to keep herself intact, for they were so close, her parents, two sides of one body. She wanted desperately to be with her, not here; wanted simply to be her mother's daughter, not someone's wife standing alone in the quiet hall at Harehope.

'We've notified the president, and of course His Majesty. We've had a personal telephone call from Arthur Stamfordham, expressing the King's regret.' Even death couldn't temper the pride in her voice, but then it trembled and broke. 'Oh, Jean. What shall I do – what shall I be – without him? I knew his health was worsening, but not so soon. I thought we had more time…'

Jean was left holding the mouthpiece after her mother had gone. She had begged to come down to London as soon as she could, but Elizabeth had urged her to spend Christmas at home and then travel down after. To be with Edward, to be with her son. *What Father would have wanted. I'll be kept busy, there will be so much to do. So many people calling by.* Elizabeth had carried on then, allowing the administration of death to take over; her husband was only four hours dead, but already she was adapting to her role as great widow, figure of grief, upright, unbent. Jean could hear it in the timbre of her voice, the new register adopted for her next incarnation. It would suit her, Jean thought ruefully.

Her back ached from standing so long, the considerable swell at her stomach now making periods of standing a trial, and she longed to go and lie down on her bed rather than find Edward, as she knew she must. But she did as she ought and walked back down the hall to her husband's study. She took in the swags of velvet and the scent of pine, the echo of carols just heard and the presents under the tree, the happy chatter of the servants as they got on with their work, the prospect of Christmas Day so close it was at its most magical. All these perfect scenes of domestic bliss she saw now as a foreigner would arriving into an unknown city; she was on the outside, looking in.

CHAPTER FOUR

Jean stood with her mother and brother on a damp slipway at Portsmouth docks, having accompanied her father's coffin by train from Victoria. Side by side, in the bite and chill of a wet January afternoon, they watched as soldiers draped the coffin in her country's flag and then heaved it onto their shoulders, faces strained under the weight of body and oak, a lone trumpeter playing a final salute. The King had offered a British armoured military vessel to carry the ambassador – esteemed emissary, valued friend – home, and his personal representative had offered condolences to Elizabeth and her children as they stood in the rain that fell in tiny shards like knives.

Her brother had come to England to accompany his mother on the voyage home, and he stood now, the collar of his coat up against the chill, his hat slick with rain. He was talking in a low voice to the captain of the ship, his face set to polite disengagement as he listened to the inevitable words of tribute. Jean hadn't seen Oliver since her wedding. His face was bloated, his body too heavy for a young man. It was clear he had been drinking the night before. She could see it in the florid patches at his cheeks and the way he was fidgeting with his cuffs, pulling at the stiff white cotton as he listened; it was a movement imperceptible to everyone but her, but she knew he was willing on the first acceptable opportunity to drink. The relief that this would bring him was real, drink no longer an indulgence but a necessity.

Jean kissed her mother briefly on the cheek, taking her gloved hand in hers. 'I'm so sorry that I can't come with you, Mama. There's only a month to go until the birth. They won't allow it.'

'Of course, my dearest, of course. And Oliver is here. He'll be a great help.' She looked across at her son, who was now nodding earnestly as he received the condolences of the chaplain. 'It's not the easiest time for him, but he is trying.'

They both watched Oliver, neither saying what they really felt. Elizabeth was adopting her standard practice of regal detachment. It was her defence against imperfection, lest it be picked up by the audience that was always, in her mind at least, somewhere at hand. She took a handkerchief from her bag and gave a valiant little blow.

'I'm sorry Edward couldn't be here.' Jean spoke quickly, keen to get the untruth out of the way.

'Don't give it another thought.'

'I know, but I—'

'Darling, he wrote me a note, and I know you've got people staying at this time of year.' It was kind of her mother not to see Edward's failure to attend as the insult it was.

Jean's hand was resting on her stomach, now distended and hard, and she felt a kick, up and under her ribcage, that caused her to shift on her feet.

Elizabeth saw her wince, and took her hand in hers once more, patting it lightly. 'You must rest, darling. Get home to

Harehope. I'll come and see you as soon after the birth as is possible. I'll have to arrange things in London, so it won't be long, I promise. I'll come back when I can.'

They bowed their heads once more as the chaplain said his final prayer. There was a desolation to the scene that Jean found unbearable, that pressed at her temples and seemed to stagnate her mind. It wasn't simply the dank brick and stone of the docks, nor the bruised sky that hung overhead, but rather a feeling, almost tangible, of deep unease, which had crept up on her since her father's death. Though a veil of black lace hid Jean's tears, she was not sure who she was crying for.

The soldiers turned, feet shuffling as they struggled once more under the weight of the coffin, and then they were up the walkway and onto the boat, where the American ensign hung, majestic as it flapped in the stiff breeze, its red, white and blue sharp against the grey. Elizabeth and her brother made their slow progress behind, Oliver keeping half a pace between himself and his mother. His head was dipped, his hat in his hand despite the persistent rain, and she saw, in that glimpse of neck above the starched white collar, the little boy of her child-hood, diminished always by the overwhelming perfection of his parents. Such brilliance butting up against such fallabillity.

Jean was accompanied to her car by a nervous young junior from the embassy, one of a number of narrow-faced and narrow-shouldered men who had hovered awkwardly, unsure how to bid farewell to this titan of their trade. He held an umbrella over her, an arm hovering discreetly at her back as he steered her gently round the potholes and puddles of the uneven road. They walked in silence, but she could tell he wanted to say something to her, shuffling the possible words in his head, and eventually he cleared his throat and spoke in a thin, cautious voice.

'I'm so sorry for your loss, Lady Warre. Your father was a great man and it was an honour to serve him.' A pause, and then the tentative step into the personal. 'It must be a wrench for you, not to be able to go back home with them.'

She kept her eyes on the ground in front of her, picking a path through the small pools of water, focusing on the damp leather of her shoes. His gentle words of sympathy were an agony to hear. She had never felt more lonely in her life; the realisation of what lay before her was overwhelming.

The young man held open the car door for Jean and she sank back into its leather cocoon, taking a last look across the docks to the vast battlecruiser that would carry her father home. His death, and her mother's inevitable departure from England for good, marked the cutting of the cord between her and America. Her life was here now, and it was for her to make of it what she could, without the comfort and protection of her parents' presence. This was what she had wished for, she reminded herself: a marriage to provide a path of her own, free from the duties, the comparisons, the requirements of life as Miss Jean Buckman. Now she watched in silence as her past set off over the ocean in that coffin of maple and oak, draped in the flag of her country, and she was left alone on the shore. A sad little mark of black, with another child in her belly, anchoring her to this place whose feelings for her were as unclear as the low, grey sky that hung overhead.

CHAPTER FIVE

An injection had been given several hours before the birth: a cocktail of drugs that promised 'twilight sleep', a poetic name for something Jean knew would be the opposite. It was the doctor's recommendation that she be kept sedated, or more likely oblivious, during the labour now upon her. There were concerns that the arrival of a second child, so close after the first, might cause complications.

There were moments when she was awake, or some parallel version of that state, but so far from herself she felt she was watching life through the wrong end of a telescope, her fingers moving but so far from her arms, her brain sending commands that got confused somewhere between decision and action. Then she would lose herself again, and a blanket of fog would come down, so thick and dense it would eclipse all thought. Pain came and went like a lighthouse beam, blinding her till she felt pinned to the bed, then disappearing as quickly as it had arrived. She was confused, her mind a quagmire where thoughts stumbled upon would then sink into the mud, lost forever.

Now she was back up to the surface, a wasp trapped in a glass, coming up against its sides, unable to reach the real air beyond. She looked at the faces before her now, of the doctor, the nurses, Edward, standing around her like a chorus, and she was aware of a throbbing at her temples. Her jaw felt tight.

'Is everything all right? Edward?' Her tongue was thick, a foreign object in her mouth. She swallowed but her mouth was dry and her throat hurt, and she realised she was desperately thirsty.

The chorus shifted and a nurse stepped forward, a bundle in her arms swaddled in white, the face a pinkish red, hair dark and streaked across the tiny head. 'It's another boy, your ladyship. Congratulations.' The drugs were still keeping Jean distanced from herself, but far away, under layers of confusion and abstraction, she felt relief.

Edward was pacing the room. 'Tell her. You can't hide it from her, for God's sake.' He walked away to the window, struggling to lift it open. 'It's horribly stuffy in here, we need some air.'

Again the assembly of faces rearranged themselves before her, and the doctor came into focus, wearing, she felt, his face for the stage, used as he must have been to delivering unwanted news.

'It turned out that your son was breech at birth, Lady Warre. Which causes difficulty when using the forceps and delivering him safely. We had something of a struggle to get him out.' The memory of battle crossed his face. 'And the excessive pressure required to deliver him while his arms were up' – here he turned to give a half-hearted demonstration to Edward, her husband's disdain evident from his resolutely turned back – 'caused damage.' The doctor attempted a smile at Jean as he turned back towards her. 'To the nerves that run from neck to left hand.'

'It's what that delightful man the Kaiser had, if you read about that.' Edward was lighting a cigarette. 'Whether one can blame the greatest war the world has known on his handicap isn't clear. But, my dear, our son is a cripple, he will have a withered arm.'

The doctor cleared his throat. 'It's called an obstetric palsy, or, more commonly, Erb's palsy.' His eyes were pleading a little now as he looked to Edward again. 'I think you will find there are several things one can attempt in childhood to ameliorate the effects, depending on how your son progresses in the next few weeks. But in all other respects, he is a healthy baby, breathing happily, taking the bottle.' The nurses nodded in unison.

'In all other respects,' Edward muttered.

Jean put out her hands for him, this little swaddle whose weight was no more consequential than a bag of sugar. Another child, another boy, the requisite spare provided – oh, the joke the gods were playing with them now.

She had been unsure of what she would feel about another child. How could her heart have room for someone else when it felt stretched to capacity with Alfie? And the manner in which he had been conceived: the physical expression of Edward's warped hate. But as she took him in her arms, put her hand to his tiny head, hair slicked from birth, as she touched that skin, improbably soft, unmarred by life, she knew her heart had miraculously grown; that there was more room, infinite space for love for him, this tiny assemblage of skin and blood and life, who needed her.

Tears slipped down her cheeks that she had no control over and the room evaporated – she was alone with him, transfixed by those tiny eyelids, the trembling grey and violet, by the skin so delicate a breath could tear it, everything impossibly small. George, her second son, but the true firstborn; the heir destined always to be in the shadows, an imperfect creature, perfect for his role.

CHAPTER SIX

He was a beautiful baby: a perfect heart-shaped face, dark hair, with long, curled lashes and eyes of a deep, almost black, brown. He occupied another room on the nursery floor, the other end to Alfie's, and she spent afternoons up there, drifting in and out of sleep in a chair meant for Nanny, as her world seemed to stretch, to twist and elongate as one birth, one son, became two, and the tiredness, the raggedness of her body, overwhelmed her.

The little left arm – the twisted sapling branch that bent out from him at its strange angle, his hand tipped back as if to receive something – became a symbol to the outside world of who he was. He was the requisite spare, celebrated for second place, and there was always a thankful look, a small sigh of relief, that accompanied anyone's learning of his condition. But for Jean, his own mother, this was the worm in the apple's flesh: the lie that ran through the convenience of it all. And it built up like a poison in Edward. Each look of sympathy, each nod as to the rightness of things, would send his self-loathing, his failure to sire nothing more than a broken spare, deeper; it would cement it, taking his cool disdain for Jean and turning it into something worse, a cold fury that frightened her.

Her mother had returned to England to close up the house on Park Lane before moving back to America for good. But she had been desperate to meet her next grandchild, to congratulate Jean and Edward on their blessings. A smaller christening had been arranged, just immediate family, with none of the pageantry and pomp that had accompanied Alfie's. Edward had been silent during her stay, sullen even, not bothering to hide his irritation from Elizabeth. He had insisted on going back to London immediately after the service. Jean knew he couldn't bear to hear the words of implicit sympathy that followed George round.

Mother and daughter sat in Jean's little salon, a fire lit, a tray of tea before them. Elizabeth had adopted a new affectation in widowhood, bringing needlepoint with her wherever she went, unpacking an elaborate bag with the current piece she was working on, skeins of wool, her case of needles, her half-moon spectacles in their maroon velvet pouch. It was a ceremonial act, a performance, letting the world know that, with her husband's death, she had bowed out from the public arena of diplomacy and was a woman now of domestic grace. How long it would last was unconfirmed.

Elizabeth set down the stiff canvas on her lap. 'It can be a difficult time for a father when babies are so young. Husbands feel that the mothers are taken elsewhere. That the love, the attention, is somehow compromised. Don't fret, though, he will cheer up.' She smiled indulgently, enjoying, Jean felt, the novelty of this scene of maternal intimacy. 'And perhaps it is a shock. Little George's arm. But I am sure you have all the best doctors. You must take him to London as soon as you feel able, make sure he sees the top man.'

Jean nodded, though her mind flicked involuntarily to where George was now, to that little crib in the nursery where he lay.

She was anxious, always, about him. A flutter in her stomach when she thought of him. She felt the fragility in him constantly, the urge to protect, amplified by Edward's disgust.

'You look tired too, my darling. It's not like you to get overcome by things. It doesn't suit you.'

'I have found it quite exhausting, this time round. And, as you say, Edward hasn't taken to it all that well.'

'Well, let's not dwell on that.' Elizabeth shifted in her seat, tapestry now forgotten. 'Why not concentrate on the things that we *can* do? I've been thinking: I know in this country that things are rather cut and dried when it comes to the division of the spoils. I think there's something that I can do to remedy that.' She leaned forward, touching Jean's face gently. 'It's in my gift. I shall make sure that he's looked after. When the time comes, he won't have to worry.' She patted Jean's hand now and smiled indulgently. 'Come, come. Cheer up! Two boys to your name. An industrious thing, like you've always been. A doer. My darling girl, the doer.'

Jean smiled up at her mother, a weak smile that only seemed to encourage the sadness that lay inside her to take hold, to put down anchor.

'Darling little things, your boys. But don't let them swallow you up. Yours is to oversee, not to do. A woman of your position must never confuse the two.' She looked across at Jean, her expression thoughtful. 'And perhaps that might apply to your marriage too. You have done a great service to Edward by providing him with two sons. And if he is' – she gave a delicate shrug – 'not always easy, then allow yourself a little respite. Life is long, God willing, and the pair of you must find a path in marriage that will take you its length. You, more than most, are blessed with independence, so don't be afraid to use it a little. As these English families love to remind us, their crumbling houses are everything to them, the symbol of who they are, and it is the same with Edward. Harehope is his. It will be Alfie's too, so allow yourself a place of your own, whether that be London or France. Your father and I weren't permanently attached to each other. He had his life and I had mine, and though we loved each other deeply, we weren't afraid to be apart. Edward won't love you any more for being by his side every moment of the day.'

Elizabeth had left two days later, the fanfare of luggage and the swirl of attendant staff and elaborate goodbyes un-dampened by widowhood. Her advice had sat with Jean, though, working away at a thought that she had tried to quell these last two years but could not: the question of David, the question of France. As much as Jean had tried to suppress the urge, her mind would go to him whenever she was alone, to that time of fulfilment, of release, when she had felt more herself than ever before. And she ached for him physically. Though the world she inhabited was now an entirely different one – mother of two boys, the nod of approval from society bestowed upon her for a job well done – still she could walk in her dreams back to that other, past life, calling to mind an image of her lover as vivid as if he was before her, of David's face in profile as they walked along the beach side by side, or the feel of her hand in his as they found each other alone. She would imagine a hundred moments more with him, an infinite pleasure to be had in the second when he was before her in her mind; but then the inevitable agony of regret would follow, knowing it must crumble to dust.

Her two boys, the family portrait that now hung for all to see, had cemented her and Edward into this life of theirs forever. But if she could dare to carve out something for herself within that; if this freedom her mother talked of – though she knew nothing of what that meant to Jean – could be reached out and touched, if she could find a way to it, it could bring her back to life.

A letter had arrived at Harehope the following week. A letter of such delicate charm that its suggestion of lunch was buried deep within its third paragraph. It was from a Professor Hinds, who had been Charles Warre's tutor at Christ Church. Having recently retired, he had taken some months to visit old friends around the country, something which his lecturing life at Oxford had prevented. One such friend lived only twelve-odd miles from Harehope and on the local line, and he wondered whether he might come and visit the house that Charles had spoken of so fondly, might perhaps meet any members of his family that happened to be there.

But this pilgrimage of love was met only with disdain, and Alice Warre had received this man – whose sole purpose was to mourn her dead son, to breathe life into his memory – as she might an unsavoury tenant. The lunch had passed in awkward silence, Alice's tone one of cut-glass disengagement. Edward was distant, tapping his cigarette into the silver dish and his foot beneath the table, willing this imposition upon his time away. Mortified by their disinterest, Jean had offered to show the professor around the house, pointing out the paintings and the tapestries of interest, doing her best to remember the artists and the names of Edward's relatives, feeling as she always did that they watched her with reproach from their gilt-framed coffins as she mangled their history. They had stood at last in Charles' library, Professor Hinds inspecting the black-figured pot on the mantelpiece, his knuckles swollen with arthritis as he held it, his hand trembling a little with age. He had looked up at Jean then, this man who seemed to her like a gentle monk, his eyes a watery blue, intense and kind, and there was a note of apology in his voice.

'I cannot emphasise enough what a fine young man Charles was. His enthusiasm was magnetic, his brilliance worn lightly. I wanted to say that in person, but I hadn't considered the things that grief can do to a family. It is a delicate thing, hard to navigate.' He put the vase back on the mantelpiece carefully. 'I hope you can pass that on to Lady Warre and to your husband. I certainly did not mean to cause upset by coming here.'

Jean had nodded. Had taken his hand warmly in hers before she said goodbye, thanked him for coming, for talking so fondly about Charles, though she shared not a drop of blood with this exceptional young man, a fact of which they were both aware. But when she lay in bed that night, each time she came close to it, sleep would evade her grasp, her mind unable to settle, her body tense. Each time she thought of the lunch – of the words of her mother-in-law, the attitude of Edward towards this gentle man; the chill of the nursery etched into every act of her husband's, handed down like a badge of honour from his mother – a rush of emotion, of fury, would return and flood her entire body so that she was wide awake, heart hammering in her chest.

She did not know if she truly believed in God. The journey of her life until now had not caused her to question him. He was someone prayed to as a child, by rote, the words mean-ingless as she ran them together, a jumble of familiar sounds that lay between bath and bed. But she felt an urge to pray now, eyes wide open in the dark, to swear to someone if they were listening that she would not bring up her boys in the same way.

That they would know – no, more than that, they would see and feel – the intensity of her love for them. However unfashionable, however unseemly that would appear to her husband and his mother, it would be her way.

Jean thought then of the different blood that her babies carried. What had so attracted her to David was the ease with which he could engage his emotions, that for him opening up was something to enjoy, not to fear. And so the prayer became a promise, became the whisper of hope to her in the dark of this unending night. She would go, she would go. Back to France, even if only for a month, with her boys. She would go with them and make a home free of the lies, the conflict, the burden, the judgement, of this place; where emotion and feeling and real life could be lived. Away from Harehope, with its stone of grey and soul of ice.

CHAPTER SEVEN

Cap d'Antibes, 1925

Jean walked up the narrow street, the walls that lined it blushing with the creep of crimson bougainvillea, Alfie's hot little hand in hers. An old man had pointed the way, his face one of bemusement as this young woman, dressed in pale pink silk and a straw hat the colour of the corn at harvest, and the little boy beside her made their journey up and away from the bustling harbour, past the *boulangeries* and *épiceries* now closed for the afternoon lull, up and beyond until they came to this quiet little street where only locals lived, nestled as it was in the oldest part of Antibes.

Alfie was defiant now that he had the ability to walk. He didn't like to be carried, would arch his back and push away if he was held against his will, desperate to be let down and to make his own slow, unsteady passage. So the pair made ponderous progress, avoiding the streak of sun – sharp as a knife's blade – that held one half of the street captive, she pulling Alfie forward when he stopped, distracted by a butterfly dancing in the still air, its wings blood red, the only thing of movement in the thick heat of midday.

She had known the house was David's as soon as she saw the bicycle leaning up against the wall outside, remembering its battered brown leather saddle and the low rack at the back where he would string whatever books he was reading at the time. As she drew closer, close enough to take in its shutters of pale blue, their paint peeling a little, and the rough, nubby stone of its walls, she felt her stomach drop at the reality of what was finally before her after months of agony and deliberation. What would David make of her, this woman he had not seen in two years, who'd left without a word; what, too, of this blonde, drunken angel at her side?

The door opened, and a young girl – no more than eighteen or nineteen, with a dark plait snaking down her back – came out and began sweeping the stone steps of the house with enthusiasm. She looked up, startled, as she sensed Jean drawing nearer. She didn't smile but tapped quickly on the window to the right of the door, terror and intrigue battling each other on her face. There was a brief pause, and then the door opened and David was before her, a look of enquiry as he looked at the girl, then over her shoulder to Jean and Alfie beyond.

He was just as he had been the last night she'd seen him. The same as he had been in her dreams, or in the moments when she lay, eyes open, in the dead black of night running over and over past scenes she had lived with him. But now he was here before her, her whole body felt charged and the air seemed to pulse with the tension she carried within her.

'Jean?' His voice was hoarse, and he rubbed his face roughly. 'I haven't heard from you in nearly two years. I thought you were never coming back.'

'I came from England last week.' Her voice caught and she had to clear her throat. 'I saw Sybil and Frank. They said they hadn't seen you for a while but that you were here, gave me your address. So I thought I would come. I'm sorry I didn't warn you.'

She watched him try to make sense of her as she scanned him for signs of change too, for revelations of anger, of coldness; she knew he would see the weight she'd lost, the dark circles beneath her eyes. He looked down at Alfie, now captivated by the girl who had gone back to sweeping the steps, though her eyes were locked on David and Jean; he was mesmerised by the broom in her hand, putting out his hands to have it.

'Wan', wan'', he said in his baby-talk way, and the girl giggled nervously, eyes flicking to David, unsure of whether to concede the broom.

Alfie's words seemed to jolt David awake and he pulled himself together, pushing the door behind him open. 'Will you come in? It's a bachelor's home really. It's tiny. I'm not sure what I've got to offer your little boy, but come, please.' He opened his arms wide, gesturing for her to follow him inside.

The narrow hallway was cool and dark after the sharp sunlight of before, and it led into a small kitchen with whitewashed walls and a rough wooden table at its centre, its low windows giving on to a small courtyard. He asked the girl, Lisette he called her, to get a jug of cold water and to cut up some bread and butter for Alfie to eat. They sat around the table, an awkward trio, Jean occupying Alfie with a spoon that he was now banging with enthusiasm on the table.

'I couldn't come back because of being pregnant with Alfie.' She looked down at her son, a mother's involuntary smile briefly lighting up her face. 'I was so sick with it – and then George, my next son, he came along so quickly after... I can't believe it's been nearly two years since I was last here. We were up north in the summers, and then back down in London. But I needed to get away for a little while, and I've thought of here, of this place, every day.' She stopped herself, checked the emotions lying just beneath the surface. 'I haven't been quite myself, felt bogged down by it all, by this change that motherhood brings.' She looked up now, embarrassed. 'And then I thought perhaps I could come back out here and... I so wanted to see you... I've left George at the house with our nanny. Brought Alfie...'

Her voice trailed off. Her hands were shaking and she laid them flat on the table to stop the movement. How to say any of this when two years of life had passed, two years in which she had lived off scraps of memory: the blue of his eyes, the timbre of his voice, the way his face changed when he smiled. These alone had sustained her. But to say any of that in the polite back-and-forth of this cramped kitchen was impossible. Each time she took a sip of water, she felt the effort of it nearly overwhelm her, the effort of keeping herself whole and not splintering into pieces on his kitchen floor.

David looked quietly at Alfie, who was kneeling now on his chair and joyfully pulling apart the bread, spreading crumbs everywhere; he took in his mop of blonde hair, his nose, that familiar blue of his eyes. 'How old is he?' His voice was quiet.

'He's nearly one and a half, he was one in March.' And as she watched him watching Alfie, she knew he understood.

He looked up at her. 'Let's go outside. I can show him something.'

Lisette's face fell. She did not need to speak English to under-stand the opera unfolding before her.

The street outside was still empty, the heat like a wall around them. There was a little lizard, its body a bright, almost lime green, frozen on the steps, sensing danger. David took Alfie's hand, and her heart caught at the sight of them together. He brought Alfie towards the lizard, and his attention was immediately caught by the creature. He stood beside his father, head bowed, brow furrowed in concentration as he watched it dart up and onto the wall of the house next door.

David turned to her and his face was drawn, the lines at his brow deeper than she remembered. 'Why did you go so suddenly? I thought I would never see you again. I wrote to anyone I could think of to find out what had happened, but all they said was that you'd gone back. Then I read in the papers that your father had died, and it nearly killed me to see your name there, in print, and to read about the funeral, and you and – Edward. But they didn't mention any children. I knew you hadn't sold the house out here, but you never came back.'

She kept her eyes on Alfie as she spoke, leaning against the wall opposite David's house. Her arms were folded, and she pulled at the sleeve of her dress. 'When I got back to England, I found out I was pregnant, and...the baby was yours...and I didn't know what to do about it. It nearly crushed me that a life was growing inside me, that I felt alive for the first time, having met you, but that...it was like this. And the only thing I could do was to paper over it all, to make it proper, and so I did. I told Edward I was pregnant as soon as I could – he knows the truth, how could he not? – and he went along with it and everyone was delighted, said how it suited me, how they hoped it would be a boy, and then Alfie came, and there he was. And he was you. And Edward can barely look at him.'

And then she broke, finally, the effort of holding it in becoming impossible, and she felt her body give at the relief of saying the words out loud. She felt David's arms around her, and it was then, as they stood together and she felt his heart beating against her own, that she knew it would begin again. That this was what she'd come for.

Eventually he let his arms drop, and they stood for a while in silence, side by side on the shabby little street, watching the boy – their son – as, bored of the lizard, he found a pile of loose stones next to the steps of the house and began stacking and unstacking them. The sun was now directly overhead, but neither could take their eyes off him. She felt drunk, light-headed at the revelation of the truth and at David's presence beside her.

David looked across at her, shy still. 'I've thought about you too, you know. Every day. Every day I remembered something from that month, till I didn't know if they were memories at all but rather dreams, of something so perfect that it couldn't have existed. Scenes from someone else's life. Those dinners where everyone else was invisible to us, the walks along your beach, an hour when we could be alone. I knew you'd never felt it before, didn't know what to do with the power of it. But there was – there was an innocence to it that made everything feel true, not like an affair. It felt more than that.'

He looked down, tracing the outline of a cobble with his shoe.

'When your husband came out, I saw what this life was that you had chosen. How unsure of yourself you were with him, how you shrank in his presence. This English boy, elegant, celebrated, who everyone was fascinated by. And I saw myself through his eyes, how someone from his world, your world, would see someone like me. An irrelevance, an imposition. It killed me. So I said that stupid thing about your money, his title. And then when you left without saying anything, I realised that you were so different to me, that all we'd had was an illusion. That you and I could never stand up to—'

'That's him. That's not me.' Jean almost shouted the words, surprising herself with their vehemence. It was so important that he understood that the part of her he had known was the real part.

Alfie turned at the noise and made his way towards her now, arms up, wanting his mother. And she picked him up, holding him at her hip. She kissed his cheek and smoothed his hair, before he wriggled down and away from her again.

Jean turned to look at David, keeping her voice measured. 'I want to stay out here for a little while. I've opened up the house, and brought help for the boys from England. Edward' – she swallowed his name like an awkward pill – 'is down in London and says I can stay out here for a while, get the boys out from under his feet.' She looked at him squarely now. 'Can't you see that this is what I want? I've come back.' And she held a tension in her body at the anticipation of what he might say.

He held her look, his face solemn, and put out his hand to hers. 'That you're here, before me, it's enough. Whatever this is, it's enough.'

CHAPTER EIGHT

So France became a haven. David had taken her back. Welcomed her with open arms, accepting her, her boys, whatever part he would play in it all. They picked up where they had left off, living for the time they knew they had, a month in July or August, the odd snatched fortnight when she would come on her own in June. Moments of bliss, streaks of joy.

Her house there was a place of refuge, and everything she touched, drank, tasted, she would draw up into herself: the simple joy of bleached heat on the beach at midday or the gentle slip and slide of the water that fringed their bay; the chill of the sea when swum at dawn, the initial touch making her gasp and then the pleasure as she swam forward to David as he treaded water in front of her, the water smooth as marble around him, willing her to come deeper; the feel of his skin on hers, still warm from the sun with salt she could taste as they lay together on afternoons where it was only them and the rest of the world was nothing. When she was back in England, back to a husband who knew where she went but said nothing, just set his face to hate, she would close her eyes and it would be there, like the flicker of film in a darkened picture house, the pleasure hers to enjoy alone.

These were summers where she would watch her boys grow, as year by year they changed from babes in arms to tousled-haired little boys that cried furious tears when tired or wronged – oh, the depths of injustice they could feel at the smallest thing – and then with a pang another year would have passed, another summer would be gone and she would return with them to England, baby fat giving way slowly but inexorably to slim, muscular bodies, golden from the sun.

And who were they, these brothers who knew nothing of themselves? At first Jean had thought to try and separate them, to make more of a gap between them so that the differences between them would be less apparent, but it was impossible. Their bedrooms at Harehope were at opposite ends of the long nursery corridor, but as soon as he was old enough, George would find his way to his brother's room in the morning, climbing into his bed, where the pair would chatter and play like puppies until Nanny came in to pull back the curtains. When questions were asked of them, George would always tilt his head, waiting for the words that Alfie would speak for both. He had been slower to learn to talk too, lacking the need when someone could do the job perfectly for him. And as the relationship grew, it became symbiotic; the more George looked to Alfie, the more Alfie would look out for George. And there was a kindness that ran through it all that made Jean's heart ache. A gentle patience with each other that remained when the rough and tumble of infancy had fallen away.

They were so close in age that they were almost twins. She had seen brothers three or four years apart who were separate characters, forming themselves in opposition to the one who came before or after. With her boys, it was different; they discovered everything together, so that opinions, passions, beliefs were somehow formed in unison. She saw it as they began to take in the possibility of Harehope and what it offered them: the river, the woods, the vast tracts of moorland that ran behind the house; endless spaces where imaginary worlds could be created away from the grown-ups – high seas for marauding pirates to sail or battlegrounds for soldiers in arms to march – worlds of delicious escape which the two brothers would voyage together.

Their father watched it all, silently, seeing the judgement the world was making and carrying his implied failure like a knife that he would pull out on his sons when tested. The brothers could never comprehend his dislike, this uneasy presence that hung like a pall over their perfect childhood.

Jean had been away in London. She hadn't been able to see David for close to five months, a stretch apart, though punctuated by letters and snatched telephone conversations, that exhausted her. In periods like this, her desire would turn to longing and then reluctantly but inevitably to a sort of vague despondency and a wheedling anxiety that she would push down, that perhaps he might not need her as much as she needed him. So she'd escaped to town for a week, finding solace in the distraction of lunches with girlfriends, of a trip to see the latest Noël Coward, a wander alone around the Royal Academy, losing herself in the shuffling strangers processing through its airy, light-filled rooms. The boys must have been eight and seven by then. Alfie was all skinny legs, perpetually bruised from adventure, a child for whom the world was an endless tree to climb or river to splash through, and the source of a million questions if he could only stand still long enough to listen to an answer. His younger brother was more hesitant, aware always of his arm, the way it hung limply at his left side; it was shorter and far thinner than his right, unable to bend fully at the elbow. The attempts that the doctors had made to improve it – so harsh, so painful for him; braces to bend him, to pull him, to straighten him – she had loathed so much that she had one day simply stopped them all. There would be no more intervention. He was just let be. So George was his brother's shadow, keeping up where he could or listening to the report, with eyes bright and face lit, of whatever he could not.

Stokes had collected Jean from the station as usual and the journey to Harehope had passed in amiable silence, but when she had walked into her house, shedding her jacket and bag, keen to find out where the children were after the time apart, she had sensed tension. She looked up the main staircase and saw two of the housemaids walking hurriedly along the first-floor corridor that gave onto the hallway below, pushing open doors as they went.

'Is everything all right?' Jean called up.

The girls stopped, looking down at Jean over the banister, unsure of what answer to give, but before they could attempt it, Alfie had appeared behind one of them, pushing his way past and then tearing down the stairs, eyes wild with fear and excitement. 'Oh, Mama, Nanny said not to say anything if we saw you.'

'Well, you've told me there's something to say now, so you'd better say it. Quickly.'

'It's George. He's been gone for nearly three hours. Nanny thought he was in his room, and she and I had gone out for a walk after tea, and when we came back, he wasn't there. And we've been looking everywhere and calling for him.'

Jean felt the vice of panic tighten around her heart and her mind began to run through every permutation of disaster that could strike; then came the voice of calm that tried, and failed, to soothe away that panic, coming up with all the alternative, harmless possibilities to explain his absence. Her mind always went to the river. Though Alfie was a strong swimmer, George still couldn't stay afloat with ease and would tire quickly, even if he was loath to admit it.

She looked at Alfie. 'I'm sure there's a perfectly reasonable explanation. Be a darling and go and see if there's anyone in the stables that can take a walk down to the river, in case he's gone there. Will you?' She gave him a push in the right direction and he dashed off, pleased to serve a purpose, too young to catch the strain in her voice.

Jean put her coat back on and began to walk quickly around the outside of the house. There was the path to the river that George could have taken, but she would leave that to the lads who would be quicker at covering the ground. She would head down the back drive instead, check in the fields to the right and left of that, where the boys sometimes played with the dogs. She began to call out his name, self-consciously at first but growing more desperate as the gentle rustle of the wind in the leaves was all that answered her.

As she turned the final curve of the drive that would lead her past the row of estate cottages and to the road to the village, shirt damp now from the brisk pace she had kept up, she stopped to catch her breath. She looked at her wristwatch: it was nearly seven o'clock. It would be light for another couple of hours at least – it was mid June, and the days were endless this far north. Further panicked calculations crossed her mind, of darkness finally coming, of George being stuck somewhere, or having fallen, being alone and shouting for her in vain.

She heard her name carried faintly on the breeze, a man's voice calling her from somewhere behind. She turned to see Stokes making his way down the drive as quickly as decorum would allow, so she jogged back to meet him.

'What is it? Have they found him?'

'No, I'm sorry, not yet, m'lady. But Alfie spoke to one of the stable lads who was riding back half an hour or so ago, and passed George. Apparently he was out in Miller's field, near where they bury the dogs. The lad should have stopped and brought him back. I'll give him a talking-to about that later. I think he was up by Kelpy's new grave.'

Relief flooded through her. It made sense that he should be there. He had always had a natural connection with animals that was much more pronounced than Alfie's, pointing to any horses or sheep he saw in a field before he had the words available to name them. She used to find him sitting by the cage in the old kitchen whenever a new puppy arrived, putting his fingers between the bars, allowing them to be nipped and licked, or simply leaning against it so the puppy could feel the warmth of his presence, knowing instinctively that it would be missing its mother.

Jean turned and walked as fast as she could, ignoring the stitch in her ribs and the rub of her shoes as she crossed over to the five-bar gate that opened onto Miller's field. There was a spot in its north-east corner under the shelter of a large oak tree whose knotted roots spread wide, where any of the many dogs that had lived and died at Harehope were buried. Usually by the keepers, with a neat cross of plain wood, their name and short dates carved into it. The gate was locked, so she scrambled awkwardly over it, cursing her London outfit, and started walking briskly up the field's rough edge, unable to relax till she could catch sight of him. The field was now grass, with a ploughed margin up the side, but the mud the plough had churned up was caked and dry, in large ruts that she tripped on as she half-ran, half-walked to the crest of the hill.

She made out his small figure as the ground flattened out. He was kneeling close to Kelpy's grave, as Stokes had suspected. No cross had been carved for the dog yet as he'd only been buried two weeks before, so George was kneeling before the mound of earth that covered the little brown spaniel he had adored since the moment he had arrived as a puppy, still blind and toothless and mewling, slick from his mother's womb. As she approached, George was in perfect silhouette, his head to one side and his left shoulder drooping down where she knew his palsied left arm would be lifted into his lap, covered by his right. The pose was a habit of his, as if to shield the world from the embarrassment of seeing it.

'George?' she called out gently.

He didn't hear at first and she called again, and this time he turned and she was close enough to see he had been crying, his skin blotched and red around his eyes. He stood, wiping his nose on his sleeve, before furiously rubbing at his eyes.

'Darling.' She walked towards him, putting out her arms, ready to receive him. He didn't come forward, though, just looked at her before looking down again, the sleeve of his jumper pulled down over his right hand from where he had been sucking it. 'You mustn't run off like that. Nanny has been sick with worry, and Alfie and everyone have been looking for you everywhere.' She looked at her wristwatch. 'It's nearly half past seven, you should be in bed by now.'

He was still watching her, distrustful somehow, his dark eyes solemn, nursing hurt.

'What is it? Come. Give me a hug, won't you? I'm not cross, I'm just glad I found you.' She dropped down to her knees; the grass was wet with dew and she felt a snag of pain where a stone dug into her. She folded him into her arms and reluctantly he hugged her back. She gave an internal sigh that she still was able to provide this; how fast it was all going. 'What is it, darling? Tell me, won't you?'

George pulled away and sat then on the ground beside her so he wasn't looking at her but looking straight ahead at Kelpy's grave; cross-legged, with brown patches at his knees from kneeling on the damp ground. They stayed as they were, silently, until eventually George spoke. His voice was quiet. 'I've been so sad about Kelpy dying, you know that. So horrid, when he wasn't even old. So unfair. And I've been missing him lots.' He gave her a quick sidelong look. 'And what I've learned about heaven is that he's up there' – he gave a nod to the sky – 'but that his body's down here, and if I want to, that it's all right to come and…think of him here. It's what we've been taught, and it made me feel all right about things. Because I knew I could come here and be with him. As often as I liked. Even if it's not his soul.' The last word was clearly new to him, and he used it tentatively.

She nodded, following his solemn words, heart aching at the sincerity of it. 'Yes, that's right. Absolutely right, darling. But you must tell people when you come out here—'

'No, no, but that's not it.' He was getting upset again, agitated that she wasn't following, and tears were building again at the edges of his eyes. 'I had told Nanny that I liked doing this and she said fine, and then she said I ought to think of him in my head too, not just by coming to the grave. Say him in my prayers at night. And when I asked her why, she said that I can't come here for ever because one day this will be Alfie's and I'll live elsewhere.' And then he started to cry, really cry. 'But if I'm not here at Harehope, then where will I be?' He was looking at her, and she could see fear and panic in his eyes. 'Am I going to be sent to live on my own when it's Alfie's? And you and Alfie and Papa and Nanny, will you all go on living here when I'm somewhere else? Where will I go? And who will come and pray for Kelpy when I'm gone?'

And he sobbed and sobbed, his nose snotty, rubbing his face with great swipes though the tears kept coming. She pulled him into her so he was on her lap, and held him tight, rocking him gently and smoothing the top of his head, allowing the rhythm to calm him.

When she felt the tears subside, she spoke. 'Darling, Nanny didn't mean that we will all be here and you somewhere else. I promise you! I promise, hope to die. When you're older, much older, it's true, Harehope will be Alfie's, but you, me, Papa, we'll all be somewhere else.'

'So Alfie will be on his own? That's not nice for him.' He looked up, confused.

'Well, I hope he might have a wife and children of his own by then. But listen, this is all so far in the future that there's no point in even thinking about it, let alone crying about it. And one thing I can promise you, whatever your age or wherever you are living when this happens, you'll never be on your own. I'll always be there – or as near as you'll have me.' She smiled, and rubbed his hair. She could see she was bringing him back, that she had soothed him, that he would soon forget this.

'Do you promise?'

'I promise.' She nodded, her face serious, giving him the certainty he needed. He smiled, a brave little smile that made her heart catch in her chest. 'Come on, let's go home and find Alfie.' She pulled him up to his feet and dusted down his jersey and shorts. 'Come, hold my hand and we'll be back in no time. Don't walk too fast though, I need to keep up.'

He smiled, the look of absolute trust now returned. And they set off down the edge of the field, a chill in the air now and both a little cold from the damp of the ground. They walked slowly and every so often George would stop, as if remembering the great sadness of before, and then just as quickly that it was all right again and would carry on, that precious hand in hers.

She felt another presence walking with them too, an uninvited guest who would appear, often without warning, but always at moments like this, when her love was at its greatest, swelling through her heart like a cresting wave. And the presence would remind her of something: of the little untruth, the poison seeping in at the edges; that underneath that fierce love, that maternal salve she could lay across any wound he showed her, there was something else. The guilt that scraped away at her for George's acceptance of a falsehood that derived entirely and only from his loving, doting mother.

CHAPTER NINE

Married life at Harehope fell into a pattern of sorts. Two lives lived under one sprawling roof, separate till necessity drove them together. It would never make sense to anyone else; how could people understand this marriage of close to ten years now, frozen somehow in the emotional ineptitude of its first? Jean supposed that an adolescence spent at her mother's elbow had trained her well. How ironic that an education in presenting the perfect flowering of American youth to the world – or to New York society, at least – should suit so neatly this life of hidden selves and untruth. Jean learned to enjoy her own company at Harehope, to take solace in the beauty that surrounded her. Her relationship with the landscape evolved. She drew strength from the endless and ever-changing skies that spread above her; from the fields, smooth as beaten gold in summer, of iron and bronze in winter, that bled always into the bruised line of moorland that lay watch beyond. They became her companion, not her judge.

In Harehope's world seasons were master, each one bringing a ritual to be solemnly marked. In August, as the harvest was being pulled in from stubble fields the colour of yolk, the moor was the epicentre of life, guns gathering each day on the hill, trudging up to the lines of stone butts that criss-crossed the heather like veins. But as naturally as day followed night, the light would change, the early-morning mists and the damp and cool of October would come, and hunting would consume the life of the house, its heart. The hunt would meet each morning at half past nine by the opened gates, sometimes thirty or forty horses at a time, plus a legion of hangers-on and whippers-in, kennelmen and terriermen. The men – and women, the more rakish long having abandoned side-saddle – would stand around waiting for the off, taking nips from their stirrup cups to keep themselves warm, or so ran the pretence, as Stokes wove between the gathering horses and swirling hounds like a swan in sail, smooth and sleek among the mass of animals and mud.

Today was damp, the ground sodden, and water seemed to run in rivulets from everything Jean looked at: the noses of the mounted men who swapped gossip and the weather in brisk voices, from the branches of the trees still bare of leaves as winter clung on with grim intent. As Jean stood in the throng of horses as they slipped and danced in the mud, she noticed a woman standing, upright and still, in the circle of whining dogs. Her hair was like lank straw, her expression sour. She turned her head as her name was called by her husband – Barrett, Jean remembered now, a coarse, hard-faced man with a terse black beard who ran the kennels. A little boy stood a pace behind her, his jacket too small, revealing pale wrists. The hounds whipped round and round the pair, pushing against each other, snarling when they got too close, desperate to get away.

The woman caught Jean watching her and as their eyes met briefly, she held Jean's stare, and there was a hint of a smile as she pushed down a dog that was jumping up at her skirts. She grabbed her son by the hand. Her voice was hard, impatient. 'Come on, Jimmy, it's time to get back. Take those two buckets out of the way.'

Jimmy, his thin little face expressionless, picked up the buckets as his mother had told him and began trudging back down the drive.

A man from the neighbouring estate, cheeks chapped and red from the cold and arm raised in greeting to Jean, was bringing his vast chestnut mare through the gathering in her direction. She smiled. James Galbraith was a sweet man, who'd always made a great effort with her at dull local affairs, and she went towards him, but the woman, Mrs Barrett, stood in her path.

'Excuse me.' Jean moved to pass the woman but she stood still, her feet set slightly apart, leaving Jean no option but to step around her, avoiding a pool of muddy water that had gathered at the side of the path.

'You'd best mind yourself, Lady Warre. Don't want to get those shoes dirty.' She kept her eyes on Jean as she passed, no effort made to hide the bite in her voice.

Edward, his horse sliding in the mud, had made his way over to where Jean was now standing talking to James. He was irritated, shifting in his seat, pulling at the reins to keep the horse still. 'Jean, I don't know why you come out when it's this wet. Stokes can do it on his own. It's clear you hate it. Just go back inside. It's pointless your being here.'

The woman was watching the conversation, her whole body turned to Jean and Edward, no attempt made to hide her interest. When Edward's horse moved off, she stared on at Jean, her hair plastered to her head by the rain, though she seemed not to notice.

*

Whether Mrs Barrett had been difficult before, Jean did not know, but she was always at the stable yard now, milling around when there was no need for her to be there, her son dragging at her heels. She was causing trouble in the house too, it seemed, making a nuisance of herself with the other women who worked there. It was her husband who was employed by the estate, but she would wander into the kitchens nonetheless, and at odd hours, swiping a roll from the table laid for the servants' lunch, in full view of whoever was in there, or taking fruit from the orchards when it was known that the picking of the apples – skins now hardened, flesh sweet and ready to eat as the frost of November came – was a privilege reserved only for Stokes and Mrs Hawkins before the gardeners came and finished the job.

Jean was standing with Mrs Hawkins beneath the porte cochère one afternoon, waving off some lingering lunch guests who were dragging out their departure with forgotten gloves and a thank you too many. As the pair watched the cars finally move off in the fading afternoon light, arms folded against the chill, Jean saw at the edge of her vision a figure leaving the stable block. She could make out only that it was a woman, dark coat belted at the waist, wheeling a bicycle beside her. Her gait was slow, and the click of the wheel and chain were the only sounds as she made a determined path from the block towards the house. As she drew closer, Mrs Barrett's face revealed itself, a bright snap of red at her lips and a flare of colour at her neck where a sliver of patterned silk emerged, jarring with the shabbiness of the rest of her outfit.

'I've told her countless times that no one is to come this way, near the front of the house. She knows that well enough.'

Jean said nothing, but they both watched Mrs Barrett as she placed her handbag in the bicycle's wicker basket in front and swung her leg over the bike's frame. They were still too far apart to make out her expression, but her head was turned in their direction. Just as she was coming close enough for their eyes to meet, she wheeled left, pushing herself high out of the saddle as she set off down the front drive.

'I don't like her.'

Jean looked across at Mrs Hawkins. Direct opinion was not a usual part of their conversation.

'She seems to think she can get away with murder here. I dislike gossip, but my husband tells me Barrett drinks and they terrorise that boy. I think they're bad sorts. I know it's been mentioned to Mr Wisden by several of the servants, but nothing seems to happen. I'm sorry to ask you, but perhaps you could say something to Lord Warre?'

Jean nodded. 'Of course.'

Mrs Hawkins went back into the house, but Jean stayed outside, unable to take her eyes off that figure as it faded into the gloaming, moving silently down the drive until it reached the bend and disappeared finally out of sight.

CHAPTER TEN

'Oh, Freddie can be fearfully forgetful when he wants to be. Our anniversary passes him by unless I have the good grace to remind him.'

Jean had been asked to lunch in London with Rose Byam-Hughes and a girlfriend of hers, a Mary Swinton, another jolly sort with pink cheeks and eyes of the same guileless blue as Rose. The three of them were sitting around the slim mahogany table in Rose's dining room that was like a shrine to her parents-in-law's cautious, faded taste. A morning's dress shopping was under their belts, as was the relief shared that the lunch of overcooked meat and boiled vegetables, prepared by the Byam-Hughes' ancient cook, had been survived. They were discussing their husbands now over coffee, swapping anecdotes to amuse as lunches like these required.

'Oh, you won't believe it. I got a nightdress from James for my last birthday, one that buttoned up to the neck and wrist and hung well below the ankle, and in the most ghastly peach rayon you've ever seen.' Mary was smiling indulgently, confident in the cosy sturdiness of her marriage. 'Of course, it used to be silk camiknickers from Harrods when we were first married. Since the children, it's never been quite the same.'

The pair looked to Jean expectantly.

What to say? That the idea of Edward buying her a nightdress was as preposterous as their hands touching? He was not, admittedly, sleeping with a tart from one of those downstairs establishments in Piccadilly which, rumour had it, Mary Swinton's husband was, but he was a stranger to her nonetheless, his inner life obscure. That only a month before, Jean had been in a hotel in Paris, the bedroom's open shutters making the rooftops of grey slate beyond voyeurs to her afternoon's lazy pleasure, as she stretched out her body for her lover to explore, giving every part of herself to this man who was not her husband?

The two women were still looking at her, mouths polite little Os, Mary no doubt waiting for a nugget from Jean's life to take home with her, or to peck over like a hen eating grain at another elegant little Mayfair lunch.

Jean gave a bland smile. 'No, Edward doesn't go in for that sort of thing much either. Presents aren't his strong point. Nor mine, actually.'

'Far too busy running that vast estate of yours – all that responsibility. Must be draining. Though I'm sure you're just making us bumpkins feel better.' Rose leaned in and poured more coffee. 'I bet you demand nothing less than the finest silk from Paris, Jean.' But she had caught something in Jean's tone and the subject of presents was dropped.

The women had passed another half an hour in idle chat, Mary's eyes flicking to her wristwatch and stifling a yawn when she realised nothing more of interest was to be revealed. But when Rose was helping Jean on with her coat – Mary now gone, having hopped in a taxi to catch the three o'clock to

Salisbury – and the pair were standing in her hall, with its lantern that hadn't been dusted for a while and that cast only a weak light on the dark walls and parquet floor below, she had stopped.

'You would say something to me, Jean, wouldn't you, if you weren't all right? Since your father died and your mama went back to America, it must seem a very different place here. I was talking to Baba Metcalfe a few weeks ago and I thought so much of you. She told me how lonely her mother had been when she was married and living over here – an American in a foreign land and all of that. That she found everyone so cold and buttoned-up. I know it's different now, but I did think of you. I'm sure you and Edward are happy, but... You can always shout if things are tricky. You don't have to carry it all. I know Mary's a frightful gossip, but I wouldn't breathe a word.'

Rose had tucked her hair behind her ear, and for a second Jean thought of the relief that would come from opening up to this woman. But then there came the click and catch of a key in the door and the wide-hipped nanny entered in a blast of cold air, pulling the vast pram behind her and shedding her hat and scarf with an elaborate display of effort.

'Oh, here he is. My darling boy. Oh, do look at him, Jean, those cheeks. He may be my third son, but he's the apple of my eye.'

And she leaned in low, fussing over the baby, whose eyes were a pair of perfect blue saucers, untying the bow of grey wool beneath his pudgy chin, delighted to get him free of his bonnet and into her arms.

Rose turned back to Jean then – her baby, only six weeks old, a tiny pellet of a thing like a dormouse, giving out little creaking sounds – and a cloud of guilt fell across her face as she remembered the words of before. She put out her hand, touching Jean's arm lightly. 'Do keep in touch, Jean. Promise me you will.'

But she was back to her baby, questioning the nanny about whether he had napped in the pram, fussing about the cool of his hands despite the mittens and several layers of thick Islay wool he had been bundled in.

Jean left Rose, a quick kiss on the cheek, a meaningless promise of another lunch which they both knew neither would push for, and she tripped down the smooth steps of the house and onto Brook Street, where the afternoon traffic was making its way slowly towards Grosvenor Square.

As she was walking back in the direction of her house, ready to cross at the corner of Brook Street and Duke Street, she found herself caught by a memory. She had been on a walk with her parents on one of her first Sundays in London, and they'd stopped at this same corner. Her father had patted her mother's hand to get her attention – absorbed as Elizabeth always was by some tiny but detailed human drama that required intricate dissection – and the trio had stood together in the weak sunshine of a spring morning, looking up at the handsome brick and stucco building before them. It had once been the home of John Adams, the first American to hold the job her father now did, in a London of another lifetime, of carriages and frock coats, powdered wigs and hooped skirts. She remembered her father's hand resting at the small of her mother's back as he told them about Adams in his gentle, unassuming way. It was the slightest of gestures, witnessed by their daughter but signifying nothing to her then. How she had taken for granted the utter assurance of affection and understanding that ran between her father and mother after decades of marriage; the minuscule acts that revealed the ocean of intimacy lying beneath. That a thousand inconsequential things passed over by others, barely of note at all, were the breath that gave a marriage voice.

The sound of a car's horn from the south side of Grosvenor Square brought her back. She was just another woman, woollen coat buttoned up to the neck; someone's wife, with her cache of London memories and her hidden inner life tucked away in her handbag. She walked on to Park Lane alone.

CHAPTER ELEVEN

They were standing now in the chill of the stables with its familiar smell of stone and straw, as one of the lads tacked up Alfie's pony. He was sliding the saddle onto the stocky little grey's back, pulling the girth tight as Alfie watched intently, desperate for everything to be as it should on this day when he knew his father's critical eye would be upon him, his first in joining the hunt. Jean had watched him dressing that morning, up when it was still dark and the rest of the house was silent, putting on his shirt and stock of white silk, a look of fierce concentration as he did up the buttons of his new little jacket of navy wool, tense at the day of adult privilege that lay ahead of him. The stable boy was smoothing the pony's coat with a pair of brushes, the movement mesmerising as he worked away, the pony's head low as Alfie rubbed its soft, velvet nose.

Jean's attention was caught by the sound of scuffling feet and then of a voice raised in anger coming through from the yard outside. Confused, she followed the noise outside, only to find a group of the stable lads, plus some of the whippers-in arriving for the day ahead, standing in a sort of half-circle.

Barrett, the kennelman, was in the middle of the group in his shirtsleeves, unsteady on his feet, wearing the air of the night before with a leering pride.

Edward was standing only a little away from Barrett. 'What's going on here?' Her husband's voice was raised.

One of the stable boys stepped forward. He had been behind Barrett, and as he made his way into the space beside him, Jean saw he was pulling Mrs Barrett with him. Her head was kept low but eventually she lifted it, revealing a face so swollen it made Jean gasp; her bottom lip was vast and misshapen, a split right through it like overripe fruit bursting, and the right side of her face was a kaleidoscope of purples. The defiance of before had been beaten out of her. A silk scarf, its jaunty pattern of pink and orange smeared with dirt, was clutched tight in the hand that hung at her side.

Jean turned to the boy next to her. 'Sid, go and get Mrs Hawkins at once. Mrs Barrett needs to be seen by a doctor.'

'What the devil is going on here? Can someone please tell me?' Despite the volume of his voice, Edward was rattled.

'You tell me, Lord Warre.' Barrett was standing, legs spread wide now, a confidence to his posture beyond the alcohol in his blood.

Edward's face blanched. 'Back to your work, Barrett. We are leaving in under half an hour.'

'I will not, m'lord.' Barrett stepped forward, chest peacock-puffed.

Edward matched him and took a step closer. His voice was low. 'I order you to go back to your work, Barrett. Do not disobey me or you'll find there is no place for you here.'

'Or my wife? It's seems you've got a special place for her, m'lord.'

The yard was silent, collective breath held, and Jean realised with a jolt that Alfie too was watching it all. She took his hand quickly in hers, and walked him back in the direction of his pony. 'Go and finish tacking up. Sid will be back in a minute.' She gave him a push.

Barrett was still talking as she returned. 'It seems it's not enough to covet someone else's wife – you've been 'aving her too. And paying her for the pleasure. I found over ten pounds stashed in her—'

'Enough, Barrett.'

'I will not be silenced.' His voice was loud, out of control. 'She says she was carrying your baby. That you knew about it and paid her to have it got rid of, promising her more money if she'd do it.' He turned back to his wife, and Jean saw that the woman's cheeks were wet with tears. 'I've seen to that myself, and I'll be keeping all that you've given her, but I'll tell whoever'll listen what kind of a man you are.'

Edward looked as if he would hit Barrett, his arm pulling back and his body squared to strike, but the sound of Stokes entering the yard checked him and he let the arm drop to his side. Sid was at Stokes' heels, cheeks flushed, enjoying his role at the centre of things, pushing his way behind Stokes through the small gathering, Mrs Hawkins following not far behind.

Stokes' voice was calm. 'Back to work, back to work, all of you. Stop this ridiculous gawping. Barrett, to your house at once, and I shall send Mr Wisden to see you as soon as he's in. Mrs Barrett, please go with Mrs Hawkins to the Hall, where she will see to you.'

The scene diffused at once with Stokes' words – looks of disappointment as the drama was being moved offstage – and the lads shuffled off, reluctantly, back to their work. Mrs Barrett was steered by Mrs Hawkins back to the house, and Stokes took it upon himself to walk Barrett out of the yard and in the direction of the back drive. Edward, however, was left standing alone while he waited for his horse to be brought out to him. He pulled a handkerchief from his breast pocket and ran it across his brow.

Jean walked up to him, her heart beating a drum in her chest.

He wheeled around to her, body snapped to attention. 'Are you going to reprimand me? You, of all people?'

She kept her voice quiet. 'Edward, these are base people. You can't possibly want—'

'What? Want what? Her? Is that what upsets you about it? Not that her face is smashed up or that he's beaten a baby out of her but that she's a rough sort. Come, Jean, you best of all understand what this is. Some low-grade writer or the kennel-man's wife. It's all the same, isn't it?'

She looked down.

'Oh, don't be coy. You have it your way, and I shall have it mine. And if this ugly little scene is too much for your delicate sensibilities, then perhaps we ought to consider sharing your arrangements in France with the wider world? See what they make of it all. How was your last little trip to Paris?' He kept his voice low, but something of the freedom of the empty yard had caught him. His eyes were bright, and he leaned in towards her. 'What is his name? David, isn't it? Is he still the one, or is it someone else? A sequence of blue-eyed boys with ink on their fingers and wallets waiting to be filled. Don't worry. It can carry on. It's clear that we are in this for the foreseeable. But don't get at me if I want to find something of my own.'

She couldn't stop herself. 'But her? Edward. She's not—'

'What? Beautiful? Rich? See where that got me. And if you're concerned merely with appearance, let me remind you that it's a damn sight better to have some woman who no one gives two hoots about than swanning around on the Riviera. I swear if I ever hear a whisper about you and him from anyone I know—'

'You know I would never do that.'

He gave a strange, twisted laugh. 'He's an odd cove then, this man David. If he's happy to hide away and be your boy for when you need him. But perhaps that's all part of the deal. Have you made a deal with him?'

This was the closest they had ever come to discussing the truth of their marriage.

'I'm sorry for you, if you want the truth. That I have someone who loves me, and you have someone you – you pay,' Jean said.

Here he gave a twisted laugh. 'And you don't pay your friend? Whose house does he stay in? Whose wine does he drink? Whose sparkling Rolls takes him up and down that beloved coast of yours?'

He knew he'd landed a blow then, because how could she explain things to him he could never understand? Emotion, connection, intimacy, knowledge. These words were from a different language to the one Edward spoke, and she thought with a sudden pang of Rose and Freddie and of the cramped chaos of their house on Brook Street. Of the looks that passed between them which they thought no one caught.

'What's the point, Edward, in doing this now? If neither of us will change.' And she turned and walked away.

Her life with David was her real life, the rest of it a performance onstage, no lights, no audience bar her boys and the household; it was a muted thing, with flashes of drama like this anger passing between the two of them. But she played the part, so that when she stepped off the stage and walked back down the dark corridor, she could push open a door and stand once more in the cool, fresh air.

Jean found Alfie waiting in the stables, his hand resting on the pony's neck, and it gave a shiver of pleasure as he patted the warm skin. He hadn't heard her, and she watched him for a second, her little boy, with his thatch of dark blonde hair; the inheritor of this place, with all of its beauty and its brokenness. 'Alfie?'

He turned, impossibly young in the formality of his hunting kit, and smiled so sweetly when he saw her that she wanted to keep him as he was for ever.

But the moment was gone, like all those moments, and she went to him, giving his shoulder a little rub and taking the pony's reins from the hook above the stable's door where they had been looped in haste by Sid.

Mother and son, and the sturdy little grey, walked out to the mounting block that stood in the yard, now empty, his father long gone.

The Barretts were moved on, but not without a final brawl at the local pub, where Barrett, it was said, broke the nose of the publican with one clean punch. Mr Wisden saw to it that another man was found for the job, a quiet, thin-faced fellow from the borders called Simons, who kept himself to himself – no wife, of course. No more was said of the scene in the yard.

One afternoon, months later, Jean was rushing around looking for some gloves and a scarf to grab to take to London, the car waiting for her outside. She had pulled open the bottom drawer of the large oak chest that held outdoor things, rifling through for a suitable pair. The top drawer held scarves, in the midst of which lay one she did not immediately recognise. She pulled it loose from the pile, a shock of pink and orange revealed. The bright splashes of colour were, as she looked now, alternating columns of a delicate pattern of tiny butterflies, each wing touching that of the next, their wings flecked with a deep bronze, printed on the finest silk, which fell like cream in her hands. The label was familiar to Jean; it was sold in all the best shops in London, was worn by many of her friends. Now here it was, laundered and returned to Jean's drawer: to the woman Mrs Hawkins had assumed was its rightful owner.

It had been not a payment then but a gift, from her husband to Mrs Barrett. Edward had gone and bought it for her, slipping away after a lunch somewhere in St James's perhaps, scanning the box the shop girl opened for him as she asked encouragingly what colour his wife liked best. So Edward had his hidden life too. Muddled and bitter, confusing sex with love because he had never learned the difference. Jean pushed the scarf quickly back into the drawer, but as she walked out to her waiting car, she carried with her now a little stone of guilt, sharp with sadness, that she put away in her pocket, buried deep.

CHAPTER TWELVE

The boys were the place where she was exposed. The rest she could shoulder, turning her face away, calling to mind the next time she could see David. But when Edward's hatred spilled out to his sons, it was an agony. The ease between the brothers somehow made him angrier; he saw Alfie's kindness to his brother as sympathy for a weakling. He loathed that Alfie was always there, helping George, aware that his arm would slow him up, or filling his cartridge bag if they were allowed out together to shoot the pheasants and partridges in the nearby hedgerows, or sitting with the keepers on wet afternoons as they modified his gun to accommodate his brother's palsy.

Jean had come upon the pair one afternoon in the gun room at Harehope. Another year was gone, the boys eight and nine now, away at prep school but home for the Christmas holidays. She adored having them back in the house, their mess and noise an ecstasy to her after weeks of creaking silence and latent tension. It was only half past three, but the days were so short here that the low afternoon sun had already bled below the horizon. Curtains were being drawn around the house and baskets of logs carried by footmen to lay the fires for the evening. The boys stood with one of the keepers as he cleaned their guns for them. He was explaining about the gun as he broke it, the stock and the barrels, both boys entranced by the sheen of the metal as he polished its smooth exterior, as he eased the pipes and cloth down the barrels.

'His lordship will show you boys, if you ask him, I'm sure. I remember the late Lord Warre used to do it with Mr Charles and your father.'

'We'd sooner learn from you, Robson,' Alfie said quickly.

George looked across at Alfie. 'He's not very patient with us.'

'I think I've got it anyway. George, let's try now, just us.' With heads bent low over the baize-covered table, the boys pieced the gun back together, handling each part with great care, while Robson stood behind watching. He looked up then, noticing Jean at the door.

'They're good lads aren't they, m'lady. Not like my boys, scrapping and whining like a pair of pups.'

Jean smiled, and stayed watching them as they carried on, engrossed in their activity, the only sound that of their gentle breathing and the satisfying click as metal hit metal and slotted back into its rightful place, a look of triumph on their small faces as they passed the gun back to Robson, correctly assembled.

Edward walked in then, dogs trailing behind him, one of the underkeepers carrying his gun slip and cartridge bag for him. The atmosphere in the room changed immediately – Robson snapped to attention, disassembling the gun and putting it back in its case, nodding his head to Edward as he made room for him at the table.

'How was your day, Papa?' Alfie asked, his face earnest with that line of worry, experience having taught him that his father's moods were often unpredictable, usually inexplicable.

'Tolerable – two useless shots from next door who couldn't hit a thing, and whose conversation was even worse. What's been going on here then?'

'I've been showing them how to clean their guns, m'lord. Took them out for a little walk through the east wood to shoot some pigeons. I should think they could do this on their own now. Little George was especially good at cleaning those barrels, weren't you, Mr George?'

It was the note of sympathy that she knew set Edward's teeth on edge. It was involuntary. The nature of the younger boy was so sweet, endearing him to everyone he met, that they couldn't help it, unaware of how it repulsed his father. It was another reminder to Edward of his own inferiority in producing a son that the world acknowledged with relief as the second, with nothing required of him but an easy temperament. How perfect it was that the younger boy worshipped his older brother and that there was no jealousy between them. *As it should be*, their kind expressions and tilted heads would say as the pair progressed through boyhood.

'It's all very well cleaning the damn thing, but can you hit anything?' He dumped his gun slip on the table and shed his jacket and boots without looking at any of them.

'A bloody waste of time with that pathetic arm, if you ask me. A bloody waste of time. And you're just rubbing it in, Alfie.' And he walked out, door slamming behind him, leaving Jean and the boys to salvage something from a scene that he had ruined like this countless times before.

Jean made sure to come by their bedrooms after scenes like this – to have an extra few minutes with them both before bed, a rub of the back, a kiss on the head, to let them know that she loved every part of them more than they would ever need. That night she went first to George's room, where he was reading, hair combed and knees pulled up, with a book open in front of him. He was happy, looking up, giving the flash of a smile that made her throat tighten when it followed the bruising of earlier. She kissed him, touched his cheek, picked up the eiderdown that had slipped off the bed, tucking it round him. 'Nanny will turn off your lights in half an hour. God bless, darling.'

She left the door ajar as he liked, and walked down the corridor to Alfie's room. His light was already off, but she knocked gently, pushing the door further open.

'Darling, are you awake?'

The shaft of light from the corridor fell across the bed and she could see he was lying on his back, his eyes open. He nodded.

'Still a kiss for me? I know you're frightfully grown-up now.'

Alfie smiled, sitting up on his elbows, and she went and sat beside him, pushing his dark blonde hair back off his face, revealing that fine, high forehead. His eyes were serious in a way that only a nine-year-old boy's could be, carrying a knowingness that belied the elfin face, and part of her didn't want to ask what was troubling him. What good would it do when she knew she was powerless to change it?

'All all right, darling?'

He nodded, saying nothing.

'Is it Papa?'

Alfie nodded again, then looked down. She put her arms around him, that slim little body, those slight shoulders. 'I hate it when he's like that to George. And George shrugs it off. What's he ever done wrong?'

'I know, I know. It's just the way your father is. He's abrupt. He's another generation, and perhaps his father was hard on him too. He doesn't mean it.'

They both knew it was a lie, but Alfie took it up anyway. He gently pulled away, looking at her with those eyes of David's, where emotion could not hide. She kissed him on the top of the head.

'I'm so glad you're both home. You have no idea how much I miss you.'

'I miss you too, Mama.' And he sank back into the pillows, and she kissed him again before leaving him.

She needed to bathe before dinner, but she paused before going downstairs, looking along the nursery corridor, with its faded carpets and hotchpotch of furniture and mismatched lamps. Though it was not done, not what mothers of her class did, she'd spent so many hours up here, lost in thought, happy simply to be near her two boys, to hear the gentle sound as they shifted in their beds or murmured in their sleep; to go and kiss them if they woke from a bad dream. Pathetic perhaps, a reflection of the emptiness of her life at Harehope. But all these moments had mounted up and it was only now, in the lull between their bedtime and dinner, that she saw how quickly it had slipped away.

Had she concentrated enough? Had she realised how lucky she was? Each moment was a blessing so fleeting it was like rain on dry ground, absorbed and gone before there was a chance to feel its impact. Alfie and George were at the far edge of childhood now, soon to leave the nursery for good. Her watch on this landing would soon come to an end; she couldn't keep them up here forever, soothing away the creases with kisses and hugs and platitudes that, one day, they wouldn't even pretend to believe.

But as her hand rested on the back of the armchair and she breathed in the familiar smell of mothballs and old wool, she knew that the greatest danger lay not in the outside world, in the realm of strangers, but right here on the nursery corridor at Harehope, in this place her boys loved with all their hearts, where the truth of who they were and their father's knowledge of it stalked them both like the wolf in a childhood fairy tale, teeth bared, fangs drawn, glinting in the light of a perfect crescent moon.

The holidays passed as they always did, patches of bliss clouded over by interludes where Edward would crush George with his dismissiveness or flatten Alfie with his rejection. Christmas Day had been wonderful, the boys so absorbed by their presents and the distraction of other guests in the house that they didn't notice his prolonged absences, or the tension between their parents. But now it was Sunday and they were to take the train back to their prep school, their trunks having already been packed and driven down. She hated the days they went back, knowing they were reluctant to leave, feeling the sadness permeating the house. Alfie would feign enthusiasm though she knew he missed her terribly. He was still so young, and it would be at least two months before she saw either of them.

George was being painfully slow, moping around the drawing room, half-heartedly looking for a book he said he was reading but couldn't find, desperate to draw out the last few moments at home.

'Come on, boys, Stokes is waiting.' She was ushering them out, hands on their backs as she steered them out into the hall where Stokes stood, the small bag with their lunch for the train in his hand. 'Mr Grieves will meet you at the other end. Stokes will see you onto the train, and then just be dears and read quietly. Don't make a nuisance of yourself. I know you won't.'

They had said their brief goodbyes to their father the evening before, a cursory shake of the hand in the drawing room before dinner as they stood before him in their flannel pyjamas, slippers on and hair, newly cut for the return to school, combed neatly to the side. They waited, unsure if he was going to kiss them, and she willed something to come from Edward that she knew would not. This morning he was out riding – he wouldn't return till they were gone – and neither boy had made mention of him, though she felt their rejection in their quiet procession past the closed door of his study, a quick sidelong look at the room that, though empty, seemed to hold his presence still.

They walked out to the car, feet crunching on the gravel, breath freezing in the air, before she gave them both a hug, a quick rub of the head, a kiss, not wanting to prolong this part they hated so much before they got in. With the door still open, she leaned in to where George sat. 'I'll write all the time, I promise. Be good. And the holidays will come around again soon.' She closed the door gently, pulled her cardigan around herself and watched the car make its slow progress down the drive. George had his eyes on her, craning his neck and turning in his seat, not wanting to break the look between them. She waved, blew him a kiss, waved again till she couldn't make out his face any more, just the reflection in the glass of Harehope behind her.

She had carved out another two weeks in Paris, at the end of January, where she would see David. She needed him. The affection, the conversation, the tenderness that was entirely absent from her life here with Edward. But what of her boys? Summer felt an eternity away, but it would come. It would come, and the sun and the warmth, and the freedom from Edward and his judgement, would do what it always did. It would open up their lungs, allowing something different to be breathed in by them, without them even knowing it was happening, without them knowing what it did for them and why.

Jean turned back to the house. Took in its breadth as it waited for her, its current mistress, to return. She felt the pitch in the pit of her stomach, the pinch at her shoulders, braced herself for the battles to come. But she drew on the image of another place, of the house where her spirit resided, if not her body; of Antibes, where the sun cast its spell on the pale yellow stone of her house, where the scent of eucalyptus hung in the air and dusk came like a veil of velvet. She closed her eyes, saw David's face before her, breathed in the smell of jasmine, felt the tension within her ease.

She exhaled and walked back through the open door of Harehope once more.

PART III

CHAPTER ONE

Cap d'Antibes, 1936

A summer's day on the Riviera: exactly as the one that preceded it and the one that would surely follow. A flat line of azure on sapphire, with a heat so intense that the edges of Jean's vision blurred. Breakfast to be had, a paper to be read, correspondence written, a house to be corralled into shape; the boys to be delighted over, fussed over, scolded, embraced; lunch in the shade of a favourite tree, crisp linen, cold wine, mild talk. Expeditions to the beach after rests taken in dark rooms with minds blanketed by the thick, shuttered sleep of the afternoon. The sweet joy of nothingness – no curbs to one's pleasure, no sharp edges to one's thoughts. Summers here followed a divine pattern, a sweet memory to be clung to on damp days and empty nights back in England.

Each year Jean had come back at the beginning of July, staying until reality could be avoided no longer and September's realities hovered insistently at the edge of every thought. There was the year Alfie had learned to swim, spluttering and gasping, head barely above water, legs and arms kicking furiously below, a look of untold joy on his face as he made it to Jean's outstretched arms. The year the boys had discovered the lighthouse at La Garoupe, mesmerised by the scale of it, making little pilgrimages there each afternoon, where they'd sit in its shadow eating sandwiches prepared by Marie and dreaming up fantastical stories of ships smashed on the rocks below, brave sailors captured by marauding pirates, always desperate to catch a glimpse of the elusive *gardien de phare*. The summer David and she had spent a magical ten days alone before the boys were brought out. They hadn't seen a soul the whole time they were there, venturing only to their beach for swimming, and for a drive down the coast one day to the hills behind the bay of Escalet, taking a picnic and a bottle of gin and making martinis that made her eyes water, watching the sun come down on a world that felt theirs alone. These were enchanted days, a blur of freedom and happiness, rolling one to the next; summers in which Jean grew up, left behind the girl who'd first arrived in London all those years before.

It was nine o'clock and the boys were asleep upstairs – bodies splayed, skin dark against the pale linen from days spent on the beach – and Jean sat alone on the terrace. David hadn't been able to leave Paris until the night before, his editor eking the last work out of him before he was moved to the Nice office for the summer. The paper David wrote for now produced its own Riviera edition for American visitors, with a weekly roll call of distinguished arrivals, so commonplace were glamorous guests in these now fashionable summer months. David was the editor of this 'pamphlet', as he called it with a roll of his eyes, but it was convenient to be based near Jean for the months of July and August, with only the odd trip back to Paris if required.

She was never good at seeing him after a long break – it had been nearly four months this time – and had poured herself a drink and smoked two cigarettes in quick succession, fussing with the gramophone in the drawing room, before there came the familiar grinding of gravel in the drive. She stood up, pushing the chair back, tucking her hair behind her ears. It always took her a day or two to find her feet with him.

But then he was there, his hand around hers, a kiss that still stopped her heart, and he had pulled out her chair and was lighting her a cigarette before one for himself, smiling as he did it.

'The train was crammed. I spotted Jim Higgins from the *Chicago Sun* in the dining car but kept my head down. Couldn't bear to hear his tales of woe for the whole damn journey.'

She smiled, knowing he would now fix her a drink.

'Martini? The boys all quiet?' He knew his way around the bar, rubbing the lip of the shaker with lemon before pouring in the gin and vermouth, shaking it casually as he looked around for the glasses he knew she liked best. 'I haven't eaten, though. I'm ravenous. Is Marie still here?'

'They've all gone home, darling – I thought you'd prefer that for tonight. But I've asked her to leave us that lamb you like, and those herbed potatoes. Let's have a drink now. Just sit beside me, will you. Let me rest my head.'

They sat as she loved most, looking out and beyond the bay that had watched over their years here, swapping stories of the last few months like old friends as they drank. They had always had the ability to do this, however long they'd been apart; it was something she prized, needed desperately after the crumbs she lived off at Harehope. This time it was the troubles with his landlady in Paris – the novelty of the simple life he led there always charmed and fascinated her – and news from home that his father's health was failing; for her, it was the boys, small milestones and silly snippets from their lives in England.

'Will you be busy with the Nice edition this summer, do you think?'

'Well, they're all excited about your new King.' He loved ribbing her for being English now. 'And his girlfriend. They're in the Eastern Med, but will they come down here? Speculation on that alone's enough to keep it going for a month. And there's that new casino and restaurant opening at Cannes in August with a lavish party. Bound to draw all my readers' favourite sort.' He smiled wryly. 'But what's happening in Spain, that's the news they should care about. What's going on in Europe, really going on, I mean. But you know Max: "In sunny places they want to read about sunny faces," so I'll be reporting on beach parties and cocktail parties while mainland Europe's tripping into the hands of the fascists...'

This was his usual gripe: that he was forced to report on trivialities when the serious news was covered by real journalists, something he was no longer considered to be; but she felt that it was more than that now. She talked on, though there was a tug of anxiety in her stomach. 'And your house? I always wonder if Lisette does anything at all while you're not there. Far too tempting to stop at that little bar they all love so much, all that delicious gossip, all those young men for her to flirt with. How she hasn't married yet, I don't know.'

That smile again of his, edged with something. Not quite sadness, but knowledge. 'I've been talking to Max about my job. It's moving someplace he wants and I don't. I'm being pigeonholed by all this gossip writing, and it's not what I do. He won't allow anything in the paper that isn't useless fluff. It's not what I came to Europe for.'

'I know, I know. But it pays the bills, doesn't it?' She was soothing him, wanting to steer him away from where this was heading.

'Barely, you know. And I've never written the book I swore I would. Father mentioned it in his last letter, in passing, but it left its mark. What have I been doing all this time? I mean, really doing?'

'Loving me?' This was meant to be playful, but it sounded so sad, Jean felt her throat tighten.

'Of course. But I only get half of you – and yes, half is so splendid it carries me through, but lately it's been seeming like it's not enough. And I can't stay in France for ever, a half-life, living with half of you. And you know what I've realised? I've only got half of me to show for it all. No book, no writing of real merit. Just a popular byline on who's who and what's going on in Paris and down here. That's not what I came here for, went to Yale for, fought in France for. God, escaped my family for. And if I don't do something about it now, it'll all be too late and everything will have come to nothing.' He rubbed his face roughly – those hands she could draw from memory, brown and smooth – and she saw now that he was tired, tired behind the eyes and in his soul, and that somehow this summer was not going to be the blur of heat and love and companionship it always had been.

'Darling, you're tired and it's late. The boys will be up early, so you'll have to be gone too. Why don't I clear up and we can go to bed, and we'll talk about all this tomorrow. I promise this isn't me not listening. I just don't know if I can do it all now.'

And he did what he was so good at: he listened and nodded and smiled that generous smile that she loved more than any-thing about him. But it had a weariness to it tonight that made her feel afraid.

CHAPTER TWO

The Riviera that Jean had stumbled upon at Antibes in those hazy summer months in the mid 1920s, away from the genteel society of Monte Carlo and Nice, had been discovered by artists, intellectuals, writers. She and David could dip in and out of this world, able to remain relatively cut off but with enough of a life to give what they had together a dimension of reality. But where artists and writers go, money and society follow, and their little enclave, sleepy Juan-les-Pins and down-at-heel Antibes, had, over the years that followed, become something entirely different. Now summer here was a Season – there were casinos, beach restaurants and nightclubs springing up everywhere – cocktail parties and dinner parties, lunches for fifty at villas that would have looked at home in Hollywood, with couples swooping down the coast in fast cars at three in the morning to find one more drink and one more dance. Rex Ingram and his Victorine Studios had burnished the sparkling coast with a film-set gloss. Packed picture houses in England and America showed glamorous blondes whipping round the hairpin bends of the Corniche, only fuelling the popular desire for more, more, more of this dazzling Côte d'Azur of high summer.

Today she and the boys had been invited to lunch by an American couple, Shirley and Eddie West. She was mouth-wash and he railroads – a blessed union to be transformed into museum wings and foundations and public art collections, to be remembered long after its more prosaic origins were faded and gone. One accepted invitation gave Jean three more she could turn down without guilt, and so she'd found herself at their home: an elaborate complex of white buildings that clung to the rocks behind the road that ran between Cannes and Antibes. The house was reached by a bridge built over the railway line that ran along this part of the coast, a feat of engineering that must have dug deep into the owners' pockets. It had a large atrium hall, furniture that was spare and pale, and the focus of the room was a pair of enormous arched doors that gave on to a terrace almost as large as the footprint of Jean's whole house, now lined with three seemingly endless rows of linen-covered tables, bristling with starched napkins and silver and glass that glittered in the midday sun.

The boys were immediately whisked away, taken to join the other children at the bathing pool by a uniformed maid of limp enthusiasm, so Jean joined Shirley West and a group of her girlfriends as they sipped cocktails and swapped gossip. Cheeks were proffered; outfits complimented upon warily. The women were all, on the surface of things, 'dear' friends, but with that edge of uncertainty that a gathering of Americans on Europe's shores could give. The hierarchy could be so unclear. Jean was hard to pin, she knew; her money, and her husband's English title, was a royal flush. Her failure to appear – but why, but why? – at major social events weakened her hand considerably.

'All she wants is to be part of everything that's going on—' Jean had no idea who they were talking about.

'I know, I know. My telephone never stops ringing.' This from a blonde with a face like whipped cream, her hair swept back in a fashionable turban that did nothing for her undefined jaw.

'And I hear from Judy Walsh that she's desperate to come today because she knows you're all coming, and there's a whisper that Maxine Elliott might come. Not that we'll know the truth in that for at least another hour… But then I hear not a thing. Not a peep. It's too peculiar.'

'I call it bad manners.' The turban-headed woman was warming to her subject now, leaning forward and pulling her sunglasses down her nose.

'You won't say that if Maxine doesn't appear.'

They all giggled, united by an incontrovertible truth that knit them together once more, and a warmth descended as they cast around for the next subject to fill the half hour before lunch was served.

'I've got a little morsel for you all.' This came from a second blonde. She had a full mouth and heavily arched eyebrows, with a made-up face that was trying its best with ordinary features.

She had the room. Eyes swivelled as one.

'I've heard, from two highly regarded sources, that a certain Mrs Simpson is making arrangements to sue for divorce.' A dramatic pause. 'On the grounds of adultery.'

'Who told you?' Shirley's voice rose in excitement. The women leaned forward as one, eyes fixed on the speaker.

'I can't say, but a friend of my husband's has a nephew at the embassy in London and apparently that's the rumour beginning to circulate. It hasn't made it into the papers in America yet – or here.' She looked at Jean. 'They don't write a thing about it in England. Isn't that so?' The collective gaze moved hungrily to Jean.

'No. But the rumours are there, you're right. I'm just not sure the establishment will be able to accept it.'

'Can't bear an American getting her hands on their King. What does your husband think? He's a peer, isn't he? You'll have a front-row seat at the coronation, surely?'

The familiar barb of jealousy.

'My husband doesn't approve. The King is head of the Church. How could he marry someone who's divorced? But they don't see each other often these days – it was much more when they were younger, before he was King, and they were only really racing friends, and Edward's fearfully discreet about all that anyway.'

'So your husband's not here today?'

'No, no. He prefers to be in England at this time of year. I can never drag him out.'

A wreath of polite smiles. 'He doesn't come at all? How marvellous for you. We should all learn your trick – I can't keep my husband away.' And the little arrow's dart made its mark.

Jean smiled, she was practised at it, and the group broke apart. All along the terrace now, guests were skirting round the tables, feigning nonchalance but eyes scanning anxiously for their place to learn how their hostess ranked them. These were the people that made up this coast now: slim women in silk pyjama pants, hair cut short to a number, faces made up, skin bronzed. The men wore elegant, collared shirts and tailored cotton trousers; gone were the rough sailor stripes and old-style bathing suits affected by the groups of artists and writers and the wealthy avant-garde that had gathered on the beach at La Garoupe. The assembled guests of today were what came after: the rich, the glamorous, those desperate to be seen.

She was looking for her seat when a scream from somewhere down below the terrace split the air. There followed a scuffle, the scraping of chairs on stone and then a distinct splash.

Shirley walked towards the edge of the terrace to see what the commotion was, the turbaned woman behind her, clearly delighted by the whiff of drama. Jean followed as Shirley's husband appeared, irritated by the distraction.

'What's going on down there. Shirley? Is this something to do with you?'

To Jean's horror, Alfie was being pulled up the stairs by the maid of before, all limpness evaporated, a firm grip at his wrist in its stead. His clothes were sopping wet, his face red and jaw set in anger. She ran down the steps that led from the terrace to the pool. 'Darling, what's happened? Where is George? Are you all right?'

'Madam, your son was extremely rude to one of the other children, and tried to hit him. The other boy defended himself, and I am afraid your son ended up in the pool.'

George was now coming up the stairs, followed by three more boys of a similar age, one of whom – the tallest, the beginnings of angry adolescent pimples appearing around his mouth – she knew to be Shirley's older boy. He looked to be enjoying the attention, rushing up the steps and pushing past the other two.

'What's going on? Harry, do stop all this commotion. We're trying to have an adult lunch up here.' Eddie was trying to take control of the situation, aware that all his lunch guests had come to watch the entertainment unfold.

Harry was breathless by the time he reached the top and had beaten Alfie, whose rage had not dissipated, although he was keeping his eyes on the ground. 'It was the Barford boys. They were ragging the other two. Teasing the one with the funny arm' – Alfie winced – 'asking him if he knew how to swim yet or if he'd sink to the bottom. All that sort of thing—'

Eddie interrupted him. 'Now listen here, Harry. I think we ought to let the boys speak before you speak for them. I'm sure they wouldn't provoke him without good cause—'

'Oh, but they did.' With the bluntness of youth, Harry carried on. 'And then Alfie asked them to stop, and they said why did he care, his brother was a cripple and everyone knew it. And that it didn't matter anyway because everyone knew that Alfie would get everything and George was just the useless spare. And that's when Alfie tried to swing a punch. Only the other boy ducked and then his brother ran at him and pushed Alfie into the pool.'

George had now made his way up the stairs, followed by the Barford brothers, glowing with pride at the victory they'd had over Alfie, a flicker of uncertainty as they took in the adults gathered on the balcony. Alfie's head was low now.

'Is this true, Alfie? Did you try and hit this boy?' Jean's voice was even, but inside her heart was hammering.

'Yes, Mama, but—'

'I asked you a question, and that was all. I'd like you to apologise to these boys for what you did, and to Mrs West for causing all this commotion, and I think we'd better make our excuses.'

'But Mama—'

'No more, thank you. Do as I say. George, come with me too, please.' Jean turned, taking George by the hand, and gave Shirley a quick kiss on the cheek. 'Darling, I'm so sorry about all this. Such a scene. And right before your lunch. I shouldn't have brought the boys – idiotic of me, without help. Would you mind awfully if I took them home? I'm not sure how the afternoon will turn out if I don't.'

She asked one of the maids for a fresh towel for Alfie to be brought to her car, and the trio made their way back through the vast hall, the sound of water dripping as Alfie trudged behind, taking up the rear. George looked up at his mother, unsure of his role in all of this drama.

CHAPTER THREE

They were sitting at the low bench on their terrace now, the boys on either side of her, towels draped over narrow shoulders, their necks brown and salty from the last swim of the day. The sun had lost its intensity, and the warmth that remained felt soft on their skin. Jean looked to each boy: Alfie, slighter, more upright, as if a string held him taut; George, softer, a curve of golden skin, damp swimsuit clinging to his thighs.

'You know that I will always love you both and look after you both, just the same, come what may.'

She had their attention now; they were looking up at her, not recognising the timbre of her voice, expecting a scolding but hearing something else. Alfie in particular was alert to her, watching her warily.

'I'm sure your father would want to talk to you about this, but after what happened today, I feel I must say something.'

George was looking at her, but Alfie had his eyes on the ground before him now, tracing a line on the stone with his toe. Patches of sand still clung to his shins and toes where he hadn't dried himself properly.

'In England, things pass from eldest son to eldest son. It's the way it is, as simple as that. How Harehope came to Papa, and to his father before him. And the same thing will happen for us too. George, we've talked about this before, about how you and I, later on, will have a different path, one that doesn't involve Harehope and everything that goes with it. But it doesn't mean anyone is better than anyone else, or more loved. It's just how our world works, always has, always will. And it's something that everyone knows about us. As known and as unchangeable as our names or the colour of our eyes. A fact: as bald as that. But those boys today' – and she looked at both of them in turn – 'they are just ignorant fools. They don't know what it means to be us, or who we really are. And that is what you must remember, must always remember.'

Alfie kept his head low. George looked briefly to his brother to say something, but when he didn't, he looked at Jean. 'I know that already, Mama. I know Harehope's not mine. It's fine, I promise.' And he shifted closer to her, resting his head against her shoulder, and, slipping his good hand into her lap, reached for hers. They sat in silence, she wasn't sure for how long, the sky moving away, the sea drawing nearer; but the tableau at some point shifted. George and her, a pair; Alfie, a breath apart, carrying his little burden of guilt, a parcel all his own, now glinting and cold, wrapped up in his brother's gentle and absolute acceptance.

That night she sat with David on the terrace, the boys asleep, her plate untouched before her.

'I couldn't be angry with Alfie – how could I be? But as much as I wanted to slap those other children, they'd only said the truth. Primogeniture, it's necessary to the survival of these estates, keeping them whole. Look at the endless counts and dukes and princes in Italy with nothing to speak of to their name, everything fragmented till worthless crumbs are left. But in England it's brutal in how it falls, cleaving brother from brother, particularly mine, so close in age, anointing one and discarding the other. In other families, I'm sure it's the father who would sit down and explain the reasoning that runs behind it all. But Edward can barely be in the same room as both of them, so it's my gift to deliver.'

'You're not new to this, though, come on.' His smile was gentle but his eyes said something different. The question of her money had begun to nag at them.

'I remember my father talking to me about my future when I was about Alfie's age. Oliver was older and a boy, so the newspaper was the natural place for him, but I was assured that I would never want for anything. I'd always known there were trusts and arrangements and responsibilities to come – every day on my way to school I passed museums where my grandfather's name was carved into the walls – but it was somehow unimportant too. I know that may seem hard to believe, but it's just different in America. My mother is the source of our money – her father put my uncle and her on a near equal footing. Here it's so stark.'

He was looking at her warily and she saw it there again, the little line drawn between them.

'And it's my guilt. I can't get away from it, the way George accepts it all so gently. I know this has happened before' – she looked down; it felt so blunt to discuss this part of it all with David – 'but you must see, when it's my life, my boys, my Alfie who always holds out his hand to help George climb over a gate, who's always looking back when they're running along the beach to make sure George is following, and now, throwing a punch at those two oafish boys who aren't worth the ground they stand on...' She stopped, took a breath. 'It makes my chest ache. The lie is in everything they do, that they will do, for ever. And it comes directly from me. The person who supposedly loves them best.'

David got up to make himself another drink. 'You can even things out, though, can't you? Make sure George gets some of your family's money?' His back was turned to her now and he said this over his shoulder, feigning nonchalance. 'I'm sure your mother would agree to that. Buy him a house somewhere, fix up another trust.' He turned back now, a hint of impatience to his voice. 'Isn't that what you people do? Settlements and trusts, trusts and settlements, getting more and more complicated until there isn't a lawyer alive that can unpick them?'

'I know she intends to leave him something. She said as much. She knows how it works in England. But I still feel that guilt eating away at me, that what those brutes said today is how the world sees it. Perfect Alfie, inheritor of the earth – defective George, never mind about him. And it's George's bloody acceptance and Edward's disgust—' Her voice cracked here, and she couldn't go on. What was the point? She had seen this scenario building and growing more real from the moment George had been born.

'But this is what frustrates me. Why not get away from it all? If it pains you so much to watch this thing grow, to see how it eats at Edward, then cut yourself off from it all. What is this marriage you are in? It's poison. Divorce.' He came and sat back down at the table, looking directly at her now. This was what had been brewing the night before.

'How could I? Edward would never allow it. You forget the wrong was mine. He may be a brute and our marriage a lie, but I am the one at fault. And what would it do to the boys?'

'Don't you see, though, that you hold the cards? This bloody money that everyone in your world is too polite and too English to talk openly about – it's all yours. He needs you for your money, and you've already given him more than enough of it. Come on, you've told me that. You've shored up that house in the country, you've paid the servants, you bought back the house in London for them, bought the art, the furniture. So you can leave him. If you go, he can keep all that, but you've got more. It's limitless, isn't it? Isn't that the whole damn point?' He was breathless now, stirred up but alive with it, as if all the listening and the talking and the gentleness was coming away and revealing the truth of what he felt, what he had covered up for so long. 'You don't know how many days and nights I've thought about what we could do if you were divorced. I could leave France, could go back to America. We could marry, make a home in New York. I could write properly. We could live together.' His voice was getting louder. 'Imagine the freedom we would have to be together, openly, and what that would give the boys.'

'You really think that could happen? With who I am, and who Edward is?' Her voice was quiet. 'You don't understand it at all.' She felt so tired. The battles ahead, the failures to come. 'People care about the exterior. They don't care if I'm miserable or spending my summers with you, or never speak to my husband, or if Alfie doesn't look quite like his father, so long as I'm still Lady Warre, outwardly doing what I ought to be doing. I'm public property. This money that you think enables me to do what I like, it doesn't, it's the opposite. It means I can't ever hide, and everyone can have an opinion and a judgement whenever they damn well like.'

She cried then, because she knew that this life she had created here, this place of freedom and happiness, was a lie. That it didn't stand up when it was pushed; it cracked, and crumbled, and fell away. What it revealed was the grubby little truth that she had always known was there – that she had slept with a man and he had fathered her child and the world could never know that. David had made it bearable, had loved her despite it, had carried her through it, but now he needed something real too, and that didn't exist.

He leaned across the table and wiped her tears with his thumbs. 'I can't give up this easily. I can't. I've spent twelve years loving you, living here, watching those boys. I can't settle for this. I can't. Then I'd be just like him, when what I want is truth and essence and real, real life. We can have that, you and I. I know we can. You just need to be strong and see that it's possible – sometimes you have to break things to remake them. Don't be some Edith Wharton Newland Archer figure, don't choose the path society wants you to choose. Break free. You are so much more than all of that.'

She nodded, her head low, hands in her lap. Her mind was a blur of alleys she knew how to run down now – God, she had done this a thousand times. Could she go to Edward, could she ask him, suggest there was a better way to live? But the alleys never led to an answer, only another turn down a darker, narrower path, where branches hung low and the ground was thick with leaves and her feet faltered beneath her.

David was talking, his voice soft. 'I watched Alfie on the beach yesterday. He was looking at the minnows darting in the shallows. He told me he loved watching them – the way they swam, that they were separate but one. I love the way he comes to the nub of things. Maybe all young boys do. But he was looking at me so straight, I had to look away. Half of him is me, and he doesn't know it. Maybe he never will. But he's my son. And I love him too.' His head was to one side, hands stretched out across the table to her. She let him take hers in his, felt the warmth and the comforting familiarity, let him soothe her, bring her back.

'Tell me what to do then, please. Just tell me.'

'Go to your mother. I've been thinking this all spring. It's the only way. I know you, and you need someone from your side to give you the strength to do this. She will listen. She must miss you hugely, being over here, and if she sees how wretched your marriage makes you, and how happy you could be, she will give you her blessing. How could she not? You're her only daughter. You've never done anything wrong before – God, look at Oliver and what he's put her through. She owes you her support. And you know how powerful her opinion is.'

'But divorce?'

'For God's sake don't tell her the truth about Alfie, that would be too much. But tell her about your marriage. Tell her your fears for George, and she can help him too. Think what would be possible then. You would have done right by everyone.'

'But what about the boys? Alfie can't leave England. What about Harehope?'

'Don't try and solve it all at once. He's twelve years old. Edward is still a young man, and Alfie's time is a long way off. He could have his holidays with us. I don't know…I just can't let this' – he looked around – 'let this be it. It's not a whole life. We deserve more than this. I know we do.'

They sat that night for another hour, maybe two. Drinking more, till the taste of the gin was bitter in her mouth; talking and smoking and then falling into silence again. Always coming back to David's need for her to go to her mother, to confess, to receive the absolution that would give her the strength to seek a divorce. The grind of the cicadas and the whisper of the sea began to wear on her. It no longer soothed but seemed to nag instead, reminding her that this place had a soul and a life that needed tending to. It was not a background; it needed nurturing, responding to, or it would turn too.

She wanted to go upstairs to bed and close her eyes, to lie with him next to her and just feel him, the weight of his body, beside her. But David didn't stay that night, kissing her instead once on the head before walking quietly round the house to where he had left his bicycle propped up against the kitchen wall. So she sat alone at the table, listened to the sound of the gate closing behind him and the light tread of the wheels on the gravel, and then he was gone, and it was just her thoughts and the slip and slide of the sea, over and over and over.

CHAPTER FOUR

Her head throbbed as she sat at the breakfast table, her coffee undrunk. All was perfection around her – the crisp linen of the tablecloth, the porcelain decorated with its motif of olives and lemons, chosen by Constance and hand-painted in Paris, the view down to the beds of lavender that lined the lawn, still green and lush despite the best efforts of the July sun – but still the dull ache at her temples lingered. And the conversation of the night before.

The door from the drawing room onto the terrace opened and George made his way down towards her, still in his pyjamas, their cotton crumpled, his hair sticking up at the back from sleep. Instinctively her arms were open and he let her hug him, leaning into her before stretching out to take a piece of bread from the basket on the table.

'Hungry, darling?'

He nodded, taking a seat beside her, and she let him be, the pair sitting in happy silence as he pulled himself back from the hold of sleep. Eventually he spoke. 'I had a nightmare, Mama. Last night.'

'Oh, darling, I'm sorry. Did you wake Alfie?'

'I didn't. I thought I'd come to you, but your room was empty. It was so late, but you weren't there. And then I looked out of your window, and you were at the table, here, you and David. You looked so sad. What were you talking about?'

'Oh, nothing, my darling, nothing at all. It was just grown-up talk.'

'I heard you say my name, and Alfie's. Why were you talking about us to him? Was it about the fight yesterday at the party?'

She kissed the top of his head and ruffled his hair. 'Honestly, nothing that need bother you. And nothing to do with yesterday's nonsense, I promise. Why don't we go and see if Alfie is up? We could go for a swim. See if anyone's about on the beach.'

He looked up and nodded, sliding off his chair and skirting back round the table and into the house. There was no sense of danger. He was still at the age where he accepted what was put before him, where what he sought was reassurance. She knew he would think nothing more of last night, would go and find Alfie and forget about the bad dream he'd had, but if it had been Alfie, now on the threshold of entering another room in his life, he would have needed and pushed to know more. He would be going to Eton in a year: another chapter for him, another step away and to adulthood.

The mother she was to these boys was something Jean had tried so hard at. Not to let them grow up as strangers, to be presented to her after bath time, washed and pressed; to be talked of as if at one remove. She had wanted, indeed had fought for, the boys to be brought up as she understood was necessary. To have a mother whose love for them was visible, unashamed and uninhibited. She could see at first hand what the accepted upbringing at Harehope had created in Edward. Jean had never seen Edward's mother more than turn her cheek upwards to receive a kiss from him; never seen her show more affection to him than she had her servants, and certainly not as much as she showed her dogs. She was still haunted by the way Alice had received Charles' old tutor like an unsavoury tenant, impervious to the emotion that he could barely contain though he'd known her son only four years.

When they were small Jean had encouraged the boys to be physical with her, much more than she knew her contemporaries did. When they went away to prep school she had written to them every day, sending them letters thick with kisses and scraps of poems and silly riddles to make them laugh, little caricatures of what was going on at home or in London. She never knew what good this would do them, this loving of them in a way so different to the absent disdain of their father. Perhaps it confused them more, drawing attention to the chasm between their parents and a marriage they must have been aware, even dimly, was cold and empty.

She had prevented David from getting too close to them at first. Had drawn a line between the time she spent with him as an adult and the time he spent with her as a mother of these two boys. But it had become impossible: if they spent an afternoon together on the beach, even as part of a large group, David couldn't hold back from slipping into a role that came so naturally. He would read with them in the shade, delighting in English stories he'd never read as a child – he adored Hilaire Belloc, reading the verses aloud, the two boys entranced by his impersonations and silly poses, laughing when he tried to ape their English accents. And so she shrugged, pushing away the doubts always watching at the periphery. It was a gift, she would tell herself resolutely, to have this generous spirit in their lives, however nebulous his role. They were just boys, and this man who was present for several weeks each summer, mainly in the background, sometimes to the fore, was a gift as welcome to them after the chill of England as the nourishing heat of the sun on their faces or the sweet pulpy flesh of the figs that they would pull from the tree and eat, skin still warm, as they ran down to the beach to swim.

They would dine out tonight, she decided. She would give David that. She would put on a dress, do her hair the way he liked it, and have a drink somewhere on their way home, perhaps listen to some music or walk along the promenade at Juan-les-Pins. They would be a couple like any other, absorbed in each other's company, a breath apart from the world around them, eyes alight for each other alone.

Jean and David walked along the seafront that ran along the main drag of the town. Now it was all bright lights and made-up faces where once it had been bedraggled and unkempt, startled by the attention it received from those early Americans who had sensed its possibilities. They had a drink at the Belles Rives, sitting in silence for a while, side by side, taking in the crowds, hands held under the table, her ankles resting against his. They walked then to dinner; she had made a reservation on the terrace at the Auberge du Pin Doré, which was popular with the fashionable set, but she had made sure to ask for a table back from the street, away from the eyes of the locals and visitors making their passeggiata in the soothing heat of the evening.

David was tired, she could tell. Ground down by the weight of their conversation the night before, her failure to give him a definitive answer. They ordered their drinks, the buzz of the restaurant only highlighting their inability to find each other's thoughts. They used to be able to start conversations in their middle, their minds keeping pace even when there were no words, their moods and thoughts as one. Tonight they were stopping and starting, missing the connections, the effect of the drinks lowering rather than lifting their spirits. There was so much noise coming from the next table that Jean struggled to make herself heard over their shouting and laughing.

Their food arrived, though she knew neither of them really wanted it, so they pushed it around their plates instead and David ordered another round of drinks. He caught a man's eye as he walked up the steps from the street onto the restaurant's terrace, a much younger woman following behind him. David looked down, irritated.

'What's the matter? Who is that?'

'It's my editor. It's Max. I knew he was in the area, but he was meant to be in Cannes with his wife.'

'Will he come over?' She looked back up again to see Max snaking his way purposefully through the sea of tables to theirs. The young woman, now wearing a sour look on her face, was being shown to her table elsewhere, piqued that he hadn't followed her. Max's features were large, with heavy brows and a hairline that began a little too far back on his head for him to be handsome.

'David, how are you?'

David smiled but did not offer to introduce Jean, and Max looked across at her, waiting for her to say something, enjoying David's discomfort.

She reached out her hand. 'Jean Warre. How do you do?'

'Max Smith. My pleasure. I'm sorry to interrupt. David always implies he's something of a hermit down here. Hates my forcing him to attend all these openings and parties.'

David pushed his fork across his plate, signalling that they were still halfway through their dinner.

'Do you mind if we join you? It's not every day I'm in Juan-les-Pins with one of my writers in such elevated company.'

Of course David's editor knew who she was. Jean's mother owned the parent paper in New York that David and Max had worked for since it had merged with its rival some ten years before. While Max was entirely autonomous as editor of the Paris edition and Elizabeth Buckman's role was purely financial, if he was an editor worth his salt he would know Jean's name and the vast sums her family ploughed into the paper that her late father had so adored, despite its now faltering profits.

'Sure, do. Jean, would you mind?'

'Of course not, please do.'

Tables were shifted, tablecloths changed, more drinks produced, and all the while Jean could see the discomfort in David's eyes at his inability to control the situation and Max's obvious delight at his unease. The woman with Max was now brought over, introduced as a 'friend' with a little smirk. Her expression had now shifted from put out to lights on, sensing Max's interest in this pair they'd joined.

Max leaned in to make himself heard over the din of the restaurant. 'So how do you know David?'

'Oh, we were introduced by mutual friends a while ago.'

'And you have a house down here?'

'Yes, not far from here, just above that little bay, l'Anse de l'Argent Faux, at Antibes, if you know it. I've had it for a while now. This town has changed so much. You could barely persuade a place to stay open for a drink when I first got here.'

'And now it's quite the scene, isn't it? Keeps David busy down here in the summer.'

'I would imagine it does.' She kept her voice even. She didn't care what this man thought, but she didn't have the spirit to change the subject.

Max leaned across the table to David now, interrupting his girlfriend. 'This calls for a celebration, David – we have Jean Warre, daughter of our esteemed paper's owner, sitting at the same table as its humble editor and star social columnist. We must have champagne!' He summoned over the waiter, whose eyes lit up at the prospect of some liberal American spending to brighten the end of an evening service. 'Champagne, monsieur, your finest.'

Jean sipped the champagne dutifully, not what she felt like drinking in the heat; reached for her cigarettes. Max talked on at her, knocking back his champagne, pouring more, waving constantly at familiar faces that passed their table. He was not popular but ubiquitous. His tenure as editor had been a long one, and he had resolutely stuck to the Right Bank society angle, steering clear of the more literary and artistic slant of his rival. He had no interest in being overtly political either. Jean knew that time and again David had put himself forward to write about what was happening in Italy and now in Spain, to draw the paper's American expat readers' attention to the shift in Europe, to the creep of fascist boots on this continent's soil, to alert them to the gathering clouds, but Max had always said no. It was a paper whose news was society, whose content was glamour and parties and an endless list of names. Privately it was known that Max was an isolationist who felt Hitler and his cronies should be left to do as they wished. He had even allowed fascist advertisements – swastikas and jackboots that he knew many of his writers had found distasteful – to creep into the paper. 'Ad money is ad money' was his response to anyone's questioning.

She eventually made her excuses, feigning tiredness, and Max called for the bill, demanding he pay for it, so delightful had been his evening spent in the company of Lady Warre. As they rose to say their goodbyes, Max shook David's hand. 'Quite a catch you've found, old sport. Won't need to worry about putting your salary up, will I?' This last comment was made just loud enough for Jean to hear, and Max patted David's shoulder chummily, giving a final oily smile to Jean before nudging his girlfriend forward through the tables, and they were away, leaving Jean and David to follow in their wake.

They walked in silence back to their car, their earlier enthusiasm for another drink after dinner now gone. Jean slipped her hand into David's, hoping the simple action would let him know she understood it all. That this summer was not the one they had thought it would be. That the road was running out beneath them.

'I'll go to my mother. At the end of this summer. Give me two more weeks here, and then I'll take the boys back to England and I'll go and see her.'

'I think we have to do this. I can't go on like this. I can't.'

His hand was tighter around hers, and they were walking now down the busy stretch of the town, between other couples leaving dinner, the night young, heading on to the casino with its brassy lights or the bars that now played jazz every night.

'We can't let all these years amount to nothing. He's my son too.' His words were almost lost in the noise of the crowds. She wished she hadn't heard them.

Eventually her hand dropped and a pair of young men, eager to get somewhere, pushed between her and David, sending her towards the metal balustrade that divided the promenade from the beach. They were far enough apart now for her to look sideways at him, tall and proud, so handsome. There was always that flicker of the physical within her when she looked at him, but then she felt a well of sorrow rise. It was becoming so hard, so full of effort, creaking and gearing up to make this thing that had begun involuntarily, like a rush of blood, keep moving. She wondered with a lurch whether this was what happened with all affairs. That the push and drive of desire and the all-consuming urge to see it fulfilled at any cost could then fall away, without either party realising it was happening, leaving them both exposed on the sand, the tide out, an incongruous pair somehow, without the swell and surge of passion to make sense of them.

She found his hand again. 'We'll find a way. I promise.'

CHAPTER FIVE

Jean kept her word, making plans for the boys' return at the end of the month and writing to her mother. She could imagine the tremble of excitement in Elizabeth Buckman's voice as she read her daughter's letter, could feel her disappointment that the boys wouldn't be joining her to be paraded around the city; could anticipate the usual rush of plans that would be put forward, who must be called upon, who it was no longer necessary for her to see. Jean's mother had somehow ossified since her husband's death, frozen before the crash, before even the war perhaps, crystallised in the old New York, when society was small and newcomers, a term Elizabeth used liberally, were treated with a ferocious disdain. Though she had moved like many of her tribe to a vast apartment on Madison Avenue, when the need to modernise – those words spoken with a shiver – had seen the demolition of many of the mansions of the city's gilded age, she lived entirely unchanged, her dresses shipped from Worth and only worn a season after they were made for fear of being seen as at the whim of fashion, keeping the same French eighteenth-century furniture, the same Sèvres porcelain and Baccarat glass, linen from Italy, running her household as she always had and as her own mother had done before her, with a suite of servants bobbing and fanning and acquiescing to this small, grey-haired woman of narrow beliefs but steely opinion.

The rest of the summer passed not in the blur of previous years but in a sequence of poignant tableaux, of which Jean and David were painfully aware. Each walk along her beach, each drive to dinner, each drink at dusk with the heat of the sun still baked into their skin had an edge of sadness; not regret, but the feeling that a change was coming, and neither knew quite what it would be. David was being called back to Paris. Finally Max had seen that the situation in Spain needed more than simply regurgitating the news feeds that came in from the US, and allowed David to coordinate reporters on the ground from the paper's main office. Not that these stories made the front page. They were relegated instead to the paper's stodgy middle, lost amid announcements of guests staying on the Croisette and photographs of Edward and Mrs Simpson sunning themselves on a boat in Croatia, her squinting into the sun, shoulders like rails, his arm around her, territorial, defiant. The battle between right and left in Spain was mere background noise.

They sat now at the table on the terrace, a glass of Pernod for David, an orange pressé for her that she knew she could not drink. The heat was oppressive, buzzing about their ears like an unwanted fly, and David was hot and uncomfortable in his clothes for the train, damp patches under his arms, checking his wristwatch involuntarily. The boys were down at the beach, playing with the gardener's son, and David had come up to the house to say goodbye. It would be the last time they would see each other for a while.

She put her hands across the table to him, as she had done countless times before, but his touch was hesitant and he let go too soon, walking over to his jacket that hung on the back of a chair instead, feeling for his cigarettes in the inside pocket. He took one from the packet, lighting it quickly, its smoke hanging in the still, hot air.

'I feel like this place is on the turn, you know. Juan-les-Pins, Antibes; they're like overripe fruit, the scent is sickly, past its best. This used to be a place of possibility, where we could be who we wanted to be. Not any more. Real life has caught up somehow. Everyone we rate has left. It used to be art, modernism, ideas, beautiful ideas that we talked about endlessly. Now it's just suntans and the stench of Europe's politics. You read *Tender Is the Night*? If that's not a metaphor for what has happened to this place, then I don't know what is.' He sat back down and took a sip of his drink, but he didn't look up at her. 'I'm broke. It was so easy when I first came out here. My salary stretched and anything was possible. Now my francs are nothing. It's embarrassing. And the words I churn out every day, I feel like they taunt me with their mediocrity.'

'Oh, come on, David. You know that's never been important. There's so much more—'

'It doesn't feel charming any more, my life out here. You've never been overt about all this' – he gestured roughly to the house behind her – 'but it's almost comic how much you have, to my dwindling little. I don't want to become some washed-out, faded copy of the man you fell in love with. This place, it's paralysing me. I need to move forward, away from here, back to America.'

'But can you see this isn't easy for me? I have to break everything up. I'm the one with so much at stake.' She snapped the last words.

He kept his voice low. 'I'm painfully aware that you have everything, that I have little to lose. But that's it, isn't it? It's the truth of it. If you don't do this – risk this – it can't ever be.'

She saw the lines under his eyes then, that he was pale beneath his tan. They weren't as young as they once had been. And he could be martyrish, doomed to be downtrodden and betrayed; someone to make others feel bad for a situation of his own making. But then came the riposte: she was nothing without David in her life, and his need for her to leave Edward was a need articulated for both of them. He was the brave one in the pair for forcing it. She had created a sham existence in England that was no good for anyone. She must leave Edward. It was no life with him, and so there she came, full circle, back on herself and her decision to seek a divorce.

Jean walked round to where he sat. He was rubbing his forehead, head down, his agitation stretched throughout his body. She knelt before him, took his face in her hands. 'I'm sorry I was angry. I'm just nervous, that's all.' She kissed him briefly, then pushed herself up to standing as the boys' voices drifted up to her from the steps. Alfie was jogging up the stairs first, ball in hand, with George following behind, one arm trailing the wall. She kissed them both, but when she turned back to the terrace, one last word of farewell on her lips, David had already gone. The ashtray, his empty glass and a reproach that seemed to hang in the air were the only remnants of their imperfect goodbye.

She travelled alone by boat to New York. The crossing was rough, great rollers in the mid-Atlantic keeping the boat, despite its size, in a constant, queasy motion. The bustling staff did their best to distract their passengers – there were dances and dinners and musical performances laid on each night, but all were at half-attendance, and only by the valiant half who talked stoically in loud voices about sea legs and English resolve, all the while looking peaky and green. Jean, for the most part, kept herself to her cabin, venturing out only on the two nights when it was impolite to decline an invitation to dine at the captain's table, an event she endured rather than enjoyed, placed at both between a retired MP who had known her father-in-law at school and insisted on telling her in great detail about the architecture of Harehope, and his near-deaf wife, who would turn sweetly to Jean every so often and smile absent-mindedly before returning to her food in happy silence.

Away from her children, away from David, from anyone who knew her well, not yet in the sphere of her mother but far from Harehope, Jean was truly alone. The sensation would momentarily soothe her, sitting in her cabin, her book unopened before her, weightless between England and America, no hands on her, no demands to be met. But this no man's land, this liner with its faceless guests busying themselves diligently with a frantic schedule of nothing, soon became a symbol of her non-existence. She was the problem, a misfit who certainly didn't belong in England to her English lord and his acres; it was his identity ground into the damp stone and rugged soil, even if her money had done the digging. But as she sat, palms down on the desk in her suite, looking towards the country of her birth, she wasn't sure if she belonged there either.

CHAPTER SIX

The morning sky was clear and blue; that hopeful Manhattan blue that she always thought of when she called to mind the city of her birth. From the cocoon of her mother's cream Phantom, Jean watched it now with a stranger's eye, and she lowered the window to breathe in the life of it all as they weaved through streets teeming with workers heading out for their day. They passed aproned shopkeepers standing, arms folded, outside grocery stores; news stands screaming with papers and pamphlets and magazines that hadn't existed ten years before; a tinker's cart clanking tin pots and saucepans and bowls and lids as it lumbered alongside a snake of schoolgirls in prim hats and pinafores, following a stern-faced nun. But this was no town for silent judgement – everything, no sooner thought, was spat out to be heard. New York had an irrepressible energy, seemingly unhampered by the crushing Depression.

Jean had read about the horrors of the crash: men throwing themselves from buildings, their bodies cartwheeling through the air like rag dolls; respectable people forced to beg on the streets of her home town, unthinkable really; she had read too of the destitution of the Dust Bowl states, seen images of women with eyes enlarged by hunger to a spectral size, children with stomachs distended by the ache for food. Yet despite all that there was still a tempo to this city – that eternal desire of those who had fought to come here, to keep the great cogs turning and to reach up their fingers till they caught the next rung of the ladder. It was a pulse so strong she could hear its beat on this bright, faultless morning.

As the car continued uptown, into the more sedate neighbourhood of her mother's apartment, she saw too how much of the city's skyline had changed in the years since she had left. She could remember when the tallest building she would crane her neck up at was the Singer Tower, almost incomprehensible to her then in its scale. The Chrysler Building and the Empire State now dwarfed it, like churches of the future, with their spires that pierced the sky. The stone majesty of her parents' building remained unchanged though, impervious to the pull and scrape of metal and steel taking place around it. The same butler, the same bobbing maids with arms outstretched for bag and coat, and there was her mother to receive her, a collar as elaborate as Elizabeth I, her face more lined than Jean remembered, her hair immobile as granite. She always held both hands out before her for Jean to take before they embraced, a little affectation adopted from her days in Europe; then a tilt of the head to receive a kiss on that skin as soft as kid, with its scent of rose and geranium worn like a wreath around her.

'Come to the drawing room, darling, you look exhausted from your trip. See that her bags go to the Chinese Room. Jean, come with me, and we'll sit and talk and have some tea. I want to hear everything, everything.' And she was off up the stairs, the servants parting for this masterful little woman, queen of her Madison Avenue realm.

The room was just as Jean had last seen it, its walls a pale yellow, a bust of her father on a marble plinth at the centre, an elaborate hang of eighteenth-century old master drawings on the wall that faced the windows. Books lined one end of the room and a fireplace sat opposite, where logs burned whatever the climate outside. Elizabeth had placed herself on the large silk sofa, a pearl in an oyster, and patted for Jean to sit beside her.

'My darling, I've been so excited to have you here. I've been making sure you can see everyone you'll need to, and I'm giving a dinner tomorrow night at the Knickerbocker in your honour. And then I thought a lunch perhaps here for the Phippses and the Goelets, and if there was anyone else you think we should ask to join. Marjorie Lawrence is closing her run of Wagner at the Met tonight too and everyone will be there, and I was hoping you might then come along to a little dinner after at Mrs Arthur's? She's so keen for you to see their new apartment. It has been done by your marvellous Constance on my recommendation and I think it would mean so much if you were to go and have a look.'

The conversation continued, with Jean nodding and accepting all the plans her mother put forward, Elizabeth patting her hand occasionally and reminding her of how tired she looked, but all the while Jean wondered when in all this lunching and dining and visiting she was to sit down and tell her why she had really come.

'And what of the boys? Are they well? At Harehope with Edward? I asked for some books to be sent to them for their next term at school – Father would have hated for them not to have some of his old Latin and Greek primers he kept all these years, though I'm sure they'd rather have new editions.'

'They are both in excellent form. As close as ever, thick as thieves sometimes. Alfie's doing very well at school, though he'd never admit it.'

'And Edward? I haven't written to him in a while, I feel terribly remiss, but one gets so caught up with life here in the city. How is Harehope?'

'Edward is well. He'll be glad to hear you've asked after him.' She paused. 'If it's all right, I might go to my room now and have a look over my things, if the girls have unpacked. I hope that doesn't seem rude. The crossing was rough and everything was put into my bags in such a hurry when we came in that I'm sure they will have left something out.'

'Oh, my dear. And I've been prattling on while you've been longing to have a rest. Do, of course, go at once. I've arranged nothing at all today. Just a lunch in a little while over at the Smiths', who were longing to see you after such a time away. And then there's the little tea we're giving here, but that's not till much later. Off you go, off you go.'

That night at the opera, among the several hundred people whom Jean was no doubt supposed to recall and her mother reintroduced her to with diligence, she spotted Edith Elcho just before the bell rang for the end of the interval and they were corralled back to their boxes. Edith was on magnetic form as always, a curtain of diamonds draped across her narrow chest, darting about, making one couple snort with laughter then leaning in to the ear of an extravagantly handsome man, with a whisper of something salacious, no doubt. Nothing had changed.

'Darling, how are you? Where's Edward?'

'I came alone this trip, just to see Mother really.'

'Well, all the more reason for you to come and have a drink later. Come to the Stork Club. I'll introduce you to Billy.'

'Who's Billy?' She always felt faintly ignorant in Edith's company.

'Darling, my new husband. I left Tommy, I'm afraid. His drinking made him such a bore, and I'd had enough of England if I'm honest. Haven't you? Anyway, do please come, there'll be so many marvellous people there who I know would adore to see you. Please?'

And so Jean had found herself in her mother's car, making her way to the corner of Fifty-Third and Park and into a room packed with diners and just as many standing, necks craning to see who was who. She spotted Edith beckoning her over to a corner table, lifting a drink to her lips.

'Drink, darling, you look like death. What's all this sobriety? I know you're with your mother but have some fun, please. We're in New York.'

Jean took the drink gladly, letting the Martini's icy cool burn its way from lips to throat. 'Thank you for rescuing me. It's been quite a day of engagements, and it's only my first.'

'I can imagine. Your mother hasn't weakened with widowhood, has she?'

'You know her too well.'

'And how is England, my dear? I'm taking it that you haven't bumped into Tommy, or you'd know about the divorce.'

'I had no idea. I'm not in London all that much. I've actually been in France the last month or so.'

'Oh, how divine. Same house?'

'Same house. I do love it.'

'And who do you and Edward see when you're there? Any of the old crowd? I miss that part of living in England, Europe on your doorstep and all that.'

'You know, Edward never comes out. Wrong time. He'd rather be at Harehope, fishing or shooting.'

The music had stopped, and another song came on that sent anyone who was still sitting onto the dance floor as one. The place was packed and Edith was leaning right in, so close Jean could smell her breath, sweet from the cocktails. Her palms were cool as she touched Jean's hand.

'I never said anything, it's been so long since I've seen you properly but – you know... I knew. About you and David Carver all those years ago. Sybil told me. Made me swear never to tell. She found it so touching, said it wasn't just a tinselly little affair. She wished you'd spoken to her about it, but she said you never did. Whatever happened to him?'

Jean was floored by her directness. The density of the room, the drink, the proximity of Edith to her, right there, looking straight at her with those dark, amused eyes, waiting for an answer, gave her the false confidence she needed.

'I'm still with him. On and off, each summer since I bought the house.'

Edith sucked in her breath theatrically. 'Does Edward know?'

'Yes, I suppose he does. We don't talk about it, and David never comes to England, so I keep it as far from him as possible. But yes, our marriage isn't much. Edward and I keep things up for appearance, but we haven't shared a room in years.'

The moment was here, she could touch it, put her fingers around it, make it real. She went on.

'It's actually the reason I'm here. I haven't told a soul this, but I've come to talk to my mother. I'm going to ask Edward for a divorce. I thought if I had Mother's blessing then I could make it all work financially, as smoothly as possible, give Edward what he wants and needs, and I could be with David.'

'Marry him?'

'Yes. We've talked about it, about trying to make a real life out of what we have.'

Edith was sitting back now, her head resting against the velvet of the banquette. 'God, how far you've come. That upright little girl I met who wouldn't say boo to a goose, come all the way out here to tell her mother she's going to get a divorce. I'm so impressed. Darling, divorce is nothing here. It's on every street corner, if you can afford it. And of course you can. But I'd be sure that Edward is of the same opinion. Tommy couldn't wait to see the back of me. We'd been to every party, drunk every drink, danced every dance there was. There was nothing left after that. He'd already marked the card of some sweet young English girl, a delightful daughter of an ageing earl, who'd give him children and turn a blind eye to the rest. And I couldn't wait to escape that place. I love it living back in New York. Come back.' She leaned in even closer. 'You must.'

'I have the boys to think about...'

'Well, presumably you've already decided that they're English – I mean, aren't they? The oldest one'll have Edward's title and the pile, and the whole shooting match. He belongs there. A veritable blue blood. You can't expect for him to come over here, can you?'

'Well, I was thinking Edward and I could come to some arrangement...' It sounded so improbable when she said it aloud.

'And has he been keeping the bed warm in your absence? Edward, I mean? Makes it easier, I should think.'

A man leaned over their table, his eyes swimming, reaching in for the bottle of champagne that sat in its middle, grabbing a glass and knocking over two next to it. He looked down at

Jean, momentarily confused, then across at Edith before he leaned forward and kissed her hard on the mouth. 'My dear, you mustn't switch places, confuses me something rotten. Dance with me, won't you? I'm drunk and you're beautiful, and they're playing that song. That one we love, though I can't for the life of me remember its name.'

He had Edith's wrist and was pulling her towards him, oblivious to the fact that Jean was in his way. She stood up to let Edith pass, and the pair were gone, disappearing into the mass of bodies heading towards the dance floor. She wanted to go home now, to the cool of her room, to get out of this place with its pulsing energy that she wasn't ready for.

Jean made her way through the dancing crowd, looking for Edith to see if she could say goodbye, but there were a hundred sleek bobs and a hundred bare, sinewy backs, golden with spines like cobras, moving to the beat of the band.

Someone grabbed her wrist and she turned, momentarily blinded by the lights from the bar.

'Jean. What a pleasure to see you here.'

It was too loud and the crowd too dense for her to make out who it was, so she followed where he led, to the edge of the dance floor.

'It's Max, David's editor. We met in Juan-les-Pins last month. I was actually on the same boat over from England but you kept yourself to your cabin, or I would have tried to ask you for dinner.'

There was something about the way he held his hand against her, letting it rest too long on the small on her back, too low for comfort. She stepped back.

'How nice to see you, I was just leaving to go home. I'm over here visiting my mother.'

'I've got a meeting booked with the board tomorrow. It's something of a big deal. Advertising and sales versus editorial from across the whole paper, America and Europe. It's not going to be pretty. Numbers down, profits non-existent. Always wanting to cut writers' jobs. Don't worry, I can put in a good word for David on your behalf, if you haven't already.'

He was looking directly at her. There was a sheen on his upper lip, and she remembered that she had disliked his stretched, wet mouth when they had met before. His eyes roamed over her face expectantly. The effect of the drink had worn off and she wanted to be out of this place, away from Max and his hands and his insinuations.

'Goodnight. I really must go.' She turned and walked away, threading her way blindly through the tables, her cheek wet from where he had kissed her. She felt repulsed by him but by herself too, that the trail of his hands was somehow accept-able because he knew. Her permissiveness was written on her body. Edith's words, *how far you've come*, were like a refrain in her head. How far she had come. How far she had come, and what a trail she had left behind.

CHAPTER SEVEN

Sitting in her father's study behind his vast desk as she waited for her mother to call her in for tea, Jean found tears sliding down her face. She hadn't cried for so long – how do tears help, she would ask herself when the urge rose in her, and she would swallow them down – but somehow, now, sitting in this room of his, in this apartment where he should have sat, in this city he had loved so much, she felt herself pulled back to childhood, shrunk and exposed. She cried for her father, for the absence of him, but she was crying for herself too. The girl that had followed him to London all those years ago was gone, snuffed out by the choices she had made. The woman who sat here in her place had made such strange decisions, had married a man she didn't love when she was too young to know herself, had loved another and had his child and now harboured a secret that she kept from the world. Who was this woman? What would her father, a man of such integrity and devotion to duty, have said to her? Living a lie as she was, day after day, watching the lie grow and grow, taking on a life of its own with feelings and demands and an identity framed in untruth. What could he have done but look away?

'Lady Warre?' A maid tapped at the study door, and Jean stood to follow her into the drawing room where her mother was already seated, a picture of benign maternal acceptance, hands folded in her lap, face upturned to receive her kiss.

'Darling, do come and sit. Tell me what it is you need to talk about. I'm so pleased you wanted some time alone. I've been meaning to discuss Oliver with you – he's been much better these last few months. I can't tell you what a relief it's been, and without your father here to talk to for advice. But first tell me what it is that's on your mind. You do look so terribly sad.'

Here was the cliff edge. She felt her heart thudding in her chest, and the air in the room seemed to vibrate with the tension she held in her body.

'I've wanted to talk to you for so long, but I've never known how even to begin. And now things have come to such a point that I need to tell you it all. But I don't want you to be saddened by it. I feel there is hope here, some hope of happiness.'

Jean looked down, her hands someone else's. Her skirt, her legs, this whole room, it was all another person's life, another woman speaking these words from a mouth now dry and scratchy with nerves.

'I don't love Edward.' A dart of air exhaled. 'I've said it. If I'm being truthful, I don't know if I ever loved him. We were so young when we met, and I was so sure that marrying him was what was best, what you wanted. It just happened, and then it was as if I woke up, and we were married, and it was so different to everything I had imagined it would be. And, you see, Edward is a damaged man – he has never allowed himself to open up to anyone and as a consequence he doesn't know how to show warmth or affection, or inspire or give love. That was a bleak world to inhabit. In a foreign country and in a marriage that to the outside world was fine and good but from within was deathly. I tried, Mother, I really did, I swear, but…I don't think I can continue any longer.'

And now her foot was on the last scrap of land before the abyss.

'I would like to see if Edward would allow me to seek a divorce. I know this is going to be shocking to you, and will involve things you will find difficult to swallow, but I have thought about it for so long and it is the only way. I want so badly to have your support. It will be immensely difficult, but I know the decision is the right one, where happiness ultimately lies, for everyone.'

She looked up, exhaled again. The words – at least the beginning of what she needed to say – had been spoken. She had placed herself in her mother's hands.

Elizabeth was upright, head still turned to her daughter, hands still folded into her lap. But a nerve was flickering by her right eye. The voice that started to speak was strangled, battling against itself to get out. 'You would like to seek a divorce?'

'Yes, Mama.'

'Because marriage has proved to be something other than you had envisaged.'

'More than that, it is not a marriage any more. We never talk, we are barely in the same house at the same time, and when we are he is a stranger to me. He is—'

'And who have you told of your plans?'

'No one, it's why I came here first to speak to you.'

'And if, as you say, you are to find happiness outside of your marriage to Edward, what do you mean by that?'

'This…this is hard for you to hear, but I met someone a long time ago, when I knew Edward and I would never… I met him in France, he's an extraordinary man, David Carver, brilliant, talented, hard-working, an American too, a writer. He loves the boys, he—'

Elizabeth stood up now, pushing herself forward with a little lurch before steadying herself, gripping the arm of the sofa for support. The flicker by her eye was still there, it seemed to dominate her face now, and she turned back to Jean, her face a mask belonging to someone else. 'You come here to tell me that your marriage is a bleak and barren place, that there is some man, a writer, an inspiration, with whom you are in love, who provides you with whatever your marriage does not. And you come for my blessing, my help, to bring this untidy situation to a close.'

Her words began to quicken, and she was standing over Jean, this diminutive woman, rigid with anger and something worse.

'My father, your grandfather, travelled the breadth of America because he had a plan. He had a plan to lay great foundations for a name that would be spoken of only in the most reverent of terms, a name that would be synonymous, yes, with wealth, with gold, but also with good. Good that would carve its name into buildings and museums, good that would further the lives of others, so that those early days of graft, of grit and steel and determination, should become the foundations for the years that would follow. And you' – her eyes were bulging now – 'you wish to divorce your husband so that that name, that name he fought for, can be cast into the gutter, can be associated with gossip and tawdry rumours and mutterings of a writer, a writer named David, to be laughed at and tossed around until everything that your grandfather, your father and I have done is left debased and in tatters.'

'But this is not about our family or your father, Mother, this is about me—'

'About *you*, and your happiness? What of your children then, if that makes matters more pertinent to you? Those boys, who carry Edward's name but our blood too – what is to become of them? When you are divorced and they are looked down upon in England for their mother's behaviour. What will happen then? A disgrace doubly endured, here and over there?'

'You would rather I was miserable for an eternity with Edward than I sought a divorce, something that is happening all over this city, all over London, with no—'

'With no consequence? Perhaps to someone like your writer, who thinks he can get his grubby hands on what is ours. Don't be naive, Jean, if you think that a divorce is something open to someone in your position without a grave blow to your public standing. Perhaps you think you have given Edward all he needs – perhaps you think you too have everything you require without him as your husband. But there is an arrogance there, Jean, that surprises me and has blinded you to the truth. Do you think anyone cares about this need of yours for happiness or personal satisfaction? No. They care that you carry the Buckman name and vast, vast wealth, and that as such you live in a manner that befits that. Well, I will not allow you to besmirch this name, I will not allow some dilution of what we are, by—'

Jean stood up. A bolt ran through her, and she spoke what she had sworn she would never, ever tell her mother. She shouted it. 'Alfie is not Edward's son. He is David's – and I will never tell a soul of that, I swear, but I cannot live with Edward any longer, I can't. It is not possible for me any longer. He despises me for what I have done, but that is the truth. He loathes me, he loathes our children, loathes the life we live, and I cannot carry on. But I can salvage something, I can...' The force that had driven her to speak petered out.

Then there was silence: a door shutting somewhere along the corridor, the hum of traffic from the street below, but not a word from Elizabeth as she sat back down on the sofa. When finally she spoke, her voice was low, choked with rage.

'You will never repeat to another living soul what you have just told me.' She cleared her throat, gathering strength as she began again. 'And I will never receive you in my house again. If you come to this city, you will not be my guest. You will pack your bags after you have heard what I am about to say. You will not talk to Edward of divorce. You will return home, and you will continue your marriage to that man until the day you die. I will see to it that you can never reveal the truth of what you have done. You will receive no further money from me, and your freedom' – the word was spoken with disgust – 'which my name, my money, has granted you, will come to an end. I will cut you off. Without your own money you will have no power over Edward to affect this divorce. And he will not accept this, without money on offer. I know that much about him now. So you will have to stand by him. And what's more: George will get nothing from me. Was that your plan? That my money would somehow absolve you of your guilt towards George. That your actions would be made good by my balancing the scales. I will not have that. I will not.' She was shouting now, her voice hoarse with rage. 'Alfie shall remain your eldest son, your heir, son of his father, and not a soul will ever know of your disgusting act of betrayal to our family. And you can live with the terrible injustice you have created.'

She gathered her strength.

'There is a code, perhaps not one as old as the code that rules your husband's country, but it is still a code that I believe should be adhered to until one leaves this earth. Your father lived by it, I live by it and your brother, with his drinking, may struggle with it, but he has a good and faithful marriage, and he tries. My God, he tries. But you, you have violated it, and I cannot – I will not – allow that violation to be made public, so that a hundred years of hard work and diligence gets tossed aside for your…your wantonness, your inability to control your impulses.'

She stared at Jean as if seeing her for the first time, waiting for her to stand.

'You will receive correspondence from me at Harehope that will set out in clearer terms how I intend to make my wishes a reality. You can reply if you feel the need, but we shall not speak again. Now leave.'

The silence again, only the ticking of the clock, the tea growing cold in the pot, the sandwiches curling a little at the edges. Jean stood up, a thousand words chasing each other through her head but none available to her to utter out loud. So she stood and walked out of the room, closing the door behind her, walked out of the apartment. She didn't have her coat or her gloves, nor her bag, and she found herself on the street, the stooped Irish doorman nodding as he did each morning. 'Would you like a cab, Lady Warre?' he asked, but she walked blindly on, not knowing where, her eyes blurred by tears.

She kept on going, her feet making a path of their own on the hard grey pavement, her eyes staring straight ahead, unable to focus. She must have walked downtown, crossing on to Fifth Avenue, because she found herself after a time by the steps to St Patrick's, its dark Gothic door a mouth ready to swallow her up.

As she made her way slowly inside, she could hear a Mass going on at the front, the muttering of the priest and his Latin making the space seem even greater as his words echoed against the stone emptiness. She walked down the central aisle, heels clicking against the polished marble floor, traversed an empty pew that took her to one of the side chapels. She knelt, comforted by the silence punctuated only by the priest and the amens of his small congregation dotted across the benches at the front, old women in black, rosaries clasped in chapped fingers, shoulders rounded in prayer. She knelt, head in hands for a while, felled by the conversation with her mother.

When she looked up again, after how long she didn't know, she found she had knelt in a recess where there stood La Pietà, its marble white as alabaster, its surface smooth as glass. The Christ's body was twisted as he looked up to his mother, his hand raised, as she, Mary, clasped it in her own, drawing up his agony, aching to relieve him of his earthly pain. Jean was transfixed by this image, its brutality and its tenderness, and she wept. For the severance of the maternal bond, her sin that would not be swept up in tender arms and absolved but returned, untouched. Jean's heart felt like it would tear then, she could feel where it sat in her chest, could feel it ache and creak. Was this the appeal of Catholicism, that absolution would always come from behind the curtain of the confessional, the voice in the darkness wiping away all sin?

She had a memory then; it must have been the first month of her marriage to Edward, when she had sat with a gentleman from Leggatt's as they catalogued the art that she and her mother had bought for the house in London. The sweet, scholarly young man, probably only a year or two older than her, had sat beside her, politely listing each painting, its provenance, its condition, looking up questioningly every few seconds as if she might decide to contradict the inconvertible truth. As his pen scratched across his ledger, his diligent hand logging each detail, she saw that the collection had been recorded as making up *The Property of Lord Warre, of —— Park Lane and Harehope, Northumberland*. The neat little leap from her money to his property, from her mother to her husband, like the tiny unseen loop in sewing, tucked behind the fabric. That was what she was: invisible, necessary to the function of things, but unseen. For all the talk of her great wealth, of her position, of the transformative power she held for a family like Edward's, she remained invisible and powerless. She was the vessel, the golden vessel, through which life poured. It made her want to scream, in the vastness of the church on Fifth Avenue, among the faceless daytime worshippers, to tell anyone who would listen that she was someone who felt – intensely, painfully – this life she was living, that she wanted to break out and make it hers. But she could not. She was just a woman, inheritor of the earth by proxy. For all the voting, and the talking and the drinking and the dancing, for every Edith who could rouge her lips and bare her shoulders and marry whomever she liked, there was a Jean, constrained by someone else's dictums, her emotions as audible as a scream in a gale.

Jean didn't know how long she sat there; she felt the light change as clouds moved across the sun outside. The worshippers drifted out, and a young novice in a long cassock, a face of quiet concentration, came past her pew to extinguish the candles that guttered before her. The wood of the bench was hard against her back and she shifted in her seat. What was she to do, now the blessing she had sought had been denied? Do it anyway, risk the battle with Edward alone, when the cards were all his? Drag her boys' name through the mud, as her mother had predicted? Be single-minded, pursue the path for herself alone, for the possibility of a life with David here in

New York, where they could live as husband and wife and let the rest be damned?

As she sat in the hush of the church, the dim light causing her eyes to lose focus, she knew she couldn't do it. Was it because she was weak, or cowed by her mother's reaction, or was she simply unable to make her children the victims of her desire for freedom from Edward? She wasn't brave enough, she knew that. She wasn't reckless. She had come face to face with a reaction to the truth, and it had stunned her. But most of all, it was the boys, her boys. They couldn't be trampled on, humiliated. Her mother was right about that. Without the force of her money behind her, Edward would never let Jean leave without dredging up all the wrongdoing, the lies, the ugly truth at the heart of it all. And they, her darling, fragile boys, for whom she was everything, would be destroyed in the process.

She walked onto the street, now filling with workers leaving their offices, slowing their pace to enjoy the last of the sun. She had to salvage something from this. She was still a mother. That would have to be her path from here, that would be the sense she would make of it all. She would give up David, would go back to Edward, would carry on with this marriage that was as hollow and senseless as the echoing Latin of this church, but it would be for her boys, and for them alone.

CHAPTER EIGHT

Her mother was gone when she returned to the apartment, and her bags, neatly packed – the clothes folded in tissue, the vanity case from the nightstand with her bottles and lotions carefully placed within – were set down beside the bed. One of the maids followed her into the room, politely asking where her bags should be sent. So this was what it was like to have the door closed, your position within your family rescinded, beautifully done of course, all neatly wrapped and carried out by a maid in uniform, but rescinded all the same. She called the Waldorf, knowing they would have rooms, and booked herself something until she could get herself on a boat home.

Jean sat in her hotel room, the blandness of its decor and its cosseted silence making the conversation of only a couple of hours before seem unreal. The only witnesses to her final departure from her parents' home had been Simms, carrying her bags into the elevator, and the maid who had packed for her, her face a blank mask as Jean walked down the hall of the apartment for the last time.

She picked up the telephone again and asked the operator to put her through to her brother's office. The pair hadn't spoken in nearly two years – they would write periodically, and usually so that he could let her know about developments at the paper, as she was nominally a part-owner. Their conversation was brief, but he was warm and sounded pleased to hear her voice, asking how she'd been and who'd she seen in town. He accepted her request to come and have a drink with her that evening at the hotel, no questions asked as to why she needed to meet, nor why she was no longer staying with their mother.

Jean waited in the bar, relishing its anonymity, filled as it already was with couples and groups of after-work men, waiters circling with trays crammed with drinks. She tried to remember the last time she and her brother had met – maybe four or five years after her father's death, when she had brought the boys to New York for a month to stay with her mother and they had all had lunch together at his apartment, a polite, uninspiring meal, everyone on their best behaviour, asking the right questions, smiling anodyne smiles, laughing tight laughs. She could remember Dee's eyes on Oliver's glass, noting each compulsive slug, each attempt at nonchalance when pouring himself another drink. The life of a drinker's wife, always on high alert for when jovial slopped over into too much fun and then bled into melancholy, regret, or worse.

She felt a hand on her shoulder and there he was, still in his overcoat, the soft wool glistening from the shower that must have caught him outside. He kissed her quickly on the cheek and then pulled his chair in to sit closer to her, gesturing to the waiter to come and take their order.

'A double bourbon for me. Jean?'

'I'll have a gin Martini. Thank you.'

As he threw his coat over a neighbouring chair and put his hat on the table, she had a chance to look at his face. He was five years older than her, tall and handsome, with the patrician nose of her father, but he was more lined than he should have been. Drink had aged him, filling out his cheeks and dulling his skin. His journey had left its mark. His suit, though, was cut to perfection, and the cufflinks at his wrist were her father's; she could see the looped letters of his initials as they moved in the light. He rubbed his face hard with his hands, sitting forward again in his seat, looking round to see if the waiter was coming. He offered her a cigarette and lit one for himself, dragging deeply on it. The sight of the tumbler placed before him relaxed him and he took a sip before sitting back and looking at her.

'Odd, isn't it. Brother and sister meeting like strangers in a hotel lobby. You would have been welcome at home, and Dee and the boys are there, but perhaps—'

'It just seemed easy to come here. I don't know how much you know about what happened this afternoon.'

'I'll put you out of your misery. I had a telephone call from Mother at around five o'clock, and a visit at the office half an hour after that. I have been informed.'

'Of what?'

'She told me that you had asked for her blessing in seeking a divorce from Edward. A blessing she was not willing to give, on the basis that you were the guilty party and that she felt you had a duty to continue on in your marriage. She didn't elaborate on what made you the guilty party – although I suppose I can guess – and she asked me to explain the situation to Dee. Which I'm afraid I haven't had time to do, as I haven't been home yet from the office. What have you done, Jean? I can't help but feel this is the wrong way round. Aren't I the source of Mother's anguish and you the golden child to be leaned upon? I don't think I can remember a day my whole life when you've been in the wrong.' He was smiling and his eyes were kind. 'Do you need my help? I'm assuming you've got a decent lawyer in England. Or are you going to stay here and try and do this from New York?'

She took a deep breath, bracing herself to speak. 'I'm not going to go through with it. I'm not going to leave Edward, divorce. I can't do it. I thought I could, but I can't without Mother's blessing. Or even with it, now I've come close to the whole thing being real. I've realised I can't destroy everything for the boys, when what's likely is I'd have to leave them in England with their father. You forget I am a woman; what standing do I have? And without the force of the family behind me, I am doubly damned. They need me, I know they do. If Mother does as she promises, Edward holds all the power.'

Oliver was looking down into his glass, rolling its heavy base from side to side, lost in thought. 'You know, in these years we've been adults, when you've been in England and I've been here, I've been a mess. I'm sure you know. I've made a mess of the paper, I only run the board because they kicked me out of editorial – too many missed deadlines and lunches that I didn't come back from, or loose words, or… God, I could go on. But Dee stuck by me, spoke for me when I couldn't, dealt with Mother and the board, and things are on more of an even keel now.' He tipped his glass. 'I can't say I am always in control, but I go home every night, I sleep in my own bed, kiss the boys goodnight. But you know what I've often thought, all this time, during all these years of self-indulgence, of struggle, of failing: that I was the defect in the line. That people would look the other way when they saw me coming, because I wasn't what

Father or Mother should have produced. That after the generation of doers, I was the inevitable ne'er-do-well, bloated by money and drink and the ease of it all. Surrounded by a family of perfect, principled people. But when I heard the fury in her voice this afternoon, saw her shake, barely able to control herself as she stood in my office, part of me wanted to clap my hands and shout for joy. You were the same! You were a rotten seed too.' He took another cigarette from his case and lit it, exhaling the smoke slowly. 'Is that terrible of me? My happiness at your downfall in her eyes?'

'So is that what we are now, ne'er-do-wells?' She was smiling, the first time she had all day. 'The pair that were meant to have – and be – everything.'

'You know, as a child, Mother would always tell me about someone who had done better than me. Even when I did all right at something, she'd bring up another fellow who'd done it first, or better, or with more charm. I remember once – how pathetic – I came back from St Paul's and I had a letter from my physics master saying I had improved that year, done better than expected, should be commended for my hard work, and she took the letter and folded it neatly, placing it on that desk of hers in the morning room, and told me that the arts were where my future lay because Father had been a scholar in the arts and no self-respecting Buckman need excel in science. I think that was the last time I remember trying at anything. What was the point? Silly now. She was probably right, what good would science do me at the *Tribune*, but all the same…'

'Do you want me to tell you what I've done? So you understand why she's so angry?'

'No, you don't owe me that. And whatever it is, when I was at my worst, about five years ago… I can't even say out loud some of the things I did. Makes me shudder. You don't need to tell me anything. I am sorry your marriage hasn't worked out, I know how easy it is for these things to break apart.'

He shifted in his seat so he was sitting forward, hands resting on his knees.

'When I think about it, Mother was always looking over her shoulder, waiting to be found out. Her worst nightmare is shame, the shame of others thinking things about her that she can't control. That's why divorce is so abhorrent to her – its public nature. Better that you're miserable in your marriage than that people know you're not perfect. Maybe that's the problem with society here. All that money but always someone coming along with more to knock you off your plinth, so you have to grip on tight, do everything you can to hold on to your position.' He sat back, took a sip of his drink. 'I'll do what I can – really, whatever I can – to help you. I know Dee will feel the same. She's a good woman, and whatever has gone on between us, we have a good marriage. Without it, I wouldn't be able to put one foot in front of the other.'

It was odd to speak like this about her mother, about her brother's marriage. The only other person who had opened himself up to her like this was David. In a fleeting moment, she saw how well he and Oliver would get on.

'I've always thought that marrying Edward was somehow not my fault. That I did what duty required. I was young, naive, all of that. Did what was expected of me. And that's the truth, you know, but I see now that it's only a part. All this money, this name of mine, it enabled what came after. These last fourteen years, this lie of a marriage, it was all because of my money, because of Mother's money. I've spent every summer in France, in a house that is mine, without my husband, because I could pay for it. And I thought that was freedom, but it's the opposite, isn't it? This money, this name, you're right, it has controlled Mother. She fears the power it gives her slipping away – the preservation of what it signifies to the world is everything to her. And now, now, it's the same for us. It controls you, controls me. There is no individual within: it is the name, to preserve at all cost. We aren't her children, not in any way I understand it, we are just the continuation of a name, a New York name.' She looked up at him, and she was surprised by how sad this made her feel. 'So if we don't continue it, then we are not to continue. I'm a dead end in history to her now.'

He looked down at his glass. 'You know she intends to change your circumstances quite dramatically. And I'm afraid, with the way the trust is set up, it is down to her. She can alter the terms, and the trustees simply have to agree. And frankly, who would argue with Elizabeth Buckman? She told me your allowance is to be stopped, your shares in the paper are to be returned to the family. You won't be able to make settlements at your discretion as you were formerly. I don't know if that matters to you, but it absolutely limits your place in the inheritance. You won't have much option but to stick with Edward and hope he's generous to you. Everything that's gone before is in his name already. But as you said, the rest, your allowance, any future money at Mother's death, that's all over. But I'll do whatever I can personally, I swear. Ask me whenever you're in trouble, promise you'll do that.'

She nodded. 'I do understand, and it's the choice I'm going to make. Thank you, though, for your kindness. It's good to talk. We never really have, have we?'

And she knew that they probably wouldn't again, that they would revert back to the old formality, to polite interchanges that were easier than honesty. But she was grateful for it now, here, in the anonymity of the Waldorf lobby, in this town that was no longer her home.

Jean took the elevator up to the eleventh floor, lay on her bed for she didn't know how long, listening to the occasional sounds of other guests passing on the corridor, the elevator doors opening and closing, the muffle of the maids turning down the rooms on the right and left. Still she lay, eyes open, looking at the ceiling, her mind drawing itself back across the water to England, to Harehope, to where she had decided, pledged, sworn in that church that her future would lie.

Before sleep overtook her, she sat at her desk, the window looking out on the avenue of lights and traffic below, a sad little sliver of a crescent moon watching over her, a thousand miles from the thrum of cicadas and dusty heat where she had left David, and put pen to paper.

David,

I have to write now because it's late, and waking up tomorrow will be the beginning of the next chapter for us.

I came here for a kind of absolution, a blessing for our relationship, a path through so that I could leave Edward finally. I had thought that the power of my feelings for you would somehow persuade Mother to our cause. But they did not. Her reaction was more extreme than anything I could have predicted. I told her the truth about Alfie. I couldn't stop myself.

She will not give her blessing. She has promised, pledged, sworn on everything she believes in that she will not allow a divorce to happen. *The trust will be changed so that my allowance is gone and I will never receive a cent more from her, and nor will the boys. She intends to leave no shred of a possibility that I leave Edward. The independence that had allowed all of this will be gone. So she will sew me into this life with thread of steel. This is what inheritance means to her. A continuation on the anointed path, at whatever human cost. She has no qualms about that.*

She will never talk to me again. She closed the door, the drawing room door that had been open to me my entire life, and said she never wanted to see my face again.

So this is what comes of trying to subvert the order of things. Of thinking I could be something I am clearly not. I am no heroine of this tale, throwing it all out and be damned. I can't do that to the boys. I'm not brave enough to watch them fall.

I am so sorry I have caught you up in all of this. What empty words to write to you of all people. Just an apology. To the man that took me in and accepted the part of me that I offered him. Well, it seems that was the most I could give, and so I must go back to Edward, to England, to the life I married.

But could I see you one last time in France at the house? Would you grant me that? Then I will close it up. End this. End this version of myself that I thought I could make real.

Jean

CHAPTER NINE

The October sun was still warm on her face as she stood alone on the terrace. The sea below her had gained a restless quality, carrying with it now the taste of winter to come, reproaching her for staying so long.

With Marie putting her final things in cases in her room, and the other women long gone, Jean allowed herself to sit down, the first time she had broken off from her day of packing up. She knew immediately that this was a mistake, and busied herself by searching for a cigarette in her purse, eventually lighting it and watching the smoke catch in the impatient breeze. Everything – the wind, the damp stone of the house, the taste of salt in the air – seemed to be willing her to leave. Her car would be here shortly and she would be on the road and away from this house: and this coda in her life would be over, as if some cheerful administrator had called time on it, had shuffled the papers and tucked them away into a box and decided that their part in it all was complete.

David had left for Paris two days before, unable to sit and watch her pack up the house. On his final afternoon he had paced the terrace and then sat at the table she was at now, his knee jigging restlessly, his jaw clenching and unclenching, his frustration unable to break out at her directly, turning it in on himself instead, a last act of decency. He should have known this was the final meeting; that he could not change her mind, make her stay. There would be no next summer, no next visit, no week in Paris carved out from somewhere that would get him through the empty months without her. And so he had raged at her then, reminding her again and again of the life that she would return to, its emptiness. But she had begged him so forcefully to stop and to salvage what little they had left that he had allowed the rage to ebb away, leaving him with just that knuckle of tension in his jaw.

They had decided then to have one last dinner together. Jean had asked Marie to leave everything prepared and take the evening off. But rather than giving them freedom, her going left a silence which neither of them had had the strength to fill. Any physical touch seemed only to isolate each from the other, leaving in its place an absence too loaded to bear. They barely talked as they ate, smoked and drank more than they normally would, and when their abandoned plates began to reproach them, moved to the drawing room.

Jean had taken him in then, a habit of hers – the beauty of him, the earnest open face with the slight furrow always at his brow. She walked over to the gramophone, leaving him sitting on the sofa, less man now, more boy, and saw that she had broken him. She put on a record and returned to him, resting her head against his chest, curling her body into him, relying on the promise of his silence.

He had handed her a slim book, its brown cloth cover worn and scuffed at the edges, the pages dog-eared. When she opened it, she could see his handwriting, its generous open script covering page after page. The first date read *April 1923*. It was a diary of their relationship. A letter to her. She closed it, unable to read the words for the tears in her eyes.

'Madam? The car is here.'

Jean looked up. Taking a final drag of her cigarette, she ground it into the dish and stood, feeling a forced energy taking hold, as if without it she would have lain her face against the cold iron of the table and given way to her grief. She followed Marie round the side of the house, its pale stone cool now, the summer's heat dissipated, past the beds of rosemary and the climbing jasmine, past the late roses, their heads bent, their petals ragged and edged with brown.

The car was waiting, engine idling. The driver's broad smile as they approached made it all seem horribly real, and the lump in her throat hurt now, making her swallow. She embraced Marie briefly – she didn't even know if she would see her again – and the look of surprise on the older lady's face gave her a brief flush of pleasure.

'Thank you so much for everything. And I will make sure the agent pays you for all your time. Just let him know anything that needs repair this winter. It will be a while until anyone is here again.'

And then she sank back into the car and gestured to the young man to move off. The car gave a little lurch and started its journey up the winding drive to the road, and though she willed herself not to, she turned and took one last look back at the house. The place that had once been her freedom was now a reminder of everything that could not be.

PART IV

CHAPTER ONE

Harehope, 1938

Harehope. She felt the name pulse like blood through her body, calling her, allowing her only so far before it pulled her back, sucked her into its thrall, unable to let her go. Harehope held them all; kept this band of disparates somehow together. Though each one's relationship with it was different, still it beat through them too, and as she watched it cast its spell upon her family, she would remind herself that this place was just that – brick and stone and chimneys and park – not a soul, sometimes tyrannical, sometimes beseeching, that would urge, push, drive them all, till in her dreams she found herself turning that curve of the drive and seeing it there before her, windows black as coal, door open, pulling her in like a siren.

If France had been her freedom, Harehope was her penance. Here she carried her cross that she must bear, that she chose to bear, in order to keep her boys protected. To give them the journey to adulthood that they deserved. Jean's mother's money, the allowance that had enabled her to go to France, to live a separate life to Edward, to love David, was gone, recalled in the stuffy afternoon heat of that drawing room on Madison Avenue. Now she was entirely dependent on Edward, dependent on his whims, his anger, his increasingly erratic behaviour.

Edward knew that she had returned to him out of necessity. He knew the reasons for the change in her finances, and it gave him a new power over her that he nursed. The cool disdain, the distrust, the self-loathing at his failure in producing George, had changed into something else, as if a new plant had been grafted onto what grew before, creating a hybrid, something of untold strength, of thick roots and great spreading leaves, that left no room for her. It found expression in secret lives away from her too, away from Harehope, away from their family. London became a place where he went, without her, as she had done with France. She had no money of her own now, and he gave her no allowance, so Harehope became the place where she lived, where she measured out time between visits from the boys; where she would invite the few friends to stay who understood the nature of their marriage.

Today the ground was frozen solid, a thick frost encasing the landscape like lead, and everything was hard, cold, impermeable. The mild winter at the beginning of December had given way, a fierce easterly wind bringing another season in its wake. She sat in silence as she was driven through a landscape where life seemed to be hiding at the edges; the flicker of movement where a robin, a splash of red at his breast, darted down in the hope of food, or a pair of fat wood pigeons, heads tucked in against the cold, ruffled their feathers, perched on a barren branch like two old men. Neither of the boys had been home since early September; they had left a world of ploughed fields and late summer harvests, a landscape scorched and dry from a searing August; they would return to moorland hardened by ice, to hedgerows with spindled fingers and skies of spectral grey.

The train was already pulling out of the station as Jean walked onto the platform, her eyes scanning the passengers milling around amid luggage and porters, desperate to light on the pair. Someone called 'Mama', and there they were, in thick overcoats of Harris tweed, woollen scarves trailing, cheeks pink from the airless carriage, and they were in her arms, and she felt something close to peace take hold of her. Alfie had grown in the summer, a spurt that required him to spend hours with the tailor in Billings & Edmonds, and though he was still slim and boyish, there was the foretelling of adulthood in the breadth of his shoulders and the uneven creak of his voice. George was still a boy, though: delicate, beautiful – truly beautiful, with his pale skin and dark, almost black hair, the limpid eyes that could not hide emotion. She pulled him to her and breathed in the smell of his skin, his hair, rubbed his cheek, kissed the top of his head.

'It's been all right, Mama. Busy but all right.'

George was tired, eyes half-closed in the warmth of the car, but she could tell he was happy, the relief at being home now tucked under his arm like a familiar toy, the strain of achievement in terms that didn't come easily to him now removed, if only for a short while.

She turned to Alfie, his head resting against the seat, looking out of the window as his eyes tracked the familiar journey home.

'This term always feels eternal. Pitch black by half past three, and it seems as if we're always at our desks in the dark. It drags. Thank God for Christmas.' He said no more, and anyway she knew he would keep any of this term's successes pitched low, not wanting to overshadow the brother he adored.

George looked across at her. 'Is anyone staying?'

'No, just us for now.'

A smile of relief spread across his face.

She turned to her elder son again. 'Darling, I know Roberts was keen to know when you were back. Says he's been holding back on the pigeons so that you could have a go.'

Alfie said nothing, but he smiled as they turned off the main road and onto the narrower network of lanes that marked the final phase of the journey. They swapped inconsequential stories as they drew closer, regaining their companionship after so long apart, but neither boy mentioned their father. He was part of the fabric of their lives, but not of the alchemy between the three of them. They existed separately to him. Their relationship was a living, animate thing. Edward's presence was still; something they came up against, like a boulder in the riverbed, that they must navigate, test themselves in relation to, edge around, till he was passed and they were out and free in the flow of water again.

As they drove through the gates, the drive and their arrival into the park silenced them as the house's presence worked on each in turn. Jean always felt something she could only describe as homesickness; the lurch as the inevitable was before her, its demands and Edward's presence within needing to be managed. For the boys it was different. It was the revelation of the eternal: its pediments and rustication, its architraves and Palladian symmetry, as familiar to them as their own faces. The house, this place, was a figure in their lives as much as any living being. But always there was the conflict, the tug of uncertainty: how would their father be? Who would he hurt?

The car drew under the porte cochère amid the familiar scrape of gravel. Doors were flung open and the boys were out of the car in a jumble of hellos and luggage and hands shaken, desperate, though, to change out of their travelling clothes, to regain the territory of their bedrooms. The dogs could always sense George's return, and they skittered out of their familiar spots, ears pricked, eager to present themselves to him, for the fur at ear and neck to be scratched by a returning friend. Alfie would want to find Roberts, keen to lose himself in the easy talk of birds and traps, rabbits and pigeons. Neither boy stopped as they passed their father's closed study door. They knew well enough not to go in.

Jean had both boys' reports in her hand. As they ran upstairs to change, she sat on the bottom step of the great staircase, leaning against the wall behind her. She opened Alfie's first, let her eyes scan the words she could predict. He was startlingly bright, with an embarrassment of talents that followed him into whatever classroom he chose to enter or pitch to walk onto. He was hard-working, conscientious; words of praise flowed from the pens of each beak that had the good fortune to teach him. George's reports were adequate, noting his kind nature, his gentle diffidence, but academic achievement and the classroom were not for him, and on anything beyond that – the playing fields, the wall game, the plays and performances – he made no mark; through inability or reluctance, they had not bothered to determine.

She knocked on Edward's study door. He didn't reply, so she opened the door slowly. He was sitting, his chair turned to the window, a tumbler of whisky before him, an ashtray filled. He didn't register her appearance, so she cleared her throat.

He looked up slowly from the newspaper he was reading. 'I hear they're back.'

'They are, and I thought I ought to show you these.' She placed the two envelopes on the desk before him.

Edward didn't touch them but looked up at her, unblinking. He had grown more handsome if anything with age, had grown into his features, the extra weight at his face making him a man of substance somehow, the moustache he wore highlighting the slant at his cheekbones.

'I am sure you can guess how they'll be.'

He pushed the envelopes aside to reach for his drink. 'I can.'

'I came to ask you, please, to sit down with them separately, to give them some of your time. Or just Alfie. And I'll do George. Alfie has done brilliantly again. He has said nothing, he won't say anything, but just give him your approval.'

She felt her throat constricting, willing herself not to reveal emotion, not to reveal Alfie's vulnerability through her own. But still he was silent, watching her with utter dispassion. It unsettled her, even though this was now so often his way.

'Edward, none of this is his fault. He can't understand why you are the way you are with him. He's only fourteen years old. It hurts him.'

He took a slow sip of his drink, relishing the silence. Eventually he spoke. 'I'm going away tonight. I'll break the journey at Bolton Abbey, and then I'll be in London by tomorrow afternoon. You can manage the boys as you like.'

'Oh, Edward, please don't. They've only just got here.'

'And look what's happened. Already you want things from me that I am not prepared to give.'

'But they'll be so confused. You haven't seen them for months.'

'Don't you think they're already confused? Why don't you go to America any more? Why don't you speak to your mother any more? Why don't you go to France? Why do you hide up here at Harehope, a recluse?'

She kept her voice quiet. 'I hide up here because I can't go to London unless it's with your approval. I am entirely reliant upon you now, as you well know.' Though she knew it was dangerous, she went on. 'What do you do when you're in London though? Who do you see? What is this life you lead away from here?'

'That's a fine thing for you to ask.'

'I know, I know I did the same, but I gave it all up. I haven't been back. I've been here. If you've wanted a wife, I've been here.'

'Oh, as if it was a thing of choice. You did it because you were forced to. And can't you see? That this family of ours, that you think you've come back to save, your beloved boys… This whole bloody set-up.' His tone was spiteful, mocking. 'Can't you see that all of this stands for nothing. This ridiculous lie we've created, now covered over. This family we've concocted. It's nothing. This whole thing has come to nothing.'

'It doesn't have to.' She should have stopped there, but she could not hold herself back. 'I know that things aren't being done here as they should be.'

'It's none of your business. It doesn't concern you.'

'But you're never here, always in London.'

'Perhaps I need to be. We need cash. Servants don't pay themselves, you know. And if you hadn't noticed, the political climate isn't looking particularly healthy. Did you read about Chamberlain's speech last night at the press dinner in London? Empty seats where the Germans boycotted it. Lines are being drawn, and as much as I believe in working with Mr Hitler rather than against him, it's a position we can't hold forever.' He looked at her directly, eyes as hard as flint. 'Does it grate, after all those years of abundance? I always knew your mother had steel beneath that veneer of American charm. If you want to pursue the spirit of truth with our boys, why don't you tell them why the funds have dried up? I can call in Alfie now, if you'd like? Go through his reports and then run through the family finances with him?'

'Have some humanity. He's just a boy!'

Before she could take stock of what was happening, his chair was back and he was up and standing over her, breathing fast. 'Humanity? Once again, it all comes down to me and my acceptance of a status quo that is not my making.' His voice was low, but he was walking her backwards towards the fireplace. 'Be kind, praise Alfie for his successes. Be kind, don't see George for the useless weakling that he is. And you say it all with that tired, sad face of yours, begging me, beseeching me.'

'Edward, I don't care if you despise me. Just don't hurt them any more. They are innocent in this.'

'And that's it. Who is really to blame for all of this? For this mess. For this lie that you rightly observe I take issue with? It's you – you – you.' He jabbed his finger into her chest and she felt his breath on her, smelt the sweet tang of whisky. And he pushed her, hard, and she fell back, the side of her head hitting the corner of the mantelpiece. She felt a spear of hot red at her temple and pain flooded through her as she hit the floor. A flash of shock crossed his face, but then it was gone and he turned away from her, walking silently to his desk, taking his seat once more.

Jean put her hand to her temple, to the source of the pain. There was the stain of blood at her fingers; the marble edge must have broken her skin. Edward's hands were shaking as he took a match from the striker and brought it to flame, lit a cigarette, pulled on it. She got to her feet, smoothing down her skirt before she spoke. 'Go to London, then. I'll tell the boys.'

And she turned away, knowing then that a contract had been made between them: that she'd take the blows to keep the truth from the boys. Edward held power over her; the thing he had wanted all along. From someone, from anyone. To control what he had never felt belonged to him. He controlled her now.

She walked out of the study, left him sitting there, staring out of the window at the landscape beyond that still remained to the outside world the signifier of who he was. The fountain was frozen and a lone cock pheasant, its plumage a streak of claret splashed onto the white behind, was making its slow passage across the lawn. The passage of time was so strange at places like Harehope, the present always deferring to who had gone before, or looking anxiously forward to who was to come. Today, under this blanket of creaking snow, it felt as if this moment of truths just covered and hatred barely kept at bay would stretch on forever, Edward's tenure at Harehope perfectly captured in the faint stain of blood at her finger and temple.

CHAPTER TWO

The week that followed was blissful. Like kisses stolen when no one is looking, each minute without Edward felt precious, snatched. The three would breakfast happily together each morning in the dining room, enjoying the simple pleasure of unburdened company. Alfie had been twice to shoot with neighbours, coming back full of who was there and the conversations of the grown-ups. It was becoming increasingly apparent that Chamberlain's triumphant claim of 'Peace for our time' would be left hanging like bunting at a party that was now only empty cups and abandoned plates.

'All anyone talked about was what Germany will do next. I think we should be firm with Mr Hitler. I don't believe he's being straight with us. Richard's father said that if we don't start rearming properly now, it'll be too late.' Alfie was leaning forward in his chair, his face solemn. He was coming to the age where boys tried on the voices of their fathers, wanting desperately to carry off the air of certainty and knowledge they'd heard in cigar-filled drawing rooms. But Edward wasn't there to listen.

She nodded. 'We've let the people of the Sudetenland down.'

'But is it too late?' He put down his knife and fork with a clatter. 'Mr Chamberlain must be told that we don't want our country to accept this, as if we think it's all right to trample over people if it doesn't affect us directly. Who will be next?'

'What do your friends think?'

'Richard agrees with his father. They were talking about a speech that man Goebbels gave yesterday, announcing to the press that Germany's territories were too small to meet the country's needs. That is a statement of intent, isn't it?' He took a sip of his water. 'They asked me what Papa thinks. I imagine he feels the same way, don't you?' He looked down, going back to his plate of eggs. 'I said as much, anyway.'

Alfie was growing up, needing this voice of independence to be heard. She nodded as he talked on as boys of his class were educated to do, believing in the absolute rightness of their opinions, the inevitability that they be heard. But there was a hesitation there, an underlying insecurity, the boy whose father had never given the approval he so desperately sought.

George was listening too, nodding quietly as he ate the pear on the plate before him, eating each hard sliver carefully. The plate had been placed there discreetly by Stokes, the fruit sliced for him in the kitchen. It was a small act they all ignored, one of the many little things that set him apart from others, that made life a little easier for him but school, friendships, fitting in, that bit harder. He was listening to Alfie, but she knew his mind was already elsewhere. Unlike his brother, he relished his time alone, the freedom simply to be. He had taken to painting in the holidays, heading off for hours at a time with a knapsack filled with oils and a small stretched canvas, a jar for his brushes, a bottle of turps. He had always had a talent, starting with pencil sketches of the dogs by the fire when he was nine or ten, or drawings of the horses in the stables, studying their heads, somehow catching something of the life of them even when the handling was naive. It was the perfect pastime for him – paper to hide behind, a justification for observing rather than participating, his left arm not required. The pencil sketches had gravitated to little oils, and he would ask for sets for birthdays and Christmas, something frowned upon by Edward – 'what kind of a boy paints as a hobby?' – but encouraged by Jean as she saw genuine ability and satisfaction gained. He had tried to learn everything else that a boy of his age ought; he could shoot with one hand, as the Kaiser had done, could play tennis adequately well, could swim, just, but he didn't really care. He had no need to prove to the world he was the same as them; he preferred, where possible, to slip to its edges and observe.

She watched now from the open front door as George headed off, wrapped up in scarf and cap and boots, satchel slung over his shoulder, a piece having been made in the kitchen to get him through to teatime.

Snow had fallen night after night since they had arrived back at Harehope and each morning they had woken to a virgin landscape, the blanket of silence broken only by the tap, tapping of pick on ice as one of the gardeners worked away at the frozen water at the base of the fountain, worrying that the birds would have nothing to drink.

Her eyes followed George as he made his way up the drive. He turned briefly to wave at her, his gloved hand held up till she raised hers back, and then he trudged on, and she could sense the happiness in the way his shoulders were, happiness for the hours of joyous solitude that stretched out before him.

*

But these dreamy days of three were to come to an end. Harehope had not had a houseful for some time, not since Edward had made London his centre of gravity, but guns had been invited for two days of pheasants that fell the week before Christmas. The house was gearing up awkwardly, stiff in its joints, preparing for the guests' arrival and Edward's return, Jean for the charade of a united family to present to the world. Meals had been planned at length with Mrs Jobson in the kitchen, and Mrs Hawkins would walk the bedroom corridors with two housemaids in her wake, a notebook and pencil in hand, jotting down each little detail that required attention. Flowers for which room, whisky on a salver for which gentlemen, which wives would be coming, who would require breakfast trays, who would need a lady's maid. Stokes oversaw the cleaning of the silver – the candelabra, the wine coolers, the endless array of knives and forks of countless sizes and encyclopaedic uses – as nervous footmen with pimples at their chin worked away under his stern eye. Appearances, it was clear, were to be kept up.

In what must have been a veiled slight by the other guns, it was only Freddie Byam-Hughes who came with his wife. As Jean walked around the downstairs rooms with Mrs Hawkins, making a final check that everything was as it ought to be before dinner, Rose was already sitting in the drawing room, drink in hand. She got to her feet quickly when she saw her hostess.

'Jean! How wonderful to see you. I hope you don't mind my coming down already. It was such a long journey, and I was gasping. Freddie takes forever, fiddling with his collar and all that wretched pomade. I think I make it worse by watching him, so I thought I'd come down. And Stokes kindly obliged.' She raised her glass happily.

Rose Byam-Hughes was relatively unchanged, though it must have been six years since Jean had seen her last. She still had that straw-blonde hair whose brushing was an afterthought and her cheeks still carried that charming flush of rose petals and cream, though she must have been nearing forty. A silk dress pulled at her hips, and a considerable bosom was visible beneath its thin fabric. She gave the hem a little tug.

'I never seemed to shift it after Billy was born. Three boys rather does something to the girlishness of one's figure.' She laughed, unperturbed. 'I would have had more, you know, but I kept losing them. Lost two more after Billy, and then Freddie said enough was enough. And I had to agree. Although I do miss it. Don't you? All that delicious pudginess and the angelic curls.'

Jean smiled, kissing her briefly on the cheek. 'I so loved that time. When they were your own. Now it feels like they'll be off and away any minute.'

'A wicked part of me longs for the day when they flee the nest. Might give Freddie and I the chance to do all the things we said we'd do and never got a chance to. They can swallow up all of one's time. And I do so yearn to travel. Do you still have that place in France? I remember Freddie telling me when you bought it. Sounded dreamy.'

'We do, we do. But it's not as easy now to get away, with one thing and another, and it's all such an expense, so we closed it up and haven't been back the last few years.'

'How very disciplined of you. I think I'd be there every moment I could, even if it was terribly profligate.'

Jean heard Edward's study door opening and the hall was filled with voices, an argument dressed as conversation making its way into the drawing room. It must have been the two guests she didn't know, friends of Edward's from London, to whom she had been told to give the best of the bedrooms and who had arrived in a sea of valets and luggage. The pair were introduced to Jean and Rose briefly – a James Faversham and a Henry Durrant – though neither man gave more than a nod as they made their way to the drinks table. Both were older than Edward, with prosperous bellies and a layer of bloat that bulged over their stiff collars like a toad's swell; Edward was listening closely to them, brow furrowed, the junior of the group.

'Surely you want to have it all in bonds at a time like this?' The taller of the two men, with a thatch of thick grey hair and hooded eyes, was scanning the room as he spoke.

The other, Henry, shook his head, dismissing his observation curtly. 'Oh, no, no. Property is the thing, old boy. Bricks and mortar. Look at the mess up here, coal and industry failing.' He fixed his eyes on Edward now. 'I see you're not all that far from Jarrow, Edward. Take heed of that. You see, I can't build houses quick enough. Costs are low, demand is high. Put anything disposable you have into housing down south.'

His friend slapped him on the back. 'Well, before you know it, Henry, you'll be buying a pile like Harehope and expecting the title to go with it.'

Henry looked at Edward a little peevishly. 'Edward's not a duke, mind you. That's what people go weak at the knees for.' A small smile spread across his porcine cheeks. 'Though a coronet on my slippers would do very nicely.'

The three men looked up. Alfie stood in the doorway, dressed in a suit for church, not old enough yet for the evening dress of the men, hesitant as to how to break in.

'Darling!' Jean was on her feet, cursing that she'd forgotten that he was to join for dinner. As his godfather was here she'd thought it would be nice, but it had slipped her mind in all the preparations.

Edward, irritated by the interruption, steered him over quickly to his two guests. 'My eldest boy, Alfie. Back from school.'

Alfie shook their hands and then stood, arms hanging awkwardly at his sides, unsure if he ought to stay and talk to his father or retreat to his mother and Rose. Edward watched him waver but did nothing, so he remained somewhere between the two, looking self-consciously at a painting.

'Lady Warre was just arriving as I came down, so she was good enough to let me steward her in.' Freddie had entered in a bluster of good cheer and *how are yous*, Edward's mother on his arm. He was still as slight as he had been in his twenties, but the intervening years had given him a modest paunch and a receding hairline, and there was a bald patch at the back of his head that was visible as he poured himself a drink. 'How are you, Jean? So kind of you to have us all so close to Christmas.'

Alfie dutifully came up and kissed his grandmother on her cheek, proffered only with the slightest of movement. Edward made the same reluctant pilgrimage, the irony not lost on Jean.

Freddie, affable as he always had been, drink now in hand, turned to Jean. 'It's been so long, Jean. And I haven't seen Edward in an age. I was quite surprised to get the nod.'

'But you see him in London, surely?'

'I do glimpse him at White's from time to time, but he's frightfully flash now.' He dropped his voice, looking over to Edward and his two friends. 'Always with swells like those chaps at Crockfords – they're awash with money, most of it new. Durrant made a fortune in construction in the south in the twenties. Spanking motors and a brand-new house in

Hertfordshire, all of that. I think they think Edward's a trophy. Something special to wheel around town. A title and an ancient pile of bricks never fails to impress.' He was smiling, but he was watching Edward curiously. 'Do you know them?'

'No. London friends, as you say. I don't get down there as much these days.'

'Well, it's a very different crowd to the old set, is all I'll say.' He smiled brightly. 'Of course, I'm sure we're all frightfully dull. Living like church mice to cling on to what we've got.' And his eyes shifted involuntarily to Alfie, standing alone and yearning for dinner to be announced.

'How odd to use the French decanters.'

Sitting by the fire after dinner, as her mother-in-law ran through the failings of the evening – the mousse not stiff enough, the meat not pink enough, the fool too tart though she would never eat more than a morsel anyway – Jean nodded and listened, so used to it now that she almost enjoyed it. She always felt as if Alice's judgements and criticisms were like a player knocking up before a set of tennis, establishing to the opposition how her game would proceed. Jean's attention, though, was on Alfie, who was sitting with Rose but counting the minutes until he could escape the drawing room. Eventually, she excused herself from Alice and went over to them.

Rose looked up, merrily patting Alfie on the knee. 'Oh gosh, am I boring him? You must stop me. He's such a dear, and only a year older than my Simon. And so handsome. My goodness, Jean. Those beautiful blue eyes. If only I had a daughter to marry off!'

As she spoke, the doors from the dining room opened and Edward was standing in the doorway, decanter of port in one hand, cigar in the other. 'What was that, Rose?' The room had fallen silent at his entrance; his voice was thick with drink, and even Alice had taken note.

Rose looked to him, embarrassed by the attention now on her, confused by his tone. 'I was just saying to Jean how utterly divine Alfie is – that he'll be breaking girls' hearts all over London soon.'

Edward's voice was too loud, his eyes on Jean. 'Well, I don't think he gets much from me.' He walked towards Alfie now, and he was looking directly at him, a strange, twisted smile on his face. 'And if you're anything like your mother, dear boy, you'd better learn to control yourself, hadn't you?' He turned and called behind him to the men who were still standing by the fireplace in the dining room.

Jean didn't want to look at Rose's kind, confused face at the periphery of her vision. 'I'm going to take Alfie up. It's late and he's got tomorrow to look forward to.' She bent down and kissed Rose briefly on the cheek, turned to say goodnight to Alice.

She walked out of the room quickly, cheeks burning, knowing Alfie was following quietly behind; knowing that she had only a moment to gather herself before she turned to look at him, only a moment to prepare another neat little basket of excuses and lies to lay at his door.

CHAPTER THREE

Edward had hit her again. After that first push in his study, which she had not questioned but had covered over with make-up and a smile, after the humiliation in the drawing room that she had not called him on, he had seemed strengthened in his resolve. She hated herself for not doing more, for not hitting back or shouting or scratching or screaming, but each time it happened was when the boys were there. She was weak, she was pathetic, but when they were in the house, how could she let them see that this was what their father had become? And that was the point that confounded her. What had he become; and what part had she played in that?

Weeks would pass, a bruise would fade then an argument flare up when she questioned Edward about their finances, about his erratic behaviour, and then another month would have gone by and Jean would stop, some glimpse of sky or a bird wheeling overhead would pull her out of herself, and she would wonder how much more she could endure; how long this strange half-life could continue. Another spring came; a summer passed, panic always beating its moth wings within her; the boys came home, Edward was away for large periods of time, and Jean began to question herself, her resilience; to wonder over and over what life this was she was living.

And then it was that morning in September and everyone was standing around the wireless; all the servants were called into the drawing room, Stokes going round the house, pulling them off whatever task was at hand, his face solemn as the grave. They were gathered around the small wooden box, a household as one, rank and class dissolved as together they heard Chamberlain's words of bitter disappointment crackling across the sun-filled room; heard his deep regret, a personal failure, his sadness that the nation was once more – too soon – at war.

She looked around at all those faces, pinched and drawn. The uncertainty of the preceding months had been lost on none of them. Hitler had flouted each agreement, each concession, till there was no excuse left that could be made for him. Grim-faced, they took stock as the inevitable became the actual. She saw Mrs Hawkins, face tight, hands clasped together as she held herself at bay, feeling her son of twenty already pulled away from her; saw one of the kitchen girls, pinafore dusted with flour, hands red from where she'd just scrubbed them clean, the little band of gold at her finger no longer a promise of happiness but a threat of loss. Jean's mind went to her boys: please, God, too young, too young. She looked to Edward, whose youth had excused him from bravery in the last war; what would be required of him now, a man of nearly forty? But as she scanned the room, scanned the faces of those men and women whose calmness and courage their prime minister now called upon, he wasn't there.

Edward didn't appear for another hour, not at lunch, nor the hour after, as Harehope lurched into action, trying to make sense of the list of duties now asked of each household: gas masks, blackouts, things that seemed so alien on a cloudless Sunday afternoon. She went to the stables to find him but was told that he had gone out riding after church with a couple of the lads and hadn't returned yet.

And it was then that Jack, the youngest of the stable boys, ran into the yard, his cheeks scarlet, hair plastered to his head with sweat, clutching his cap in his hand. 'He's fallen, m'lady. Lewis has stayed with him, but he's not moving. The horse bucked and he went over him and landed so awkward. Lewis told me to come back here and call for the doctor.'

Jean telephoned for the doctor as if in a dream. She was driven out in silence to the place where the fall had happened. It was his horse she saw first, tied to a gate in the corner of the field, one leg crooked awkwardly with no weight on it, pulling its head back in distress. She got out of the car and walked along the lane, flanked with high hedgerows still thick with cornflowers; she entered the field where the gate was held open by Lewis, cap in hand, his head bowed. She walked on through the wet grass, the sun at her back, the beauty of Eden stretched out before her. There had been a massive thunderstorm the night before, a month's rain falling in a matter of hours, and the ground was soft beneath her feet. She walked on, though she felt no contact with the earth, and then something inside her gave when she saw him: Edward, pale and prone and somehow so tidy and precise against the dark, smeared ground beneath him.

She knelt by him and instinctively put her hand to his face. His skin was cold and flaccid, and she felt a surge of nausea. It wasn't him. Where had he gone – where had all that anger and hate gone? She heard the doctor's car on the lane behind the hedge and she stood in a cloud of confusion as he told her that Edward's neck had broken on hitting the ground, that he had died immediately, would have felt no pain. Still she stood, the September sun warm on her face as her husband of seventeen years was pronounced dead, words funnelled to a mind lost beneath a blanket of shock.

Jean sat in the hall later, shoes black with mud that was now caked and dry, the telephone receiver in her hand. She had to tell Alice. Her mother-in-law received the news with only a momentary release of control. Jean heard her exhale, a strange dart of air, then she let out a strangled cry somewhere between a moan and a growl. She gathered herself almost immediately. 'I see. How awful. I see. I must tell Charlotte at once.' And then with a click she was gone, leaving Jean alone in the silence of her house, on a day when the whole country was stunned into silence, to work out how to tell her boys. The irony was not lost on her that once again her husband had missed his chance to fight for King and country.

While the house came to terms with the news – how strange, how unreal, she knew they all thought as they waded through this day of double calamity, the nation and Harehope's fortunes aligned – Stokes set about discreetly removing the day-to-day detritus of Edward's life from his home. There were his cigarettes left on the side of a table, his cap by the door, his jacket flung on a sofa, a book left half-open on a side table, his fingers having only just left the page. And a dress of black bouclé was laid out for Jean to put on: the costume for her next incarnation.

As she unclipped the diamonds at her ear, slipped out of her skirt and stepped into the shift of black, she saw herself in the looking glass. A widow, in the discreet uniform of mourning, at the age of thirty-eight: too young, she would hear people say, too young to lose a husband in his prime. But what could they know of the chaos, of the tangle of emotions that lay beneath?

Regret, a sadness so bitter she could taste it; a flare of relief that he was gone, chased by hounds of self-loathing for feeling it; images of what she had done to him, memories of what he had done to her. The mess and ugliness of it all, now dressed up as something that would be written about in obituaries, talked of in London clubs, passed around in polite did-you-hears around the county to ease the mutterings of a truth that hung in the air, almost undetectable but there nonetheless, that all had not been quite as it seemed.

The funeral that followed was small. Everything was so strange during the weeks and months that followed Chamberlain's announcement. The Bore War, people took to calling it, when no one was quite sure how to behave, when everything and nothing had changed. England had been expecting German bombers to come streaking through the sky, raining death and destruction as they'd seen in *The Shape of Things to Come*. But that hadn't happened, and life had carried on much as before. There was a small service at the family chapel, the promise of a larger memorial in London that would never materialise. Edward's mother invited neighbours but not tenants, any family who would travel, and of course the boys, brought up from school. Alfie and George – hair cut short, best coats on – stood beside Jean as Edward's coffin was lowered into the ground next to the graves of his brother and father, their young heads bowed, their hands clasped in front, so close their shoulders were touching.

As the straggle of mourners picked their path slowly through the sodden ground back to the house, Jean sensed the hesitation in Alfie as he politely shook the hands of well-wishers and estate workers who had lined the way between the chapel and the house. They tipped their caps or bobbed a curtsy as he passed, and she was momentarily confused until she realised that the page had already turned, the blank one smoothed and ready, ink poised to mark it, for the new Lord Warre. Alfie, in suit and tie, shoes shining and hair combed, had been unsure of how to respond, the crown not yet fitting, shoulders too narrow to carry the weight of expectation.

The boys cried that night, tears they tried to hide, muffled into pillows, but she went to them, sat with them, stroked their heads in the strange, forced dark of the blackout, until they drifted off, the soothing touch somehow making her feel real again. She knew that their grief, like hers, was a conflicted one. For a father who had shown no warmth or affection, who had seemed repulsed by George and enraged by Alfie, for reasons they could never understand. Theirs were tears of confusion, of guilt, of shame, but not of loss. Because how you could you be bereft of something that had never really been yours?

And Jean? The weeks of shock receded, fading into months of public mourning and private regret. But in the bleeding light between dreams and wakefulness, there began to form in her mind a name. It was still only a question, a possibility as fine as gauze, as intangible as the mist at dawn that rolled across the park as she stood in her dressing gown, looking out from her bedroom window, from a house that now felt, as she did, nomadic, rudderless.

David. Of course. It was David.

CHAPTER FOUR

Alfie's inheritance of his father's title – of the house, the land, the responsibility – came so quickly it caught them both off guard. Jean was Edward's widow, and as such had a role to play, but Alfie, though still at school, was his heir, and in the world of primogeniture, the age-old mechanism that kept these English estates together, he was called upon at once. He was now Lord Warre, and though he would not take full control until the age of eighteen, the agent, the trustees, the bank looked to him. Jean had become a sort of Prince Regent, hands bound by virtue of her sex, to a boy whose father's rejection of him cast his reign into shadow and uncertainty, though the outside world bestowed its solemn approval.

Mother and son sat together at a meeting arranged by the trustees in London. The house at Park Lane had been unused for months, and they were gathered in the drawing room in the flat light of a December morning. The trustees were a pair she'd had little to do with, whom she felt had met her as one person, wreathed in wealth and the inviolability of her Buckman name, and now as she sat next to Alfie – fifteen, with dark rings beneath uncertain eyes – were to discover as someone quite other.

Richard Holdsworth sat opposite Jean, adjusting his tie nervously before he spoke, shifting forward in his seat. He had been handsome when they first met but somehow age had hollowed him out and left him with a face that was narrow and pinched. He cleared his throat, looking to Alfie, looking back at Jean. 'We feel obliged, in the light of events, to discuss with Alfie – and with you, of course, Lady Warre, Jean if I may – the financial circumstances in which we find ourselves.'

Simon Marjoribanks leaned forward, slowly removing his glasses and giving them a leisurely rub. His tone was one of mild condescension: Alfie and Jean's role was to listen to the wisdom he would impart; to relax, safe in the knowledge that a man of intellect and substance was their guide. 'The question of expenditure, however indelicate, must always be raised as each new generation takes up the reins. And capital sales are always helpful to inject a little petrol into the tank.' He smiled generously, amused by his own lightness of touch. 'With the political situation as it is, I suspect it would be prudent to consider a few sales. And given the sudden nature of your father's death, there were sadly large pockets of property and land that had not yet been passed down from your father's trust to your own. The trust structure does not protect those, and there will be significant death duties to pay. Sales will need to be made in light of this' – and here the swell of a smile appeared at his well-padded cheeks – 'but we will always do our utmost to retain the core of the estate, the house, the land. What is rightfully yours and has been handed down from eldest son to eldest son for so many years—'

Richard, face like a ferret as he watched Simon closely, interrupted. 'It must be noted, Lady Warre' – he had dropped his feeble attempt at familiarity – 'that your personal circumstances undertook a marked change. A change of which, of course, Edward was aware, and which made you more reliant on the estate for your living. This has added a little strain to circumstances.' He gave a constipated smile as he looked at Alfie.

Simon took over again, voice smooth as cream. 'Without wanting to be presumptuous, Jean, if there were to be some settlement from your family in America in due course, it could be put to great use by your son, by the estate.'

What had Edward made them do, she wondered, in these last few years, for them both to be sitting here with their magpie eyes.

Simon knit his hands together amiably, addressing Alfie now with an avuncular smile. 'But in the meantime, Alfie, I think it is worth remembering that in these days of uncertainty, it is advisable to cut one's cloth a little. Your father did have a way of life in London that caused something of a pull on the estate, that we, as trustees, of course did our best to manage.' He went on. 'As you are a minor, Alfie, we are what is termed as administrators until you reach the age of eighteen. As such, we shall keep you informed of any significant changes that might be necessary, although we hope that won't be the case.'

Richard gave a queasy smile at the conclusion of Simon's speech.

Alfie sat there, nodding quietly, his eyes flicking to Jean occasionally. His face was serious, feigning confidence when she knew there was so little there. And at the age of fifteen, confronted by these men in suits, representatives of his father though they claimed to be his, what was left for him to do but nod?

The group parted in jovial bonhomie, Simon patting Alfie on the back, the men relieved to be back on the safe ground of the weather and the war, far away from the grubby talk of monies owed.

'Lloyds is laying odds that this will all be over by Christmas,' Simon observed breezily, before wishing Alfie well at school, kissing Jean on each cheek.

They took a taxi back to Waterloo. 'I'll be fine, Mama. You don't need to come with me,' Alfie had said, but she had ignored his request, and they sat together as they made their way through streets now lined with sandbags, past the park where trenches were being dug, past letterboxes being painted over, past workers carrying gas masks as they went to get their lunch, all of this activity a little self-conscious, for it was set against a backdrop of nothing much out of the ordinary at all. No planes screaming overhead, no poison gas streaking through the city, no enemy on the streets, just an endless roll-call of announcements to listen to, warnings to heed, preparations to make.

'It'll be good to be back at school, with your friends.' Though other schools had moved to safer locations, Eton had stayed put, promising anxious parents that it had invested in the best possible shelters. 'But try not to think about this morning too much. It's a lot for you to take on board: Papa's death, all this change. I wished we could have postponed the meeting, but they were adamant.'

'It's all right. It's just an odd time. Everywhere.' He hesitated. 'And Papa never talked about any of this to me.'

'No, I know he didn't. No bad thing really – you could get on and not get bogged down in the detail of it before it was necessary.'

'You don't always have to make it better, you know,' he snapped. 'I'm not a child any more. You don't have to try and do that all the time.'

Jean chose her words carefully. 'I understand that now. But it's hard not to sometimes. I suppose it's because I'm sorry for my part in it.' She hesitated. 'There might have been someone else who made things easier for him. We weren't—'

'Why do you always make excuses for him? I can't bear it.' His voice began to waver. 'You were always making it better for us. What a waste, always having to make up for him. And he's dead now anyway.' The words fell out of him, and he looked away. He rubbed his eyes roughly, hating himself for letting tears fall. 'I don't want to cry.' He sniffed loudly, wiping his nose on his hand, not looking at her. 'I don't want to cry,' he said again, gathering himself. 'I just don't understand why he seemed to hate us.' He looked up at her. 'There. I've said it. But now you look so sad, and then I'll cry again, and I really don't want to.' And his voice rose and then she laughed and so did he, and the mood was broken. He sniffed and rubbed his eyes again.

'Oh, darling, you are so good. What did I do to deserve you?' She put her hand out to him, knowing that he was too old for this but that he would let her. And he did; he put his hand in hers, and a thousand memories of that most pure of connections, the simplest of gestures, blew through her like the gentle breeze through trees in summer. He let her rub his hand gently with her thumb but then he let go, and his hand was back in his lap as he turned away to look out of the window, as they wound their way through the streets of Belgravia, driving past men carrying their briefcases, poppies pinned to their raincoats for Armistice Day which was nearly upon them, now signifying not just the memory of loss but the fear of its return.

Alfie was still looking out of the window as he spoke, his voice unsure. 'Why didn't Papa ever talk to me? It was like it was poison to him that it would come to me.'

'He was a complicated man. Things that came easily to you, they weren't the same for him. I know it's difficult to hear, but he might not have been able to.'

He laughed, a sad, wry laugh which she hated for coming from one so young.

'And inheritance, this handing on of things, it's not always easy. It can be a reminder of one's own failings, how they will always be set against what comes after or before. I think your father felt that strongly.'

'I won't be like him.' His voice was low. 'Don't hate me for saying that about my own father. But I won't.'

Jean said nothing, and they continued in silence. She was mesmerised by the lies and truths that Alfie was coming up against as he grew up; like a blind man feeling in the dark, he was coming into contact with a form that was hard, that felt to him impassable; he was mistaking it for a closed door, though the cold draught of truth was there at its edge.

Her son saw it all: the pieces of a childhood puzzle, tipped out of the box and strewn across a table, meaningless in their scattered isolation. He saw it all; he just did not see the whole.

CHAPTER FIVE

1939 drifted on into the next year – still no drama, just a slow slide into a new normal of blackouts and the drip, drip of mild deprivation, of margarine where butter had been, of train scheduling now a mess, of museums closing then opening again, of evacuees heading half-heartedly, like parcels, out of the city, of gas masks that were no longer carried but sat, gathering dust on shelves, reminding one always of the war to come hovering in the wings, waiting to enter the stage. But then as slow as the first act had been, the one that followed was so rapid it left the country reeling: Germany's invasion of the lowlands; the surrender of the Belgian army; the horror of Dunkirk; the day the German tanks rolled into Paris, causing Londoners a collective shiver of fear at the prospect of a city so majestic, so untouchable, now in the hands of the enemy; then the shock, the absolute horror at the surrender of France; the Battle of Britain; all of it happening like bricks falling in a burning building, so fast it was hard to imagine that the whole thing wouldn't come down upon them too.

And then the bombs fell on London.

One night of bombing in mid September of the Blitz ripped

a hole right through the roof of the house on Park Lane. It had been empty at the time, the boys at school and the skeleton staff that worked there home by then, but Jean felt she had to go. She had been driven from King's Cross along the Marylebone Road, the taxi threading its way through the streets of Soho, avoiding roads blocked by debris, where ARP wardens were funnelling traffic cheerfully down new routes. They passed a cordon to a warren of streets now closed off and evacuated. 'There'll be one of the Engineers down there,' her driver said proudly over his shoulder, for Londoners were all now compatriots in the shared nocturnal hell that rained down on them. 'Heroes those lads, using their mathematics and their nerves to deal with those godawful time bombs.' On they went, a journey through a nightmare. She saw a church on Dean Street, its clock tower standing, though the rest of it had been obliterated. Defiant, improbable, it was like a lone skittle about to topple, the driver whistling through his teeth as they passed.

She stood in that magnificent hallway on Park Lane, where great chunks of plaster lay like icebergs on the chequered marble floor and a sky of cobalt blue looked down on them through the vast hole in the ceiling.

'Finding skilled workmen to do a decent job of repairing the roof at this time will be nigh on impossible.' Simon was standing beside her, politely waiting, she could tell, for her to make the decision he would not leave without.

'The size of it. And unused by anyone really. I'm not sure how you might feel...' Richard looked to Simon.

'The thing is, Jean, if we sold the lease back to the Grosvenor estate, the money would be extremely useful. I've had words with a pal there and he hinted they would take it off our hands very quickly.'

They were both different men to the ones she had met only months before. The jokes made then about a quick end to the war belonged to another life; and London too was another city, where every one of her citizens found him or herself called upon, where the pomposity of a man like Simon had been obliterated by the air raid's wail and the decimation of her streets.

As Jean walked through the house with them, inspecting the damage, up the staircase with its runner of burgundy and gold – the finest wool, the richest braiding – she thought of that September afternoon after her wedding, when she and Edward had first entered as husband and wife, past parcels and boxes from Asprey's and Garrard's, Thomas Goode and Harrods, all these presents piled up and waiting, society's benediction of their perfect marriage. The hollowness of it all echoed back to her now from the walls of every one of its grand, imposing rooms.

They stepped into what had been Edward's bedroom with its curtains of deep green silk, chosen by her mother. Jean hadn't slept in there for years; God, hadn't even walked through its door for an age. Simon and Richard watched her in silence as she walked over to its double-height windows that looked down and across to the park, now sandbagged, with deep trenches dug along its edge. They were right. What was its purpose, this vast house that now stood, reproachful and silent? Some empty symbol that the Warre family still held the position it once had?

She turned back to Simon and Richard, but something struck her as she did. The paintings that had hung on either side of the door were no longer there. A pair of pastoral scenes by Boucher, rococo gems that her father had insisted on giving Jean on her marriage. They had hung in his study in New York and she had loved them as long as she could remember, coming up with silly little stories for the pink-cheeked, romantic figures that reclined in their hazy, idealised world. On her wedding day, her father had arranged for them to be hung here in their bedroom, with a small handwritten note left on her desk: *May your children and your children's children derive the same pleasure from them as we did. Yours ever, Papa.* The paintings were gone, a pair of bland hunting prints hanging in their place.

She looked to the two men standing in the doorway, their eyes on her. 'Where did the pair that hung there go? I haven't been in this room for so long. I know Edward sold some things at Christie's, but not these. I never saw anything about the Bouchers. He wouldn't. You wouldn't.' Her voice rose, and she felt anger like a rod of heat within her.

Neither answered, but Richard cleared his throat.

'They were given to me by my father. There will be a record of them in the catalogue of paintings for this house.'

Simon gave a nervous smile. 'I understand that your parents were extremely generous to you upon your marriage, Jean, in buying this house, in furnishing it. I'm not sure Edward took that as a permanent state of affairs.'

'These paintings weren't part of that. For God's sake. They were my childhood.' She took a breath, steadied herself. 'What are you not telling me, Simon? I am entitled to know the truth. As Alfie's mother at least, I am entitled to know what went on.'

Simon forced a smile. 'I do see that this is frustrating, Jean. Not easy to hear. But Edward understood his possession of the estate, the house here in London and all of its contents, in an absolute sense. Ultimately, on marriage, it all became his.'

'I know that, I know that. But can't you see that these paintings were different. They were mine, from my father on my wedding day. For me...and yet everything became Edward's, Edward's to fritter away – it makes me so angry.'

The eyes that watched her were utterly flat, like mirrors. What was the point? The clock in the corridor outside chimed two.

'Do we need to sell this house?'

They both nodded, faces washed out in the thin afternoon light.

'I will talk to Alfie. I'm assuming that you can arrange this on his behalf?'

'Absolutely. We will sign the papers as soon as we can. We can arrange for the paintings and furniture to go into storage. Although Alfie might consider some judicious sales there too – when the time is right.' Richard's voice was almost wheedling.

And when they stood in the chequered hallway once more, pulling on coats and hats, she saw their relief: in the release at their shoulders, the vigorous shaking of her hand. 'Be assured, the money will be put to good use,' Simon added greasily as he turned to go.

Jean nodded as she watched them hurry down the steps and onto Park Lane, wondering if they had any real sense of the absurdity of it all. That this great gift from her mother – a house befitting the person her daughter had become on marriage, lined with paintings, groaning with Paul Storr silver and Chippendale furniture – should now be consigned to sale, authorised by the briefest of handshakes from two Englishmen whom Elizabeth Buckman had never even laid eyes on.

Edward's parting gift to his wife had been a fitting one.

CHAPTER SIX

The morning after a raid, Jean and Constance Holmes walked up
Regent Street from Piccadilly Circus. Shop upon shop had had
its front blown in, and they passed a window display of ladies'
stockings hanging like bunting blowing in the breeze. Their
feet crunched across a film of broken glass that sparkled in the
morning light like frost, the destruction strangely mesmerising.

Jean looked across at her old friend. The pair had remade
their acquaintance a month or so before, having lost touch since
those days in France. Constance was unchanged by the intervening years, the skin at her cheeks a little looser perhaps, the
arch at her eyebrow drawn a little more severely – 'it helps the
structure of one's face, darling. Scaffolding, if you like' – but
she was still a dynamo, with an address book and work ethic
undented by the advent of war.

They crossed the street, stepping over a stream of water
pouring out from a burst main.

'Do you know Stella Reading?'

'Darling, who doesn't? The woman is like a force-nine gale
at sea. One can't avoid her.'

'What do you think? Shall we do it?'

'Oh, it'll be like a cocktail party – without the cocktails, of course. But I think we must. Of course we must.'

Stella Reading's WVS – or the Women's Voluntary Service, to give it its full name, as Lady Reading apparently preferred – had turned out to be run rather like a club on St James's, with Who Knew Who mattering a lot more than any kind of training or skill. And before long, Jean and Constance had been called to an office off Whitehall, given the address of a school in Paddington, where they were given some perfunctory training the next morning, and issued with their authority to wear voucher and instructed to head to Harrods or Fenwick's to purchase their suit, blouse and overcoat of grey-green tweed and their distinctly sensible felt hats.

'She managed to persuade Digby Morton to design them, for goodness' sake.' Constance laughed, as they stood together by the counter at Fenwick's, an assistant parcelling up their clothes in tissue and string. 'The woman is a marvel!'

The work was piecemeal at first, but as the bombing intensified that winter, so too did what was asked of them. Raids were happening each night, and every morning, not much after the all-clear had sounded, they and a team of ladies would set off to an area that needed them. The first time Jean went out, the group of four women were packed into a grocer's van, still painted with the name of its previous owner but with a large sign declaring its management by the WVS propped up behind the windscreen. They had been told to set up their mobile canteen on a street in Battersea, and having hauled themselves into the van, bleary-eyed from lack of sleep, they made their journey through a city that was almost unrecognisable, past craters in the road so large they could have swallowed a bus whole. Entire sides of buildings had been stripped off like skin, revealing strange details of daily life beneath: a photograph still on a mantelpiece; a dress in a wardrobe; an old stuffed toy, patched and worn, surveying the wreckage from a child's neatly made bed. Incendiaries had left fires burning everywhere, thankfully by this time down to a smoulder, while firemen with faces black from smoke stood, hoses in hand, wearing the long stare of a night without sleep.

A young woman knelt on the cracked pavement, rifling through a small holdall. Jean crouched down beside her. 'Are you all right? Can I get you a cup of tea?'

'I've just come up from the shelter.' The girl shook out a cardigan roughly, pulled out a dress. Now her hands were running frantically around the inside edges of the bag.

'My husband's away, you see, posted somewhere on the west coast. And I packed this case for the shelter last night, and I swear I put my ration book, my money, and – and a photograph of Jim and me, from our wedding day.' There was a slight waver in her voice and she stopped, pulling herself together, not wanting her emotions to spill out onto the rubble of the pavement with her clothes. She looked at Jean directly now. 'How am I to get word to him of this? And what would I say? That we've lost everything. The whole bloody building's gone.'

Jean pulled her to her feet and walked her to the van, where Constance passed her a mug of tea, and the three stood in silence. Jean put her hand on the girl's arm and watched a tear slide down her cheek, wiped away as soon as it appeared.

The queue for their van was growing now, snaking down the street as more and more emerged from the safety of shelters only for the grim new reality above ground to be revealed.

There was a mother, a baby of no more than eight or nine months in her arms dressed in only a vest, little socks and bootees poking out from under the blanket. 'Where am I going to bathe him, when my home of fifteen years is nothing but dust and rubble?'

'My ration book's lost,' another woman muttered as she filed into line. She was wheeling what was left of her belongings in a perambulator, her baby at her hip.

And so, as each day bled into the next in that seemingly endless winter, Jean would pat a hand or put an arm around a shoulder, would find a sandwich for a hungry child, a handkerchief for a tear, direct the now homeless to an office for rehousing or a place to get replacement ration books, uttering all the while what she felt were useless words of comfort, of encouragement, of commiseration. But always she was confronted by the same spirit. A cheeriness in the face of extraordinary, shocking loss. Unbroken, unbowed, the people she would meet might gripe about the inconvenience, would grumble about the lack of facilities in shelters or the scrum that would now form at the Underground stations in the early afternoons to find a spot for the night, but still they would keep going, with a resolve and a strength of purpose that was astounding, though each night held the promise of more to break them.

That winter, Jean lived the grind that all Londoners lived, and though being in the city could have killed her a hundred times over, though it wore her down and her nails were bitten to the skin, it kept her alive. It brought a sense of purpose, she now came to realise, to a life that had for too long lacked it. She took on the lease of a two-bedroomed flat in the north-east corner of Berkeley Square, though the letting agent thought her mad; it was up on the first floor, with a drawing room that got the morning sun and looked out and onto the square below. And she would sit in the shelter each night there was a raid, whispering childhood prayers she had thought long forgotten, alongside people with whom her only connection was a shared wish to survive the night, coming up when the all-clear sounded to another bombed-out dawn, where she was needed and she could do good. And she felt herself repair, felt an incremental shift within her, away from the darkness, after the damage of the years before.

Jean and Constance were sitting in a crowded pub in a square somewhere behind Victoria station. It was a cold and dank afternoon and they couldn't face the walk home, trudging back to Mayfair among the commuters who now left work earlier, their day shifting back by an hour or so to accommodate life in a bombed-out city where journeys were unpredictable and your bus route of only the day before might not exist. They had decided to stop for a shandy instead, something to gee them up for the long evening ahead. In this London of blackouts and raid, it was tiredness, not fear, that ground one down.

'I envy you your energy.' Jean was sitting down in a seat in the window, her coat still on, and she smiled wanly at her friend. 'I feel shattered by today. In-my-bones tired.' She took a sip from the glass Constance had put before her, looked at her friend, incongruous somehow in the smeary warmth of the pub, with its hard benches and wood panelling, wedged in as they were among railway workers and taxi drivers on their breaks. Despite the day's efforts Constance was as pulled together as ever, a jaunty pheasant's feather now tucked under the band of red on her standard-issue green felt hat, a silk scarf of green and red polka dots knotted neatly at her neck.

'It suits you though, all of this.'

Jean smiled. 'What sort of a woman must I be for war to suit me!'

'No, but really. It's good. I can see it. To have a life of your own. I know that Edward only died a year ago, but it's important to make something of the here and now. And not always be fretting about your boys.' She took a sip of her beer, raising the glass to Jean, smiling at the funny pair they made. 'Alfie'll be a man before you know it and then he'll marry some nymph of a girl who'll fill his head with nonsense about his beloved mother, and you'll be cast out in the shadows.'

'Constance, you are awful!'

'But it's true. You're nearly forty, not an old crone of sixty-something like me. Find some delicious diplomat who's lonely and needs a shoulder to cry on. Or a nice brigadier who's looking for a warm bed for the night.' Her face grew serious. 'I know the last years before Edward died weren't the easiest. You slid away from things. I see it now. From life really. You're coming back to it now, though. Keep doing that, won't you?'

Jean laughed. 'I'm not sure I'm the enticing prospect I once was.'

'Oh, come, come. I always felt you wanted to shrug all that off anyway.'

Jean hesitated. They were friends, she was a grown-up. What was there to lose in being honest? She took a sip of her drink before speaking. 'You're going to think me mad, but do you remember David Carver, from all those years ago in France?'

'Of course, how could I not? That evening when you sobbed and sobbed, told me all about it. It was heart-breaking.' Constance frowned. 'You can't still hold a torch for him, surely? That was aeons ago.'

'The thing is – it carried on, beyond that summer.'

'Oh?'

337

'For a long time. I did break it off with him eventually, but I've thought about him since. About finding him. And now I'm on my own, well, the door somehow feels open again.'

'Oh, but darling, I know what's become of him. Or something of it, at least. I was doing up a house in Palm Springs, it must have been three years ago, and I'd see him playing tennis or at the Colonial for drinks. We spoke a couple of times, in fact. He was charming still, handsome still, and he was with Thelma Duke, had been I think for some time. Thelma's quite something. Pots of money.' She gave Jean a wry smile. 'Laurence Duke is much older, you see, and fearfully rich – oil, or was it tobacco? Gosh, my mind isn't what it was, imagine me forgetting a thing like that. Anyway, David Carver was Thelma's walker... Not that that means everything, but, well, you know...'

Jean felt her chest cave. 'Oh. I see. I had no idea. I feel idiotic for even mentioning it.'

Constance put her hand across the table to Jean's, giving it a pat. 'Oh my love, is that a frightful disappointment? I'm so sorry. But what's the point in hiding these things? I feel so much now that we should live in the present. Don't you? Not go back to dredge up the past.' She smiled kindly. 'And what did you have in common with him anyway, beyond *la grande passion*? And one does wonder whether he was a little too interested in the good life. You're English now, and living in England. Find someone here. Do, please.'

The room seemed to shrink a little, and Jean became aware of the conversation of the two men who were sitting so close to them their elbows could almost touch. So David had found someone else. Of course he had. Why would he not, when she had ended it all? She felt a fool for even thinking about him after so much time had passed. But her heart took a blow nonetheless; she felt the bruise right there in the centre of her chest.

Constance was right. She ought to try to be part of this life in London. It was exhilarating to have one's nerves on edge, to reach out and touch life in all its pain and imperfection, to share a drink with a friend at the end of the day, here in the fug of a pub somewhere in Pimlico. London was where she ought to find sustenance, in the camaraderie of danger and privation; find connection in the anonymity of a city that lived each day on a knife's edge.

So she went to a club, the Café de Paris, one night after dinner. It was a week or so later, with Constance and her husband and a group of their friends who she didn't really know. She sat at a small round table with a little lamp at its centre that cast a waxy glow, next to a man of forty with a neat moustache and grey-green eyes. He had fixed them on Jean as they talked and the evening wore on; he'd bought her a drink, had held her eyes as he handed it to her, and when they had danced together as he seemed to know they would, his cheek against hers, he'd whispered something that she couldn't quite catch but knew its meaning. He had pulled back to look at her then, his eyes unafraid of the message they held.

But she had walked back to her flat that night with Constance and her husband, not the man with the grey-green eyes. He hadn't been disappointed when she had made her excuses. He'd just smiled, a rueful smile, and had turned to another woman now sitting next to him, leaning in to light her cigarette. That was what people did now.

Next time she'd try. She promised herself this as she lay down on the right side of the bed, the sheets on the left smooth as marble, tucked in tightly, as she waited for sleep to take her. It was a lie, but she told it to herself anyway.

A woman of considerable means, who he squired around tennis clubs and talked with at tables strewn with cocktail glasses and bathed in the clean, bright sunshine of California. The images of David and this woman shuttered across Jean's mind till she wasn't sure if she was there with him too. Did he love this woman; did he want her? Was Jean even a memory to him, called to mind fleetingly by the way this woman held her cigarette or laughed at some joke while a crowd of hangers-on smiled indulgently? Jean tormented herself, imagining these scenes over and over. But then came that tide of tiredness – something she'd never experienced before the war, an overwhelming thing that one could not fight – sweeping over her, leaving her mind an empty blank, till dawn should come again to drag her back up to the present.

CHAPTER SEVEN

The young man from the Ministry of Works was making slow progress up the main staircase at Harehope with Jean, Stokes following behind at a polite distance. He was a neat soul, in a suit of grey wool, with a pair of round spectacles perched on a snub of a nose, and he carried a ledger tucked under one arm and a pencil and a tape measure in the other. He had been methodically noting down dimensions of rooms, widths of doorways, the height of the cellars, the kitchens, the pantry, even taking notes in Stokes' sparse little anteroom that Jean had never been into the whole time she had lived there.

He had been particularly taken by Harehope's enormous oak front door. 'It's almost eight feet across. Marvellous, really marvellous.' He gave Jean a bright smile, as if she had somehow been involved in the door's construction. 'A wonderful thing to see.'

He carried on taking enthusiastic notes as they worked their way up the great staircase into the best bedrooms, which were to be made over for officers and their batmen, their beds now stripped of all but their mattresses, the furniture hastily covered in dust sheets. They threaded their way past uniformed young men as they bumped and heaved paintings and chairs, lamps and rugs down the stairs and into the yard, which was to be turned over for storage of items of 'particular value' – 'There is not much in this house that would not meet that classification,' Stokes had announced with a look of imperious disdain on his face – as room upon room was emptied to make way for the men of C Company that would soon occupy them.

A young soldier, only eighteen or nineteen, an enormous Chinese vase in his arms, was struggling to pass them. Stokes' eyes followed the boy as he spoke. 'A little more time might have been preferable. For her ladyship to prepare the house for their arrival.'

The man from the ministry nodded, a face of polite concern. 'I do understand. But with events moving so quickly, any houses that are suitable are to be requisitioned with the utmost urgency. I am afraid your position, on the edge of the moors here, is enviable. For training and manoeuvres. The civil service seem to be paired up with schools and hotels, buildings of a more public nature. Houses such as yours, gems really, have been marked up for the army.' He smiled sheepishly. Jean had taken to this young man, his tie impossibly straight, hair neatly combed, manners precise to a fault. He turned to Jean. 'I've been asked by the War Office to come up with a reasonable market rent to pay your ladyship's family. I can't promise that it will be huge, but I hope it will go some way towards expressing our gratitude for your generosity in opening your doors.' He cleared his throat, eyes flicking nervously to Stokes. 'I should probably also add at this point that the Ministry of Works only suggests implementation of protective works in houses where the architecture is of the Elizabethan or medieval period. It seems rather a crude rule, given the number of Georgian and Victorian houses I have seen on the list, but I will stress to the new occupiers that this is a home that has been in your family for hundreds of years, and as such should be treated with the greatest of respect.'

And so, with those polite words of warning, he had departed, the army had moved in and Harehope had been reborn. Her new incarnation was one of khaki and paperwork, of hammering typewriters and men everywhere, of the tread of heavy tyres on her gravel and the appearance of Nissen huts like measles on her skin. One became two became ten, till the whole park was dotted with them and Jean struggled to remember what that placid and Arcadian expanse of green, grazed by docile sheep and trimmed in its neat black railings, had looked like before.

'It's actually come as something of a relief,' she confided to Constance one afternoon when she was back in London. 'After Edward died, I could finally admit what I think I'd always known. That Harehope, the estate, it's not mine. Never was. Edward had never invited me to feel as if it could be. I was the interloper. The flash American that his mother always thought me. You know, unless the boys are there and it's the holidays, I long to be back here. The house being requisitioned gives me the perfect excuse to leave.'

So when the school holidays came, she would meet the boys at the station and drive them back to their new digs in the east wing – an area of the house that still enabled them to have Edward's old study as a smaller drawing room as well as perfectly acceptable bedrooms up the back stairs. In the evenings, Stokes would push a trolley carrying an enormous candelabra and a plate of Cook's best down a barely lit back corridor that ran from the old kitchen, making sure, with a less than gentle ram, that any soldier he encountered gave him sufficient space to pass. The trolley would give a loud thunk as it met uneven floorboards, giving Stokes additional pleasure, she thought, that his pilgrimage was not going unnoticed by their new, unwelcome guests.

On the war dragged; more was asked of them, more was taken. People talked of a tiredness that sat somewhere behind the eyes. A tension, tucked away or studiously ignored, that worked away at them nonetheless, day after day, grinding them down, stretching them out. One year rolled into the next, autumn into winter, a Christmas passing, then another spring that brought more rationing, more restrictions, and then it was her turn – when that prayer she had made on the day war broke out was returned unanswered. Her turn, as mother of a son of fighting age, had come.

Conscription was now for anyone aged eighteen and over, and Alfie had celebrated his birthday in his last term at school. Most of his friends were heading for the RAF, which was smarter, more louche somehow, for boys desperate to be like the Spitfire pilots of 601 Squadron, who would walk into the Four Hundred like young movie stars, wreathed in gold. He should have gone to the Life Guards, the right sort of place in the army for boys like Alfie, where his uncle and grandfather had held rank, where his father would have had he been alive. But he had not wanted to take that route, had been adamant about wanting to join the new parachute regiments that Churchill had established the year before. All the talk of discipline, grit and determination had spoken to him. He'd had a beak at school who had connections to the training school in Derbyshire, and he had written letters and got anyone he knew with clout to request that Alfie get accepted, though it was unorthodox. And so Alfie's school record, his focus, his dedication and the countless invisible threads that linked someone like her son to almost anyone in the English establishment meant that he had, inevitably, got his way.

He had left in September to start his training at Hardwick Hall, fired up by the challenge, desperate to get his teeth into something. Had written home each week, wanting to keep abreast of everything at the house, asking always about George, about her. And now it was Christmas, and he had a week of leave that they would spend together at Harehope.

The few months he had been away had changed him. She could see it in the way he held himself, in the broadening of his shoulders, in the gentle curve of muscle in his slim arms and the quiet efficiency with which he now got on with things. She could see too that he had benefited hugely from being away, a sense of self solidifying away from Harehope, from her perhaps.

They were sitting around the fire in Edward's old study, the wireless on in the background, the chunter of the men in the officers' mess coming in through the open door. Dinner was over and Stokes was giving the boys a glass of port, unwilling as ever to allow any small standard to slip, despite Hitler's best efforts. He had managed too to pull together a garland for the mantelpiece, and Mrs Hawkins had studded it with cinnamon sticks which she'd squirrelled away God knows where and tied two great bows of red velvet at each end.

'There was one boy whose leg splintered like a twig when he'd landed, I heard the crack. It was his first dummy jump.'

George was mesmerised, a boy's fascination with pain and injury spread across his face.

'He was stretchered off, screaming, before he fainted – and my God, the noise he made. Like an animal trapped in a snare. Made us all go sheet white at the thought of that happening to one of us. But you have to put it aside, not think about it. Keep doing the practice jumps. At first we did them from converted barrage balloons, familiarising ourselves with the equipment, learning how to work it all, before the real jump. One poor lad was moved on after that. He got the jitters when the moment came to haul out of the plane for the first time. He just refused, clinging onto the side, with the commanding officer yelling blue murder in his face.'

'You weren't frightened?' His brother's voice was quiet, tinged with awe.

'Of course I was, but then the exhilaration that comes after is extraordinary. The wind screams in your ears, this rushing feeling until you pull the cord and there's the tremendous yank of the chute behind you. And then you're sailing down, at a totally different pace, the world spread out beneath you like some snakes and ladders board, not real at all – but then the smack of earth beneath your feet and it's real all right.' He grinned. 'It's extraordinary. I can't explain it, but it's something I never thought I'd love as much as I do.'

'What are the others like?'

'Most of them are all right. It's quite a rum bunch, different sorts from all backgrounds. And I got gyp from some of them. One boy's younger brother is training here at Harehope now, so he's heard all about it from him. That there's countless rooms and gardens that go on for miles, all that sort of nonsense. But I like a lot of them.'

'You've lost weight though, darling. Are they feeding you properly?'

Alfie smiled at his mother, rolling his eyes. 'It is pretty filthy. Grey meat if we're lucky, and indiscriminate veg. But it's the exercises that do it. They drill into us, over and over, that what the parachute regiments are to be known for is self-discipline, self-reliance, aggressiveness. That our job is to be dropped in behind enemy lines, that we might be separated from each other and need to establish targets on our own, under enemy fire, in extreme conditions. So in reality that's miles and miles walked with packs on our scrawny backs, feet numb from cold and from pounding on the frozen ground for hours on end. It's not all bad, though. On the route back to camp on the last sortie before Christmas leave, we were given half an hour to drink as many pints as the girl behind the bar at the local pub could pour for us.'

As Jean watched George listening to his brother, tales from a wartime experience he would never have, she could tell that her younger son was truly happy to be home. He was sunk deep in his armchair, face turned to Alfie, with Yip, the smallest of their spaniels, asleep across his feet. School and the scrum of boys – lessons to be rushed to, one's social self called upon at all times – drained him. He loved Harehope for giving him the space simply to be: to read, to paint, to walk. And there was a bond between the three of them that had strengthened since Edward's death. As if they were the war-wounded, survivors of something, who shared the scars though they would never talk about it. It meant that there was a real tenderness in moments like this, in the quiet companionship as they sat around the fire, the familiar ornaments laid out as they were every year, the cherub hanging from the mantelpiece, with his trumpet of chipped gold, the miniature Christmas tree that one could wind up so that it turned, jerkily, to the creaking tune of 'O Tannenbaum'.

Alfie was standing with his back to the fire now, hands behind him as he warmed them. 'There's a fraternity among us, if that's the right word. It's different to what there was at school, it's different to anything I've experienced before. I like it. There's a sense of purpose.'

He stopped then, and though she didn't know where his mind had gone, she could make a good guess. Despite the path so clearly mapped out for him, Alfie had never felt entirely at ease with it all. His father had seen to that. But this training, the learning, the camaraderie, this was something of his own. Not handed to him, but chosen. To be worked at, fiercely, and the rewards to be reaped were personal ones, the losses all his own. She understood it. It was what she had felt in the worst days in London.

Christmas came and went, the fourth without their father, the fourth of the war. A strange Christmas, in a house no longer their own, where the service on Christmas Day in their chapel was notable for the absence of men, where the presents were scant, the food simple, but the moments together somehow all the sweeter.

Then Alfie was gone again, as quickly as he had come. His leave was over, the six days he spent in the house a memory as she and George packed up for his return to school. Her eldest son was gone. She would hear his voice in her study, or see him walking up the back stairs to his room, or talking in that serious, polite way he had with Stokes or Mrs Hawkins, asking how they were, offering assistance, or laughing with George about some stupid thing that would have them both in fits, great belly laughs that no one else could pull from them.

He would still write, though. Jean would devour his letters and share them with George when he was home from school and the pair would talk for hours after about his news, wondering anxiously where he might be sent as his training drew to a close. His was the 4th battalion, soon to be joined into a new regiment, the 2nd Independent Parachute Brigade. He was so proud of his achievements, she could tell, though always there hung the spectre of the man who had never praised him for anything.

For the left-behind, for Jean and George, guessing was the game now, piecing together news from the papers and what they could glean from the radio and any snippets from that hallowed group, those who Really Knew, to find a plausible place for deployment. And Jean found herself just a number, one of those thousands upon thousands of mothers, powerless in the face of the inevitable call to arms that was coming ever closer; their only defence was distraction and the sharing of privation, each pang of hunger or putting on of last year's winter coat, each wait for a train delayed or cancelled, each inconvenience at home became something to cherish, a connection to her boy soon to be suffering far worse.

CHAPTER EIGHT

The boys would be here soon. Jean stood at the window, looking down and onto Berkeley Square below her. The mess of Number 30 was no longer as shocking as it had been when she first saw it; the whole house, save for the lift's shaft, reduced to a pile of rubble. There hadn't been serious bombing in the city for a while now. London had taken a pummelling in January, a reaction to the Allied assault on Berlin, but since then the ack-ack boys had been doing their job and there was almost a nonchalance to life. Couples would dawdle as they left the theatre or groups of friends spill out onto the streets from the cinemas – *The Life and Death of Colonel Blimp*, with Deborah Kerr in all her technicolour glory, was the film of the moment – and they would stop for a moment before walking home or making their way to the Underground, looking up at a sky that was clear but for the silhouette of barrage balloons, great silvered moons that gave such comfort to those beneath, savouring the simple pleasure of the light of a summer's evening and the heavens at peace above.

A taxi door opened outside, there was the sound of low voices, and she was at the window and Alfie was there in his khaki uniform, maroon beret already off his head and in his hand, craning his neck to see if he could make her out at the window. She waved, her heart lifting as it always did at the sight of him. Though several buildings nearby had been turned over for offices for American war departments, her building was often empty, much to the annoyance of those who knew what a housing crisis the bombing of London had caused. Her neighbours above and below preferred to keep heads down in the country, unless a shopping trip to London called, but there was still a doorman, too old to be called up, who would greet Alfie cheerfully and send him upstairs.

'Darling.'

She kissed him, held his hand briefly in hers. He looked thinner, slight shadows under his eyes. It was nearly six, so she let him open a bottle of gin and fix them a drink. She watched him as he stood over the tray in the corner of the room, always the man now, adding the bitters for his mother, knowing how she liked it. He brought hers over first, and as she looked across at him she could sense his distraction. He sat in the armchair opposite, tapping his foot, turning the tumbler in his hand.

'I've missed you so much. The weather's been so lovely in London this last week, and I've wondered what you've been up to as I've sat here in the evenings.'

He barely acknowledged her comment. 'I don't want to be serious. Tonight's our last evening, I know. But I need to get this out of the way before George gets here.'

She knew she had seen something. The shadows were not just from the training and troubled sleep before heading off to fight. She listened, leaning against the window, the pane still warm from the afternoon's sun.

'I just feel, without Papa, that my going away, whatever might happen – I don't want to leave you in the lurch. There's a lot to do and Harehope has become something of a burden. I can see that, even though you do your best to pretend it's not.'

She was distracted by the poignancy of his appearance; his uniform, so crisp and clean, the buttons gleaming, his shoes polished – had he done that this morning? – even his hair, combed neatly to the left and trimmed short at the back, a strip of pale skin newly exposed.

'Darling, you're so kind and sweet to fret, but I'll be all right. You'll see when you come back. It's not going to be easy, and we'll have to take a pull, but it's what the whole country's having to do, don't forget.'

'I know, I know. I just hate the idea that it's all on you when it's my responsibility now. It all happened so much more quickly—' He stopped himself, looking down at his nails, bitten right down, the skin red at the edges.

She took a sip of her drink and turned her head to look out again onto the square. There was a couple walking across it, the man in the dark blue of the RAF, the girl in tidy blouse and skirt, their heads almost touching as they shared a sandwich, he passing the neat square to her, waiting for her to take a bite and pass it back. Jean turned back to Alfie.

'You're not rid of George and me yet. I'll keep it all straight while you're away.' She didn't want them to get into all of this tonight, not their last night together for who knew how long.

'I know. I don't want to be a bore, but I want to go away with things in order. And I had a letter last week that came to me at camp. It had gone to Harehope and then been sent on, so it was dated nearly a month ago.'

Alfie stood up and pulled an envelope from his top pocket. He handed it to Jean, watching her closely as she pulled out two pieces of paper, one typed and the other looking like some sort of statement of account. The letterhead was the Buckmans' trust lawyers in New York, the author a man she had never heard of. She scanned the letter, her heart in her mouth, not knowing what information it might contain. The text was curt and to the point, essentially a settling of accounts and the termination of a trust to which Alfie was a minor beneficiary. The amount it alluded to was one hundred and fifty pounds, and it was being wired to their bank in London.

'I don't understand what this is – Grandma Buckman died nearly four months ago, and this is all that's come? I hate to sound mercenary, but Papa used to talk about your trust, this vast amount that was all that came between Harehope and the debtors back in the day. He once showed me some gossip piece in the *Express* from when you got engaged, all about Grandma's money, that her father was the richest man in California. And the trustees mentioned in that first meeting, do you remember... And it might help, mightn't it? With all of this headache? So I wasn't sure what this cheque was.'

She handed the paper back to him, looking at that solemn face, at her boy trying to be a man; no example to follow, no pattern to take up. 'I'm afraid Grandma had a change of tack a while before she died and altered her will. Felt, for right or wrong, that we had our own life in England that your father ought to look after, and that things in America should be kept separate to that. My brother had the newspaper to consider, and I think things haven't been so easy there – and Mother's money will have been a huge help to him. We'll get some money through from the London house sale soon—'

'But one hundred and fifty pounds – Mama, I saw the last set of household accounts for Harehope. It runs at almost ten times that a year. And with the death duties, how will there be enough?' He looked down at his drink again. 'You see, there's a hill farm and a big parcel of land up at Holyburn that was always earmarked for George. That would have been Papa's if Charles hadn't been killed. I thought that with some of the American money we could take back the house, set him up there when he's a bit older. I think he's going to find it all so hard, and I want to look out for him, without making him feel like he's some sort of broken thing that needs fixing. I just want to get things straight.'

'You're so responsible—'

'It's not responsibility, it's the reality of it. That it's all mine and I don't always feel, maybe like you' – he looked up warily – 'that it's mine at all, or that…or that I even want it sometimes. I saw a painting George did at Christmas, a little oil of a ruined fell cottage, on some part of the estate that I don't know and that Papa probably never even went to. Don't you see the way he finds some corner of the house, and he'll sit, with one of the dogs at his feet, now Papa's gone, and he can just be.'

'But this is how it is in England, how it is in a family like ours. How it's always been.'

'But it feels odd sometimes. I understand it in the general sense, of course I do. It's the only way for this whole thing to carry on. How it came to Papa. But when the world is upside down with war, when Harehope's filled with soldiers and when it's my brother who will need more help than others, it just feels…' He floundered for the words. 'Feels at odds sometimes. Doesn't sit that well with me. I know that probably makes me strange.' His shoulders were low, and Jean went and sat on the chair's arm, put her hand on his shoulder.

'You can't make it all fair, Alfie. You can't. It's out of your hands. And I'll look after George. That's my job. I'm his mother. You've got your own life to think about.'

She felt the truth then, tapping at the window, wanting to come in. Could she tell him? Would she? The glimpse of another room like this, where another conversation took place, when the truth was broken out, where he knew. But she couldn't. What would it do to the three of them? So she pushed it down, gave him a kiss, promised to herself that somehow she would make it right; she would look after George, however she could, till the day she died.

There was a gentle knock and George was standing in the open door, a small holdall in his hand. He was smiling, his face a little flushed. He gave his mother a quick kiss on the cheek, looked to his brother, sensed the tension in the room.

'You both look so serious. All right? Nerves?' He went and stood next to his brother. 'It must be hard to prepare. I don't know how you do it.'

'No, no, I just wanted to make sure everything was straight before I went away. I got a letter from Grandma's lawyers in America that I was confused by. I don't want to leave Mama in the lurch.'

'I'll still be here, you know. I know I'm still at school, but I shan't think the army will be knocking down the doors to have me with this come the summer.' He gestured to his arm with a weak smile. 'I've already spoken to the recruitment officer that came to school and it was all he could do not to laugh when I mentioned wanting to do my bit.'

Jean went over to him and linked her arm through his. 'I need you, George, and Harehope does too. The house is a mess, and it seems each day that the soldiers are doing their level best to tear the whole place down. They don't take too kindly to my requests for them to treat it a little more gently. And it would be so helpful to have someone to discuss everything with. Keeping it all straight is tough, as Alfie says, and I feel it really is a job for two. Would you do that for me, Georgie, darling? I know it doesn't sound terribly glamorous, but Alfie is right.'

His face was serious as he nodded. 'I'll do it. Of course.'

They both turned to Alfie, who had put the letter back in his pocket, and he gave a quick smile when he saw their eyes on him.

She needed tonight to be about the three of them and so they sat while she cooked, inexpertly, a whole chicken she had paid a fortune for on the black market – a challenge Stokes had taken up with relish, knowing whose stomachs the haggled-over bird would ultimately end up in – and some almost-on-the turn potatoes from Harehope, whose floury insides they chose to ignore, but the prize, too, which she'd held as carefully in her lap as if they were Venetian glass for the five hours on the train, of tiny tomatoes, pulled from the vine that morning, skins soft but the pulpy sweetness within sublime. The three talked in the fading light at a small table, an old dressing table from a spare room at Park Lane, now laid with more thought and care than the finest spot at the Savoy, and they drank a little more, and George made them laugh and laugh about his journey down to London opposite a group of elderly matrons, red-faced and stout-kneed, sweating in their tweed suits, clutching the clothing coupons they were desperate to spend. She watched them both, so sweet and easy in each other's company, so pleased to be together after the last months apart. In some ways they were better when they were alone. With other people around, who they were seemed to impinge and things that were expected of them were duly performed. George would recede, allowing

Alfie, whether he wanted to or not, to come to the fore. Alone, though, they were just the pair of brothers they had always been, scrapping, laughing, teasing.

When it got dark – it must have been nearly ten, as they were on double summertime now – they had helped her hoist up the blackout blinds and draw the curtains closed, and she kissed them both and left them to carry on talking, urging them not to stay up too late. She went into her room and changed into her nightdress, pulling back the covers as the night was warm but making sure to leave the door ajar before she got into bed, so she could fall asleep hearing their voices, the sweetest sound she knew.

CHAPTER NINE

Jean and George stood in a jumble of well-wishers and those pushing to make their way onto the train. The station was busy, the air clammy and Jean felt flushed and too hot. To be a mother waving off her son, the moment upon her, yet the rub of her blouse and the scurf on the shoulders of the man in front felt more real than the fact that this could be the last time she might see Alfie. But this is what people did, what they had to do. She kissed him on each cheek, then clasped his hands in hers, and then there were no words, only the sting of tears at the corner of each eye as she looked straight into his and willed him to come back to her. Another squeeze of his hands and another kiss and he was onto the train and she and George could only see his back disappearing into the carriage and then another soldier in another uniform was in his place, jostling to get on, and he was gone.

They waved as the train pulled away from the platform, waved even though neither of them could see Alfie, carried on waving until they felt foolish and the platform was all but empty, and they turned to walk back down to the main concourse. She linked her arm through George's and they walked in silence through the bustle and noise of Paddington Station, both of them unable to articulate the swirl of sadness and fear, the exhaustion at the prospect of their nerves being stretched till they saw him safely back home again.

'Let's have a cup of tea somewhere, shall we? You don't have to be back at school yet, and it seems too mean to pack you straight off when you've only just said goodbye to Alfie. Besides, I need the company. We can be glum together.'

They sat at a cramped table in the window of a nondescript tea shop on Praed Street, wedged next to two young women, secretaries on a break, she guessed, eking out the time away from their desks. They ordered a pot of tea and George asked for a scone, which was hard as rock when it came, although he ate it quickly, pulling it apart with his right hand, his other resting limp on the table. She'd seen the girls next to them register his palsied arm, as people always did. It was warm and he was in his shirtsleeves and they could see the left arm narrow and taper away; she watched the look of confusion she'd seen a hundred times, at the hand tipped back, then that smile of sympathy when they saw George's face with its melancholy beauty, those sensitive brown eyes, the gentleness that leached out of him.

She leaned in to hear him over the chatter and the clattering of plates from behind the counter.

'Shall we talk about something else, Mama? Might be easier?'

'No, you're sweet. I don't think I could. Are you all right though? I mean, will you be all right at school, or will you worry terribly?'

'I'll be fine. I've got exams, though I'm not sure what I'll do once I've finished. But that'll keep me busy. It's just – I suppose I'm so used to having Alfie around... Pathetic to say it, but we talk a lot. I'm not used to being apart from him as much as we have been recently.' He pulled at the last chunk of scone and then put it down, looking up at her directly. 'What if something did happen to him? I know I'm not meant to say this, but I can't stop thinking about it. He's brilliant and brave and he won't do anything stupid, but what if he did?'

There was something so fragile, almost breakable, about him. Opting out of the normal push and shove of adolescence had left him somehow untested against the harshness of things; it caused her chest to tighten, the thought of him worrying about his brother while he went about his lessons at school or sat doing his prep at night.

'You don't have to imagine. What good has that ever done anyone, to imagine the worst? So think about how much he wants to go and how he loved his training and how desperate he'll be to use all of that now he can.'

The girls at the next table were getting up to leave now, scraping chairs and smiling politely as they squeezed past George and Jean to get out. She put her hand on George's.

'We just have to put all our efforts into keeping busy.' She knew that it was utterly meaningless, something she ought to say. She'd said it a hundred times over to poor souls who'd lost everything in the Blitz, like putting a jaunty little sticking plaster over a mortal wound.

He was watching her thoughtfully now, stirring the teaspoon in his cup. 'What was all that about Grandma and the letter? You know I thought about her the other day – I never talked to you when she died. We hadn't seen her for so long, and you didn't make any fuss. It sort of passed me by.'

'It was a shock. And a sadness not to be able to go to her funeral.'

'But before, when she was still alive, did you ever think about sending us over there? There were children being sent off to America – you'd have thought we might have gone to visit and maybe even stayed on with your family, been safer away from England. I'm glad we didn't, but did you ever think about it? Three boys in my year left because they were told it was better to sit out the war over there. I know the Mountbatten girls were sent to New York—'

'I didn't always do what was the absolute best. I did what was best for us at the time, and keeping you both close to me, when Papa had died and you were all I had...' Her voice cracked.

'Oh, Mama, I'm sorry.'

'No, don't be – you're right to ask.'

She poured them both another cup from the metal pot in front of them, the tea tepid now, its taste bitter from having stewed too long. Of course she was lying about one part. Even if she could have travelled to her mother's funeral, there had been no invitation. In fact, there had been an explicit request from her mother's solicitors that she not attend. A telegram from Mssrs Smith, Cope and Freeman that followed immediately after the one from her sister-in-law informing Jean of her mother's sudden death. Elizabeth Buckman had died in her box at the Met, a heart attack apparently, suitably baroque and no doubt with jewels at wrist and neck and a loyal servant or three at hand to ensure dignity was retained to the last.

Her mother's death had made real the final part of her promise in her drawing room those seven years before. As she had vowed that day, Elizabeth Buckman had changed her will and Jean had been left nothing, not a cent. Jean's allowance had been cut off following their last meeting, but this last act was the most brutal of all. The cheque Alfie had shown her the night before was the sum total of her bequest. Although Jean shouldn't forget the letter that had followed about a month after Elizabeth's death, informing her only daughter of a small annual cheque that would be made out to the Harehope estate for 'the maintenance of any burial plots relevant to the Buckman Family at Harehope Hall', which she supposed was intended for when Jean was next to Edward six feet under, so that whoever should find themselves visiting that graveyard in years to come should know that the Buckmans looked after their own, even in death. The precision of it was her mother to a tee.

George was pulling at his sleeve and wasn't looking at her as he spoke. 'If I'm being straight with you, Mama, there has been a lot of talk at school about what everyone will do next – the army, the navy, all of that.'

She nodded, encouraging him.

'I can't help thinking, even without the question of fighting, of doing my bit, what will I do? I know what people say about me. That I'm quiet. That I'm so different to Alfie. I do sometimes feel different.' Colour rose in his cheeks, and he swallowed. 'I heard a boy describing me as strange the other day. I don't mind, but, well…I suppose I do mind, in fact.' He shrugged, his head low, pushing at the remaining crumbs on his plate with his thumb. 'I know Alfie wants me to help you at Harehope, but that's just for now and because he's being kind. He feels sorry for me. But I've got to do something for myself. I don't want to be hanging around Harehope for ever. It's his, not mine.' He looked up. 'I would like to make a go of painting if I could. But maybe you don't think that's something proper, or what young men like us ought to do.' He gave a weak smile. 'I know Papa didn't. But then he's not here.'

His eyes were filled with uncertainty. Her little boy who so desperately needed the path ahead to be carved for him. And life seemed to have become harder for him as he grew older. When the road of childhood ran out, he did not know where to go. He carried a little burden at his back now, one that contained nothing more than the simple weight of being. She'd give everything to take it up for him, but she couldn't because it would always be there, it was who he was.

'What do you think, Mama?'

'Oh, George, you're only just eighteen.' And she laughed, though her heart gave a little. 'You don't need to decide it all now. Let me look after you for a little while longer, won't you? And what I said last night. I really do mean it. I'd love it if you came to Harehope and helped me keep on top of things. I worry so much about there being a chimney fire or something ghastly like that. It would mean an awful lot to Alfie too.'

'Of course I will – I'd like to. Although you'll be in London half the time.'

'I know you hate it, but it's hard not to and there's so much still to do down here. And I love my flat. It feels like home now.'

And it did. Two years she'd had it now, two years that had brought so much change to their lives. A widow and her eldest boy away to fight and she and George left to cling together and wait and hope that he would come back to them. She wasn't sure where he was going, though it would likely be Africa, and then Italy. After Monty's victory, Italy was talked of as the next front for invading Europe. The pair of them would have to do as everyone else was doing: put one foot in front of the other, deal with the matters at hand, suppressing always the thoughts of the boys over there, dealing with God knows what.

They finished their tea, and she walked George back up to the Bayswater Road to find a taxi to take him to Waterloo. She put out her hand, and while the driver pulled over, Jean hugged George tightly to her before pressing some money into his hand. 'In case you need anything before the holidays come. I'll miss you. Be good. And write to me, won't you?'

She shut the door and watched as the taxi joined the line of traffic making its way to Marble Arch. She could have got a lift with him some of the way, but it was warm and she wanted to walk through the park, down along the Serpentine, with the friendly squawk and splutter of the birds that dabbled at its edge. As Jean walked, her coat now over her arm, she tried not to think that each minute was taking Alfie further and further from her and from safety. With him gone, she felt physically different, as if the chemistry of her body had been altered by his departure. She had a sense of herself in one place, in the park as she was now, people around her, and then there was this lighter feeling in her stomach and around her skin, an absence that was difficult to articulate, of another self that had gone to the space where her boy was. A little part of her hovering above Alfie, wherever he was, whatever he was seeing, doing, enduring. She couldn't say it to other people. They mightn't understand, but she felt it now as she walked beside the plane trees and silver birch, their leaves shivering as the warm breeze blew through them. She was no longer quite whole, a sliver of herself pared off, gone elsewhere.

CHAPTER TEN

The flat was too quiet, the water in the tap loud as it splattered against the sink when she went to pour herself a glass of water. She went into the boys' room, hoping for a mess of blankets and sheets for her to tidy, but both beds had been made neatly – the army's influence, she thought with a smile – with the eiderdowns folded at the foot of each. She ran her hand over the smooth top sheet and it was then that she saw an envelope propped against the bedside lamp. It was in Alfie's scratchy writing, addressed to her.

She sat down on the bed, thrilled at the unexpected shred of his presence.

Mama,

It's after two in the morning – I woke up and couldn't get back to sleep again. I couldn't say everything I wanted to say because George arrived and it seems too crude when he's so powerless in it all.

The thing is, I had a meeting with the trustees yesterday morning. I'm sorry I didn't tell you. Simon did most of the talking;

told me he's having discussions with the National Trust about giving them Ashworth when the war's over as he can't see how he can make it work. And then he turned to Harehope, and that seems to be the nub of it all. They've been trying to sort things out quietly behind the scenes, but now that I'm going away, they felt they had to come clean about the whole lot.

To be blunt, Papa had racked up huge debts that they've been keeping from us. From about '36 or so he went from gambling a little to a serious habit. He started playing cards with those men that came to Harehope, do you remember them? Using land and property to pay them off when he lost – handing over hill farms, small plots which were not worth too much, even that little estate that I had always thought would be for George. Simon and Richard helped him settle the sales discreetly.

When he died, though, they uncovered much more that he hadn't told them about; he'd gone into business with Henry Durrant. Promising him sums he didn't have. Sold paintings, furniture, anything he could to persuade him he had money for the deal. And now, with the war, it's all crashed and we – I – owe so much more. They've tried to get out of some of it, they've paid off part, but with the death duties there just isn't enough to do it.

Simon says we can fix it, with more judicious sales. He has a plan, he promises – the Park Lane sale is nearly through, the house in France when he can, all of that and more – but they keep talking about how everything can be worked out for me. So that's the point. When I come back I will find a way to give George something of his own, even if nothing more comes from

Grandma. But promise that you'll look after him in the mean-time, whatever happens. If Papa couldn't, then I will. You see, George said something to me at Christmas that I can't shake off: that he couldn't imagine himself beyond twenty. Couldn't picture where he'd be. It made me feel so sad. I love him so much, Mama – I can't say it out loud, but I can write it. He's like the other side of me.

When I say goodbye to you tomorrow, that's my family, you and George and me. Papa never was. It never felt like he loved me – liked me even. So we've got to look after each other, the three of us, when the world is upside down.

Simon wants me to explain the sales to Grandma Warre too. Will you do that for me? I don't envy you the task.

I'll write as often as I can. Don't worry about me – I know you will – but I'll be fine. I always am.

A x

Jean folded up the letter as she sat on the edge of the neat turned-down bed. There were times when she could forget the lie at the heart of it all. Where she could tell herself that this was what happened in these families, where the inequality was sewn in and it was left for a pair of brothers, sons like hers, to swallow down the pill given to them, however unfair it felt, however bitter the taste. That was life. But as she sat, holding this letter that throbbed with sentiments half-understood, where Edward's loathing of his boys was expressed in the unravelling mess he had left behind for them, she knew this tableau was different. The portraits were so vivid, the chiaroscuro so intense, each character bleeding for the other.

But as the sound of the afternoon traffic dragged her back to the surface, Jean knew that whatever Edward had done to try and destroy it all, whatever horrors there were still to uncover, the truth about her boys would stay locked within her for ever. Because to speak it now, to break the box open, would be to set a hundred birds up into the sky, a hundred crows with wings of black and beaks of shining ebony, whose shrieking and flapping would beat away what shreds of good and hope there lay in the sliver of sky behind.

CHAPTER ELEVEN

The Dowager Lady Warre's drawing room was airless. A fire was burning in the grate despite the warmth of the day outside and as Jean waited, her ancient housekeeper returned, lumping a desultory log on the fire before standing up with an awkward lurch as her mistress entered the room.

Jean hadn't seen Alice for months; the last time had been at church as they both filed out, stopping to say goodbye to the parson at the end of the service. She was a little more stooped and the collar of her silk shirt gaped, revealing the crag of her neck. Her hand gripped a brass-topped stick and the skin on her hands was purple and chapped, her knuckles swollen. The indignity of ageing: however imperious Alice's attitudes, however scathing her belief in the world's slipping standards, time had chipped away at her till all she could do was fix it with a disparaging eye.

The housekeeper had barely re-entered, hands shaking beneath a tray with tea and a Victoria sponge, before its offer was impatiently declined with an irritated bat of the hand. Lady Warre had always let it be known that appetites – or indeed too much of an interest in anything – were sub-par. Passions were considered extraordinary. She had lived in the old rectory for more than twenty years, leaving Harehope the day after Edward and Jean were married, evicting the parson from his home of a decade in the process. She had subsequently established a little court under its tidy Dutch-gabled roof, among the local ladies of note. They would meet for bridge, lips pursed in disapproval, eyes shining with the zeal of the wronged as they lamented the catastrophic changes taking place in society and, of far greater importance, in the houses they had once ruled over. Most of those women were now dead and Alice was the group's lone survivor, thin as she always was but so brittle now she might snap, her bones worn down to their finest point. The same pearls hung low on her chest, three looping strands with an enormous ruby like an angry eye in their middle.

Conversation was something made for Alice, not by her, and so she allowed Jean to talk, her face one of bare tolerance, before she gave a sudden jerk forward in her seat, interrupting her daughter-in-law with a raising of her stick. 'Surely you didn't come here to discuss the weather?' Her voice, weakened by lack of use, caught.

'No, I didn't. And if you'd rather I got to the point, I will. I thought it best to let you know that there have been some – upheavals, shall we say – in the finances of the estate. Alfie has been advised by the trustees that there are a lot of outstanding debts, and so there'll have to be some significant sales.'

'Well, I heard you're selling the London house.'

'Yes, as soon as we can.'

'Not much good without a roof.'

'Quite.'

Another silence ensued, so Jean persevered.

'The death duties couldn't be helped. But the more awkward issue is that of other debts which only recently came to light. Gambling debts – of Edward's.'

This was met with silence and a pursing of lips.

'Money is still owed despite recent sales and…it may well be that several of the houses in the village and some land closer to the Hall might need to go too.'

Still there was silence.

Jean soldiered on. 'These sales do have to be made, and you will obviously always have a house—'

'How kind,' Alice said acidly.

'But I think we are all going to have cut our cloth a little – there are some rather "historic", if that is the word, allowances that we have been accustomed to living on, and these might have to be altered—'

'My dear, you sound like the agent.'

Silence followed again, broken only by the quiet ticking of the clock and the shuffle of the housekeeper outside, anxious ear no doubt to the door. Assuming the conversation was over, Jean was taking a sip of her tea when Alice leaned forward on her stick again.

'If we are being frank, and everything shall be discussed openly as if we were reading from a railway timetable, then I do have something I should like to say that has been vexing me these last few months.' She fixed Jean with a watery eye. 'Where, may I ask, has all your family's precious money gone?'

She hadn't raised her voice at all, but she moistened her lips with a darting movement of her tongue. Jean was too shocked to speak. Alice had never said anything as frank to her in the twenty years they'd known each other. They had only ever spoken like a pair of reluctant acquaintances, enquiring about health, the weather, anything that negated the need for actual emotion.

'Indeed, how has it come to this? Where is all your beloved Mama's money? I shall never forget the letter she wrote to me after you and Edward were married. Full of warmth and delight at the match, drenched in it. I've never told anyone this, but it stuck in my craw. She couldn't see how I abhorred this great wash of money coming over here, supposedly to save our poor ennobled souls. None of you could. I loathed that whole little dance. Was I supposed to be grateful for her generosity? And then to see the paltry affection between you and Edward. The idea that it would somehow last was laughable.'

'I don't think that's fair. When we met—'

'Oh, Edward didn't want a cosy little marriage, minds and bodies and all of that nonsense. I know that much. He wanted a wife to provide an heir and look the part. But I knew it would turn out as it did. You had to want things, need things. I could see it in the way you moped around the house, waiting for someone to take you by the hand and show you what to do. Do you think anyone had the decency to do that for me when I married his father?'

The way she was holding herself, one hand on her stick, the other folded in her lap, so removed from the impact of her words, gave Jean the impulse to throw it all out then. She didn't feel sympathy towards this old woman; she felt hatred, if she was honest, for the years of cold disdain she had experienced at the hands of this fine-boned, perfectly bred, diminutive tyrant.

'But do you think, Alice' – Jean noted the slight wince at the use of her first name, and it gave her a little thrill – 'that you might have played a part too? You say you thought our marriage was dead from the beginning. But why was that? I don't think I ever saw you smile at Edward, let alone—'

'And where does that get one in life?' Alice's eyes were black and bright now, a little water gathering at their rheumy edges.

'Embracing and kissing and smothering people in affection and approval until they can't breathe. What's wrong with containment, a little restraint to one's affections? You may have thought that Edward and I barely spoke and that I was distant. But I was more reliable than you turned out to be.' She paused and then spat out the next words as if they had risen like bile from her stomach. 'He told me the truth – about who Alfie's father is. That delightful little gift you so thoughtfully brought into the Warre family. If you want to lay blame for the state of your marriage, lay it there.' Alice shifted in her seat, pleased at the punch she'd landed. She reeled herself back in then, as if she lacked the capacity, or the desire, to emote further. She gave a tight smile. 'Edward took your money and he used it, I give you that, but now you tell me it's all gone.'

'Gone because he gambled it all away. Gambled away an estate—'

'...that was to be passed on to a bastard boy.'

'That bastard boy is still my son.' Jean shouted these words, and she stood up. 'Don't you feel anything? What is wrong with you all? I have loved my boys. Have loved them from the moment they were born, and I will go on doing it until I am dead and there's nothing left of me. You say I was never enough for this place, with my money and my...with what I did. Well, if the truth be told, I am glad. I don't want to be like you. Scrub me out of your family's history if you prefer, I don't care. But I came here on behalf of my son, to tell you of the trustees' decisions. Should there be a need to sell this house, you will be moved to another house on the estate, until—'

'Until I'm dead. Yes, until I'm dead.' Alice smiled the last words before ringing a silver bell that sat on the side table next to her.

Jean didn't wait for the housekeeper to show her out. She needed air, to get away from the stifling, cold judgement that she had felt from that woman since the day they had first met. Jean had once thought that the animosity had come from her usurping of Alice's place by moving into Harehope, but now she saw it was more than that. More than a dislike in handing on the reins of power, in relinquishing status, more than the change from one chatelaine to the next. It was that Jean was other. Her money, though she had never been ostentatious in herself, had marked her out as somehow unbecoming and unfitting for the faded, implicit grandeur of Harehope. Her attitudes had only affirmed that. To emote, to express, to struggle, to falter. This was not the stuff of life to Alice Warre, a woman who needed the world to reflect her own frigid image.

Now she had reached the gates of Harehope, and as her eyes ran down the curve of the drive, that familiar sweep, she shivered. She felt the end of it all, as if she could touch it: its occupation by the soldiers and their tanks, their files and papers and cigarette ends, was the house stumbling towards its inevitable end. So Edward couldn't bear for it to go to a bastard boy bathed in glory, wreathed in talents, nor the fragile, imperfect creature that was his own. Better to smash and destroy, to hate and burn, than to admit the truth that lay at the heart of him: that he, too, felt like he didn't belong. That it wasn't really his either.

As she approached the servants' entrance, the stone now honey-yellow in the late-afternoon sun, there was Stokes in his shirtsleeves. He was leaning against the wall, eyes closed. His pale arms were exposed, the skin loose, blotched with age, and she realised she'd never seen them in all these years. She slowed so as not to disturb him, but he started when he heard her footsteps on the stone.

'Ah, your ladyship. Apologies—'

'Don't let me stop you, Stokes. Please.' She paused as she was level with him. 'It'll be a beautiful evening, won't it?'

She walked on alone into the hollow quiet of the back hall with its faint smell of damp and moss, as if centuries of wet clothes, shrugged off and left to pool on the floor till someone came to whisk them away, had left an indelible mark on the air there. Harehope would remain, of course. Survival was the essence of these places. Look at her mother-in-law, widowed, two sons dead and gone, but with a grip of iron still on what she felt was rightly hers. Hadn't these estates survived family feuds, religious battles, bloodshed, civil war that ripped the country apart, in their eternal circle of reincarnation. Theirs was to endure, shrinking or expanding but always retaining just enough to cling on. This war, like all the others before it, would one day come to an end, the soldiers would pack up their things and go, the grass would come back, the passage of time would soothe and mend Harehope's trampled soul. Alfie would do what was required of him.

But when Jean turned out the light by her bed that night and lay, eyes open in the inky dark, she had a strange, unsettled feeling that played on her, keeping sleep always just out of reach. She had felt a shift in the air that moved through Harehope, through its great rooms inlaid with memory and its corridors hollowed out by the tread of those long gone; it was as if the house had sighed and the whisper of goodbye had been carried in its breath.

CHAPTER TWELVE

The fight with her mother-in-law was like a line drawn. This question of what she ought to do – of what society thought she owed this life she had married, of what someone like Constance felt was right – no longer held her, and in the weeks that followed, Jean gained a clarity of purpose that she had not had for years, perhaps ever.

A month or so later, she had accepted an invitation to lunch at the Savoy given by Ambassador Winant. All the bigwigs were there – Averell Harriman, Anthony Eden, the cream of American society in London – and it amused Jean to find herself still among their number. As the guests stood around waiting to be seated, she spotted Max tucked away in the corner of the room, deep in conversation with two of the embassy officials. Ever the hack, he had an eye on the rest of the room, scanning it for interest, and their eyes met briefly. He smiled, raising an eyebrow, and she smiled back. The sight of him was like being woken, a jolt at the shoulder in the night. The France of her past had been tipped into the present and with it came David, and she could not now push him from her mind. The question of him, the possibility of him, despite what Constance had told her. She would see him in a restaurant, taking off his coat, his face briefly caught in profile, but he would turn and the face would be all wrong, the jaw too wide, the nose too pinched, and he would be gone again.

And the thing was, you were as likely to hear an American accent in London as an English one. On every street corner there was a GI with a southern drawl, white teeth and the flash of gum as he chomped and chatted, or a serviceman with a Boston lilt, shooting the breeze on a damp September morning as he waited for a bus on Piccadilly. Even the paper seller at the top of St James's, who would yell a cheery 'Welcome to England, lads' to any US soldier that passed him, had grown tired of it, unable to keep up with the influx onto the city's streets. The Americans in town, with their money and energy, not yet ground down by years of war, had changed the city's tempo. Round Grosvenor Square, or Eisenhower Platz as it was nicknamed, it felt like Fifth Avenue, with American generals and officials, office workers, correspondents and editors, all buzzing round the square and surrounding streets.

Max had been easy to track down again. He drank, like many of his contemporaries, at the American Bar at the Savoy most nights, so she got a message to him there. Would he like to have lunch with Jean Warre? She was keen to catch up. He telephoned the next day: he'd love to see her; he was so sorry to hear about her husband – though his voice had not a hint of sorrow to it – and they'd set the date, lunch at The Dorchester in two days' time.

Other than the wall of sandbags that bookended the hotel entrance like sagging bricks, it would be easy to forget there was a war on. There were women chatting, hair set, lipstick on, as they shrugged coats off shoulders to a sea of waiting staff. The tables in the dining room were full, a now familiar patchwork of blue and green, of uniforms and suits, served by a battalion of starched-collared, Brylcreemed waiters. The Dorch, as it was chummily called, had a reputation for being a little risqué, with its mix of society hostesses camping upstairs in suites, cheek by jowl with politicians, generals and showgirls. It was known that Lord Halifax used to stand about in the lobby, talking loudly about things one really oughtn't to know, without a worry as to who might be listening, and so it had gained a reputation for flapping ears – and illicit behaviour. At night, the ballroom would be chock-full of men and women dancing, drinking, escaping. More importantly, it was a fortress, known for the strength of its concrete and iron structure and its supposed inviolability against any bombs that Hitler should choose to rain down on it. At night, during air raids, the underground gymnasium served as a veritable who's who, a dormitory of snoring duchesses and dignitaries and those who simply happened to be chasing a good time when the heavens opened and fire rained down.

As Jean handed over her coat and glanced at herself in the mirror, she felt a wave of nostalgia for the Park Lane of her past. The hotel had been a grand old house when she had first moved to London; she'd had dinner in its vast dining room, walked its picture gallery, danced in its ballroom. It had been one of those Park Lane palaces that seemed like a dream now, torn down to make way for change and its need for en suite bathrooms and porters and practical plumbing, not creaking liveried footmen and an endless enfilade of rooms that her mother and father's generation had thought the only way to live. But things moved on, her parents were long dead, and cities shrugged off old skins like serpents. That was how they survived; how they kept people coming.

Jean hadn't eaten there for a while, and certainly didn't know the staff, but as she scanned the room for her date, a hand was raised, and there was Max, already seated at one of the better tables in the centre, lit cigarette in the ashtray, a drink being worked on before him.

He stood for her, pulling out her chair and kissing her on one cheek. If age had taught her to worry less about others' opinions of her, it had also taught her that strangers, and particularly men, found her attractive. Max was no different; his eyes took her in for a fraction too long. He was as she remembered – tall and broad-shouldered, with large hands, though perhaps a little less hair and a little more paunchy, the lunching life having taken its toll – but he had an undeniable presence; an ease in the world of dining and talking and charming.

The waiter appeared and she ordered a White Lady. The buzz in the room was magnetic. London was a city beleaguered by war, but you wouldn't know it from the fun being had in the hundred feet around her.

He leaned forward to light her cigarette. 'You look fantastic, if you'll allow me to say that.'

'I'm not so sure. I feel deprived of a lifetime of sleep. And my eldest son is somewhere in Africa right now, preparing for whatever's going to happen next. You must have a better idea than most of what's going on?'

'I'm not with the paper any more. I got hired by NBC about four years ago. I'd had enough of newspapers – not enough money in it for me. Radio's where it's heading. You're right though. We did initially get some preferential treatment from the Brits when it came to information. They were desperate for us to let every-one back home know the truth: the nightmare of the Blitz, the rationing, the fuel, the blackouts. The Yanks didn't have a clue.'

'Well, it seems you did your job. I feel like there are more Americans here now than there are English.'

'That's not too much of a hardship for you, is it? Or do you consider yourself an Englishwoman now?'

He smiled, beckoning the waiter over. Menus were produced quickly – he was clearly a regular, no need to exert himself to get attention – while all the while he kept up easy conversation about her, about London, about her life, nothing too heavy, nothing too political. He was a lunching professional. She scanned the menu, knowing that the elaborate French was an elegant disguise, *lapin a la campagne* no doubt slivers of grey meat fanned out on a pile of turnip purée.

'I was sorry to hear about your husband.'

'Yes, it was a shock. He wasn't even forty. Young, too young. And—'

'You've learned to live with your grief?' His smile was bold, but something about the way he said it was not rude. She took it as an offering, a suggestion of where the lunch could go, and she sipped the drink in front of her.

'You could say that. And as you must have gathered, it's not done here to dwell too much on one's feelings. I've had to adopt this country in other ways too. I haven't been able to go home for a while, and my family and I have…drifted. It was a pleasant surprise to see you at that lunch. A face from another time.'

'You know, they say this place' – he gestured to the room around them – 'is like the Riviera when we were there. Shady people, money on the move, people on the make. A certain grubbiness to it.'

She laughed. 'Do you miss it? I mean the paper and life out there, the South of France?'

'You know, I don't. There was a time and a place, and maybe I'll go back one day to visit, but I'm not sure if it hadn't had its day. And you?' The invitation was there for her.

'You know, in the spirit of honesty' – she leaned forward, looking him straight in the eye – 'I think you might have an idea as to why I wanted to see you.'

He smiled, saying nothing.

'I last saw David Carver in '36, that summer I met you in Juan-les-Pins. I closed up the house there – haven't sold it yet, though we will have to soon, but I haven't been back. And he and I, we lost touch. I—'

'I thought that might be the reason for this. I didn't flatter myself that it was purely for my good company you tracked me down. Do you know anything about what's happened to him since?'

She shook her head. What Constance had told her was not enough.

He went on. 'When I was in New York, that September when I bumped into you at the Stork Club, a big meeting was called about the direction of the paper. I was asked to stick around for that before heading back to Paris. I got a request about that time from your brother – quite a rare thing. I mean, it was unusual for there to be much involvement from your family in editorial matters, in fact it was frowned upon by then. Impartiality and all that. But when we met, I was informed by Oliver that there probably ought to be some changes to the staff at the European paper, that perhaps some writers and editors weren't best suited to the job, was it necessary to have such a large gang of them out there, things like that. And then David's name came up. He didn't seem to be doing much of interest, perhaps he ought to be moved on. He might be better suited to another paper.'

'Oh my God. That's horrendous.'

'Well, it wasn't much fun letting David know, that's for sure. But if I'm honest, he hated the job by then. You must have known that. He didn't like me much either. Loathed the way I ran the paper like the social pages. No meat on the bone, he'd always say to me. But I did ask him what he'd do next, and he said he was going to carry on writing. Although he said what was the point in writing a novel when the way the world was going was crazier than fiction.'

The plates of food arrived – the fanfare with which it was delivered in contrast to the drab assemblage revealed – and she took a deep breath. 'Did you hear more after that? I heard he was living in California for a while. Look, I'm sorry if you think I'm awful, mining you for all this—'

Max shook his head. 'I lost track of him after he left France and I went back to the States. I know he was very friendly with that fellow Gil Smith, who moved across to NBC and is in London now. God, for all we know David could be here too. It feels like you can't walk a block without hearing an American. Have you walked past the Rainbow Corner at night? It's madness.'

'I would like to try and find him.'

'Pick things up?' He was curious.

'Not necessarily. So much has changed, so much water under the bridge. But it would be good to see him again, at least. It all ended so abruptly.' She felt coy then for revealing so much of herself to this man she barely knew, but his eyes were kind and he was nodding.

'I'll talk to Gil and I can put word out – at the embassy, if you'd like? I'm there most days seeing someone or other or getting a briefing.' He paused. 'You could ask your brother if anyone at the paper knows, but I don't know how things are with your family?'

'You don't know, or you'd like to know?'

'Well, I am admittedly one of a small number who take an interest in that kind of thing.' He grinned.

'Well, perhaps the little that you know is all there is. We aren't as close as we were, and my looking for David isn't something I would go to my brother about… You know, if we are to be honest, that dinner we had in France when I first met you, I thought you were odious. The way you knew what was going on between David and me and were watching him squirm.'

'Oh, come on, it was too good to be true. My bleeding-heart writer, always at me for not being interested in the right stories, and there he was, love-struck, on the arm of one of the wealthiest women our good country had to offer.'

'But you wanted to make us both uncomfortable. It was so childish.'

'Well, I'm sorry. I really am. And I'll make amends by trying my best to put the two of you back in touch.' He was smiling, and she didn't have the energy to dislike him for it. In truth, she was enjoying his company, and talking freely about David was liberating.

They stayed there for another hour or more, the neighbouring tables gradually emptying, the waiting staff standing at the edges of the room, limp like wilted salad, willing lunchtime service to draw to a close.

Max lit a cigar and ordered a brandy. This man that she had found repellent on first meeting, with his assumed knowledge of who she was, was someone quite different. Perhaps she was too.

'It's extraordinary, this city right now. To be at the centre of things. I wouldn't want to be anywhere else in the world. Dinner with the Murrows, lunching with the embassy staff, drinking with those fellows in Whitehall who really know what's driving decision-making.' He leaned back in his chair, taking her in. 'It's taken its toll, though.'

'How so?'

'My marriage. It's broken down, for good, I'd say, if I were a betting man. Sally, my wife, she's still living in New York with my two boys, and I think I've got a taste for freedom. Being unencumbered.' He smiled, a little sheepishly.

She could tell he would make a pass at her if he could, but the fact that he knew she would never reciprocate gave the lunch an easiness she enjoyed.

'You must feel it, though. This sense that we're all in it together, all living so much in the here and now, that anything is possible. That you've got to take every chance you're given.'

'I do, I do. It's part of the reason why the question of David has come to the surface again. I feel that I have to know, even if it amounts to nothing. Otherwise, what's the purpose of all of this? Everything so haphazard, the losses so senseless, happiness so brief.'

As they said their goodbyes on the pavement outside, he promised once again to do anything he could to locate David for her: 'I'll make up for that dinner. I can't have the prettiest widow in London thinking I'm a chump.'

Jean walked back up Park Lane amid the noise of cars and people making their way to the Underground. So much had changed for London since she had arrived, and so much for her too. Who was there left that she cared about now? She had no relationship with her brother to speak of. The last exchanges with her family had been via the lawyers. She never saw Edward's crowd any more, though that had been happening even when he was still alive. It was surprisingly easy to drift out of society: one just stopped going to things, and then people stopped remembering to invite you. If they didn't see you, you gradually became peripheral to their thoughts. She had a small group of friends, but she'd made no effort to find someone after Edward. Her two sons, they had been her everything, but now at the edge of the frame there was the possibility of David. A man whose existence she could not guarantee, whose feelings towards her after seven years of silence were entirely unknown, who might well love someone else. If they could meet again – and if Alfie could stay out of trouble – if, if, if... But these were days of deep uncertainty, where bombs could drop or sons be snatched away, feelings of dread and anxiety worn like an invisible cloak while one carried on, getting through the daily drudge of life at home.

She was nearing Berkeley Square, almost at the end of Mount Street, passing the wrecked roof of Farm Street. She knew they still said Mass there every day, though the roof had been all but destroyed by incendiaries and though they faced a monumental task in rebuilding it.

Hope, or faith – whatever you chose to call it – was all one had to rely on these days. Hope that the roof could one day be mended, that God would still be listening to your prayers, that the sky wouldn't fall in. That a man you once loved might still be out there, that something might still be found amid the rubble, something long-buried that could be picked up, wiped clean, maybe even mended, fixed, treasured once more.

CHAPTER THIRTEEN

That winter passed in a blur of news, or lack of it, from Alfie, Jean's nerves on tenterhooks when she read in the papers about the landing in Sicily in September. It was chalked as a success, though Alfie's letters revealed next to nothing and so few details were reported that she barely knew anything at all. Italy's surrender, the mystery of Mussolini's escape from jail, rumours about a new German secret weapon that would be used against London and the decision by the government to continue with the blackout – all of these meant tensions were never allowed to slack off.

She continued to see Max, and she went to the embassy every couple of weeks to try and find any information on David. There were several D. Carvers, but she was eventually directed to another office on Grosvenor Square, where they took more details from her, although the lack of formal relationship between them caused the matronly secretary recording her request to raise an eyebrow which Jean studiously ignored. Max promised he was trying on her behalf, and had got hold of Gil Smith, who confirmed that David had signed up straight after Pearl Harbour.

The bombings started up again in February. They were now strange, daytime affairs, unlike the late afternoon and evening raids of the Blitz. George had finished school and was now living at Harehope. When she went back for a week to visit, it was a relief to know he was safe but to see too the changes he was effecting, the quiet pleasure gained from the sense of purpose and the knowledge that he was helping his brother. Major Graves, the burly redhead in charge of the camp at Harehope, had clearly taken to him. George was easy, his diffident manner enabling him to get on with things quietly without putting noses out of joint.

'He's a funny little chap, isn't he?' The major caught her as he passed her in the corridor outside his office one morning. 'Terribly reserved, but goodness me, he's been efficient. Gets an awful lot done in his quiet way.' He paused then, unable to help himself. 'Such a shame about that wretched arm, it will hold him back in life. But then again,' he added brightly, 'your other boy's out there doing his bit. So that must be something.' And he was off down the passage, a trail of cigar smoke drifting behind him.

And George had achieved a great amount, working through what needed doing methodically and without drama. They were talking as they sat in the study one night, the crackle of the evening news on the wireless their companion, and she watched that face of his, its expression painfully earnest as he sat across from her, leaning forward in his seat as he explained his last few weeks.

'Whether what's already been done is reparable, I don't know, but I've managed to halt some of the damage at least. I've got the men to rejig some of the rooms they were using as storage for furniture. It was all done so quickly and badly when they first came, so now, with some moving around, I've freed up a bit more space. It's opened up the old garage as another room for the soldiers to spend their rec time in. It means they're not using the yellow drawing room any more, causing more damage to the tapestries. And they far prefer it because they can listen to the wireless without the officers getting irritated about the noise.'

He had hesitated, though, when he was heading up for bed, lingering in the doorway.

'What is it, darling?'

He turned back into the room, nosed the floor with his shoe. 'I don't want to meddle. It's not my business. I know that, I promise. It's just that I found a box of papers while I was sorting one of the storage rooms. They belonged to Papa, and I shouldn't have looked, but I wanted to know whether they ought to be kept or chucked, and then I started going through them properly and I saw what they were. It's only that I think you might want to take a look?'

The next morning before breakfast, he took her out to one of the old potting sheds that backed onto the walled garden. They pushed hard at the door, its paint cracked and peeling at the edges, the wood at its bottom split and dry. He took the torch hung on a nail behind the door and wove a path through the neat stacks of boxes and ghostly outlines of upturned furniture covered in dust sheets. At the back of the room was a battered box, no bigger than a hatbox, pushed into the corner.

'It's these.' He looked at her warily before kneeling. 'It was just that there were so many of them. Piles and piles of them. Records of conveyance, deeds of sale, letters from the lawyers, all jumbled together and shoved into this box in no particular order.'

The pair crouched together in the semi-darkness and Jean's eyes struggled to adjust to the light as she scanned the pages that had, as George rightly observed, been stuffed into the box, never to be seen again. There were papers relating to places whose names she was ashamed she didn't recognise at all: Carrshill, Nunthanton, a set of farm buildings and three hundred acres at Clydesdown; deeds of sale, changes to title, all thrown together without care. Then came names of places she did know, of hill farms familiar from walks taken up near Dinnyford and along the furthest eastern flank of the moor. Papers registering the sale of huge swathes of moorland, five or six thousand acres at a time, neatly recorded on headed paper from the lawyers in London; then that piece of land that Alfie had mentioned at Holyburn, signed off and dated as sold February 1936, its title now belonging to a John Fairfield of Rothbury, Northumberland; more houses sold that she knew had sat in Alfie's trust; houses that her parents had bought for them on marriage; several houses in the village that nudged right up to the gates of Harehope. The pile of papers was vast, seemingly unending, place after place, house after house, farm after farm, land and more land; nearly a decade of sales that seemed scattergun at first but had clearly grown more flagrant as the years progressed. And at the bottom of so many of the pages and documents there sat the unmistakable, confident loop of Simon Marjoribanks' signature and then just below it Richard's neat, apologetic scrawl. The anger rose in her like bile.

George was watching her closely, his face unsure. 'Did you know?' His voice was panicky as he tried to read her face. She felt him casting around for something he could understand.

How pathetic she was at this moment: the vessel she had always been now cracked, the contents emptied, spilled out as scraps for someone to rake over in the mossy dark of a long-abandoned shed. She pulled herself in before she spoke.

'I had an idea he was selling some things, but not to this extent and certainly not at the time.' She needed to soothe him, soothe herself. 'I swear I didn't know at the time.'

'But could he do that? Could Papa simply sell whatever he wanted? Did Alfie have no say?'

'Alfie was still so young at the time of much of this, and Harehope was ultimately your father's, to do with as he wished.'

'But mustn't it make life difficult now? This was what Alfie was worrying about, wasn't it? Before he went…' His voice trailed off.

Jean nodded. 'But we'll be all right. Of course we will.' She touched his arm. 'I know you won't believe me, but I promise you. With a proper plan, we can make it right. Things might not be as easy as they have been, but we'll be all right. And you did the right thing in showing me.'

She smiled at him, willing him to feel safe again, the ground beneath him secured, but he wasn't looking at her, picking up instead the last of the papers and putting them back quickly into the box as if doing so would take away their existence.

'It feels so strange. I could walk so many of those places with my eyes shut. I know them like they're my own skin. I have a little oil of that ridge near Dinnyford, it's in my room. Showed it to Papa once, though I knew he wouldn't be interested. You know I painted it from memory.' He looked up at her now, the boy he still was pushing at the surface. 'Why would he do that, Mama? When he didn't have to. To Alfie. To all of us. It's just so strange.'

They walked back through the shed in silence. And what could her answer be? She couldn't tell him that it wasn't strange at all. That this pile of papers was a perfect summary of what George's father had thought of his two sons. Of their perfect family portrait of four.

CHAPTER FOURTEEN

A glass of water was poured for her and Jean sat, hands folded in her lap, as Simon Marjoribanks talked on with no need for an answer. The room was noisy, every table full, with several men standing at the bar that ran along the restaurant's far side, smoking with enthusiasm as they waited to be seated. Simon had pointed out the backs of two prominent members of the cabinet who were hunched over their tumblers, deep in conversation, entirely oblivious to the din of the room around them.

'It amazes me that one still struggles to get a table here. It's like the old days. Rather wonderful, actually. Though sadly no plovers' eggs to be had.' His eyes, which had been scanning the room greedily for people he knew, now returned to Jean. 'I trust you're coping at Harehope? Its requisition can't be easy. How clever Rosebury's wife was in getting the housing of art for Mentmore. She's terribly chummy with Kenneth Clark, which must have swung it for them. I hear the army can be a little heavy-handed.' The menu now open before him, he smiled indulgently. 'They are frightfully creative these days, aren't they? Now, a drink. Most important. And do tell why such an honour has been bestowed upon me, Jean. I think I can count on one hand the number of times we've lunched together.'

A waiter came to take their order and Simon gave a discreet nod to a pair of diners passing their table, men of a certain age, faces the colour of vintage port.

'I've had George up at Harehope with me, helping me keep on top of things while Alfie's away. He's been marvellous. Got to grips with an awful lot.'

'Oh, splendid. He's just left school, has he? Absolutely the sort of thing for him to get his teeth into.' He was talking to her but had his hand raised for the waiter. 'A bottle of the Clos de Bèze, if you have it? Harold often keeps a case or two back for those of us who come here too often for our own good. You were saying, Jean?' His smile was absent, mind still on the wine.

'The thing is, it has all been such a mess since the army came, as you say. And that's why I wanted to talk to you.'

'Oh?' Simon sat back expectantly.

'Well, in all of this sorting, George managed to unearth a whole lot of papers that I'd never seen. That Alfie certainly hadn't. Documents from sales made over the last ten years. From long before Edward died and there was the need to pay those wretched death duties. Alfie told me about the meeting you had before he went away. This hasn't come as a surprise to me, that Edward was selling things off, but the extent is quite staggering. And the boys – well, I want to understand your part in it all. You see, as trustees, it's your name on pretty much all of the paperwork. Not Edward's, and certainly not Alfie's.' She took a breath. 'Did you and Richard simply agree to everything Edward said?'

Their wine had been poured for them, but Simon did not move. He simply stared at Jean, unblinking.

She went on. 'This may sound direct, but was there not a point at which you thought to prevent Edward from doing what he was doing? To steer him away from his course, to discuss with Alfie what was going on? I know I was his wife, but as you well know, that counts for nothing. Even though so much came from me, or my family at least.' Again she felt that flicker of rage, which had taken hold of her since George's discovery, at the smoothness of this man who had presided over this mess yet acknowledged no part in it.

Simon caught the waiter's eye again, beckoning him over to refill his now near-empty glass, and gave a tight smile. 'I had thought this lunch was a social one. But I see that I was mistaken. If you wish to be blunt, Jean, is its purpose the suggestion of our negligence as trustees?' His tone, the warmth and bluster of a minute ago extinguished, caught her off guard.

'I simply want to know how it came to this. I see that it is too late to change a lot, but there are certainly some sales that relate to property that was part of Alfie's trust. Should you not have spoken to him about these? Could we not try and claw them back on those grounds, if they were sold to pay gambling debts? He would have been fifteen at the time of some of them. Not a baby, but a sentient boy with opinions and an interest in the future of Harehope. These sales will undoubtedly have made his tenure more difficult. I need to understand what exactly Edward was doing and, more importantly, what you knew of it.'

'Jean, perhaps it is worth reminding you, as an American' – ah, how quick they were to remind her, when it suited them, of this subtle but unforgettable difference – 'that the role of trustee here in England is a delicate one. One is party to a wealth of information that a family might not wish to share with the wider world. In this instance, I would say that discretion was what Edward always looked to Richard and I for.' He leaned forward now, giving a quick glance to the table of two men next to them before dropping his voice. 'And let me tell you it is a nonsense, an absolute nonsense, this idea that someone like Edward would ever be at the mercy of his trustees. We were appointed by him, and as such were told by him to agree to whatever he wanted, whether we thought it advisable or not.'

'But you didn't ask Alfie's permission. Surely that is not—'

He spoke over her, his voice hard. 'His father asked us to make these sales. Alfie was still a minor and we were therefore administrators of his estate and answerable to Edward—'

'But didn't you feel that it was wrong?' Her voice had risen and she found this man, with his condescending drawl and his innate, unbreakable confidence, unbearable. He would have stood by and let the place burn if it meant the claret kept flowing.

'It was clear to me that Edward was not a happy man in the last decade or so of his life, although it seems strange that I need to point this out to you. He gambled, increasingly heavily, he made ludicrous promises to that man Durrant, from whom he desperately sought approval. But he was not mad, nor out of his senses. If anything' – here he shifted in his seat – 'he had a singularity of purpose, the root cause of which perhaps you might be better positioned to explain. And to be frank, it was his estate to do whatever he damned well liked with.'

'I understand that. I understand that he instructed you to sell things, to pay off his debts, to do his bidding, as you so clearly felt was your duty, but I am asking you now, at this table, where there are only the two of us here, when much of what was sold off had been bought by my parents upon our marriage, whether you thought it was—'

Simon leaned forward with a jerk, knocking his wine glass so that a stain of bright red bloomed on the white damask between them. He hissed the next words. 'Jean, I wonder if we should talk a little more about George, who has so diligently drawn your attention to the details of the past few years.'

She sat back and noticed how flushed Simon's cheeks were; that the hand that now encircled the wine glass before him was clenched tight, its doughy knuckles pink. 'Go on.'

'He is a fragile boy, you would agree.'

'I am aware of his palsy, if that's what you mean.'

'I mean in temperament. Life does not come as easily to George, it seems, as it does to his older brother Alfie, with his embarrassment of talents.' He had regained control of himself, and he set his chin defiantly. 'If you choose to drag up the question of these distasteful sales, sales made at the direct expression of your husband's wishes, and my possible negligence, I might find myself duty-bound to alert people to the tricky question of your sons' parentage. And where do you think that would leave Alfie, and where your darling, sensitive George?' He wiped his upper lip with his napkin as he watched Jean take in his words, his trump card now left on the table for Jean to do as she liked with. 'This information would, I am in no doubt, cause great, and grave, scandal. Might ultimately lead to the ruin of the reputation of one son, perhaps of the whole family. Might cause Harehope – that, I should add, I have done my utmost to protect over the years – to falter, perhaps to fail.' His face was triumphant; he called over the waiter with a flick of his hand. 'Not an appetising thought, is it? I think the lunch is over, Jean, don't you? I've rather lost my enthusiasm for it.'

The waiter appeared with the bill, and Simon took out his wallet from his inside pocket. But Jean would not let him have the last word. She kept her voice low, mindful of a lull in conversation as the table next to them lingered over the menus. 'Do not talk to me, ever, of George's character, or of what you deem to be Alfie's successes. You know nothing of either of them, or me. I can see that I am the American who doesn't understand the English way, a woman to whom this world of yours is a closed book. Have it. Take it. Talk about me in your club if you like, make insinuations about what kind of woman you think I am. But know that I see you for what you are.' She stood, the waiter pulling the chair out from behind her.

Simon had set his face once more to polite; his voice returned to one of casual confidence. 'If Alfie would like for us to retire from our role and to appoint new trustees, that can be arranged when all of this is over. But I suggest for now that we remain in place. As I said to Alfie before he left, with some further judicious sales the estate's future will be secured and he can remain living at Harehope, perfectly adequately, for his lifetime, and quite possibly his children's.'

She found men like Simon repellent. Always had, she realised, although in her youth she would have thought that she was somehow at fault. How she wished she could go back and whisper the truth into the ear of her twenty-year-old self.

'Goodbye, Simon.'

As she walked through the room of diners, past clusters of men to whom Simon's revelation would no doubt have been meat to fall upon, and stepped onto the pavement of King Street, she knew she would not speak to him again. She would tell George that she had spoken to him; would promise her younger son that despite all these sales everything would be all right. That Alfie had a plan, that Simon was aware of his brother's wishes, that they would all be looked after and life would carry on when this wretched war was over. But she could not speak to that man again. For what he had said. For the power he thought he had over her.

They were twenty and nineteen now, her boys, and still the urge to protect them was animal within her. In her loneliest moments, when she thought of what she had given up, of the pearl of sorrow within her, when she felt there was no one on this earth who could truly hold the whole of her, in all its mess and untruth, in their open palm, she would remind herself of this one thing. That if this was all her life had amounted to – the creation and the protection of these boys – it would be enough; it would be enough.

CHAPTER FIFTEEN

Spring came, and with its loveliness, with its air of whimsy and promise, it seemed to taunt a people ground down by the relentless stretching of nerves, by the rationing of food, of clothes, of life, for what had now been four gruelling years. Jean's feet would crunch across broken glass on her daily walk to the WVS canteen that she was now running behind Bayswater and, with a stiff back and a knot between her shoulders, she would trudge home in the early afternoon, past crowds gathering outside Underground stations once more, making life difficult for the commuters who would force their way past the families with their bundles of bedding and food waiting patiently for the safety of a subterranean bed, however uncomfortable, for the night.

Most nights were interrupted and Churchill's warnings about pilotless rockets strung her out, while the news from Italy was so uncertain. It seemed that the easy arrival Allied troops had encountered had morphed into a gritty and gruelling battle, up in the country's spiny centre, near Cassino. Alfie still wrote as often as he could, though sometimes there would be agonising gaps, and she would snap when someone asked her how she was, then two letters would arrive together and she would read them over and over, buoyed briefly by his cheery good humour but knowing how much of it was an act put on for her benefit.

On a bright May morning, when she was rushing out of the flat with a splitting headache after a bad night, she took the post from the tray and there among the usual mass of bills and dull correspondence was a letter with the official stamp of the US embassy on it. She opened it where she stood, oblivious to the draught blowing in, tore it open, scanning it greedily for information. They had tracked down a D. Carver, DOB 15 June 1899. He was now Captain David Carver of the 29th Infantry Division that was currently stationed on the south-west coast; the address for post to reach him was enclosed.

Jean had kept the letter in her pocket, checking it every so often as she sat in the sorting office, helping the next round of exiles from the previous day's bombing, passing them new ration books, steering them to the housing office tucked into the back of an old Salvation Army building around the corner, making tea for those who looked distressed, but every so often taking the letter out of her pocket, smoothing out its creases, reading the name D. Carver over and over again. She walked back home in the afternoon sun in a daze, pausing to take in the tulips on display in Hyde Park, their brave heads of pink and yellow quivering in the breeze, as in her head she started and restarted the letter she would write to him. What would she find? Would he want to hear from her after years of silence? When she sat down to write to him that evening, she kept it brief. That she was spending her time in London; that she was now a widow. Here was her address, should he wish to look her up.

The weeks that followed slowed to stagnation, and the news from Italy stretched her out like she was on a rack. The wireless gave little away, but it was clear to everyone that their boys were bedded in, had been lured into that mountainous terrain some-where in the centre of Italy and had lost any advantage they'd had with their relatively easy arrival in the south. Armchair experts sprung up everywhere, spouting opinions to anyone that would listen, desperate to suggest something that would break the deadlock.

And then it came. She had been out of London for nearly a week, visiting George again at Harehope, and she returned late one Tuesday evening, cross from a delayed train that had sat for more than an hour in a siding somewhere outside London, the air in the carriage stale from reuse, the polite English silence souring into something else as the delay grew and grew. She had finally made it back to the flat at nearly eight o'clock, tired and hungry. The strap from her suitcase had broken and she had had to pull it awkwardly and readjust her position every few yards as she looked around in vain for a taxi. When she pushed open the door to the building and leaned back against it to pull in her bag, she scooped up the pile of post that lay on the floor. She flicked through the pile absently, bills and personal correspondence of the family on the floor above, when she saw it, stamped with the PASSED BY US EXAMINER stamp and the mark of his base. The envelope was a little battered and looked as though it had been folded in half at one point. She hurried up the stairs, dragging her case and fumbling with her keys to get the wretched thing into the lock.

She opened the envelope, reading it where she stood in the middle of the room, her jacket still on, her handbag dangling lifelessly from her shoulder.

Jean,

How strange to receive your letter on a day that is so quintessentially English: the sky a pale, restrained blue, the sun shining politely, a chill in the breeze. The cottage where I've been billeted for the past six months is rather damp, but the sweet childless couple in their seventies whose home it is are so kind and treat me almost as their own.

Those years in France we shared, they feel like they belong to another world. The possibility of it all. Now I feel drenched in reality. I suppose we all do.

You tell me Edward died; that you are a widow. Well, I am married, although it hasn't been for long and hasn't come to much. Thelma is Californian, a widow of considerable means, a fact which it may charm or repel you to learn. We have not been blessed with children, a fault laid clearly at my door and the cause of a great deal of her unhappiness; I chose to forego the truth that I have a son of my own.

Life has been so strange, a series of false starts and things unfinished. I wrote my first novel, but it didn't do much. I'm toiling away at the next, but nothing seems to come. Maybe it was never there. I am not sure what will be waiting for me in California when all of this is over.

Jean, I have this awful fear – it's grown as the years have passed – that you never really wanted what was between us to last. That perhaps I wasn't what you had hoped for. That your mother's decision came as a relief, that she gave you a way

*out. I don't know if this letter means that is not the case. But
I would like so very much to see you again, if you still would
me, knowing what you do now.*

*This war, so much time away from anyone who knows you –
who really knows you – it does strange things to a man. Can
make one maudlin. I think of Alfie, I dream of him sometimes,
of the boy he was. What man is he, Jean? Is he fine, and good,
and strong? I feel in my heart he is.*

David

Jean read the letter, read it again and again, till she knew the
blot where the pen had stuck and the ink had spread, blooming
out across the thin paper, till she knew each loop and line.

She needed to tell him it hadn't been convenience, that she
had loved him. That what had come after, the reality of it all,
had been impossible for her to surmount, but that what had
come first was true. It was important to her that he knew that.
Desperately important. Whatever the here and now, whatever
the reality and the tiredness and the ugliness of this life, she
needed David to know that she had loved him then, had loved
him deeply and that borne of that love was a boy of integrity
and beauty, of intelligence and grace; that no part of their past
could ever be regrettable, when Alfie was its future.

But the day that had been talked of, worried over, debated
around every wireless and kitchen table and pub and factory
for month upon month, was now here. Jean heard the thunder
of planes overhead when the sky was still a bruise of dark and
violet, as the bombers headed out over the rooftops to the
coast, and somehow London became stretched out so that the

streets of Mayfair and Kensington, of Lambeth and Putney, were joined to the narrow lanes of Hampshire, to the early summer hedgerows and fields of that quiet corner of England that looked across the Channel to France. Every woman, mother or sister, daughter or lover, was transported to that shore, her heart and mind ready to travel its thin stretch. It felt to Jean that day as if the whole country was holding its breath, going about its business, shopping bag or briefcase or lunchtime sandwich wrapped in waxed paper in hand, chest tight, not yet ready to exhale.

That afternoon, people waited on street corners, anxious for deliveries of the evening news, and Jean snatched at any crumb she could find: it had gone well, the landings had taken place, there were 'few' casualties – that word, 'few': she did a mental tot of averages, someone had to be one of the few, but who, not David, not David – and then she sat alone that evening in the flat, listening to the King on the wireless as he urged his exhausted people on and made his earnest request, in that jerking, halting voice that gave such comfort, for a vigil of prayer; she took it to heart and she knelt, hands clasped before her, on the kitchen floor till her knees hurt, the discomfort giving her something that she could share with them, the boys and men fighting, falling, dying, struggling on, on the other side of that small sliver of the Channel.

She wrote to David the next day, not knowing when he'd get the letter. Saying she was thinking of him and that she wanted to see him, despite what he had said, wanted to see him so very much. It became so important to let him know that there was something from those years, something unblemished and true. Her letter was short. She wanted to get it to the post so that she could get home and write another, as if each letter allowed her to reach across the sea and touch him. Then she had a letter from Alfie – another burst of relief, her heart blooming; he was on his way to Rome, the misery of Cassino behind them, the prospect of some time away from the front lines for him, the men lost too many to bear. She was here in workaday London, but her heart, her mind, her nerves were stretched across the continent.

Then three days had passed. The newspapers were full of progress in France, a foothold, fierce fighting near Caen; then five days, a week; ten days, and still nothing from David. Why wouldn't he write back to her? A thousand reasons were plausible; she would create a thousand more if it meant he was safe. And then her letter was returned from his base. The envelope that lay on the tray that morning felt like an alien had crept into her flat overnight, some dark and shadowy presence that brought with it worry and anxiety and the whiff of death that she could not bear to allow in. She threw the letter in the wastepaper basket, then picked it back out and tore it into pieces, ripping it up into halves, quarters, eights, tiny pieces so that it didn't exist, wanting to destroy the possibility of what its reappearance at her flat might mean.

It was now the fourteenth day since the invasion, and the third since her letter to David had been returned. Jean was walking up Berkeley Street in the late-afternoon sun, her mind a tired blank, her neck stiff from another night of no sleep at the return of the sirens and the arrival of the buzz bombs. She looked up as she came along the east side of the square, and saw a man standing outside the door to her building. She kept walking, head down now, but as she got closer she couldn't avoid it any longer and, looking up again, she could make out that it was Max. He had seen her then too, and he took off his hat and started walking towards her, but something about the way he took it off, the apologetic dip of his head, a hesitance in his first step, and she knew that he knew something.

Max kissed her quickly on the cheek. 'Can we go somewhere, to talk? Up to your flat, or we can get a drink somewhere.'

But she didn't want him to speak. She didn't want this last moment, before truth was uttered, to end. 'Don't say anything. Please.'

He nodded and walked her back down Berkeley Street in silence, and her feet felt odd and heavy and flat. They crossed Piccadilly and into the Ritz, the lobby quiet, and he steered her towards the upstairs bar, to a small table for two, and ordered them both a whisky. Still he waited for her to give him a sign.

Finally, she looked at him. 'Tell me.'

'I heard this morning. It's David. He's dead, Jean. I'm so sorry. There's no other way to say this. He was killed on the beaches. It was a mess. They landed too far out, some drowning straight away, those that managed to wade in were sitting ducks. It was so heavily fortified, they didn't stand a chance. We were given a list of the dead yesterday, and his name was on it. I didn't know how else you would find out.'

The waiter appeared with two tumblers of whisky. Jean took a sip, and something about its taste and the strength of it made her stomach heave and she had to run to the bathroom. She was ill, violently ill, her stomach emptying itself. She slumped down to the floor afterwards, her head lying against the cool porcelain, the tiled floor cold against her stockinged legs.

After she didn't know how long, there was a gentle knock and a woman's voice, hesitant, came through the door: 'Ma'am, there is a gentleman outside asking if you are all right. If you'll come out.'

Jean stood up slowly and opened the door, catching herself in the mirror. Her face was pale and greasy. She straightened her skirt, following the woman out.

Max was sitting on a little chair outside the bathroom, his body looking vast on its narrow frame, his head held in his hands. He looked up when he heard her and stood slowly, opening his arms. She leaned into him, and his arms were around her, and then the tears came.

The end of the relationship. It hadn't ended on that terrace in Antibes, a thing of choice. Instead it was this thing of ugliness, a horrid block of nothing, dumped before her outside the bathrooms of the Ritz, amid the noise and the chatter and the sound of glasses being washed, and with it came the unbearable realisation of all that waste. The misunderstanding. That he had died not knowing that she had loved him.

Jean pulled back from Max, cheeks swollen. He walked her back to the table, and they sat together in silence. She lit one of his cigarettes, smoking half of it before stubbing it out, the taste making the nausea return, and she thought she would be sick again.

Max was talking to her. She looked up.

'Don't be alone at a time like this. Could you go to the country and see your son? What good will being here in London do you? I don't know who you can talk to about this, but don't stay here and suffer on your own.'

She nodded. 'It's ridiculous, what I feel now. I'm forty-three, I hadn't seen him in so long. He was married, for God's sake.'

He nodded. 'I heard that too, a couple of weeks ago. I wasn't sure if you knew.'

'Some heiress, he said. From California.'

He smiled, awkwardly. 'You were in good company then.'

'Don't.' But he had made her smile, a weak smile that he could raise in her because they were friends now. She looked at him. 'It wasn't that we were going to be together again – I don't know. I'm another person now. He had made another life too. But he sounded sad about it all. You know, we were together for thirteen years on and off. The period of my life where I grew up.' She took a deep breath. 'He's the only man I've ever loved. And I don't think he realised what he meant to me back then. And to know that he was moved on from the paper because of me. All of that. It's an awful thing. An awful thing.' She stopped, tired at the prospect of ordering all of this into something that could be presented to the world. The parts of it that no one else could know. And she thought then of Alfie. A future where he and David met, embraced, talked, laughed, blotted out as David's body sunk beneath the water, in the nightmare of dying men and gunfire and the ghastly flotsam of bodies; or did he make it to the beach, was that chapter torn to shreds on the sand of his beloved France, with hands clawing at him, the breath snatched from him, enemy bullets piercing his skin, meeting muscle, bone, heart, lung. She rubbed at her face to push away the images. 'Can we just sit here for a while?'

'Of course. I can sit here as long as you like.'

Jean kept thinking of the tone of David's letter to her – the regret, the sadness. She felt the nausea welling up in her again.

Max had lit a cigarette and was looking at her; he looked almost shy, unsure of himself. 'You know, it will have meant a lot that you tried to find him. Imagine if he'd never known that. Never known you'd been looking for him. Even if you didn't get to explain it all. Remember that. Will you?'

A tall man in a charcoal-grey suit came over to their table then, coughed gently to announce his presence. Max stood up, shook his hand; they must have been work acquaintances. The pair stood a little away from the table while they talked in low voices. Max kept flicking a concerned eye back to Jean, but clearly the two needed to talk. This was what happened then, Jean realised. The world moved on, with business to attend to, answers to be given, plans to be made – and she would be carried along in its slipstream. Still a widow to Edward, mother to her two boys, appearing to the outside world as someone not changed at all but with this strange hole within her, filled with a secret grief, swilling around in guilt and dreadful what-ifs.

Because what could anyone know? What could she share? An old boyfriend, a lover she hadn't seen in years, had been killed in this war that killed people every day, children sleeping in their beds, whole families sheltering from bombs that tore off their roof and ripped the skin from their bodies, young men only just out of school fighting in the scrub on a mountainside in Italy, so what did her personal tally mean?

He wasn't even her husband. He was someone else's husband, some rich woman in California who was keeping their bed warm while he was away. It was so tawdry.

So she would have to turn it all in, tuck this feeling of washed-out grief somewhere underneath her ribcage, carry it with her every day, not let out the thought that he was Alfie's father, hold it in tight, stuff it down.

When Max returned to the table, an apologetic smile, a pat to her hand, it had already begun.

CHAPTER SIXTEEN

'Mama, it's me.' George had telephoned her. It was only a couple of days after she'd heard the news and she was alone in her flat.

'Darling.' Her voice felt like someone else's entirely. She had been sitting, hands in her lap, staring ahead, and she had to use all her energy to stand, the blood rushing to her head and flecks of bright light obscuring her vision.

'Please will you come up to Harehope? I can't bear that you're there when you don't have to be. It's driving me mad with worry. That it'll be you. Come back, please, Mama. I beg you. This is madness.'

The receiver felt so heavy in her hand as she stood, and the effort of an answer made her want to cry. 'I just have to finish up a few things and I'll come as soon as I can. By the end of the week, I promise.' The words were stones in her mouth.

Her mind had been with David in the France of before. He was standing on their beach, hat in hand, turning to say something to her over his shoulder as she lay on a rug, leaning back on her elbows, the sun warm on her face, her feet bare on the shingle beneath her. Then she'd feel the sadness well up again within her, overwhelm her. That she had been here, eating lunch, walking to work, putting her head to the pillow at night while he had been there dying his ghastly death in Normandy, thinking that the love between them had been a thing of convenience, that it had meant nothing. Her mind would go over and over the other iterations, what could have happened for it not to end like this, tripping over itself to escape the inescapable, her mind butting against itself like some wounded animal in flight, and yet she would be there on that sofa, perfectly still, head upright.

George was talking. She had to make herself focus on his words.

'Or else I'll come down and live with you in the flat.'

'No, you can't do that. I'll come up. I'll come up, I promise.'

He rang off, and she went and sat back down on the sofa – limbs of lead, heart of lead – but this time she pushed off her shoes and pulled up her feet beneath her to lie down. Her neck was cricked and uncomfortable, but she didn't want to shift herself. She would allow herself a few more hours like this, just to lie, to let the sadness possess her, before dragging herself back to the demands of today.

It was lunchtime the following day and she was in Kensington, walking past St Mary Abbots on her way to deliver a birthday present to Constance, a silly thing really, a bar of lavender soap that had taken all her energy to wrap in brown paper and old string; it didn't merit the journey, but it had given her a reason to leave the flat. She had stopped for a cup of tea on Kensington Church Street, sitting at the scrubbed wooden table with the bang and clatter of cups and pans and the chatter and noise of the other customers around her but she had felt nothing, heard nothing, as if glass surrounded her and the rest of the world were trapped on the other side.

Jean heard the strange buzzing sound as she left the cafe, engines pulsing overhead, coming directly over her, loud and low. The woman in front of her stopped, shopping bag limp by her side, and they both looked up at the sky, a smeary grey, dense with rain. The plane was flying directly over them, so low Jean thought it might touch the tops of the buildings. Louder and louder the sound grew, and time seemed to stretch as all around her people watched it carry on its path, and then came the eerie silence as the engines cut, as the finger of Death idled for a second as it scanned the citizens beneath to choose its prey. And then the bomb dropped what must have been only a thousand yards away from where Jean was standing.

The sound was extraordinary. It was like a solid thing, and Jean felt it strike her body like a punch. In a dream she carried on in the bomb's direction as people ran in strange scattergun paths, not knowing where it had fallen, and her ears were ringing as vans and ambulances and fire engines started streaming down past her and turning right and she found herself following them onto Kensington High Street. A woman came towards her, her shirt ripped off the shoulder and only one brown sensible shoe on her left foot, her legs bloodied and black, and then there were more of them coming in Jean's direction, limping and shouting and crying as they flooded towards her.

Jean felt no connection to her body, felt no connection at all to what was happening around her. But then a man pushed past her hard and the shove at her shoulder jolted her back into the moment. It was a priest, come from one of the churches nearby to help, the black of his cassock flapping behind him as he passed her, and the force of him brought her to.

She stood amid the chaos of the doodlebug's destruction. Her chest was heaving and her cheeks were wet with tears. She would go back to Harehope. Go back to her boy.

Jean pulled herself together then, for George, for both of them. It was what people did when all this death and loss mounted up, set against the backdrop of another summer's day. She set herself small challenges to overcome: to concentrate on a mundane task at hand that she could get through, tick off, that could demonstrate to the outside world that she was operating as she ought. To talk to George about the future, about when Alfie would be back and the soldiers gone; to make a plan for Harehope, an attempt to think of life when some semblance of normalcy would return.

But the war was still going on, and it seemed that Alfie would have to be moved into another field of battle after the reprieve he'd had in Rome. His last letter had been cheerful, more detailed than the last few. He'd had dinner the night before in a trattoria in the Trastevere with some fellow officers. They'd drunk some decent red wine and chatted about home and he'd wished she and George could have seen the church they walked around that night tipsy and full-stomached, looking up at the mosaics that covered the basilica's interior, the kindly priest giving them candles and leaving them to wander alone, the warmth of the gold and the solemn medieval faces flickering in the low light, transporting them all far, far away from the chaos and carnage, the gruesome relentlessness of death that had threatened to overwhelm them in the months at Cassino.

July had become August, most of the soldiers had moved out from Harehope and there were mainly desk clerks left behind, hammering away on typewriters, always walking round with sheaves of paper in their hands, looking absently for somewhere to file them. The mud that had covered the park was now caked and hard, great ridges of it, sometimes a foot or so high. George was always anxious, checking the post for letters, returning to the study to listen to the news morning and evening in case he missed anything important. They were both wary of talking about the future in case they jinxed it, but somehow Alfie's letters would come just when they were needed, bringing him back into the room, reviving the pair of them with his almost-presence.

She ended up telling George about David, one evening as they sat in the study at twilight, the two of them, reading in companionable silence. They'd listened to the news together but had fallen quiet as they read for a while, Jean lost in her thoughts, the book open before her but the pages a blank, when she realised George was talking to her.

'You seem so far away.'

'Oh, darling, I'm sorry. My mind's elsewhere.' She paused, a flicker of hesitation, before going on. 'I heard the other day that a friend, from those summers in France, had been killed. On D-Day. An American friend, killed on the beaches. It came as a shock.'

'Who? Did I meet him?'

'Do you remember a man called David? You were ten or eleven when we last went back, so maybe you do? He'd come to our little beach, or to the house for lunch. For dinner sometimes. Tall, with dark blonde hair, blue eyes.'

He was thinking, and then he smiled. 'I do, I do. Did he read to us? I have a memory of him reading to me and Alfie on a rug on our beach. Did we sit with him sometimes in the afternoons and read?'

She nodded, tears forming at the edge of her eyes.

'I loved that house, you know. Why did we stop going? I remember that beach, and warm bread thick with butter that we'd have in the mornings. A terrace with a long table, was that right?'

They went on like this, Jean filling in the gaps in his memory, little snapshots coming back to George that she would make sense of for him. Talking about David and about France, even in this abstract manner with the truth mostly hidden, was a release for her. It allowed the sadness to go somewhere rather than to reside pent-up in her chest, trapped like a bee in a bedroom in summer, tapping hopelessly against the glass.

Another letter came from Alfie to tell them he'd be leaving Italy in the next day or two, he couldn't say more, sending love, asking for more letters and news from home. He was at an airfield somewhere outside Rome, the men complaining that the heat was unbearable but it reminded him of those August afternoons in France as children, the air thick, the sky a pulsing blue above them. *Love to both of you, all is well with me. More soon, A x.*

Then a week went by, and nothing. She felt the flutter of panic but wouldn't allow herself to acknowledge it. It was like the whine of an unseen mosquito near her ear, its presence impossible to ignore. The whine grew louder as the days of silence mounted and she and George would eat breakfast without talking, the wireless always on, knives scraping against plates, the absence of news bearing down on them both till they could barely take it.

There had been a second landing in the South of France on 15 August, mainly US and French forces, but some British paratroop regiments, which it was likely Alfie was part of; it had been hugely successful, practically unopposed. They were calling the landing near Le Muy an outright success. German opposition was weak, and some areas were being taken without guns being fired. A few casualties – that word again, now bitter in her mouth – but the news continued to improve and they began to breathe more easily. The troops were making their way along that strip of coast, liberating from Hyères to Marseille, and as far as Fréjus and Saint-Raphael.

They sat, toast getting cold, Stokes painstakingly clearing around them as they heard about the fighting near Draguignan on 18 August, then near Fayence. These towns and villages of Jean's past, places she could picture without effort: the little hilltop towns, with their red tiled roofs and the way they caught the evening sun so that the sand-coloured stone seemed to glow, where she had sat on warm evenings sharing a pastis with David, the smell of cigarette smoke filling the air. Then the liberation of Cannes was announced on the 23rd, and more days passed and it was nearly the end of August and still no word. The liberation of Nice came next and she could see the promenade as if it were yesterday, the tables and chairs of the Negresco, the hum of music, the chatter of voices, the swaying of hips as ladies sauntered down its sun-drenched streets. Now it was a place of liberation and freedom once more, but at what cost? Her thoughts went to those people of her past, to Marie and her family. What would have happened to them after all they had endured?

The evenings at Harehope were long. It didn't get dark until nearly ten o'clock this far north, and she and George had taken to walking the same route each night after their dinner. Tonight was warm, neither of them needing a jacket as they took in the path that ran alongside the river. Its water was low, barely covering the smooth stones at the edges, and there was the gentle chaff of warblers in the fading light. They looped round and back down the front drive, its bend and turn so familiar that they could have walked it with their eyes shut. The gloaming light before night fell had softened the damage.

'If I blur my eyes, it could be twenty years ago. The house and grounds as they were.' She looked at George as he walked beside her, glancing back every so often to Yip, who was following them, darting off to follow some scent or other, skittering back when George called to him.

'It's going to end, isn't it? Soon, I mean. They're talking about it being over by Christmas.'

'I think so, although I hate to jinx things.'

They walked on in silence, Yip now trotting happily between them. She thought then of what Simon had said about George; about his fragility. She had never felt closer to him. He was different, he did carry things in him, she could tell. Feelings that were difficult for a nineteen-year-old boy to express. What he required was quiet companionship, a place simply to be.

'Where do you think he is now?'

She smiled at him in the almost-black. 'That's what I do. Try and picture him, somewhere safe, alongside men he likes. Thinking of us, taking comfort in those thoughts. You know I tell him in my letters what a help you're being to me here, to him, to the house.'

He dipped his head. 'If it just brought him home safely.'

'I know, I know. He'll be back soon. I promise.' She put her arm through George's and they carried on without speaking, their minds now in France with Alfie. And it was so strange and confusing to her that all her tensions and focuses should fall at this point in life on that one, small part of the world where all of this had begun.

*

She woke, the morning of 29 August, to news on the wireless of the Allied forces pushing north and east, the Battle of Normandy over, another victory, another mention of the possibility that the war might be over by the end of the year. She had finished her breakfast, was going to go and find George to tell him there'd been more good news as she hadn't seen him yet, and then he was there in the doorway.

His face was grey, drained of everything. The room was dark and light at the same time – the air in it seemed to contract and expand till Jean didn't know where she was in it, and she didn't know how to move.

A door must have been open somewhere, because a gust of wind blew through the room and there was a slam. The sound made her lurch forward, and it was then she saw an older man, in officer's uniform, cap in hand, standing behind George. He stepped forward into the room. 'Lady Warre, I am so sorry to inform you—'

She couldn't focus.

'Your son, Alfred. His battalion was scattered along a wide area of land. He never made the drop zone.'

Her hands were clammy and she realised that she was holding the newspaper in her hand, its paper sticking to her palms.

'Action around Fayence... An attack from one of the few remaining strongholds. Fierce gunfight... The body of a private in his battalion was found alongside some of your son's things.'

She heard things only in patches; saw through the window another officer, standing by his car, parked on the gravel. He was taking the last drag of his cigarette, grinding it now into the ground beneath his foot.

'We will do everything we can in the coming weeks to recover his body. Your son was a fine officer, one of the best. Admired by his men.'

She didn't know if she was still standing, felt nothing of the room around her.

'His service to this country will never be forgotten.'

No boy from the post office with brown legs and a scab on his knee, no whir of wheels and snap of chain. But still the Angel of Death, dressed in an officer's uniform, with clipped hair and cut-glass voice, had come to take her boy.

CHAPTER SEVENTEEN

How to catalogue grief. Could one compare and contrast, slotting into sections pain that struck one part of your heart, or obliterated one conception of self, versus another kind of sorrow? Which self was the truest self, which part the most vulnerable to loss – was it the daughter, the lover, the mother? The death of David was something in which she felt so complicit; the guilt, the feeling of loss like ashes in a grate, cold and grey and empty. But the loss of Alfie – this was something so different, so total. The order so wrong, the failure to protect him hitting her anew each minute. Her waking hours were nightmarish, stretched and twisted so that time passed in meaningless slots, as if she was wading through mud; at night, when she would eventually fall asleep as dawn light appeared reproachfully at the curtains' edge, her mind would go blank, snuffed out, exhausted.

Grief was so inventive the way it could hit you, each moment, each hour, catching you with a fresh blow. She would ache for him physically, the yearning excruciating; ache for the touch of her son at all the ages she had held him: as a toddler, when his head would come into her shoulder and his fine hair would brush her skin and she would instinctively rub her face against his to feel that velvet touch; the little boy, arms wrapped around her neck when he would kiss her goodnight, sitting up in the dark of the bedroom, with just the light of the open door across his face, the little body so slight still, the tiny heart hammering in his chest. The young man, his arm linked in hers as they walked together down a street, the pride at his presence, so strong and handsome and vital beside her.

She'd always had lurches as the boys grew up, when the 'what-if' flitted across her thoughts like a ghost across a grave. She would think of the story of Solon the Wise she'd read as a child – 'call no man lucky till he is dead' – and she would shiver, counting her blessings, knowing that life was so arbitrary, that one could never be sure of what lay ahead. But then the officer had come to Harehope and she was really in it, alone, struggling to get the air into her lungs, to breathe, to keep afloat.

She had felt strange and somehow naked in front of George, exposed by her grief. Another failure of herself as a mother as she stood on that dreadful morning, bare and raw in front of her younger son, as if she was inflicting more pain by revealing her own anguish. But he was so gentle; he had put his arm around her shoulder and he had known somehow that she wouldn't want to be inside and so they had sat together on the stone steps outside the camellia house in that late August sun, and she had smoked cigarette after cigarette, and he had somehow kept his tears in as hers rolled out of her and she didn't want him to leave her side.

Afterwards, years later, she would remember the look George wore those first weeks and months. His face was slack with grief, grey. But where she saw only a mirror to her own state, what she had missed was the acceptance – as if he knew he couldn't live with this pain, a world without his brother, for long. His loyalty in a strange way had always been to Alfie; that was his other half, the lens through which he chose to see life. Without it, what was the point, really? She didn't know it then. All she saw was a nineteen-year-old boy who had no language available to him to express the enormity of his loss. And he seemed to retreat from the shift of things to him that Alfie's death brought about. He was now Lord Warre, his shoulders to bear whatever the future of this place was; it was his responsibility, his to shape or break. She saw him shrinking physically before her and he would listen and nod and do all that was expected of him, but there was a raw fear in his eyes.

One night, past midnight, unable to sleep, she had walked along the boys' corridor. She had stopped outside George's door and heard a shift in the bed within. She gently pushed open the door a little further. He was lying in bed, elbows behind his head, eyes wide open in the dark.

She sat down on the edge of the bed next to him, and he looked at her but didn't seem able to speak. She nudged him over and lay on the bed beside him, this slim young man – but he was still just her boy, and she pulled the covers over them both. They lay there in silence for a while, looking up at the ceiling. And he cried in the dark next to her; she could hear him trying to hold it in. Eventually he spoke.

'I don't think I can do the funeral. I can't hear those words said about him. I can't do it.'

'You don't have to do it. I'll be there for both of us.' And she put her hand out for him to take.

But of course he did have to be there, and he had forced himself to stand beside Jean in the family chapel. Another small service, another Lord Warre whose soul they prayed for, in this place that seemed to be swallowing them up like a fairy-tale monster. The service was tiny, Alfie's loss too tragic to countenance anything bigger. The few remaining older staff who had worked under Edward and were still living in the village came: Stokes, of course, his sadness a dreadful thing to see, a part of him he'd never shown to any of them, his face struggling desperately to contain its grief; Charlotte, her new husband and her daughters-in-law, her sons away fighting; and of course Alice. Jean couldn't look at her, and nor could she Jean.

To Jean, life now felt like the stage at the end of a Greek tragedy, with the characters left standing devastated, bereft, but still blind to who they really were. The truth lay at the edge of her thoughts, and when she was alone at night the whisper would become a scream and Jean would panic that she would blurt it out to George, let him know that while the pain of Alfie's death would never go away, his guilt at inheriting his brother's destiny was all based on lies. But she couldn't. Couldn't debase the memory of one to save the other. To do so, she felt, would make Alfie's death somehow all right, convenient, a word too ghastly to contemplate as the agony of his absence seeped into every single thing she did, every room she walked into, every conversation she had. And so she kept the truth hidden, buried it further, pretended not to see the sideways look Alice gave her at the funeral, tried to immure herself to the comments and comparisons people couldn't help themselves but make about her boys.

Her boys. George was nineteen. At the cusp of everything, with the confusion of adult emotions all just coming to the surface, woefully ill-equipped to deal with any of it. He had no one to whom he could truly articulate his feelings of loss. He was too considerate to open up to Jean. She was too consumed by her own sorrow to see what it was doing to him. That he felt he was nothing without his brother. That all he wanted – deserved, could face really – was to be Alfie's younger brother. Without Alfie, he was so dreadfully exposed.

There were days when grief swallowed her entirely and she would stay up in her room, alone, curtains drawn against the day. She wanted to be there for George, to involve herself in life, but she kept coming up against this overwhelming wall of guilt that Alfie's death was the universe's way of snuffing out the lie at the heart of him. The lie that was her doing. It would become too much for her to bear, and she felt herself struggling to breathe, her chest tightening as if it would cave in, and she had to leave a room if too many people were in it, if she couldn't see an escape. The grief crushed her, aged her, trampled on her; and left behind a person in shreds, overwhelmed by the senselessness of life when her child – her boy, her baby, her heart – was gone.

Another Christmas came. She couldn't remember now what they did, where they ate, if they saw anyone. Another January, another February. The army making plans to leave Harehope entirely within the next month or two, the reality of the estate now falling to George. There were ameliorated death duties as Alfie had been killed fighting for his country, the letter so prosaic in how it expressed the tax savings that she had to read it through several times to understand it. People were talking about the war being over by the summer. She watched George talk to the agent, heard him dealing with the bank on the telephone, plans that he had made to help Alfie now his own to voice.

Richard had come up by train – Simon was too much of a coward to come – and she stood with him in the hall as they waited for George to come downstairs. It was only a week after

VE Day, and Richard had been in London, had joined in among the exultant crowds.

'Sarah and I waited for hours, packed in, thousands upon thousands of us, waiting just to hear the roar as the King and Queen came onto the balcony. I'll never forget it as long as I live. And the girls, dancing in the streets, ribbons of red, white and blue around their waists, poppies and cornflowers in their hair. It was marvellous, the stuff of dreams.'

Jean smiled, wanted to feel the jubilation, as she had when she had listened to the wireless that day, to Churchill's words; knew the significance of this moment, for all eternity, but felt it as if from the bottom of a well, looking up at the shimmering light of a cloudless sky from the darkness of far, far below.

Richard had run through the list of properties that would be sold. The trustees had come upon the idea of selling the rest of the moorland too when the right buyer came along. Confident that it would cover the majority of the outstanding debts and death duties. Settle things for the future.

'Now Alfie is gone,' he said quietly to her, as they waited, 'there might not be such a need for all that land, all that sport.'

When it came to explaining the plan to George when the three sat in Edward's old study, Richard smiled kindly. 'You might feel all of it as quite a weight upon you, all those days to fill, with guns and house parties and all of that. The world has changed so much – that all belongs to another time, don't you think?' The implication was left delicately for George to take up if he wished; the stark difference between the brothers and their talents, the future that might have been, the future that was. George had signed the papers quickly, agreed with all the plans without question, wanting Richard gone.

Jean couldn't distinguish one day from the next, and the house had started to make her feel deeply uneasy. As if, at last, it had uncovered her ambivalence towards it and was watching her now, reproachfully, as she struggled to hold herself together under its roof. She was the cause of its uncertain future; she the one to blame for its demise.

A letter arrived one morning from her brother, wholly unexpected. Oliver was travelling to London: could he come and see her? He had heard the news about Alfie, he wanted to offer his condolences in person. He would travel to Harehope if Jean would have him. She hadn't thought once about him, nor of what remained of her family when it had all happened. Her grief had eclipsed everything. But he had, of course, been informed.

He came at the appointed hour, immaculate in his raincoat, soft as sand; his perfectly cut suit beneath. She could see he was well: his face was lean, his body fit. He must have been dry for a while, though she felt no happiness for him. She struggled to feel anything much at all. Just the pull of sadness that dragged at her as she walked from room to room, from day to day.

Oliver declined a drink from Stokes, and they walked together around this house he had never visited. Its condition wasn't much given its recent past, but he was full of admiration about its architecture, the paintings, asking the right questions about the right objects, acknowledging all the house's best aspects.

When they reached her study and she sat down in her armchair, he sat across from her, palms together, hands resting lightly on his knees.

'It's futile for me to attempt to understand your loss, Jean, and I would never attempt to. A mother's pain when a child dies. It is unthinkable, unspeakable.'

She nodded, numb to the words of condolence she had heard a thousand times, always receiving them as if they were addressed to someone else. Not for her, never for her.

He went on. 'The eternal gratitude the world will owe Alfie and boys like him. Who gave their lives to defend our way of life. It's a sacrifice that will never be forgotten.'

But she sensed there was more he wanted to say, something he was edging towards.

'Jean, I came here too to tell you I know the truth about Alfie, about who his father is, about everything that happened in France. Mother told me all those years ago in New York, swore me to secrecy. She was adamant about cutting you off and it was not in my power to change it then, nor is it today. It may all seem irrelevant to you now, we haven't spoken in so long, but I wanted to tell you that I lay no judgement on you, I never have and I never will. I am still your family.'

He looked down, frowned. Gathering himself for what was to come next. But she didn't want to hear it, she wanted to scream over his voice as it went on, smooth and confident in the truth of what he now said.

'Perhaps, though it's hard to feel it now in the depths of your despair, perhaps there is a greater plan at work. Something that is not ours to design but rather to do our best to accept. You see, George will now be able to play his rightful part. The estate will be his, the duty that comes with it his to take up. Perhaps you may ultimately take some solace in that.'

He talked on – so earnest, his words utterly meaningless to her. Told her that he would try and come to London again soon, that he would like for them to build on their relationship now there were only the two of them left. She listened, nodded, kissed him lightly on the cheek before he stepped into the car waiting for him on the gravel outside.

Jean walked back through the house, past a pair of officers in uniform talking in the hall, barely noticing her as she passed. On she walked, through corridors that had been her home for more than twenty years, through a house that was tired in its bones, its walls marked, its carpets worn. But it had survived, its future secured, just; another son here to take his turn.

She took a seat at her desk, looking out of the window as the sun sank low and those ancient trees cast their long shadows on the lawn. The timelessness of it all, the shift and creak of it, the sighs, the breaths like whispers in the breeze, the shiver of past lives that ran through the leaves here, of happiness, of sadness, of a succession of stories, laid over and over one another till each one was indistinguishable from the last, an enfilade of memories opening onto more memories, until there was just darkness.

She sat there for an hour, maybe two, watching the sky change, dusk come, night fall. And still she sat in the near darkness, with just the light from an almost perfect moon as her companion, unable to countenance the way all of this could be read, misread, construed, twisted, till what was her life could be explained away by someone else as something so far from the truth. They could never understand it – perhaps she didn't understand parts of it herself – but she felt it. She felt it all.

Before he'd left, Oliver had given her a photograph of her family, one he'd found when clearing out their mother's apartment. It was of her mother and father, Jean and her brother; it must have been taken at their house on Rhode Island, a formal photograph of the four of them on the large stone terrace that led down to the ornate Italianate garden below. Jean was fourteen or fifteen, hair soft and cut around her shoulders, squinting into the sun from a chair placed in front of her parents. Her mother's hand was on her shoulder, and though a lifetime ago, she could feel the pressure of it now.

Jean took the photograph and walked over to the fireplace, where a neat pile of logs had been laid by Stokes. She struck a match and knelt by the fire, holding the match till the flame caught and spread and the fire began to lick and curl in the grate. Then came the crack and spit as the fire grew and took hold and she placed the photograph in there. She watched the flame take hold of its stiff edge, watched it singe till it blackened and the fire took it entirely and then she dropped it, kneeling in silence until she saw the image of them all swallowed up and gone.

She closed the door to the study and walked up the stairs alone.

PART V

February 1963

Jean walks up the steps from the Underground in a jostle of commuters and day-trippers and into the dull light of a nondescript afternoon. It is one of those London days where colour has bled away and all that is left are a thousand variations of grey. Marble Arch is at the periphery of her vision, a grimy smudge in front of which a few squalid pigeons are attacking a packet of crisps. There are rain clouds, low and heavy – old flannels to be wrung out – that hang in the sky above her and she wraps her scarf more tightly around herself as she turns to make her way down Park Lane. The change in the city still confounds her, buildings completely gone that had once seemed as permanent as the earth itself, and cars pass her in a thin stream. There's the clang and wrench of scaffolding being erected and a run of houses at the bottom of Piccadilly, whose owners she once knew, now boarded up, ready for demolition. Buses with smeary windows cough up fumes that catch in her throat but her heart lifts as she finds herself approaching Berkeley Square: the neat parcel of calm it always was, with benches where she sits when the afternoons are warm, allowing her eyes to close and her mind to drift. But today winter clings on and the square's plane trees are skeletal as she approaches the building at the north-east corner that still holds her home.

She is up in her kitchen, making a cup of tea, the lid of the kettle rattling with the bubbles rising within, when the sound of movement in the corridor outside interrupts her thoughts. She takes it off the stove. She isn't expecting anyone, so she goes to the door, opening it and looking out into the empty hall.

At the far end is the figure of a man, tall, broad-shouldered, hat in hand. 'Can I help you?' she hears herself say. 'The Gordons are away, if you're looking for them.'

The man comes closer, and he is only fifteen feet or so away now. Something happens to her skin, to the blood beneath the surface, as he approaches. She knows him, knows this face, though she does not know it: it is sharper at the cheekbones, with creases and lines that are unfamiliar. She is frozen, and she swallows.

'It's me. Mama, it's me. It's Alfie.'

Jean stares on and he repeats his name again. It is him but it is not him. She is aware of her breathing, rapid and shallow. She leans back against the door – her legs won't hold her – and it hits the wall behind her, and then she slides down till she is sitting, her knees bent in front of her. 'Am I mad? Am I mad?' she says finally, muttering the words to herself.

'No, Mama, no, you're not mad.' He takes her hand in his. 'It is me.'

She finds herself sobbing now, great heaving sobs that take over her whole body. Her hand is still in his and he cries too, this man before her, but silently, and he lets go of her hand to wipe the tears from his face. They are both sitting on the floor in the doorway.

After she doesn't know how long, she becomes aware of herself again, looks around. He stands to help her to her feet and they walk into her flat together. She sits on the sofa, her knees out straight in front of her, her body not her own. The drawing room is dark, and she can hear rain outside drumming against the windows. He sits down next to her. He is muscular, broader at the shoulders, and his skin is brown from the sun.

'I don't know how to start.' His voice catches when he speaks, and he clears his throat. 'You're not mad. How can I explain where I've been or what happened? But you're still here, and that's all I've wanted, to see you and George again.'

He knows nothing. Nothing of any of it, but he is talking to her, and she pulls herself to focus on what is before her. It is Alfie, his eyes the blue of a July sky, though one is covered by a patch of dark cotton and one side of his face is so strange, the skin hardened, like plastic, its surface smooth. The timbre of his voice is one she knows, but the accent shifts and something of it eludes her.

'If I tell it to you from the beginning then maybe it will make sense. Where I've been. I never meant to hurt you, I just – I found out everything and it seemed the only way, or the only way to do things right by you...by George...'

He is looking at her and his expression is so gentle, apologetic. It is him: she knows it now. He is here.

'Do you want me to tell you it all? Can I?'

Jean nods, transfixed by his face. The fineness of youth has gone, hardened into something else, squarer lines, a definition at his jaw she does not know.

'I have to go back, to that August, to the landing in France.'

She nods again, her hands folded in her lap. He doesn't look at her, keeping his eyes on the low table in front of them instead.

'Time away from Harehope had done things to me. It was the training at first, the focus of it, experiences that spoke to parts of me I hadn't known existed. And then when I was in Italy, even in the worst of it at Monte Cassino, even amid the chaos and the death and the unbearable strain, the distance gave me something, a feeling of freedom. We all talked about going home at the end of it all, sweethearts missed or families longed for, but I remember feeling this pull within me. That I missed you and George but that something in me was breaking away, that I wanted to keep the distance from Harehope. I had time to think, you see, nights when I lay awake sifting through memories, and I would find myself coming back to Papa. To his hatred of me that he carried like a knife. His loathing of George. Of you. It ran through everything. All the sales he made and the debts he ran up, turning them over in my mind, seeing it all as if for the first time.

'We were told that we were going to be part of the second landing in the South of France. I wrote to you from Italy, do you remember? That was my last letter. After Rome, we were to be flown to Southern France to land ahead of the mainland invasion. It was mainly American and French troops but about five British battalions too. It was so strange because I kept thinking, I know this part of France where we're headed – those summers of my childhood – but we hadn't been back for so long.'

She knew all of this. She'd gone to talk to his commanding officer one dreary September morning, sat in an airless office in Whitehall as he, distracted and time-pushed with heavy bags beneath his eyes, gave her what details he could about the manner of Alfie's death. Just points on a map to him; to her, pieces of her heart scattered across the red-pink rocks of Esterel.

He is talking again. 'We were dropped, miles off course. It was a disaster. The fog was so thick and our pilot was way, way off and though I didn't know it then, our stick had ended up nearly twenty miles away from the drop zone, flung like coins over a huge swathe of ground. I was on my own, with no idea where I was and where the rest of my battalion were. I managed to link up eventually with a private who'd broken his ankle on landing and we were trying desperately to work out our bearings, no idea where we were, signs covered over, none of the landmarks we were expecting, and it was then that I saw the outline of a lighthouse in the distance. A great tower of a thing, visible even in the dark of night. And it was so familiar to me. And I knew it. I knew it from childhood, and—'

'La Garoupe?'

He nods.

'So you were near the house?' She is in a trance listening to his words, this version of her son, before her. Older, but lean and somehow in sharp focus, his hands spread out over his knees before him.

'We were probably only a mile away at most from the house. I told the private, Bill was his name, that we needed to find our way there before dawn came, to sit it out while we worked out what the hell to do next. Everywhere was deserted, and we kept to the ditches that ran along the roadside until we came to those gates, their metal rusted, jammed shut with bricks. The lavender along the front of the house had run wild, the table on the terrace was on its side, the chairs upturned, the front door was barred and shuttered, but we found a way in, through Marie's old back entrance.'

'You were there?' Her voice is dry. She has been there in her dreams too. Found herself on that beach, the sea a wash of violet before her, the water soft and translucent at her feet, the pale stones uneven beneath her. But it is so fragile a memory that it escapes her even as she dreams it.

'I hadn't been there since I was eleven or twelve, maybe eight years before. In that way one never does as a child, I hadn't questioned why we'd stopped going there, and then war had broken out, so of course we couldn't. But to have found it like that, to be walking through those rooms of my childhood. The furniture still as it had been, everything just the same, as if we'd only just left. Images of the past—' He looks up at her now. He is shy with her; they are strangers still. 'Of playing draughts with George when it was too hot to be outside and we didn't want to sleep. Do you remember? And you would lie on the sofa with a book, your head resting in the crook of your arm, hair still damp from a swim.'

She smiles and the flicker of memory passes between them, becoming something tangible.

He talks to her directly now. 'I had let Bill sleep, exhausted from the pain, and I sat in that room. Lost in memories, I suppose. And it was then I saw the diary in a pile of books on the table; it looked so out of place that I opened it, thinking it might be yours, hoping it might be. There was a photograph tucked inside – of me, I was probably nine or ten at the time, you were standing beside me, and there was a man smiling behind me, his hand on my shoulder.' He reaches into the inside pocket of his jacket. 'I've kept it with me. I always have it on me. He'd written the date on the back.'

She looks at the photograph in her hand, bleached and faded, traces the outline of her boy; she can feel his skin, smooth and supple, the narrow neck with its down of fine hair where David's hand rests; the sun is high above them in that indigo sky, the grind of the cicadas is inside her head and spread across the ground, and everywhere is pine and eucalyptus and salt and freedom.

'This diary, it was like a love letter to you. The first time he met you on the beach below the house – your beauty, your charm, how young you were. You would have been only a little older than I was when you met, and I couldn't stop reading it: about this past of yours and this man who loved you although you were married to someone else. And then I came to a part where you came back, with two little boys in tow, me and George…and then I saw it all. He, this man, was David.' His face is washed out. 'I do remember him. David was funny, gentle. Different to the grown-ups I knew. And I remember the way he looked at you. I swear I remember thinking that was how you ought to be looked at, that Papa never did, and then I read more, I read it all.'

'I'm so sorry.' Jean speaks, finally, and her voice cracks. She takes his hand, this man before her who is Alfie though she does not understand how. But her heart knows it is him. How could you not know your son, however he comes to you?

'I found out David was my father. That you'd had George afterwards with Papa. And then it all fell into place. So much… so much you wouldn't believe that had felt so wrong and awkward about Harehope and Papa, and how he was to me and how he was to George. He must have hated me so much. He did, I knew it. I wasn't his, and all those successes and things people would say – how proud he must have been of me – it made him sick, didn't it?'

She nods, slowly. 'Did it make you hate me, too? For all this mess, for all the lies I had created—'

'How could I hate you? I loved you. You were our mother, and you were the most wonderful, perfect thing in our lives.

It was the rest that had seemed so dark, so confusing. I kept reading. I couldn't stop. He wrote about me. Watching me play and hoping that the part of him that was in me would grow... Reading this made me understand myself for the first time. It was strange – I felt euphoric – I had loved you and I had loved George, but I hadn't ever felt that Papa loved me, nor that Harehope was mine. I had felt this strange unease about it all, and always this guilt about George, that he was cast aside. Maybe some hidden part of me knew... But I read on, about you wanting to ask for a divorce and going to Grandma, and her vitriol, and your decision to come back and to give David up. For us, for our happiness. And the guilt that you told him you felt about this awful lie, this untruth, and George at its heart. My brother that I loved more than anything. Your over-whelming love for us both, but this guilt that you struggled to bear.'

'But why?' Jean feels herself falling again, and all the pain, the loss, is coming up and she feels panic spreading across her chest through veins of ice.

'I took the diary. I put it in my pack, and I woke Bill and told him we needed to get going. That we couldn't stay in this house waiting for someone to discover us. I don't know what I thought it all meant but I kept thinking over and over about your guilt and the injustice for George, and about this part of me that was other, that belonged somewhere else, not in England, not at Harehope, not weighed down by titles and trusts and inheritance but somewhere entirely different. We made our way through the back country, because there was a network of the maquis running information across this stretch of coast. We would have to do as they said, follow closely, and they would get us to safety. My mind was all over the place – memories of

Papa, of you, images of my past seen as if for the first time as I pieced it all back together.

'Nearly a day later we met up with four or five trucks full of Americans who'd landed at Fréjus and were part of the force working their way east along the coast. We explained what had happened, that we'd been dropped miles off course, had failed to meet up with the rest of our battalion. We were told to join them and then I remember we were on a road – we were safe, high up in the back of a jeep – driving up to the outskirts of a small town, the soldiers singing some song I didn't know, and it was as the approach narrowed and the landscape started tapering uphill that we were attacked. German snipers and gunfire, and I remember the men were panicking as the road was narrow and we'd struggle to reverse quickly enough. And then came the blast. Darkness. No pain but black.'

He stops. She watches him, frozen in this moment with him – the split second before the end came.

'Then I heard a buzzing in my ears, a whine that grew, and I don't know how long I was out for but I came to and I remember seeing Bill about three feet in front of me and a great chunk of his face was missing, his cheek blown off, a shard of bone exposed like porcelain. And then the darkness came again and I don't remember any more.'

She needs to touch him now, to push back that darkness, to bring him back to life. 'Your face? Is that what happened?' Jean puts her hand out to it, touches where he must have felt the pain. She feels her heart spread through her, out to her fingers; everything is different now, tinged with light.

He nods. 'I must have been in and out of consciousness. I was moved to a larger field hospital. It was chaotic, and things were being packed up around me – we needed to move on to keep up with the progress north that the troops were making. I was so confused, but it became apparent they didn't know who I was. That the truck I had been travelling in had been carrying American soldiers from different battalions and from across two different divisions – that the convoy had been pretty much wiped out. They told me there'd been two British paratroopers with them, but they'd been killed. That only I'd survived, found under a mess of bodies several hours later, uniform in shreds from the blast. They kept saying how unlucky we'd been. That the landing had been so easy and the Allies were liberating towns all up the coast, calling it the Champagne Campaign as they took back town after town as they moved east.' Here he shifts in his seat. Looks up at her slowly. 'They had nothing. And I said nothing. Stayed quiet. In the hospital there were all these American boys. No one seemed to mind that I couldn't remember anything, they didn't have the time, so they gave me temporary papers, put me down as being part of the 36th Infantry Division that had lost men at Fayence.

'I must have got an infection then, because I lost a week or more. I remember so little, but then I was in Paris and it was quieter there, a big hospital, a room where injuries were bad. There was a boy who'd lost both his arms and who would scream in pain all night, phantom limbs that haunted him and his cries were torture. I had been ill, I was losing weight. The burns on my face were not healing well, I would need grafts. There was quiet concern, and that was when a little voice started to whisper something while I lay there alone and so removed from everyone and everything I knew. I let assumptions be made, let people talk for me, waited to see what would happen if I stayed quiet. The voice grew louder. People with not enough time and more pressing concerns were happy to pass me on. I was eventually brought back to an American base in England, alongside soldiers who needed time away from the fighting. There was talk about going back home: nerves, combat fatigue, the jitters. And I knew I was on to something. I was a person unknown. Body someone else's, though whose didn't seem to be a concern. I was light suddenly, unbound. Free.'

Her voice is frail, uncertain. 'They told me you were missing, presumed dead. That you had never found your battalion, and then two weeks after the landing they identified the body of a private from your squadron, a Bill Strong, with an American convoy that had been attacked. Found some of your things there with his body. Later your commanding officer told me that you must have landed near Antibes, made your way up through the Var – you would have been so near to the house, so near to our past. That you must have linked up with this convoy, been killed with Bill in the explosion. They talked about your bravery, the achievements made as a consequence. But the pain—' She can't say more, engulfed by memories.

He speaks again. 'It's so hard for me to explain, but when I lay there in the darkness I began to feel a different path was possible. That the truth of me had come to the surface and I couldn't go back to before. Not only had it all been a lie, but I didn't want it either. I didn't want this thing that my father had hated me for. I could get away. From this place that wasn't mine, from this life that didn't belong to me. Abandoning things, escaping things. The line between them blurred. But I knew that if I did go, in the mess and madness of it all, then what was George's could be his, what he had deserved all along instead of always being overlooked. That he and you could look after each other – and I could be free of all this and put things right. There was a feeling that was so entwined with Harehope, I thought it would crush me at times, a weight that hovered over me, that I had to push off by doing or achieving. I didn't want it any more.' His voice trails off.

'So you don't know?' She feels her heart hammering in her chest.

He looks confused.

'About George.'

'What? What? Is he all right?'

'Oh, I can't do this to you. Let me…' She takes his hand and holds it. Though he is a grown man, he is somehow nine again and there is a connection in the warmth of his hand, the feel of his skin, that makes nothing of the years that have passed, that they have lost. She puts her fingers up to his face, the scars and the dark patch that covers his left eye. She touches the strange, puckered skin and then speaks. 'George is dead.'

Jean watches as his mind unravels and he struggles to find firm ground, to make sense of her words. She holds his hand tight. She must tell him this. She needs to tell him this.

Her voice is small. 'George and I were torn apart by your death. He tried, and he clung onto your memory, but he was slipping away somehow. We both were. I didn't realise it then but the grief was separating us, doing different things to us. I wasn't watching closely enough. And – the reality was that George couldn't bear that he had inherited what he thought was yours. Felt he was undeserving of it. That's the ghastly truth.'

She lets go of Alfie's hand and rubs her face roughly. She can't look at him.

'He grew quite withdrawn after you'd gone, I only saw how much after. But when we were alone together and we would talk about you, he would speak always of your brilliance, your bravery, your honesty. I told him all the time, I swear I did, that you would have wanted him to be in charge. But the whole thing was such a mess. I was lost and the house was in a state by the time the army left – doors broken off hinges, furniture smashed to pieces, paintings damaged beyond repair. No one came back, not a single person who worked at the house, apart from Stokes, who'd never left.

'There were so many decisions to be made. We were both underwater with your loss but I didn't realise how much…and then one day George went to London. Said he had a meeting with the bank. And then I got a telephone call that evening, telling me to come to London at once. He'd – he'd stepped in front of a train. At Green Park station. Walked out in front of it as it came in. The middle of the afternoon, an empty platform.' She sees it, though she has tried and tried to stop her mind from taking her there. From watching his foot falter, then propel itself forward: the suck of air from the tunnel, the screech of brakes on rails, the horror of the driver's face as her boy's body is tossed like a rag doll into the air.

'When was this?' His voice is a whisper.

'September 1946. He was twenty-one. He left a letter for me at the flat, but I couldn't bear to read it for months afterwards because I knew what it would say. And when I did finally open it… He didn't feel up to the job. Couldn't bear to have what should have been yours. The third Lord Warre to die in seven years.'

His voice is panicky. 'Why didn't you tell him the truth? That it should have been his all along—'

She crumples then, head in her hands. This is what she must confront. 'I don't know, I don't know. It felt so disloyal to you. As if it was all right now that you were dead and out of the way. I felt so torn. But I regretted it so deeply after. I didn't really cope after he was gone. Kept going over what I could have done differently, but it always went back to the fact that the only thing I could have done differently was not to have had you two boys.' She looks up. 'And what life would that have been? You were my everything. The breath in my body, my heart, my soul. And then I would break anew – that I had created you and then destroyed you. Maternal guilt, amplified until it grew so great it blotted me out.'

'Where is he buried?'

'There is a plot at Harehope for you and him, but I gave you a shared gravestone. I wanted you to be together even though there was no body for you – you were my boys, my boys...'

She is back at the grave, shoulders low, the burden of it unfathomable, the path ahead impassable.

Alfie goes on, his voice uncertain. 'I wanted to give George what was his. Those letters you sent when I was fighting, telling me how well he was getting on, how involved he was becoming at Harehope. That I could be freed of all that stuff, the money, the obligation, that hatred Papa had for me because I wasn't his, because it shouldn't have been mine. But what did it get George? I should have known that it was too much for him. I thought I'd saved him by going away but I made things worse, far worse. I killed him—' He is sobbing now, and she puts her arms out to him, touches his face again, pulls him to look at her.

'No, no. Never think that. Never say that.'

'But I did. I abandoned him.'

'Alfie, you're here. You're here now. You loved him, and you carry him with you. That's not abandoning. How could you know that he couldn't live with the world once you'd gone? He was so gentle, truly, in his soul – he needed a defender, a ballast against it all. And that was you.'

'And you? What did you need?'

'I think so many parts of me were extinguished, like lights going out in a building. One by one. The last went out with George. I lost the few years after his death, after you'd both gone. I put one foot in front of the other, got out of bed in the morning, went to lunch with someone here or dinner there, the next day did the same and the same and the same, until one day I didn't have to remind myself to breathe in the morning, and then the moment came when I could look at a picture of the two of you without feeling the ground disappearing beneath me.'

'And Harehope?'

'Harehope went to Charlotte's oldest son. He sold it and the estate as soon as he could. So I had this flat, and I had friends who kept me going. And I would go to the graveyard at Harehope every year, on the anniversary of George's death. It's a school now, though I don't know for how much longer. And I would sit and talk to you both. Talk about those summers in France when it was the three of us – and David.'

'I know David was killed. That he died at Omaha on D-Day.' He stands then, going to his holdall and opening it. 'This should be yours.'

He hands her the cloth-covered diary. She takes it, rubs the cover with her thumb, opens it slowly. That handwriting, her name there on every page; she can hear Billie Holiday on the gramophone, can taste the chill smoothness of the Martini he has fixed her, the gentle kiss to her forehead. The minuscule acts that are the purpose of it all.

'I got to New York and I walked away. It was so easy. I'd fallen between the cracks of life. The old me was missing, presumed dead, and I had become this non-person, unclassified, and in the mess of soldiers and the last months of the war no one followed where I went. I was in America, and the mad thing was, in reality I was as American as the next person. I had my watch – from your father – which was enough to get me a bus ticket and a few months to set myself up. I headed to the Midwest, got a job on a farm in Bismarck, North Dakota, working horses, ranching for an old farming family. They could never get over my riding. Said I looked like I'd been born in the saddle. What was my story, who was I? But I learned to avoid questions, keep myself to myself. People stopped asking after a while or I'd move on if they didn't, and everywhere I went they needed cheap labour, the war was over, families were broken. And each day that passed, I thought was a gift I was giving George. Each day a clean start for me and for him too. He was my brother, I loved him so much. It was my gift.

'I went on to New Mexico after that, to another ranch up near Santa Fe, another family. I settled eventually when I met someone, fell in love. She's from a totally different background, grew up in a small town where her family had never travelled more than ten miles. I told her the crazy truth – that it was something I never wanted to return to – and she understood that, she really did. But then we had a child, a son, you see.'

He stops, distracted. So he is a father. She sees that change in him now so clearly. Another life carried always within, that part of self always to be shared, to be sacrificed should there ever be a need.

'He's six – and he's so full of life and of questions about everything, and something in that relationship with him…it kept bringing me back to you, to memories of my childhood, memories of George. I knew I had to come back, even if it was to see you just once. That you were all right.' He looks at her directly. 'I live a happy life. I promise I do. I had begun to feel so restless, hemmed in by everything...and knowing that I had done the right thing for George—'

He breaks then, and he can't speak. The reality of what he has learned seems to hit him like a punch to the stomach and she watches him, powerless to help.

'Perhaps it would have been better if you hadn't come, hadn't learned the truth.'

He shakes his head roughly. 'It's better to know.' And he rubs his face with his palms. 'I think something in me knew it wasn't me, before France, before I found out.'

This is the truth of it, what she has come to understand as she looks back on Alfie's journey to adulthood. Something in him knew.

Silence falls between them, and she is unsure of what he is feeling. And there is a finger of anxiety tapping at her chest. Was the truth too much for him? But he is looking across at her now.

'Would you let me sit here a little while?'

Something about the simplicity of his request, after the intensity of what he has learned, is overwhelming. He is a boy, asking his mother for something that only she can provide. Her body gives, a tension that she has been carrying all this time, and there is a beautiful release, an ecstasy after all the loss; a valve has been opened and she is holding him in her arms, in the fog of birth, and it is only them in the world. What would a mother do for her child but protect, but love, and, when they are gone, only endure.

She looks across at him. The mother within her had never died, even when her boys were gone. Her arms were there to hold them, her thumbs to wipe away their tears. 'Please stay,' she hears herself say. 'Please stay, Alfie. Won't you?'

But he cannot. She knows that he cannot.

*

Jean gets up from her bed, feels the throb of pain at the small of her back from where she has been lying still for too long. She puts a hand now to her hip, rubs at the stiffness, walks over to the window before her. She pulls back the curtain and lifts the sash; breathes in the cool of the night air. The moon is full, she can see it suspended high above the rooftops of Piccadilly, lighting up the streets below like a stage. All is quiet, the evening's revellers long gone. This hour belongs to the fox, slinking through deserted streets in search of food, or the lost soul who must find shelter in a doorway, head nodding into drawn-up knees till dawn comes to release him. It is a lonely hour when a city's comfort evaporates, for while sleep comes to the content, it is the rest – the fearful, the lonely, the grieving – that it evades.

She had gone back to France, to the house, one last time. It was 1946, only a month after George had died and fifteen months after Alfie. She was an empty shell, walking through rooms leached of all colour, of all sound. The trustees had been approached by a buyer for the house; had pounced on the offer. Charlotte, in a rare moment of grace, had resolved that the money from the sale should go to Jean despite what Simon Marjoribanks would have liked, and so it was made clear that Jean should go out to sign the paperwork. In truth, she was greedy for any trace of them all that might still be there.

When her car had reached the gates of the house, though, all courage evaporated, and she wasn't sure if she could go in. It felt as if the past was barring her way, a mass of memories too dense to pass through. Her mind was thick with them, endless iterations of lunches and dinners, layered one over another, of conversations and arguments and scraps and make-ups and kisses and laughter – the collage of their life – all of it somehow still trapped inside the house. But when she entered, nothing of them was there. It was cold, where in her mind it had always been a place of gentle warmth; rooms were mostly empty of furniture, all was hard angles and bare floors, and she wanted to leave. She stood in her bedroom and looked out on her little bay, scarred now by loops of barbed wire and an abandoned pillbox. She watched a small fishing boat pulling up its nets as it headed in for the day, and she found she couldn't breathe. The air just would not come.

The remaining furniture in the drawing room had been pushed roughly to the corners, her rugs gone, the parquet floor exposed and unswept. But she was hit then by a memory so acute it made her stop, made a strange strangled sigh escape her mouth.

She saw herself lying on the sofa, her feet on David's lap as they both read one night, bodies loose from wine and their lovemaking. He had one hand resting on her foot, the other pinning open a page of a book he was reading, and his face was so present to her then, his brow so smooth, his skin brown and freckled from the sun, that his death, all of this horror and loss that came after, was the impossibility. The empty room she stood in, in this house that war had seeped into and grown over: this was the dream. The reality was her memories, these pictures in her mind.

Where has he gone? Where have they gone? Those four simple words tapped at her heart. *Where have they gone?* For where do people go when they die; what can possibly happen to that life's force, to that concentration of thought and passion, of observation and opinion, to their anger, their humour, their love? Even if you see a body – as she had George's; the horror of it, grey and flaccid on a cold metal slab – it can seem a trick, an impossible vanishing act, a cruel joke, where you are left waiting always for the sound of their feet returning, for their laughter at the door.

Her books lay abandoned in piles in the corner of the room, valueless to the new buyers, pulled from the shelves and left for someone to take pity on. She sifted through them as she knelt. Novels she knew she'd read though their plots now escaped her; novels David had urged her to read, covers torn. What a fool she was not to have read them, it would have given her another thread to connect them now. Then her eyes fell on a pile of the boys' books: annuals of comics, battered *Just Williams*, a *Robinson Crusoe*, its back half ripped off and the spine split.

Then she saw a cover of rough brown. It was not a book, it had no title, no heft to it. A slip of a thing. As she opened it up, her heart shifted in her chest. The gift David had given her that last night when they'd said goodbye, the gift she had been unable to read. She picked it up then, and the photograph tucked inside slipped out onto the floor: her little boy, frozen in a moment where possibility was everywhere; where the ending had not yet been written.

The next day she drove out to Fayence. She stood on the steep, narrow road that wound up to the hilltop town, a wooden cross the only sign that this arbitrary spot was where her eldest boy had died. She found herself kneeling on the ground and scraping up a handful of the grit there on the roadside, putting it in her coat pocket. She kept it in her hand, rubbing it between her fingers, working away at it as she walked through the quiet cobbled streets of the little town, lined with its houses with their roofs of red tiles and apricot plaster walls. The streets were slick and deserted in the wet of a February afternoon. She had drunk a pastis, standing alone at the bar in a shop whose shelves were half-empty and whose owner wore a stained shirt and a weary smile, as a black cat with a white-tipped tail watched her warily.

Her son's death was as arbitrary, as pointless, as that. An explosion, then darkness. Life. Then no life.

Her boys. Only she knows the truth of them, and so she frees them. Harehope is gone, France only fragmented memories. What remains of them all, of that time, is like the back of the drawer of some long-forgotten desk: just that worn-out diary, David's words within hieroglyphs to anyone who might read it now; bleached photographs of people and places unrecognisable even to themselves; a sparse assembly of possessions whose meaning has faded, like coins no longer in currency – but the truth of them all is inside her. Because that is what she did with her sorrow. When the years after their deaths had circled on, when people no longer asked how she was, or even knew of her boys' story, this was what happened. She subsumed them into her: her heartbeat slowly became richer with their heartbeats, her dreams saturated with their words, their faces. They didn't fade from her grasp, as they did for the rest of the world. They became part of her. But the tempo was different, the cadence shifting from the mad cacophony of the first years to something softer, sad still but with a beauty, something that she learned slowly, gradually, to live with. For Grief had sat at her shoulder, a rook with feathers of black, weighty with sorrow, but then one day he had flown away.

Their lives were cut short, not even in half; a generous quarter was all they got – lives stopped like a watch whose mechanics had given out. There were no wives to share them with, no grandchildren to coo over their likeness in. She alone is the keeper of the flame; it is for her to do as she wishes with it. And so, secretly, away from anyone, she liberates Alfie in her mind. In her dreams she makes sense of the hatred he knew Edward felt for him though he couldn't understand why; she gives him resolution, mends his troubled man-boy heart.

Tonight she had opened the door of her flat to Alfie, had held his hand in hers; had given him another ending to tell her, where he knew the truth of who he was. She had told him of George's death, had shared her grief at the horror of it – the unbearable, unchangeable tragedy of it. For only Alfie would understand her pain. She lets him stand before her in her mind as a man, a scarred but vital man. She gives him those years he never had, an ending where he did not die: so beautiful, so entrancing. She soothes George too some nights, strokes his hair, feels his head on her chest, tells him that he could have done it, could have managed things, but she understands that he did not feel able. 'You needed peace, my love. You needed peace.'

She dreams another ending. She frees them in her mind.

And so she stands now, alone, at the window and looks out onto an empty, moonlit Berkeley Square. She leans her head against the glass and puts her arms around her boys.

ACKNOWLEDGEMENTS

To Eugenie Furniss at 42 for taking me on and working tirelessly on the manuscript with such insight and dedication, and for making the process a joy, always.

To Jenny Parrott and the team at Oneworld, for publishing this novel and championing it with such enthusiasm. To Sarah Terry for her painstaking and faultless copy-editing. To Kate Appleton, Lucy Cooper, Beth Marshall Brown, Paul Nash and Mark Rusher. I know it takes an army to get a book out there, so thank you so much to you all.

To my mother, Eithne, for encouraging me to write, for reading endless drafts and for giving constructive advice: a precarious tightrope for a mother to walk... Get on and write yours now.

To my father, Peter, though I can't bear that you're not here to see it published, thank you for being so encouraging of all my endeavours always. I think, Dad, you would have applauded me if I'd written the phone directory.

To the Short Ladies, for starting me on my publishing journey and for helping me along the way, with advice, love and humour.

To my best girlfriends – you know who you are. You are my sisters and I couldn't do a thing without you, nor, in fact, would I want to.

To my brothers – thanks, Tom and Jack, for making me eternally ballgirl, wicketkeeper, goalie, in all our games growing up: a bookworm's dream. And for all the rest too.

To Arys and Jemima, for all your help keeping the show on the road.

To Scroopey and to Sarah. It was at your house that I first saw those two de László portraits all those years ago: the early, early kernel of a story.

To the Beaumonts: for allowing me in to Bywell – and for being the absolute opposite of the family that Jean marries into. You are all heart and love and laughter, and I adore you all.

To Wenty, thank you for encouraging me when I first told you I was going to write this; thank you for your patience, and for giving me the time and the support to see it through – and for much, much more.

And lastly to my children – Wenty, Walter and Nancy – for putting up with my squirrelling myself away for a long, long time, particularly when I am not sure you had a clue what I was up to. You can now buy the book in a shop, which I think is all you really wanted to know.

Photo credit: © Ben Kelway

VANESSA BEAUMONT studied Classics at Oxford University before joining Short Books, the independent publisher in London, where she was Commissioning Editor for eight years, editing both fiction and non-fiction. She co-ran the literary agency Prentice Beaumont, before deciding to take the reckless decision to embark on a novel. She lives between West London and Northumberland, and is married with three children.